TESS GERRITSEN

OMNIBUS

In their Footsteps

Stolen

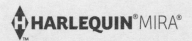
HARLEQUIN® MIRA®

Published in Great Britain 2014.
Harlequin MIRA, an imprint of Harlequin (UK) Limited,
Eton House, 18-24 Paradise Road,
Richmond, Surrey, TW9 1SR.

In Their Footsteps © 1994 Terry Gerritsen
Stolen © 1995 Terry Gerritsen

ISBN: 978-1-848-45278-7

60-1013

Harlequin (UK) Limited's policy is to use papers that are natural, renewable and recyclable products and made from wood grown in sustainable forests. The logging and manufacturing processes conform to the legal environmental regulations of the country of origin.

Printed and bound by
CPI Group (UK) Ltd, Croydon, CR0 4YY

In their Footsteps

To Misty, Mary and the Breakfast Club

Prologue

Paris, 1973

He was late. It was not like Madeline, not like her at all.

Bernard Tavistock ordered another café au lait and took his time sipping it, every so often glancing around the outdoor café for a glimpse of his wife. He saw only the usual Left Bank scene: tourists and Parisians, red-checked tablecloths, a riot of summertime colors. But no sign of his raven-haired wife. She was half an hour late now; this was more than a traffic delay. He found himself tapping his foot as the worries began to creep in. In all their years of marriage, Madeline had rarely been late for an appointment, and then only by a few minutes. Other men might moan and roll their eyes in masculine despair over their perennially tardy spouses, but Bernard had no such complaints—he'd been blessed with a punctual wife. A beautiful wife. A woman who, even after fifteen years of marriage, continued to surprise him, fascinate him, tempt him.

Now where the dickens *was* she?

He glanced up and down Boulevard Saint-Germain. His uneasiness grew from a vague toe-tapping anxiety to outright worry. Had there been a traffic accident? A last-minute alert from their French Intelligence contact,

Claude Daumier? Events had been moving at a frantic pace these last two weeks. Those rumors of a NATO intelligence leak—of a mole in their midst—had them all glancing over their shoulders, wondering who among them could not be trusted. For days now, Madeline had been awaiting instructions from MI6 London. Perhaps, at the last minute, word had come through.

Still, she should have let him know.

He rose to his feet and was about to head for the telephone when he spotted his waiter, Mario, waving at him. The young man quickly wove his way past the crowded tables.

"M. Tavistock, there is a telephone message for you. From *madame*."

Bernard gave a sigh of relief. "Where is she?"

"She says she cannot come for lunch. She wishes you to meet her."

"Where?"

"This address." The waiter handed him a scrap of paper, smudged with what looked like tomato soup. The address was scrawled in pencil: 66, Rue Myrha, #5.

Bernard frowned. "Isn't this in Pigalle? What on earth is she doing in that neighborhood?"

Mario shrugged, a peculiarly Gallic version with tipped head, raised eyebrow. "I do not know. She tells me the address, I write it down."

"Well, thank you." Bernard reached for his wallet and handed the fellow enough francs to pay for his two café au laits, as well as a generous tip.

"Merci," said the waiter, beaming. "You will return for supper, M. Tavistock?"

"If I can track down my wife," muttered Bernard, striding away to his Mercedes.

He drove to Place Pigalle, grumbling all the way.

What on earth had possessed her to go there? It was not the safest part of Paris for a woman—or a man, either, for that matter. He took comfort in the knowledge that his beloved Madeline could take care of herself quite well, thank you very much. She was a far better marksman than he was, and that automatic she carried in her purse was always kept fully loaded—a precaution he insisted upon ever since that near-disaster in Berlin. Distressing how one couldn't trust one's own people these days. Incompetents everywhere, in MI6, in NATO, in French Intelligence. And there had been Madeline, trapped in that building with the East Germans, and no one to back her up. *If I hadn't arrived in time…*

No, he wouldn't relive that horror again.

She'd learned her lesson. And a loaded pistol was now a permanent accessory to her wardrobe.

He turned onto Rue de Chapelle and shook his head in disgust at the deteriorating street scene, the tawdry nightclubs, the scantily clad women poised on street corners. They saw his Mercedes and beckoned to him eagerly. Desperately. "Pig Alley" was what the Yanks used to call this neighborhood. The place one came to for quick delights, for guilty pleasures. *Madeline,* he thought, *have you gone completely mad? What could possibly have brought you here?*

He turned onto Boulevard Bayes, then Rue Myrha, and parked in front of number 66. In disbelief, he stared up at the building and saw three stories of chipped plaster and sagging balconies. Did she really expect him to meet her in this firetrap? He locked the Mercedes, thinking, *I'll be lucky if the car's still here when I return.* Reluctantly he entered the building.

Inside there were signs of habitation: children's toys in the stairwell, a radio playing in one of the flats. He

climbed the stairs. The smell of frying onions and cigarette smoke seemed to hang permanently in the air.
Numbers three and four were on the second floor; he
kept climbing, up a narrow staircase to the top floor.
Number five was the attic flat; its low door was tucked
between the eaves.

He knocked. No answer.

"Madeline?" he called. "Really now, this isn't some
sort of practical joke, is it?"

Still there was no answer.

He tried the door; it was unlocked. He pushed inside,
into the garret flat. Venetian blinds hung over the windows, casting slats of shadow and light across the room.
Against one wall was a large brass bed, its sheets still
rumpled from some prior occupant. On a bedside table
were two dirty glasses, an empty champagne bottle and
various plastic items one might delicately refer to as
"marital aids." The whole room smelled of liquor, of
sweating passion and bodies in rut.

Bernard's puzzled gaze gradually shifted to the foot
of the brass bed, to a woman's high-heeled shoe lying
discarded on the floor. Frowning, he took a step toward
it and saw that the shoe lay in a glistening puddle of
crimson. As he rounded the foot of the bed, he froze in
disbelief.

His wife lay on the floor, her ebony hair fanned out
like a raven's wings. Her eyes were open. Three sun-
bursts of blood stained her white blouse.

He dropped to his knees beside her. "No," he said.
"No." He touched her face, felt the warmth still lingering in her cheeks. He pressed his ear to her chest, her
bloodied chest, and heard no heartbeat, no breath. A sob
burst forth from his throat, a disbelieving cry of grief.
"Madeline!"

As the echo of her name faded, there came another sound behind him—footsteps. Soft, approaching...

Bernard turned. In bewilderment, he stared at the pistol—Madeline's pistol—now pointed at him. He looked up at the face hovering above the barrel. It made no sense—no sense at all!

"Why?" asked Bernard.

The answer he heard was the dull thud of the silenced automatic. The bullet's impact sent him sprawling to the floor beside Madeline. For a few brief seconds, he was aware of her body close beside him, and of her hair, like silk against his fingers. He reached out and feebly cradled her head. *My love,* he thought. *My dearest love.*

And then his hand fell still.

1

Buckinghamshire, England
Twenty years later

Jordan Tavistock lounged in Uncle Hugh's easy chair and amusedly regarded, as he had a thousand times before, the portrait of his long-dead ancestor, the hapless Earl of Lovat. Ah, the delicious irony of it all, he thought, that Lord Lovat should stare down from that place of honor above the mantelpiece. It was testimony to the Tavistock family's sense of whimsy that they'd chosen to so publicly display their one relative who'd, literally, lost his head on Tower Hill—the last man to be officially decapitated in England—unofficial decapitations did not count. Jordan raised his glass in a toast to the unfortunate earl and tossed back a gulp of sherry. He was tempted to pour a second glass, but it was already five-thirty, and the guests would soon be arriving for the Bastille Day reception. *I should keep at least a few gray cells in working order,* he thought. *I might need them to hold up my end of the chitchat.* Chitchat being one of Jordan's least favorite activities.

For the most part, he avoided these caviar and black-tie bashes his Uncle Hugh seemed so addicted to throwing. But tonight's event—in honor of their house guests, Sir Reggie and Lady Helena Vane—might prove more interesting than the usual gathering of the horsey set. This was the first big affair since Uncle Hugh's retirement from British Intelligence, and a number of Hugh's former colleagues from MI6 would make an appearance. Throw into the brew a few old chums from Paris—all of them in London for the recent economic summit— and it could prove to be a most intriguing night. Anytime one threw a group of ex-spies and diplomats together in a room, all sorts of surprising secrets tended to surface.

Jordan looked up as his uncle came grumbling into the study. Already dressed in his tuxedo, Hugh was trying, without success, to fix his bow tie; he'd managed, instead, to tie a stubborn square knot.

"Jordan, help me with this blasted thing, will you?" said Hugh.

Jordan rose from the easy chair and loosened the knot. "Where's Davis? He's much better at this sort of thing."

"I sent him to fetch that sister of yours."

"Beryl's gone out again?"

"Naturally. Mention the words 'cocktail party,' and she's flying out the door."

Jordan began to loop his uncle's tie into a bow. "Beryl's never been fond of parties. And just between you and me, I think she's had just a bit too much of the Vanes."

"Hmm? But they've been lovely guests. Fit right in—"

"It's the nasty little barbs flying between them."

"Oh, *that*. They've always been that way. I scarcely notice it anymore."

"And have you seen the way Reggie follows Beryl about, like a puppy dog?"

Hugh laughed. "Around a pretty woman, Reggie *is* a puppy dog."

"Well, it's no wonder Helena's always sniping at him." Jordan stepped back and regarded his uncle's bow tie with a frown.

"How's it look?"

"It'll have to do."

Hugh glanced at the clock. "Better check on the kitchen. See that things are in order. And why aren't the Vanes down yet?"

As if on cue, they heard the sound of querulous voices on the stairway. Lady Helena, as always, was scolding her husband. "*Someone* has to point these things out to you," she said.

"Yes, and it's always you, isn't it?"

Sir Reggie fled into the study, pursued by his wife. It never failed to puzzle Jordan, the obvious mismatch of the pair. Sir Reggie, handsome and silver haired, towered over his drab little mouse of a wife. Perhaps Helena's substantial inheritance explained the pairing; money, after all, was the great equalizer.

As the hour edged toward six o'clock, Hugh poured out glasses of sherry and handed them around to the foursome. "Before the hordes arrive," he said, "a toast, to your safe return to Paris." They sipped. It was a solemn ceremony, this last evening together with old friends.

Now Reggie raised his glass. "And here's to English hospitality. Ever appreciated!"

From the front driveway came the sound of car tires on gravel. They all glanced out the window to see the first limousine roll into view. The chauffeur opened the door and out stepped a fiftyish woman, every ripe curve defined by a green gown ablaze with bugle beads. Then a young man in a shirt of purple silk emerged from the car and took the woman's arm.

"Good heavens, it's Nina Sutherland and her brat," Helena muttered. "What broom did *she* fly in on?"

Outside, the woman in the green gown suddenly spotted them standing in the window. "Hello, Reggie! Helena!" she called in a voice like a bassoon.

Hugh set down his sherry glass. "Time to greet the barbarians," he said, sighing. He and the Vanes headed out the front door to welcome the first arrivals.

Jordan paused a moment to finish his drink, giving himself time to paste on a smile and get the old handshake ready. Bastille Day—what an excuse for a party! He tugged at the coattails of his tuxedo, gave his ruffled shirt one last pat, and resignedly headed out to the front steps. Let the dog and pony show begin.

Now where in blazes was his sister?

AT THAT MOMENT, the subject of Jordan Tavistock's speculation was riding hell-bent for leather across a grassy field. *Poor old Froggie needs the workout,* thought Beryl. *And so do I.* She bent forward into the wind, felt the lash of Froggie's mane against her face, and inhaled that wonderful scent of horseflesh, sweet clover and warm July earth. Froggie was enjoying the sprint just as much as she was, if not more. Beryl could feel those powerful muscles straining for ever more speed. *She's a demon, like me,* thought Beryl, suddenly laughing aloud—the same wild laugh that always made poor Uncle Hughie cringe. But out here, in the open fields, she could laugh like a wanton woman and no one would hear. If only she could keep on riding, forever and ever! But fences and walls seemed to be everywhere in her life. Fences of the mind, of the heart. She urged her mount still faster, as though through speed she could outrun all the devils pursuing her.

Bastille Day. What a desperate excuse for a party.

Uncle Hugh loved a good bash, and the Vanes *were* old family friends; they deserved a decent send-off. But she'd seen the guest list, and it was the same tiresome lot. Shouldn't ex-spies and diplomats lead more interesting lives? She couldn't imagine James Bond, retired, pottering about in his garden.

Yet that's what Uncle Hugh seemed to do all day. The highlight of *his* week had been harvesting the season's first hybrid Nepal tomato—his earliest tomato ever! And as for her uncle's friends, well, she couldn't imagine *them* ever sneaking around the back alleys of Paris or Berlin. Philippe St. Pierre, perhaps—yes, she could picture *him* in his younger days; at sixty-two, he was still charming, a Gallic lady-killer. And Reggie Vane might have cut a dashing figure years ago. But most of Uncle Hugh's old colleagues seemed so, well... used up.

Not me. Never me.

She galloped harder, letting Froggie have free rein.

They raced across the last stretch of field and through a copse of trees. Froggie, winded now, slowed to a trot, then a walk. Beryl pulled her to a halt by the church's stone wall. There she dismounted and let Froggie wander about untethered. The churchyard was deserted and the gravestones cast lengthening shadows across the lawn. Beryl clambered over the low wall and walked among the plots until she came to the spot she'd visited so many times before. A handsome obelisk towered over two graves, resting side by side. There were no curlicues, no fancy angels carved into that marble face. Only words.

Bernard Tavistock, 1930–1973
Madeline Tavistock, 1934–1973

On earth, as it is in heaven, we are together.

Beryl knelt on the grass and gazed for a long time at the resting place of her mother and father. *Twenty years ago tomorrow,* she thought. *How I wish I could remember you more clearly! Your faces, your smiles.* What she did remember were odd things, unimportant things. The smell of leather luggage, of Mum's perfume and Dad's pipe. The crackle of paper as she and Jordan would unwrap the gifts Mum and Dad brought home to them. Dolls from France. Music boxes from Italy. And there was laughter. Always lots of laughter...

Beryl sat with her eyes closed and heard that happy sound through the passage of twenty years. Through the evening buzz of insects, the clink of Froggie's bit and bridle, she heard the sounds of her childhood.

The church bell tolled—six chimes.

At once Beryl sat up straight. Oh, no, was it already that late? She glanced around and saw that the shadows had grown, that Froggie was standing by the wall regarding her with frank expectation. *Oh Lord,* she thought, *Uncle Hugh will be royally cross with me.*

She dashed out of the churchyard and climbed onto Froggie's back. At once they were flying across the field, horse and rider blended into a single sleek organism. *Time for the shortcut,* thought Beryl, guiding Froggie toward the trees. It meant a leap over the stone wall, and then a clip along the road, but it would cut a mile off their route. Froggie seemed to understand that time was of the essence. She picked up speed and approached the stone wall with all the eagerness of a seasoned steeplechaser. She took the jump cleanly, with inches to spare. Beryl felt the wind rush past, felt her mount soar, then touch down on the far side of the wall. The biggest hurdle was behind them. Now, just beyond that bend in the road—

She saw a flash of red, heard the squeal of tires across pavement. Froggie swerved sideways and reared up. The sudden lurch caught Beryl by surprise. She tumbled out of the saddle and landed with a stunning thud on the ground.

Her first reaction, after her head had stopped spinning, was astonishment that she had fallen at all—and for such a stupid reason.

Her next reaction was fear that Froggie might be injured.

Beryl scrambled to her feet and ran to snatch the reins. Froggie was still spooked, nervously trip-trapping about on the pavement. The sound of a car door slamming shut, of someone running toward them, only made the horse edgier.

"Don't come any closer!" hissed Beryl over her shoulder.

"Are you all right?" came the anxious inquiry. It was a man's voice, pleasantly baritone. American?

"I'm fine," snapped Beryl.

"What about your horse?"

Murmuring softly to Froggie, Beryl knelt down and ran her hands along Froggie's foreleg. The delicate bones all seemed to be intact.

"Is he all right?" said the man.

"It's a she," answered Beryl. "And yes, she seems to be just fine."

"I really *can* tell the difference," came the dry response. "When I have a view of the essential parts."

Suppressing a smile, Beryl straightened and turned to look at the man. Dark hair, dark eyes, she noted. And the definite glint of humor—nothing stiff-upper-lip about this one. Forty plus years of laughter had left attractive creases about his eyes. He was dressed in formal black tie, and his broad shoulders filled out the tuxedo jacket quite impressively.

"I'm sorry about the spill," he said. "I guess it *was* my fault."

"This is a country road, you know. Not exactly the place to be speeding. You never can tell what lies around the bend."

"So I've discovered."

Froggie gave her an impatient nudge. Beryl stroked the horse's neck, all the time intensely aware of the man's gaze.

"I do have something of an excuse," he said. "I got turned around in the village back there, and I'm running late. I'm trying to find some place called Chetwynd. Do you know it?"

She cocked her head in surprise. "You're going to Chetwynd? Then you're on the wrong road."

"Am I?"

"You turned off a half mile too soon. Head back to the main road and keep going. You can't miss the turn. It's a private drive, flanked by elms—quite tall ones."

"I'll watch for the elms, then."

She remounted Froggie and gazed down at the man. Even viewed from the saddle, he cut an impressive figure, lean and elegant in his tuxedo. And strikingly confident, not a man to be intimidated by anyone—even a woman sitting astride nine hundred muscular pounds of horseflesh.

"Are you sure you're not hurt?" he asked. "It looked like a pretty bad fall to me."

"Oh, I've fallen before." She smiled. "I have quite a hard head."

The man smiled, too, his teeth straight and white in the twilight. "Then I shouldn't worry about you slipping into a stupor tonight?"

"*You're* the one who'll be slipping into a stupor tonight."

He frowned. "Excuse me?"

"A stupor brought on by dry and endless palaver. It's a distinct possibility, considering where you're headed." Laughing, she turned the horse around. "Good evening," she called. Then, with a farewell wave, she urged Froggie into a trot through the woods.

As she left the road behind, it occurred to her that she would get to Chetwynd before he did. That made her laugh again. Perhaps Bastille Day would turn out more interesting than she'd expected. She gave the horse a nudge of her boot. At once Froggie broke into a gallop.

RICHARD WOLF STOOD BESIDE his rented M.G. and watched the woman ride away, her black hair tumbling like a horse's mane about her shoulders. In seconds she was gone, vanished from sight into the woods. He never even caught her name, he thought. He'd have to ask Lord Lovat about her. *Tell me, Hugh. Are you acquainted with a black-haired witch tearing about your neighborhood?* She was dressed like one of the village girls, in a frayed shirt and grass-stained jodhpurs, but her accent bespoke the finest of schools. A charming contradiction.

He climbed back into the car. It was almost six-thirty now; that drive from London had taken longer than he'd expected. Blast these backcountry lanes! He turned the car around and headed for the main road, taking care this time to slow down for curves. No telling what might be lurking around the bend. A cow or a goat.

Or another witch on horseback.

I have quite a hard head. He smiled. A hard head, indeed. She slips off the saddle—bump—and she's right back on her feet. And cheeky to boot. *As if I couldn't tell a mare from a stallion. All I needed was the right view.*

Which he certainly had had of her. There was no doubt whatsoever that it was the female of the species he'd been looking at. All that raven hair, those laughing green eyes. *She almost reminds me of...*

He suppressed the thought, shoved it into the quicksand of bad memories. Nightmares, really. Those terrible echoes of his first assignment, his first failure. It had colored his career, had kept him from ever again taking anything for granted. That was the way one *should* operate in this business. Check the facts, never trust your sources, and always, always watch your back.

It was starting to wear him down. *Maybe I should kick back and retire early. Live the quiet country life like Hugh Tavistock.* Of course Tavistock had a title and estate to keep him in comfort, though Richard had to laugh when he thought of the rotund and balding Hugh Tavistock as earl of anything. *Yeah, I should just settle down on those ten acres in Connecticut. Declare myself Earl of Whatever and grow cucumbers.*

But he'd miss the work. Those delicious whiffs of danger, the international chess game of wits. The world was changing so fast, and you didn't know from day to day who your enemies were....

He spotted, at last, the turnoff to Chetwynd. Flanked by majestic elms, it was as the black-haired woman had described it. That impressive driveway was more than matched by the manor house standing at the end of the road. This was no mere country cottage; this was a castle, complete with turrets and ivy-covered stone walls. Formal gardens stretched out for acres, and a brick path led to what looked like a medieval maze. So this was where old Hugh Tavistock had repaired to after those forty years of service to queen and country. Earldom must have its benefits—one certainly didn't acquire this much wealth in government service. And Hugh had struck him as such a down-to-earth fellow! Not at all the country nobleman type. He had no airs, no pretensions; he was more like some absentminded civil servant who'd wandered, quite by accident, into MI6's inner sanctum.

Amused by the grandeur of it all, Richard went up the steps, breezed through the security gauntlet, and walked into the ballroom.

Here he saw a number of familiar faces among the dozens of guests who'd already arrived. The London economic summit had drawn in diplomats and financiers from across the continent. He spotted at once the American ambassador, swaggering and schmoozing like the political appointee he was. Across the room he saw a trio of old acquaintances from Paris. There was Philippe St. Pierre, the French finance minister, deep in conversation with Reggie Vane, head of the Paris Division, Bank of London. Off to the side stood Reggie's wife, Helena, looking ignored and crabby as usual. Had Richard *ever* seen that woman look happy?

A woman's loud and brassy laugh drew Richard's attention to another familiar figure from his Paris days— Nina Sutherland, the ambassador's widow, shimmering from throat to ankle in green silk and bugle beads. Though her husband was long dead, the old gal was still working the crowd like a seasoned diplomat's wife. Beside her was her twenty-year-old son, Anthony, rumored to be an artist. In his purple shirt, he cut just as flashy a figure as his mother did. What a resplendent pair they were, like a couple of peacocks! Young Anthony had obviously inherited his ex-actress mother's gene for flamboyance.

Judiciously avoiding the Sutherland pair, Richard headed to the buffet table, which was graced with an elaborate ice sculpture of the Eiffel Tower. This Bastille Day theme had been carried to ridiculous extremes. *Everything* was French tonight: the music, the champagne, the tricolors hanging from the ceiling.

"Rather makes one want to burst out singing the 'Marseillaise,' doesn't it?" said a voice.

Richard turned and saw a tall blond man standing beside him. Slenderly built, with the stamp of aristocracy on his face, he seemed elegantly at ease in his starched shirt and tuxedo. Smiling, he handed a glass of champagne to Richard. The chandelier light glittered in the pale bubbles. "You're Richard Wolf," the man said.

Richard nodded, accepting the glass. "And you are...?"

"Jordan Tavistock. Uncle Hugh pointed you out as you walked into the room. Thought I'd come by and introduce myself."

The two men shook hands. Jordan's grip was solid and connected, not what Richard expected from such smoothly aristocratic hands.

"So tell me," said Jordan, casually picking up a second glass of champagne for himself, "which category do you fit into? Spy, diplomat or financier?"

Richard laughed. "I'm expected to answer that question?"

"No. But I thought I'd ask, anyway. It gets things off to a flying start." He took a sip and smiled. "It's a mental exercise of mine. Keeps these parties interesting.

I try to pick up on the cues, deduce which ones are with Intelligence. And half of these people are. Or were.'' Jordan gazed around the room. ''Think of all the secrets contained in all these heads—all those little synapses snapping with classified data.''

''You seem to have more than a passing acquaintance with the business.''

''When one grows up in this household, one lives and breathes the game.'' Jordan regarded Richard for a moment. ''Let's see. You're American....''

''Correct.''

''And whereas the corporate executives arrived in groups by stretch limousine, you came on your own.''

''Right so far.''

''And you refer to intelligence work as *the business*.''

''You noticed.''

''So my guess is...CIA?''

Richard shook his head and smiled. ''I'm just a private security consultant. Sakaroff and Wolf, Inc.''

Jordan smiled back. ''Clever cover.''

''It's not a cover. I'm the real thing. All these corporate executives you see here want a safe summit. An IRA bomb could ruin their whole day.''

''So they hire you to keep the nasties away,'' finished Jordan.

''Exactly,'' said Richard. And he thought, *Yes, this is Madeline and Bernard's son, all right. He resembles Bernard, has got the same sharply observant brown eyes, the same finely wrought features. And he's quick. He notices things—an indispensable talent.*

At that moment, Jordan's attention suddenly shifted to a new arrival. Richard turned to see who had just entered the ballroom. At his first glimpse of the woman, he stiffened in surprise.

It was that black-haired witch, dressed not in old jodh-purs and boots this time, but in a long gown of midnight blue silk. Her hair had been swept up into an elegant mass of waves. Even from this distance, he could feel the magical spell of her attraction—as did every other man in the room.

"It's her," murmured Richard.

"You mean you two have met?" asked Jordan.

"Quite by accident. I spooked her horse on the road. She was none too pleased about the fall."

"You actually unhorsed her?" said Jordan in amaze-ment. "I didn't think it was possible."

The woman glided into the room and swept up a glass of champagne from a tray, her progress cutting a no-ticeable swath through the crowd.

"She certainly knows how to fill a dress," Richard said under his breath, marveling.

"I'll tell her you said so," Jordan said dryly.

"You wouldn't."

Laughing, Jordan set down his glass. "Come on, Wolf. Let me properly introduce you."

As they approached her, the woman flashed Jordan a smile of greeting. Then her gaze shifted to Richard, and instantly her expression went from easy familiarity to a look of cautious speculation. *Not good,* thought Richard. *She's remembering how I knocked her off that horse. How I almost got her killed.*

"So," she said, civilly enough, "we meet again."

"I hope you've forgiven me."

"Never." Then she smiled. What a smile!

Jordan said, "Darling, this is Richard Wolf."

The woman held out her hand. Richard took it and was surprised by the firm, no-nonsense handshake she returned. As he looked into her eyes, a shock of recognition went through him. *Of course. I should have seen it the very first time we met. That black hair. Those green eyes. She has to be Madeline's daughter.*

"May I introduce Beryl Tavistock," said Jordan. "My sister."

"SO HOW DO YOU HAPPEN to know my Uncle Hugh?" Beryl asked as she and Richard strolled down the garden path. Dusk had fallen, that soft, late dusk of summer, and the flowers had faded into shadow. Their fragrance hung in the air, the scent of sage and roses, lavender and thyme. *He moves like a cat in the darkness,* Beryl thought. *So quiet, so unfathomable.*

"We met years ago in Paris," he said. "We lost touch for a long time. And then, a few years ago, when I set up my consulting firm, your uncle was kind enough to advise me."

"Jordan tells me your company's Sakaroff and Wolf."

"Yes. We're security consultants."

"And is that your real job?"

"Meaning what?"

"Have you a, shall we say, *unofficial* job?"

He threw back his head and laughed. "You and your brother have a knack for cutting straight to the chase."

"We've learned to be direct. It cuts down on the small talk."

"Small talk is society's lubricant."

"No, small talk is how society avoids telling the truth."

"And you want to hear the truth," he said.

"Don't we all?" She looked up at him, trying to see his eyes in the darkness, but they were only shadows in the silhouette of his face.

"The truth," he said, "is that I really am a security consultant. I run the firm with my partner, Niki Sakaroff—"

"Niki? That wouldn't be Nikolai Sakaroff?"

"You've heard the name?" he asked, in a tone that was just a trifle too innocent.

"Former KGB?"

There was a pause. "Yes, at one time," he said evenly. "Niki may have had connections."

"Connections? If I recall correctly, Nikolai Sakaroff was a full colonel. And now he's your business partner?" She laughed. "Capitalism does indeed make strange bedfellows."

They walked a few moments in silence. She asked quietly, "Do you still do business for the CIA?"

"Did I say I did?"

"It's not a difficult conclusion to come to. I'm very discreet, by the way. The truth is safe with me."

"Nevertheless I refuse to be interrogated."

She looked up at him with a smile. "Even under torture, I assume?"

Through the darkness she could see his teeth gleaming in a grin. "That depends on the type of torture. If a beautiful woman nibbles on my ear, well, I might admit to anything."

The brick path ended at the maze. For a while, they stood contemplating that leafy wall of shadow.

"Come on, let's go in," she said.

"Do you know the way out?"

"We'll see."

She led him through the opening and they were quickly swallowed up by hedge walls. In truth, she knew every turn, every blind end, and she moved through the maze with confidence. "I could do this blindfolded," she said.

"Did you grow up at Chetwynd?"

"In between boarding schools. I came to live with Uncle Hugh when I was eight. After Mum and Dad died."

They rustled through the last slot in the hedge and emerged into the center. In a small clearing there was a stone bench and enough moonlight to faintly see each other's face.

"They were in the business, too," she said, circling the grassy clearing slowly. "Or did you already know that?"

"Yes, I've…heard of your parents."

At once she sensed an undertone of caution in his voice and wondered why he'd gone evasive on her. She saw that he was standing by the stone bench, his hands in his pockets. *All these family secrets. I'm sick of it. Why can't anyone ever tell the truth in this house?*

"What have you heard about them?" she asked.

"I know they died in Paris."

"In the line of duty. Uncle Hugh says it was a classified mission and refuses to talk about it, so we never do." She stopped circling and turned to face him. "I seem to be thinking about it a lot these days."

"Why?"

"Because it happened on the fifteenth of July. Twenty years ago tomorrow."

He moved toward her, his face still hidden in shadow. "Who reared you, then? Your uncle?"

She smiled. "'Reared' is a bit of an exaggeration. Uncle Hugh gave us a home, and then he pretty much turned us loose to grow up as we pleased. Jordan's done quite well for himself, I think. Gone to university and all. But then, Jordie's the smart one in the family.''

Richard moved closer—so close she thought she could see his eyes glittering above her in the darkness. ''And which one are you?''

''I suppose…I suppose I'm the wild one.''

''The wild one,'' he murmured. ''Yes, I think I can tell….''

He touched her face. With that one brief contact, he left her skin tingling. She was suddenly aware of her pounding heart, her quickening breath. *Why am I letting this happen?* she wondered. *I thought I'd sworn off romance. But now this man I scarcely know is dragging me back into the game—a game at which I've proved myself a miserable failure. It's stupid, it's impulsive. It's insanity itself.*

And it's leaving me quite hungry for more….

His lips grazed hers; it was the lightest of kisses, but it was heady with the taste of champagne. At once she craved another kiss, a longer kiss. For a moment, they stared at each other, both hovering on the edge of temptation.

Beryl surrendered first. She swayed toward him, against him. His arms went around her, trapping her in their embrace. Eagerly she met his lips, met his kiss with one just as fierce.

''The wild one,'' he whispered. ''Yes, definitely the wild one.''

''Demanding, too…''

''I don't doubt it.''

''…and *very* difficult.''

''I hadn't noticed….''

They kissed again, and by the ragged sound of his

breathing, she knew that he, too, was a helpless victim of desire. Suddenly a devilish impulse seized her.

She pulled away. Coyly she asked, "Now will you tell me?"

"Tell you what?" he asked, plainly confused.

"Whom you really work for?"

He paused. "Sakaroff and Wolf, Inc.," he said. "Security consultants."

"Wrong answer," she said. Then, laughing wickedly, she turned and scampered out of the maze.

Paris

At 8:45, as was her habit, Marie St. Pierre patted on her bee pollen face cream, ran a brush through her stiff gray hair, and then slipped under the covers of her bed. She flicked on the TV remote control and awaited her favorite program of the week—"Dynasty." Though the voices were obviously dubbed and the settings garishly American, the stories were close to her heart. Love and power. Pain and retribution. Yes, Marie knew all about love and pain. It was the retribution part she hadn't quite mastered. Every time the anger bubbled up inside her and those old fantasies of revenge began to play out in her mind, she had only to consider the consequences of such action, and all thoughts of vengeance died. No, she loved Philippe too much. And they had come so far together! From finance minister to prime minister would be such a short, short climb....

She suddenly focused on the TV as a brief news item flashed on the screen—the London economic summit. Would Philippe's face appear? No, just a pan of the conference table, a five-second view of two dozen men in suits and ties. No Philippe. She sat back in disappointment and wondered, for the hundredth time, if she should have accompanied her husband to London. She hated to fly, and he'd warned her the trip would be tiresome. Better to stay home, he'd told her; she would hate London.

Still, it might have been nice to go away with him for a few days. Just the two of them in a hotel room. A change of scenery, a new bed. It might have been the spark their marriage so terribly needed—

A thought suddenly crossed her mind. A thought so painful that it twisted her heart in knots. *Here I am. And there is Philippe, alone in London....*

Or was he alone?

She sat trembling for a moment, considering the possibilities. The images. At last she could resist the impulse no longer. She reached for the telephone and dialed Nina Sutherland's Paris apartment.

The phone rang and rang. She hung up and dialed again. Still it rang unanswered. She stared at the receiver. So Nina has gone to London, too, she thought. And there they would be together, in his hotel room. *While I wait at home in Paris.*

She rose from the bed. "Dynasty" had just come on the TV; she ignored it. Instead she got dressed. *Perhaps I am jumping to conclusions,* she thought. *Perhaps Nina is really home and refuses to answer her telephone.*

She would drive past Nina's apartment in Neuilly. Check the windows to see if her lights were on inside.

And if they were not?

No, she wouldn't think about that, not yet.

Fully dressed now, she hurried downstairs, picked up her purse and keys in the darkened living room, and opened the front door. Just as she felt the night air against her face, her ears were blasted by a deafening roar.

The explosion threw her off her feet, flinging her forward down the front steps. Only her outstretched arms beneath her prevented her head from slamming against the concrete. She was vaguely aware of glass raining down around her and then of the soft crackle of flames. Slowly she managed to roll over onto her back. There she lay, staring upward at the fingers of fire shooting through her bedroom window.

It was meant for her, she thought. The bomb was meant for her.

As fire sirens wailed closer, she lay on her back in the broken glass and thought, *Is this what it's come to, my love?*

And she watched her bedroom burn above her.

2

Buckinghamshire, England

The Eiffel Tower was melting. Jordan stood beside the buffet table and watched the water drip, drip from the ice sculpture into the silver platter of oysters below it. So much for Bastille Day, he thought wearily. Another night, another party. And this one's about run its course.

"You have had more than enough oysters for one night, Reggie," said a peevish voice. "Or have you forgotten your gout?"

"Haven't had an attack in months."

"Only because *I've* been watching your diet," said Helena.

"Then tonight, dear," said Reggie, plucking up another oyster, "would you mind looking the other way?" He lifted the shell to his mouth and tipped the oyster. Nirvana was written on his face as the slippery glob slid into his throat.

Helena shuddered. "It's disgusting, eating a live animal." She glanced at Jordan, noting his quietly bemused look. "Don't you agree?"

Jordan gave a diplomatic shrug. "A matter of upbringing, I suppose. In some cultures, they eat termites. Or quivering fish. I've even heard of monkeys, their heads shaved, immobilized—"

"Oh, please," groaned Helena.

Jordan quickly escaped before the marital spat could escalate. It was not a healthy place to be, caught between a feuding husband and wife. Lady Helena, he suspected, normally held the upper hand; money usually did.

He wandered over to join Finance Minister Philippe St. Pierre and found himself trapped in a lecture on world economics. The summit was a failure, Philippe declared. The Americans want trade concessions but refuse to learn fiscal responsibility. And on and on and on. It was almost a relief when bugle-beaded Nina Sutherland swept into the conversation, trailing her peacock son, Anthony.

"It's not as if Americans are the only ones who have to clean up their act," snorted Nina. "We're none of us doing very well these days, even the French. Or don't you agree, Philippe?"

Philippe flushed under her direct gaze. "We are all of us having difficulties, Nina—"

"Some of us more than others."

"It is a worldwide recession. One must be patient."

Nina's jaw shot up. "And what if one cannot afford to wait?" She drained her glass and set it down sharply. "What then, Philippe, darling?"

Conversation suddenly ceased. Jordan noticed that Helena was watching them amusedly, that Philippe was clutching his glass in a white-knuckled fist. What the blazes was going on here? he wondered. Some private feud? Bizarre tensions were weaving through the gathering tonight. Perhaps it's all that free-flowing champagne. Certainly Reggie had had too much. Their portly houseguest had wandered from the oyster tray to the champagne table. With an unsteady hand, he picked up yet another glass and raised it to his lips. No one was acting quite right tonight. Not even Beryl.

Certainly not Beryl.

He spied his sister as she reentered the ballroom. Her cheeks were flushed, her eyes glittering with some unearthly fire. Close on her heels was the American, looking just as flushed and more than a little bothered. Ah, thought Jordan with a smile. A bit of hanky-panky in the garden, was it? Well, good for her. Poor Beryl could use some fresh romance in her life, anything to make her forget that chronically unfaithful surgeon.

Beryl whisked up a glass of champagne from a passing servant and headed Jordan's way. "Having fun?" she asked him.

"Not as much as you, I suspect." He glanced across at Richard Wolf, who'd just been waylaid by some American businessman. "So," he whispered, "did you wring a confession out of him?"

"Not a thing." She smiled over her champagne glass. "Extremely tight-lipped."

"Really?"

"But I'll have another go at him later. After I let him cool his heels for a while."

Lord, how beautiful his baby sister could be when she was happy, thought Jordan. Which, it seemed, wasn't very often lately. Too much passion in that heart of hers; it made her far more vulnerable than she'd ever admit. For a year now she'd been lying doggo, had dropped out entirely from the old mating game. She'd even given up her charity work at St. Luke's—a job she'd dearly loved. It was too painful, always running into her ex-lover on the hospital grounds.

But tonight the old sparkle was back in her eyes and he was glad to see it. He noticed how it flared even more brightly as Richard Wolf glanced her way. All those flirtatious looks passing back and forth! He could almost feel the crackle of electricity flying between them.

"...a well-deserved honor, of course, but a bit late, don't you think, Jordan?"

Jordan glanced in puzzlement at Reggie Vane's flushed face. The man had been drinking entirely too much. "Excuse me," he said, "I'm afraid I wasn't following."

"The Queen's medal for Leo Sinclair. You remember Leo, don't you? Wonderful chap. Killed a year and a half ago. Or was it two years?" He gave his head a little shake, as though to clear it. "Anyway, they're just getting 'round to giving the widow his medal. I think that's inexcusable."

"Not everyone who was killed in the Gulf got a medal," Nina Sutherland cut in.

"But Leo was Intelligence," said Reggie. "He deserved some sort of honor, considering how he...died."

"Perhaps it was just an oversight," said Jordan. "Papers getting mislaid, that sort of thing. MI6 does try to honor its dead, and Leo sort of fell through the cracks."

"The way Mum and Dad did," said Beryl. "They died in the line of duty. And they never got a medal."

"Line of duty?" said Reggie. "Not exactly." He lifted the champagne glass unsteadily to his lips. Suddenly he paused, aware that the others were staring at him. The silence stretched on, broken only by the clatter of an oyster shell on someone's plate.

"What do you mean by 'not exactly'?" asked Beryl.

Reggie cleared his throat. "Surely...Hugh must have told you...." He looked around and his face blanched. "Oh, no," he murmured, "I've put my foot in it this time."

"Told us what, Reggie?" Jordan persisted.

"But it was public knowledge," said Reggie. "It was in all the Paris newspapers...."

"Reggie," Jordan said slowly. Deliberately. "Our understanding was that my mother and father were shot in Paris. That it was murder. Is that not true?"

"Well, of course there was a murder involved—"

"*A* murder?" Jordan cut in. "As in singular?"

Reggie glanced around, befuddled. "I'm not the only one here who knows about it. You were all in Paris when it happened!"

For a few heartbeats, no one said a thing. Then Helena added, quietly, "It was a very long time ago, Jordan. Twenty years. It hardly makes a difference now."

"It makes a difference to *us*," Jordan insisted. "What happened in Paris?"

Helena sighed. "I told Hugh he should've been honest with you, instead of trying to bury it."

"Bury *what?*" asked Beryl.

Helena's mouth drew tight.

It was Nina who finally spoke the truth. Brazen Nina, who had never bothered with subtleties. She said flatly, "The police said it was a murder. Followed by a suicide."

Beryl stared at Nina. Saw the other woman's gaze meet hers without flinching. "No," she whispered.

Gently Helena touched her shoulder. "You were just a child, Beryl. Both of you were. And Hugh didn't think it was appropriate—"

Beryl said again, "No," and pulled away from Helena's outstretched hand. Suddenly she whirled and fled in a rustle of blue silk across the ballroom.

"Thank you. All of you," said Jordan coldly. "For

your most refreshing candor.'' Then he, too, turned and headed across the room in pursuit of his sister.

He caught up with her on the staircase. "Beryl?"

"It's not true," she said. "I don't believe it!"

"Of course it's not true."

She halted on the stairs and looked down at him. "Then why are they all saying it?"

"Ugly rumors. What else can it be?"

"Where's Uncle Hugh?"

Jordan shook his head. "He's not in the ballroom."

Beryl looked up toward the second floor. "Come on, Jordie," she said, her voice tight with determination. "We're going to set this thing straight."

Together they climbed the stairs.

Uncle Hugh was in his study; through the closed door, they could hear him speaking in urgent tones. Without knocking, they pushed inside and confronted him.

"Uncle Hugh?" said Beryl.

Hugh cut her off with a sharp motion for silence. He turned his back and said into the telephone, "It *is* definite, Claude? Not a gas leak or anything like that?"

"Uncle Hugh!"

Stubbornly he kept his back turned to her. "Yes, yes," he said into the phone, "I'll tell Philippe at once. God, this is horrid timing, but you're right, he has no choice. He'll have to fly back tonight." Looking stunned, Hugh hung up and stared at the telephone.

"Did you tell us the truth?" asked Beryl. "About Mum and Dad?"

Hugh turned and frowned at her in bewilderment. "What? What are you talking about?"

"You told us they were killed in the line of duty," said Beryl. "You never said anything about a suicide."

"Who told you that?" he snapped.

"Nina Sutherland. But Reggie and Helena knew about it, too. In fact, the whole world seems to know! Everyone except us."

"Blast that Sutherland woman!" roared Hugh. "She had no right."

Beryl and Jordan stared at him in shock. Softly Beryl said, "It *is* a lie. Isn't it?"

Abruptly Hugh started for the door. "We'll discuss it later," he said. "I have to take care of this business—"

"Uncle Hugh!" cried Beryl. "Is it a lie?"

Hugh stopped. Slowly he turned and looked at her. "I never believed it," he said. "Not for a second did I think Bernard would ever hurt her...."

"What are you saying?" asked Jordan. "That it was Dad who killed her?"

Their uncle's silence was the only answer they needed. For a moment, Hugh lingered in the doorway. Quietly he said, "Please, Jordan. We'll talk about it later. After everyone leaves. Now I really must see to this phone call." He turned and left the room.

Beryl and Jordan looked at each other. They each saw, in the other's eyes, the same shock of comprehension.

"Dear God, Jordie," said Beryl. "It must be true."

FROM ACROSS THE BALLROOM, Richard saw Beryl's hasty exit and then, seconds later, the equally rapid departure of a grim-faced Jordan. What the hell was going on? he wondered. He started to follow them out of the room, then spotted Helena, shaking her head as she moved toward him.

"It's a disaster," she muttered. "Too much bloody champagne flowing tonight."

"What happened?"

"They just heard the truth. About Bernard and Madeline."

"Who told them?"

"Nina. But it was Reggie's fault, really. He's so drunk he doesn't know what he's saying."

Richard looked at the doorway through which Jordan had just vanished. "I should talk to them, tell them the whole story."

"I think that's their uncle's responsibility. Don't you? He's the one who kept it from them all these years. Let him do the explaining."

After a pause, Richard nodded. "You're right. Of course you're right. Maybe I'll just go and strangle Nina Sutherland instead."

"Strangle my husband while you're at it. You have my permission."

Richard turned and spotted Hugh Tavistock reentering the ballroom. "Now what?" he muttered as the man hurried toward them.

"Where's Philippe?" snapped Hugh.

"I believe he was headed out to the garden," said Helena. "Is something wrong?"

"This whole evening's turned into a disaster," muttered Hugh. "I just got a call from Paris. A bomb's gone off in Philippe's flat."

Richard and Helena stared at him in horror.

"Oh, my God," whispered Helena. "Is Marie—"

"She's all right. A few minor injuries, but nothing serious. She's in hospital now."

"Assassination attempt?" Richard queried.

Hugh nodded. "So it would seem."

IT WAS LONG PAST MIDNIGHT when Jordan and Uncle Hugh finally found Beryl. She was in her mother's old room, huddled beside Madeline's steamer trunk. The lid had been thrown open, and Madeline's belongings were spilled out across the bed and the floor: silky summer dresses, flowery hats, a beaded evening purse. And there were silly things, too: a branch of sea coral, a pebble, a china frog—items of significance known only to Madeline. Beryl had removed all of these things from the trunk, and now she sat surrounded by them, trying to absorb, through these inanimate objects, the warmth and spirit that had once been Madeline Tavistock.

Uncle Hugh came into the bedroom and sat down in a chair beside her. "Beryl," he said gently, "it's time… it's time I told you the truth."

"The time for the truth was years ago," she said, staring down at the china frog in her hand.

"But you were both so very young. You were only eight, and Jordan was ten. You wouldn't have understood—"

"We could've dealt with the facts! Instead you hid them from us!"

"The facts were painful. The French police concluded—"

"Dad would *never* have hurt her," said Beryl. She looked up at him with a ferocity that made Hugh draw back in surprise. "Don't you remember how they were together, Uncle Hugh? How much in love they were? *I* remember!"

"So do I," said Jordan.

Uncle Hugh took off his spectacles and wearily rubbed his eyes. "The truth," he said, "is even worse than that."

Beryl stared at him incredulously. "How could it be any worse than murder and suicide?"

"Perhaps...perhaps you should see the file." He rose to his feet. "It's upstairs. In my office."

They followed their uncle to the third floor, to a room they seldom visited, a room he always kept locked. He opened the cabinet and pulled a folder from the drawer. It was a classified MI6 file labeled Tavistock, Bernard and Madeline.

"I suppose I...I'd hoped to protect you from this," said Hugh. "The truth is, I myself don't believe it. Bernard didn't have a traitorous bone in his body. But the evidence was there. And I don't know any other way to explain it." He handed the file to Beryl.

In silence she opened the folder. Together she and Jordan paged through the contents. Inside were copies of the Paris police report, including witness statements and photographs of the murder scene. The conclusions were as Nina Sutherland had told them. Bernard had shot his wife three times at close range and had then put the gun to his own head and pulled the trigger. The crime photos were too horrible to dwell on; Beryl flipped quickly past those and found herself staring at another report, this one filed by French Intelligence. In disbelief, she read and reread the conclusions.

"This isn't possible," she said.

"It's what they found. A briefcase with classified NATO files. Allied weapons data. It was in the garret, where their bodies were discovered. Bernard had those files with him when he died—files that shouldn't have been out of the embassy building."

"How do you know *he* took them?"

"He had access, Beryl. He was our Intelligence liaison to NATO. For months, Allied documents were showing up in East German hands, delivered to them by someone they code-named Delphi. We knew we had a mole, but we couldn't identify him—until those papers were found with Bernard's body.''

''And you think Dad was Delphi,'' said Jordan.

''No, that's what French Intelligence concluded. I couldn't believe it, but I also couldn't dispute the facts.''

For a moment, Beryl and Jordan sat in silence, dismayed by the weight of the evidence.

''You don't really believe it, Uncle Hugh?'' said Beryl softly. ''That Dad was the one?''

''I couldn't argue with the findings. And it *would* explain their deaths. Perhaps they knew they were on the verge of being discovered. Disgraced. So Bernard took the gentleman's way out. He would, you know. Death before dishonor.''

Uncle Hugh sank back in the chair and wearily ran his fingers through his gray hair. ''I tried to keep the report as quiet as possible,'' hc said. ''The search for Delphi was halted. I myself had a few sticky years in MI6. Brother of a traitor and all, can we trust him, that sort of thing. But then, it was forgotten. And I went on with my career. I think...I think it was because no one at MI6 could quite believe the report. That Bernard had gone to the other side.''

''I don't believe it, either,'' said Beryl.

Uncle Hugh looked at her. ''Nevertheless—''

''I *won't* believe it. It's a fabrication. Someone at MI6, covering up the truth—''

''Don't be ridiculous, Beryl.''

''Mum and Dad can't defend themselves! Who else will speak up for them?''

''Your loyalty's commendable, darling, but—''

''And where's *your* loyalty?'' she retorted. ''He was your brother!''

''I didn't want to believe it.''

"Then did you confirm that evidence? Did you discuss it with French Intelligence?"

"Yes, and I trusted Daumier's report. He's a thorough man."

"Daumier?" queried Jordan. "Claude Daumier? Isn't he chief of their Paris operations?"

"At the time, he was their liaison to MI6. I asked him to review the findings. He came to the same conclusions."

"Then this Daumier fellow is an idiot," said Beryl. She turned to the door. "And I'm going to tell him so myself."

"Where are you going?" asked Jordan.

"To pack my things," she said. "Are you coming, Jordan?"

"Pack?" said Hugh. "Where in blazes are you headed?"

Beryl threw a glance over her shoulder. "Where else," she answered, "but Paris?"

RICHARD WOLF GOT THE CALL at six that morning. "They are booked on a noon flight to Paris," said Claude Daumier. "It seems, my friend, that someone has pried open a rather nasty can of worms."

Still groggy with sleep, Richard sat up in bed and gave his head a shake. "What are you talking about, Claude? Who's flying to Paris?"

"Beryl and Jordan Tavistock. Hugh has just called me. I think this is not a good development."

Richard collapsed back on his pillow. "They're adults, Claude," he said, yawning. "If they want to jet off to Paris—"

"They are coming to find out about Bernard and Madeline."

Richard closed his eyes and groaned. "Oh, wonderful, just what we need."

"My sentiments precisely."

"Can't Hugh talk them out of it?"

"He tried. But this niece of his…" Daumier sighed. "You have met her. So you would understand."

Yes, Richard knew exactly how stubborn Miss Beryl Tavistock could be. Like mother, like daughter. He remembered that Madeline had been just as unswerving, just as unstoppable.

Just as enchanting.

He shook off those haunting memories of a long-dead woman and said, "How much do they know?"

"They have seen my report. They know about Delphi."

"So they'll be digging in all the right places."

"All the dangerous places," amended Daumier.

Richard sat up on the side of the bed and clawed his fingers through his hair as he considered the possibilities. The perils.

"Hugh is concerned for their safety," said Daumier. "So am I. If what we think is true—"

"Then they're walking into quicksand."

"And Paris is dangerous enough as it is," added Daumier, "what with the latest bombing."

"How is Marie St. Pierre, by the way?"

"A few scratches, bruises. She should be released from the hospital tomorrow."

"Ordnance report back?"

"Semtex. The upper apartment was completely demolished. Luckily Marie was downstairs when the bomb went off."

"Who's claiming responsibility?"

"There was a telephone call shortly after the blast. It

was a man, said he belonged to some group called Cosmic Solidarity. They claim responsibility.''

"Cosmic Solidarity? Never heard of that one.''

"Neither have we,'' said Daumier. "But you know how it is these days.''

Yes, Richard knew only too well. Any wacko with the right connections could buy a few ounces of Semtex, build a bomb, and join the revolution—any revolution. No wonder his business was booming. In this brave new world, terrorism was a fact of life. And clients everywhere were willing to pay top dollar for security.

"So you see, my friend,'' said Daumier, "it is not a good time for Bernard's children to be in Paris. And with all the questions they will ask—''

"Can't you keep an eye on them?''

"Why should they trust me? It was *my* report in that file. No, they need another friend here, Richard. Someone with sharp eyes and unerring instincts.''

"You have someone in mind?''

"I hear through the grapevine that you and Miss Tavistock shared a degree of…simpatico?''

"She's way too rich for my blood. And I'm too poor for hers.''

"I do not usually ask for favors,'' said Daumier quietly. "Neither does Hugh.''

And you're asking for one now, thought Richard. He sighed. "How can I refuse?''

After he'd hung up, he sat for a moment contemplating the task ahead. This was a baby-sitting job, really— the sort of assignment he despised. But the thought of seeing Beryl Tavistock again, and the memory of that kiss they'd shared in the garden, was enough to make him grin with anticipation. *Way too rich for my blood,* he thought. *But a man can dream, can't he? And I do owe it to Bernard and Madeline.*

Even after all these years, their deaths still haunted him. Perhaps the time had come to close the mystery, to answer all those questions he and Daumier had raised twenty years ago. The same questions MI6 and Central Intelligence had firmly suppressed.

Now Beryl Tavistock was poking her aristocratic nose into the mess. And a most attractive nose it was, he thought. He hoped it didn't get her killed.

He rose from the bed and headed for the shower. So much to do, so many preparations to make before he headed to the airport.

Baby-sitting jobs—how he hated them.

But at least this one would be in Paris.

ANTHONY SUTHERLAND STARED out his airplane window and longed fervently for the flight to be over and done with. Of all the rotten luck to be booked on the same Air France flight as the Vanes! And then to be seated straight across the first-class aisle from them— well, this really was intolerable. He considered Reggie Vane a screaming bore, especially when intoxicated, which at the moment Reggie was well on the way to becoming. Two whiskey sours and the man was starting to babble about how much he missed jolly old England, where food was boiled as it should be, not sautéed in all that ghastly butter, where people lined up in proper queues, where crowds didn't reek of garlic and onions. He'd lived too many years in Paris now—surely it was time to retire from the bank and go home? He'd put in many years at the Bank of London's Paris branch. Now that there were so many clever young V.P.s ready to step into his place, why not let them?

Lady Helena, who appeared to be just as fed up with her husband as Anthony was, simply said, "Shut up, Reggie," and ordered him a third whiskey sour.

Anthony didn't much care for Helena, either. She reminded him of some sort of nasty rodent. Such a contrast to his mother! The two women sat across the aisle from each other, Helena drab and proper in her houndstooth skirt and jacket, Nina so striking in her whitest-white silk pantsuit. Only a woman with true confidence could wear white silk, and his mother was one who could. Even at fifty-three, Nina was stunning, her dark, upswept hair showing scarcely a trace of gray, her figure the envy of any twenty-year-old. *But of course,* thought Anthony, *she's my mother.*

And, as usual, she was getting in her digs at Helena.

"If you and Reggie hate it so much in Paris," sniffed Nina, "why do you stay? If you ask me, people who don't adore the city don't deserve to live there."

"Of course, you *would* love Paris," said Helena.

"It's all in the attitude. If you'd kept an open mind..."

"Oh, no, we're much too stuffy," muttered Helena.

"I didn't say that. But there is a certain British attitude. God is an Englishman, that sort of thing."

"You mean He isn't?" Reggie interjected.

Helena didn't laugh. "I just think," she said, "that a certain amount of order and discipline is needed for the world to function properly."

Nina glanced at Reggie, who was noisily slurping his whiskey. "Yes, I can see you both believe in discipline. No wonder the evening was such a disaster."

"We weren't the ones who blurted out the truth," snapped Helena.

"At least *I* was sober enough to know what I was

saying!'' Nina declared. ''They would have found out in any event. After Reggie there let the cat out of the bag, I just decided it was time to be straight with them about Bernard and Madeline.''

''And look at the result,'' moaned Helena. ''Hugh says Beryl and Jordan are flying to Paris this afternoon. Now they'll be mucking around in things.''

Nina shrugged. ''Well, it was a long time ago.''

''I don't see why you're so nonchalant. If anyone could be hurt, it's you,'' muttered Helena.

Nina frowned at her. ''What do you mean by that?''

''Oh, nothing.''

''No, really! What do you mean by that?''

''Nothing,'' Helena snapped.

Their conversation came to an abrupt halt. But Anthony could tell his mother was fuming. She sat with her hands balled up in her lap. She even ordered a second martini. When she rose from her seat and headed down the aisle for a bit of exercise, he followed her. They met at the rear of the plane.

''Are you all right, Mother?'' he asked.

Nina glanced in agitation toward first class. ''It's all Reggie's bloody fault,'' she whispered. ''And Helena's right, you know. I *am* the one who could be hurt.''

''After all these years?''

''They'll be asking questions again. Digging. Lord, what if those Tavistock brats find something?''

Anthony said quietly, ''They won't.''

Nina's gaze met his. In that one look they saw, in each other's eyes, the bond of twenty years. ''You and me against the world,'' she used to sing to him. And that's how it had felt—just the two of them in their Paris flat. There'd been her lovers, of course, insignificant men, scarcely worth noting. But mother and son—what love could be stronger?

He said, "You've nothing to worry about, darling. Really."

"But the Tavistocks—"

"They're harmless." He took her hand and gave it a reassuring squeeze. "I guarantee it."

3

From the window of her suite at the Paris Ritz, Beryl looked down at the opulence of Place Vendôme, with its Corinthian pilasters and stone arches, and saw the evening parade of well-heeled tourists. It had been eight years since she'd last visited Paris, and then it had been on a lark with her girlfriends—three wild chums from school, who'd preferred the Left Bank bistros and seedy nightlife of Montparnasse to this view of unrepentant luxury. They'd had a grand time of it, too, had drunk countless bottles of wine, danced in the streets, flirted with every Frenchman who'd glanced their way—and there'd been a lot of them.

It seemed a million years ago. A different life, a different age.

Now, standing at the hotel window, she mourned the loss of all those carefree days and knew they would never be back. *I've changed too much,* she thought. *It's more than just the revelations about Mum and Dad. It's me. I feel restless. I'm longing for...I don't know what. Purpose, perhaps? I've gone so long without purpose in my life....*

She heard the door open, and Jordan came in through the connecting door from his suite. "Claude Daumier finally returned my call," he said. "He's tied up with the bomb investigation, but he's agreed to meet us for an early supper."

"When?"

"Half an hour."

Beryl turned from the window and looked at her brother. They'd scarcely slept last night, and it showed in Jordan's face. Though freshly shaved and impeccably dressed, he had that ragged edge of fatigue, the lean and hungry look of a man operating on reserve strength. *Like me.*

"I'm ready to leave anytime," she said.

He frowned at her dress. "Isn't that…Mum's?"

"Yes. I packed a few of her things in my suitcase. I don't know why, really." She gazed down at the watered-silk skirt. "It's eerie, isn't it? How well it fits. As if it were made for me."

"Beryl, are you sure you're up to this?"

"Why do you ask?"

"It's just that—" Jordan shook his head "—you don't seem at all yourself."

"Neither of us is, Jordie. How could we be?" She looked out the window again, at the lengthening shadows in Place Vendôme. The same view her mother must have looked down upon on *her* visits to Paris. The same hotel, perhaps even the same suite. *I'm even wearing her dress.* "It's as if—as if we don't know who we are anymore," she said. "Where we spring from."

"Who you are, who I am, has never been in doubt, Beryl. Whatever we learn about them doesn't change us."

She looked at him. "So you think it might be true."

He paused. "I don't know," he said. "But I'm preparing myself for the worst. And so should you." He went to the closet and took out her wrap. "Come on. It's time to confront the facts, little sister. Whatever they may be."

At seven o'clock, they arrived at Le Petit Zinc, the café where Daumier had arranged to meet them. It was early for the usual Parisian supper hour, and except for a lone couple dining on soup and bread, the café was empty. They took a seat in a booth at the rear and ordered wine and bread and a *remoulade* of mustard and celeriac to stave off their hunger. The lone couple finished their meal and departed. The appointed time came and went. Had Daumier changed his mind about meeting them?

Then, at seven-twenty, the door opened and a trim little Frenchman in suit and tie walked into the dining room. With his graying temples and his briefcase, he could have passed for any distinguished banker or lawyer. But the instant his gaze locked on Beryl, she knew, by his nod of acknowledgment, that this must be Claude Daumier.

But he had not come alone. He glanced over his shoulder as the door opened again, and a second man entered the restaurant. Together they approached the booth where Beryl and Jordan were seated. Beryl stiffened as she found herself staring not at Daumier but at his companion.

"Hello, Richard," she said quietly. "I had no idea you were coming to Paris."

"Neither did I," he said. "Until this morning."

Introductions were made, hands shaken all around. Then the two men slid into the booth. Beryl faced Richard straight across the table. As his gaze met hers, she felt the earlier sparks kindle between them, the memory of their kiss flaring to mind. *Beryl, you idiot,* she thought in irritation, *you're letting him distract you. Confuse you. No man has a right to affect you this way—certainly not a man you've only kissed once in your life. Not to mention one you met only twenty-four hours ago.*

Still, she couldn't seem to shake the memory of those moments in the garden at Chetwynd. Nor could she forget the taste of his lips. She watched him pour himself a glass of wine, watched him raise the glass to sip. Again, their eyes met, this time over the gleam of ruby liquid. She licked her own lips and savored the aftertaste of Burgundy.

"So what brings you to Paris?" she asked, raising her glass.

"Claude, as a matter of fact." He tilted his head at Daumier.

At Beryl's questioning look, Daumier said, "When I heard my old friend Richard was in London, I thought why not consult him? Since he is an authority on the subject."

"The St. Pierre bombing," Richard explained. "Some group no one's ever heard of is claiming responsibility. Claude thought perhaps I'd be able to shed some light on their identity. For years I've been tracking every reported terrorist organization there is."

"And did you shed some light?" asked Jordan.

"Afraid not," he admitted. "Cosmic Solidarity doesn't show up on my computer." He took another sip of wine, and his gaze locked with hers. "But the trip isn't entirely wasted," he added, "since I discover you're in Paris, as well."

"Strictly business," said Beryl. "With no time for pleasure."

"None at all?"

"None," she said flatly. She pointedly turned her attention to Daumier. "My uncle did call you, didn't he? About why we're here?"

The Frenchman nodded. "I understand you have both read the file."

"Cover to cover," said Jordan.

"Then you know the evidence. I myself confirmed the witness statements, the coroner's findings—"

"The coroner could have misinterpreted the facts," Jordan asserted.

"I myself saw their bodies in the garret. It was not something I am likely to forget." Daumier paused as though shaken by the memory. "Your mother died of three bullet wounds to the chest. Lying beside her was Bernard, a single bullet in his head. The gun had his fingerprints. There were no witnesses, no other suspects." Daumier shook his head. "The evidence speaks for itself."

"But where's the motive?" said Beryl. "Why would he kill someone he loved?"

"Perhaps that is the motive," said Daumier. "Love. Or loss of love. She may have found someone else—"

"That's impossible," Beryl objected vehemently. "She loved him."

Daumier looked down at his wineglass. He said quietly, "You have not yet read the police interview with the landlord, M. Rideau?"

Beryl and Jordan looked at him in puzzlement. "Rideau? I don't recall seeing that interview in the file," said Jordan.

"Only because I chose to exclude it when I sent the file to Hugh. It was a...matter of discretion."

Discretion, thought Beryl. Meaning he was trying to hide some embarrassing fact.

"The attic flat where their bodies were found," said Daumier, "was rented out to a Mlle Scarlatti. According to the landlord, Rideau, this Scarlatti woman used the flat once or twice a week. And only for the purpose of..." He paused delicately.

"Meeting a lover?" Jordan said bluntly.

Daumier nodded. "After the shooting, the landlord was asked to identify the bodies. Rideau told the police that the woman he called Mlle Scarlatti was the same one found dead in the garret. Your mother."

Beryl stared at him in shock. "You're saying my mother met a *lover* there?"

"It was the landlord's testimony."

"Then we'll have to talk face-to-face with this landlord."

"Not possible," said Daumier. "The building has been sold several times over. M. Rideau has left the country. I do not know where he is."

Beryl and Jordan sat in stunned silence. So that was Daumier's theory, thought Beryl. That her mother had a lover. Once or twice a week she would meet him in that attic flat on Rue Myrha. And then her father found out. So he killed her. And then he killed himself.

She looked up at Richard and saw the flicker of sympathy in his eyes. He believes it, too, she thought. Suddenly she resented him simply for being here, for hearing the most shameful secret of her family.

They heard a soft beeping. Daumier reached under his jacket and frowned at his pocket pager. "I am afraid I will have to leave," he said.

"What about that classified file?" asked Jordan. "You haven't said anything about Delphi."

"We'll speak of it later. This bombing, you understand—it is a crisis situation." Daumier slid out of the booth and picked up his briefcase. "Perhaps tomorrow? In the meantime, try to enjoy your stay in Paris, all of you. Oh, and if you dine here, I would recommend the duckling. It is excellent.'' With a nod of farewell, he turned and swiftly walked out of the restaurant.

"We just got the royal runaround," muttered Jordan in frustration. "He drops a bomb in our laps, then he scurries for cover, never answering our questions."

"I think that was his plan from the start," said Beryl. "Tell us something so horrifying, we'll be afraid to pursue it. Then our questions will stop." She looked at Richard. "Am I right?"

He met her gaze without wavering. "Why are you asking me?"

"Because you two obviously know each other well. Is this the way Daumier usually operates?"

"Claude's not one to spill secrets. But he also believes in helping out old friends, and your uncle Hugh's a good friend of his. I'm sure Claude's keeping your best interests at heart."

Old friends, thought Beryl. Daumier and Uncle Hugh and Richard Wolf—all of them linked together by some shadowy past, a past they would not talk about. This was how it had been, growing up at Chetwynd. Mysterious men in limousines dropping in to visit Hugh. Sometimes Beryl would hear snatches of conversation, would pick up whispered names whose significance she could only guess at. Yurchenko. Andropov. Baghdad. Berlin. She had learned long ago not to ask questions, never to expect answers. "Not something to bother your pretty head about," Hugh would tell her.

This time, she wouldn't be put off. This time she demanded answers.

The waiter came to the table with the menus. Beryl shook her head. "We won't be staying," she said.

"You're not interested in supper?" asked Richard. "Claude says it's an excellent restaurant."

"Did Claude ask you to show up?" she demanded. "Keep us well fed and entertained so we won't trouble him?"

"I'm delighted to keep you well fed. And, if you're willing, entertained." He smiled at her then, a smile with just a spark of mischief. Looking into his eyes, she found herself wavering on the edge of temptation. *Have supper with me*, she read in his smile. *And afterward, who knows? Anything's possible.*

Slowly she sat back in the booth. "We'll have supper with you, on one condition."

"What's that?"

"You play it straight with us. No dodging, no games."

"I'll try."

"Why are you in Paris?"

"Claude asked me to consult. As a personal favor. The summit's over now, so my schedule's open. Plus, I was curious."

"About the bombing?"

He nodded. "Cosmic Solidarity is a new one for me. I try to keep up with new terrorist groups. It's my business." He held a menu out to her and smiled. "And that, Miss Tavistock, is the unadulterated truth."

She met his gaze and saw no flicker of avoidance in his eyes. Still, her instincts told her there was something more behind that smile, something yet unsaid.

"You don't believe me," he said.

"How did you guess?"

"Does this mean you're not having supper with me?"

Up until that moment, Jordan had sat watching them, his gaze playing Ping-Pong. Now he cut in impatiently. "We are definitely having supper. Because I'm hungry,

Beryl, and I'm not moving from this booth until I've eaten.''

With a sigh of resignation, Beryl took the menu. ''I guess that answers that. Jordie's stomach has spoken.''

AMIEL FOCH'S TELEPHONE rang at precisely seven-fifteen.

''I have a new task for you,'' said the caller. ''It's a matter of some urgency. Perhaps this time around, you'll prove successful.''

The criticism stung, and Amiel Foch, with twenty-five years' experience in the business, barely managed to suppress a retort. The caller held the purse strings; he could afford to hurl insults. Foch had his retirement to consider. Requests for his services were few and far between these days. One's reflexes, after all, did not improve with age.

Foch said, with quiet control, ''I planted the device as you instructed. It went off at the time specified.''

''And all it did was make a lot of bloody noise. The target was scarcely hurt.''

''She did the unexpected. One cannot control such things.''

''Let's hope this time you keep things under better control.''

''What is the name?''

''Two names. A brother and sister, Beryl and Jordan Tavistock. They're staying at the Ritz. I want to know where they go. Who they see.''

''Nothing more?''

''For now, just surveillance. But things may change at any time, depending on what they learn. With any luck, they'll simply turn around and run home to England.''

"If they do not?"

"Then we'll take further action."

"What about Mme St. Pierre? Do you wish me to try again?"

The caller paused. "No," he said at last, "she can wait. For now, the Tavistocks take priority."

OVER A MEAL OF poached salmon and duck with raspberry sauce, Beryl and Richard thrusted and parried questions and answers. Richard, an accomplished verbal duelist, revealed only the barest sketch of his personal life. He was born and reared in Connecticut. His father, a retired cop, was still living. After leaving Princeton University, Richard joined the U.S. State Department and served as political officer at embassies around the world. Then, five years ago, he left government service to start up business as a security consultant. Sakaroff and Wolf, based in Washington, D.C., was born.

"And that's what brought me to London last week," he said. "Several American firms wanted security for their executives during the summit. I was hired as consultant."

"And that's all you were doing in London?" she asked.

"That's all I was doing in London. Until I got Hugh's invitation to Chetwynd." His gaze met hers across the table.

His directness unsettled her. *Is he telling me the truth, fiction or something in between?* That matter-of-fact recitation of his career had struck her as rehearsed, but then, it would be. People in the intelligence business always had their life histories down pat, the details memorized, fact blending smoothly with fantasy. What did she really know about him? Only that he smiled easily, laughed easily. That his appetite was hearty and he drank his coffee black.

And that she was intensely, insanely, attracted to him.

After supper, he offered to drive them back to the Ritz. Jordan sat in the back seat, Beryl in the front—right next to Richard. She kept glancing sideways at him as they drove up Boulevard Saint-Germain toward the Seine. Even the traffic, outrageously rude and noisy, did not seem to ruffle him. At a stoplight, he turned and looked at her and that one glimpse of his face through the darkness of the car was enough to make her heart do a somersault.

Calmly he shifted his attention back to the road. "It's still early," he said. "Are you sure you want to go back to the hotel?"

"What's my choice?"

"A drive. A walk. Whatever you'd like. After all, you're in Paris. Why not make the most of it?" He reached down to shift gears, and his hand brushed past her knee. A shiver ran through her—a warm, delicious sizzle of anticipation.

He's tempting me. Making me dizzy with all the possibilities. Or is it the wine? What harm can there be in a little stroll, a little fresh air?

She called over her shoulder, "How about it, Jordie? Do you feel like taking a walk?" She was answered by a loud snore.

Beryl turned and saw to her astonishment that her brother was sprawled across the back seat. A sleepless night and two glasses of wine at supper had left him dead to the world. "I guess that's a negative," she said with a laugh.

"What about just you and me?"

That invitation, voiced so softly, sent another shiver

of temptation up her spine. After all, she thought, she was in Paris....

"A short walk," she agreed. "But first, let's put Jordan to bed."

"Valet service coming up," Richard said, laughing. "First stop, the Ritz."

Jordan snored all the way back to the hotel.

THEY WALKED IN THE Tuileries, a stroll that took them along a gravel path through formal gardens, past statues glowing a ghostly white under the street lamps.

"And here we are again," said Richard, "walking through another garden. Now if only we could find a maze with a nice little stone bench at the center."

"Why?" she asked with a smile. "Are you hoping for a repeat scenario?"

"With a slightly different ending. You know, after you left me in there, it took me a good five minutes to find my way out."

"I know." She laughed. "I was waiting at the door, counting the minutes. Five minutes wasn't bad, really. But other men have done better."

"So that's how you screen your men. You're the cheese in the maze—"

"And you were the rat."

They both laughed then, and the sound of their voices floated through the night air.

"And my performance was only...adequate?" he said.

"Average."

He moved toward her, his smile gleaming in the shadows. "Better than adquate?"

"For you, I'll make allowances. After all, it was dark...."

"Yes, it was." He moved closer, so close she had to tilt her head up to look at him. So close she could almost feel the heat radiating from his body. "Very dark," he whispered.

"And perhaps you were disoriented?"

"Extremely."

"And it *was* a nasty trick I played...."

"For which you should be soundly punished."

He reached up and took her face in his hands. The taste of his lips on hers sent a shudder of pleasure through her body. *If this is my punishment,* she thought, *oh, let me commit the crime again....* His fingers slid through her hair, tangling in the strands as his kiss pressed ever deeper. She felt her legs wobble and melt away, but she had no need of them; he was there to support them both. She heard his murmur of need and knew that these kisses were dangerous, that he, too, was fast slipping toward the same cliff's edge. She didn't care—she was ready to make the leap.

And then, without warning, he froze.

One moment he was kissing her, and an instant later his hands went rigid against her face. He didn't pull away. Even as she felt his whole body grow tense against her, he kept her firmly in his embrace. His lips glided to her ear.

"Start walking," he whispered. "Toward the Concorde."

"What?"

"Just move. Don't show any alarm. I'll hold your hand."

She focused on his face, and through the shadows she saw his look of feral alertness. Swallowing back the questions, she allowed him to take her hand. They turned and began to walk casually toward the Place de la Concorde. He gave her no explanation, but she knew just by the way he gripped her hand that something was wrong, that this was not a game. Like any other pair of lovers, they strolled through the garden, past flower beds deep in shadow, past statues lined up in ghostly formation. Gradually she became more and more aware of sounds: the distant roar of traffic, the wind in the trees, their shoes crunching across the gravel...

And the footsteps, following somewhere behind them.

Nervously she clutched his hand. His answering squeeze of reassurance was enough to dull the razor edge of fear. *I've known this man only a day,* she thought, *and already I feel that I can count on him.*

Richard picked up his pace—so gradually she almost didn't notice it. The footsteps still pursued them. They veered right and crossed the park toward Rue de Rivoli. The sounds of traffic grew louder, obscuring the footsteps of their pursuer. Now was the greatest danger—as they left the darkness behind them and their pursuer saw his last chance to make a move. Bright lights beckoned from the street ahead. *We can make it if we run,* she thought. *A dash through the trees and we'll be safe, surrounded by other people.* She prepared for the sprint, waiting for Richard's cue.

But he made no sudden moves. Neither did their pursuer. Hand in hand, she and Richard strolled nonchalantly into the naked glare of Rue de Rivoli.

Only as they joined the stream of evening pedestrians did Beryl's pulse begin to slow again. There was no danger here, she thought. Surely no one would dare attack them on a busy street.

Then she glanced at Richard's face and saw that the tension was still there.

They crossed the street and walked another block.

"Stop for a minute," he murmured. "Take a long look in that window."

They paused in front of a chocolate shop. Through the glass they saw a tempting display of confections: raspberry creams and velvety truffles and Turkish delight, all nestled in webs of spun sugar. In the shop, a young woman stood over a vat of melted chocolate, dipping fresh strawberries.

"What are we waiting for?" whispered Beryl.

"To see what happens."

She stared in the window and saw the reflections of people passing behind them. A couple holding hands. A trio of students in backpacks. A family with four children.

"Let's start walking again," he said.

They headed west on Rue de Rivoli, their pace again leisurely, unhurried. She was caught by surprise when he suddenly pulled her to the right, onto an intersecting street.

"Move it!" he barked.

All at once they were sprinting. They made another sharp right onto Mont Thabor, and ducked under an arch. There, huddled in the shadow of a doorway, he pulled her against him so tightly that she felt his heart pounding against hers, his breath warming her brow. They waited.

Seconds later, running footsteps echoed along the street. The sound moved closer, slowed, stopped. Then there was no sound at all. Almost too terrified to look, Beryl slowly shifted in Richard's arms, just enough to see a shadow slide past their archway. The footsteps moved down the street and faded away.

Richard chanced a quick look up the street, then gave Beryl's hand a tug. "All clear," he whispered. "Let's get out of here."

They turned onto Castiglione Street and didn't stop running until they were back at the hotel. Only when they were safely in her suite and he'd bolted the door behind them, did she find her voice again.

"What happened out there?" she demanded.

He shook his head. "I'm not sure."

"Do you think he meant to rob us?" She moved to the phone. "I should call the police—"

"He wasn't after our money."

"What?" She turned and frowned at him.

"Think about it. Even on Rue de Rivoli, with all those witnesses, he didn't stop following us. Any other thief would've given up and gone back to the park. Found himself another victim. But he didn't. He stayed with us."

"I didn't even see him! How do you know there *was* any—"

"A middle-aged man. Short, stocky. The sort of face most people would forget."

She stared at him, her agitation mounting. "What are you saying, Richard? That he was following us in particular?"

"Yes."

"But why would anyone follow you?"

"I could ask the same question of you."

"I'm of no interest to anyone."

"Think about it. About why you came to Paris."

"It's just a family matter."

"Apparently not. Since you now seem to have strange men following you around town."

"How do I know he wasn't following you? You're the one who works for the CIA!"

"Correction. I work for myself."

"Oh, don't palm off that rubbish on me! I practically grew up in MI6! I can smell you people a mile away!"

"Can you?" His eyebrow shot up. "And the odor didn't scare you off?"

"Maybe it should have."

He was pacing the room now, moving about like a restless animal, locking windows, pulling curtains. "Since I can't seem to deceive your highly perceptive nose, I'll just confess it. My job description is a bit looser than I've admitted to."

"I'm astonished."

"But I'm still convinced the man was following *you.*"

"Why would anyone follow me?"

"Because you're digging in a mine field. You don't understand, Beryl. When your parents were killed, there was more involved than just another sex scandal."

"Wait a minute." She crossed toward him, her gaze hard on his face. "What do you know about it?"

"I knew you were coming to Paris."

"Who told you?"

"Claude Daumier. He called me in London. Said that Hugh was worried. That someone had to keep an eye on you and Jordan."

"So you're our nanny?"

He laughed. "In a manner of speaking."

"And how much do you know about my mother and father?"

She knew by his brief silence that he was debating his answer, weighing the consequences of his next words. She fully expected to hear a lie.

Instead he surprised her with the truth. "I knew them both," he said. "I was here in Paris when it happened."

The revelation left her stunned. She didn't doubt for

an instant that it was the truth—why would he fabricate such a story?

"It was my very first posting," he said. "I thought it was incredible luck to draw Paris. Most first-timers get sent to some bug-infested jungle in the middle of nowhere. But I drew Paris. And that's where I met Madeline and Bernard." Wearily he sank into a chair. "It's amazing," he murmured, studying Beryl's face, "How very much you look like her. The same green eyes, the same black hair. She used to sweep hers back in this sort of loose chignon. But strands of it were always coming loose, falling about her neck...." He smiled fondly at the memory. "Bernard was crazy about her. So was every man who ever met her."

"Were you?"

"I was only twenty-two. She was the most enchanting woman I'd ever met." His gaze met hers. Softly he added, "But then, I hadn't met her daughter."

They stared at each other, and Beryl felt those silken threads of desire tugging her toward him. Toward a man whose kisses left her dizzy, whose touch could melt even stone. A man who had not been straight with her from the very start.

I'm so tired of secrets, so tired of trying to tease apart the truths from the half truths. And I'll never know which is which with this man.

Abruptly she went to the door. "If we can't be honest with each other," she said, "there's no point in being together at all. So why don't we say good-night. And goodbye."

"I don't think so."

She turned and frowned at him. "Excuse me?"

"I'm not ready to say goodbye. Not when I know you're being followed."

"You're concerned about my welfare, is that it?"

"Shouldn't I be?"

She shot him a breezy smile. "I'm very good at taking care of myself."

"You're in a foreign city. Things could happen—"

"I'm not exactly alone." She crossed the room to the connecting door leading to Jordan's suite. Yanking it open, she called, "Wake up, Jordie! I'm in need of some brotherly assistance."

There was no answer from the bed.

"Jordie?" she said.

"Your bodyguard stays right on his toes, doesn't he?" said Richard.

Annoyed, Beryl flicked on the wall switch. In the sudden flood of light, she found herself blinking in astonishment.

Jordan's bed was empty.

4

That woman is staring at me again.

Jordan stirred a teaspoon of sugar into his cappuccino
and casually glanced in the direction of the blonde sitting
three tables away. At once she averted her gaze. She
was attractive enough, he noted. Mid-twenties, with a
lean, athletic build. Nothing overripe about that one. Her
hair was cut like a boy's, with elfin wisps feathering her
forehead. She wore a black sweater, black skirt, black
stockings. Fashion or camouflage? He shifted his gaze
ahead to the street and the evening parade of pedestrians.
Out of the corner of his eye, he spied the woman again
looking his way. Ordinarily it would have flattered him
to know he was the object of such intense feminine scru-
tiny. But something about this particular woman made
him uneasy. Couldn't a fellow wander the streets of Paris
these days without being stalked by carnivorous females?

It had been such a pleasant outing up till now. Minutes
after sending Beryl and Richard on their way, he'd
slipped out of his hotel room in search of a decent wa-
tering hole. A stroll across Place Vendôme, a visit to the
Olympia Music Hall, then a midnight snack at Café de
la Paix—what better way to spend one's first evening in
Paris?

But perhaps it was time to call it a night.

He finished his cappuccino, paid the tab, and began

walking toward the Rue de la Paix. It took him only half a block to realize the woman in black was following him.

He had paused at a shop window and was gazing in at a display of men's suits when he spotted a fleeting glimpse of a blond head reflected in the glass. He turned and saw her standing across the street, intently staring into a window. A lingerie shop, he noted. Judging by the rest of her outfit, she'd no doubt choose her knickers in black, as well.

Jordan continued walking in the direction of Place Vendôme.

Across the street, the woman was parralleling his route.

This is getting tiresome, he thought. *If she wants to flirt, why doesn't she just come over and bat her eyelashes?* The direct approach, he could appreciate. It was honest and straightforward, and he liked honest women. But this stalking business unnerved him.

He walked another half block. So did she.

He stopped and pretended to study another shop window. She did likewise. *This is ridiculous,* he thought. *I am not going to put up with this nonsense.*

He crossed the street and walked straight up to her. *"Mademoiselle?"* he said.

She turned and regarded him with a startled look. Plainly she had not expected a face-to-face confrontation.

"Mademoiselle," he said, "may I ask why you're following me?"

She opened her mouth and shut it again, all the time staring at him with those big gray eyes. Rather pretty eyes, he observed.

"Perhaps you don't understand me? *Parlez-vous anglais?*"

"Yes," she murmured, "I speak English."

"Then perhaps you can explain why you're following me."

"But I am not following you."

"Yes, you are."

"No, I am not!" She glanced up and down the street. "I am taking a walk. As you are."

"You're dogging my every step. Stopping where I stop. Watching every move I make."

"That is preposterous." She pulled herself up, a spark of outrage lighting her eyes. Real or manufactured? He couldn't be sure. "I have no interest in you, *Monsieur!* You must be imagining things."

"Am I?"

In answer, she spun around and stalked away up the Rue de la Paix.

"I don't think I am imagining things!" he called after her.

"You English are all alike!" she flung over her shoulder.

Jordan watched her storm off and wondered if he had jumped to conclusions. If so, what a fool he'd made of himself! The woman rounded a corner and vanished, and he felt a moment's regret. After all, she had been rather attractive. Lovely gray eyes, unbeatable legs.

Ah, well.

He turned and continued on his way toward the Place Vendôme and the hotel. Only as he reached the lobby doors of the Ritz did that sixth sense of his begin to tingle again. He paused and glanced back. In a distant archway, he spied a flicker of movement, a glimpse of a blond head just before it ducked into the shadows.

She was still following him.

DAUMIER ANSWERED the phone on the fifth ring. *"Allo?"*

"Claude, it's me," said Richard. "Are you having us tailed?"

There was a pause, then Daumier said, "A precaution, my friend. Nothing more."

"Protection? Or surveillance?"

"Protection, naturally! A favor to Hugh—"

"Well, it scared the living daylights out of us. The least you could've done was warn me." Richard glanced toward Beryl, who was anxiously pacing the hotel room. She hadn't admitted it, but he knew she was shaken, and that for all her bravado, all her attempts to throw him out of her suite, she was relieved he'd stayed. "Another thing," he said to Daumier, "we seem to have misplaced Jordan."

"Misplaced?"

"He's not in his suite. We left him here hours ago. He's since vanished."

There was a silence on the line. "This is worrisome," said Daumier.

"Do your people have any idea where he is?"

"My agent has not yet reported in. I expect to hear from her in another—"

"Her?" Richard cut in.

"Not our most experienced operative, I admit. But quite capable."

"It was a man following us tonight."

Daumier laughed. "Richard, I am disappointed! I thought you, of all people, knew the difference."

"I can bloody well tell the difference!"

"With Colette, there is no question. Twenty-six, rather pretty. Blond hair."

"It was a man, Claude."

"You saw the face?"

"Not clearly. But he was short, stocky—"

"Colette is five foot five, very slender."

"It wasn't her."

Daumier said nothing for a moment. "This is disturbing," he concluded. "If it was not one of our people—"

Richard suddenly pivoted toward the door. Someone was knocking. Beryl stood frozen, staring at him with a look of fear.

"I'll call you back, Claude," Richard whispered into the phone. Quietly he hung up.

There was another knock, louder this time.

"Go ahead," he murmured, "ask who it is."

Shakily she called out, "Who is it?"

"Are you decent?" came the reply. "Or should I try again in the morning?"

"Jordan!" cried a relieved Beryl. She ran to open the door. "Where have you been?"

Her brother sauntered in, his blond hair tousled from the night wind. He saw Richard and halted. "Sorry. If I've interrupted anything—"

"Not a thing," snapped Beryl. She locked the door and turned to face her brother. "We've been worried sick about you."

"I just went for a walk."

"You could have left me a note!"

"Why? I was right in the neighborhood." Jordan flopped lazily into a chair. "Having quite a nice evening, too, until some woman started following me around."

Richard's chin snapped up in surprise. "Woman?"

"Rather nice-looking. But not my type, really. A bit vampirish for my taste."

"Was she blond?" asked Richard. "About five foot five? Mid-twenties?"

Jordan shook his head in amazement. "Next you'll tell me her name."

"Colette."

"Is this a new parlor trick, Richard?" Jordan said with a laugh. "ESP?"

"She's an agent working for French Intelligence," said Richard. "Protective surveillance, that's all."

Beryl gave a sigh of relief. "So that's why we were followed. And you had me scared out of my wits."

"You *should* be scared," said Richard. "The man following us wasn't working for Daumier."

"You just said—"

"Daumier had only one agent assigned to surveillance tonight. That woman, Colette. Apparently she stayed with Jordan."

"Then who was following us?" demanded Beryl.

"I don't know."

There was a silence. Then Jordan asked peevishly, "Have I missed something? Why are we all being followed? And when did Richard join the fun?"

"Richard," said Beryl tightly, "hasn't been completely honest with us."

"About what?"

"He neglected to mention that he was here in Paris in 1973. He knew Mum and Dad."

Jordan's gaze at once shot to Richard's face. "Is that why you're here now?" he asked quietly. "To prevent us from learning the truth?"

"No," said Richard. "I'm here to see that the truth doesn't get you both killed."

"Could the truth really be that dangerous?"

"It's got someone worried enough to have you both followed."

"Then you don't believe it *was* a simple murder and suicide," said Jordan.

"If it was that simple—if it was just a case of Bernard shooting Madeline and then taking his own life—no one would care about it after all these years. But someone obviously does care. And he—or she—is keeping a close watch on your movements."

Beryl, strangely silent, sat down on the bed. Her hair, which she'd gathered back with pins, was starting to loosen, and silky tendrils had drifted down her neck. All at once Richard was struck by her uncanny resemblance to Madeline. It was the hairstyle and the watered-silk dress. He recognized that dress now—it was her mother's. He shook himself to dispel the notion that he was looking at a ghost.

He decided it was time to tell the truth, and nothing but. "I never did believe it," he said. "Not for a second did I think Bernard pulled that trigger."

Slowly Beryl looked up at him. What he saw in her gaze—the wariness, the mistrust—made him want to reach out to her, to make her believe in him. But trust wasn't something she was about to give him, not now. Perhaps not ever.

"If he didn't pull the trigger," she asked, "then who did?"

Richard moved to the bed. Gently he touched her face. "I don't know," he said. "But I'm going to help you find out."

AFTER RICHARD LEFT, Beryl turned to her brother. "I don't trust him," she said. "He's told us too many lies."

"He didn't lie to us exactly," Jordan observed. "He just left out a few facts."

"Oh, right. He conveniently neglects to mention that he knew Mum and Dad. That he was here in Paris when they died. Jordie, for all we know, *he* could've pulled the trigger!"

"He seems quite chummy with Daumier."

"So?"

"Uncle Hugh trusts Daumier."

"Meaning we should trust Richard Wolf?" She shook her head and laughed. "Oh, Jordie, you must be more exhausted than you realize."

"And you must be more smitten than you realize," he said. Yawning, he crossed the floor toward his own suite.

"What's that supposed to mean?" she demanded.

"Only that your feelings for the man obviously run hot and heavy. Because you're fighting them every inch of the way."

She pursued him to the connecting door. "Hot?" she said incredulously. "Heavy?"

"There, you see?" He breathed a few loud pants and grinned. "Sweet dreams, baby sister. I'm glad to see you're back in circulation."

Then he closed the door on her astonished face.

WHEN RICHARD ARRIVED at Daumier's flat, he found the Frenchman still awake but already dressed in his bathrobe and slippers. The latest reports on the bombing of the St. Pierre residence were laid out across his kitchen table, along with a plate of sausage and a glass of milk. Forty years with French Intelligence hadn't altered his preference for working in close proximity to a refrigerator.

Waving at the reports, Daumier said, "It is all a puzzle to me. A Semtex explosive planted under the bed. A timing mechanism set for 9:10—precisely when the St. Pierres would be watching Marie's favorite television program. It has all the signs of an inside operation, except for one glaring mistake—Philippe was in England." He looked at Richard. "Does it not strike you as an inconceivable blunder?"

"Terrorists are usually brighter than that," admitted Richard. "Maybe they intended it only as a warning. A statement of purpose. 'We can reach you if we want to,' that sort of thing."

"I still have no information on this Cosmic Solidarity League." Wearily Daumier ran his hands through his hair. "The investigation, it goes nowhere."

"Then maybe you can turn your attention for a moment to my little problem."

"Problem? Ah, yes. The Tavistocks." Daumier sat back and smiled at him. "Hugh's niece is more than you can handle, Richard?"

"Someone else was definitely tailing us tonight," said Richard. "Not just your agent, Colette. Can you find out who it was?"

"Give me something to work with," said Daumier. "A middle-aged man, short and stocky—that tells me nothing. He could have been hired by anyone."

"It was someone who knew they were coming to Paris."

"I know Hugh told the Vanes. They, in turn, could have mentioned it to others. Who else was at Chetwynd?"

Richard thought back to the night of the reception and the night of Reggie's indiscretion. Blast Reggie Vane and his weakness for booze. That was what had set this off. A few too many glasses of champagne, a wagging tongue. Still, he couldn't bring himself to dislike the man. Poor Reggie was a harmless soul; certainly he'd never meant to hurt Beryl. Rather, it was clear he adored her like a daughter.

Richard said, "There were numbers of people the Vanes might have spoken to. Philippe St. Pierre. Nina and Anthony. Perhaps others."

"So we are talking about any number of people," Daumier said, sighing.

"Not a very short list," Richard had to admit.

"Is this such a wise idea, Richard?" The question was posed quietly. "Once before, if you recall, we were prevented from learning the truth."

How could he not remember? He'd been stunned to read that directive from Washington: "Abort investigation." Claude had received similar orders from his superior at French Intelligence. And so the search for Delphi and the NATO security breach had come to an abrupt halt. There'd been no explanation, no reasons given, but Richard had formed his own suspicions. It was clear that Washington had been clued in to the truth and feared the repercussions of its airing.

A month later, when U.S. Ambassador Stephen Sutherland leaped off a Paris bridge, Richard thought his suspicions confirmed. Sutherland had been a political appointee; his unveiling as an enemy spy would have embarrassed the president himself.

The matter of the mole was never officially resolved.

Instead, Bernard Tavistock had been posthumously implicated as Delphi. Conveniently tried and found guilty, thought Richard. Why not pin the blame on Tavistock? A dead man can't deny the charges.

And now, twenty years later, the ghost of Delphi is back to haunt me.

With new determination, Richard rose from the chair. "This time, Claude," he said, "I'm tracking him down. And no order from Washington is going to stop me."

"Twenty years is a long time. Evidence has vanished. Politics have changed."

"One thing hasn't changed—the guilty party. What if we were wrong? What if Sutherland wasn't the mole? Then Delphi may still be alive. And operational."

To which Daumier added, "And very, very worried."

BERYL WAS AWAKENED the next morning by Richard knocking on her door. She blinked in astonishment as he handed her a paper sack, fragrant with the aroma of freshly baked croissants.

"Breakfast," he announced. "You can eat it in the car. Jordan's already waiting for us downstairs."

"Waiting? For what?"

"For you to get dressed. You'd better hurry. Our appointment's for eight o'clock."

Bewildered, she shoved back a handful of tangled hair. "I don't recall making any appointments for this morning."

"I made it for us. We're lucky to get one, considering the man doesn't see many people these days. His wife won't allow it."

"Whose wife?" she said in exasperation.

"Chief Inspector Broussard. The detective in charge of your parents' murder investigation." Richard paused. "You do want to speak to him, don't you?"

He knows I do, she thought, clutching together the edges of her silk robe. *He's got me at a disadvantage. I'm scarcely awake and he's standing there like Mr. Sun-*

shine himself. And since when had Jordan turned into an early riser? Her brother almost never rolled out of bed before eight.

"You don't have to come," he said, turning to leave. "Jordan and I can—"

"Give me ten minutes!" she snapped and closed the door on him.

She made it downstairs in nine minutes flat.

Richard drove with the self-assurance of a man long familiar with the streets of Paris. They crossed the Seine and headed south along crowded boulevards. The traffic was as insane as London's, thought Beryl, gazing out at the crush of buses and taxis. *Thank heavens he's behind the wheel.*

She finished her croissant and brushed the crumbs off the file folder lying in her lap. Contained in that folder was the twenty-year-old police report, signed by Inspector Broussard. She wondered how much the man would remember about the case. After all this time, surely the details had blended together with all the other homicide investigations of his career. But there was always the chance that some small unreported detail had stayed with him.

"Have you met Broussard?" she asked Richard.

"We met during the course of the investigation. When I was interviewed by the police."

"They questioned you? Why?"

"He spoke to all your parents' acquaintances."

"I never saw your name in the police file."

"A number of names didn't make it to that file."

"Such as?"

"Philippe St. Pierre. Ambassador Sutherland."

"Nina's husband?"

Richard nodded. "Those were politically sensitive

names. St. Pierre was in the Finance Ministry, and he was a close friend of the prime minister's. Sutherland was the American ambassador. Neither were suspects, so their names were kept out of the official report.''

''Meaning the good inspector protected the high and mighty?''

''Meaning he was discreet.''

''Why did your name escape the report?''

''I was just a bit player asked to comment on your parents' marriage. Whether they ever argued, seemed unhappy, that's all. I was only on the periphery.''

She touched the file on her lap. ''So tell me,'' she said, ''why are you getting involved now?''

''Because you and Jordan are. Because Claude Daumier asked me to look after you.'' He glanced at her and added quietly, ''And because I owe it to your father. He was...a good man.'' She thought he would say more, but then he turned and gazed straight ahead at the road.

''Wolf,'' asked Jordan, who was sitting in the back seat, ''are you aware that we're being followed?''

''What?'' Beryl turned and scanned the traffic behind them. ''Which car?''

''The blue Peugeot. Two cars back.''

''I see it,'' said Richard. ''It's been tailing us all the way from the hotel.''

''You knew the car was there all the time?'' said Beryl. ''And you didn't think of mentioning it?''

''I expected it. Take a good look at the driver, Jordan. Blond hair, sunglasses. Definitely a woman.''

Jordan laughed. ''Why, it's my little vampiress in black. Colette.''

Richard nodded. ''One of the friendlies.''

''How can you be sure?'' asked Beryl.

''Because she's Daumier's agent. Which makes her

protection, not a threat.'' Richard turned off Boulevard Raspail. A moment later, he spotted a parking space and pulled up at the curb. ''In fact, she can keep an eye on the car while we're inside.''

Beryl glanced at the large brick building across the street. Over the entrance archway were displayed the words *Maison de Convalescence*. ''What is this place?''

''A nursing home.''

''This is where Inspector Broussard lives?''

''He's been here for years,'' said Richard, as he gazed up at the building with a look of pity. ''Ever since his stroke.''

JUDGING BY THE PHOTOGRAPH tacked to the wall of his room, ex-Chief Inspector Broussard had once been an impressive man. The picture showed a beefy Frenchman with a handlebar mustache and a lion's mane of hair, posing regally on the steps of a Paris police station.

It bore little resemblance to the shrunken creature now propped up, his body half-paralyzed, in bed.

Mme Broussard bustled about the room, all the time speaking with the precise grammar of a former teacher of English. She fluffed her husband's pillow, combed his hair, wiped the drool from his chin. ''He remembers everything,'' she insisted. ''Every case, every name. But he cannot speak, cannot hold a pen. And that is what frustrates him! It is why I do not let him have visitors. He wishes so much to talk, but he cannot form the words. Only a few, here and there. And how it upsets him! Sometimes, after a visit with friends, he will moan for days.'' She moved to the head of the bed and stood there like a guardian angel. ''You ask him only a few questions, do you understand? And if he becomes upset, you must leave immediately.''

"We understand," said Richard. He pulled up a chair next to the bedside. As Beryl and Jordan watched, he opened the police file and slowly laid the crime-scene photos on the coverlet for Broussard to see. "I know you can't speak," he said, "but I want you to look at these. Nod if you remember the case."

Mme Broussard translated for her husband. He stared down at the first photo—the gruesome death poses of Madeline and Bernard. They lay like lovers, entwined in a pool of blood. Clumsily Broussard touched the photo, his fingers lingering on Madeline's face. His lips formed a whispered word.

"What did he say?" asked Richard.

"*La belle.* Beautiful woman," said Mme Broussard. "You see? He does remember."

The old man was gazing at the other photos now, his left hand beginning to quiver in agitation. His lips moved helplessly; the effort to speak came out in grunts. Mme Broussard leaned forward, trying to make out what he was saying. She shook her head in bewilderment.

"We've read his report," said Beryl. "The one he filed twenty years ago. He concluded that it was a murder and suicide. Did he truly believe that?"

Again, Mme Broussard translated.

Broussard looked up at Beryl, his gaze focusing for the first time on her black hair. A look of wonder came over his face, almost a look of recognition.

His wife repeated the question. Did he believe it was a murder and suicide?

Slowly Broussard shook his head.

Jordan asked, "Does he understand the question?"

"Of course he does!" snapped Mme Broussard. "I told you, he understands everything."

The man was tapping at one of the photos now, as

though trying to point something out. His wife asked a question in French. He only slapped harder at the photo.

"Is he trying to point at something?" asked Beryl.

"Just a corner of the picture," said Richard. "A view of empty floor."

Broussard's whole body seemed to be quivering with the effort to speak. His wife leaned forward again, straining to make out his words. She shook her head. "It makes no sense."

"What did he say?" asked Beryl.

"*Serviette.* It is a napkin or a towel. I do not understand." She snatched up a hand towel from the sink and held it up to her husband. "*Serviette de toilette?*"

He shook his head and angrily batted away the towel.

"I do not know what he means," Mme Broussard said with a sigh.

"Maybe I do," said Richard. He bent close to Broussard. "*Porte documents?*" he asked.

Broussard gave a sigh of relief and collapsed against his pillows. Wearily he nodded.

"That's what he was trying to say," said Richard. "*Serviette porte documents.* A briefcase."

"Briefcase?" echoed Beryl. "Do you think he means the one with the classified file?"

Richard frowned at Broussard. The man was exhausted, his face a sickly gray against the white linen.

Mme Broussard took one look at her husband and moved in to shield him from Richard. "No further questions, Mr. Wolf! Look at him! He is drained—he cannot tell you more. Please, you must leave."

She hurried them out of the room and into the hallway. A nun glided past, carrying a tray of medicines. At the end of the hall, a woman in a wheelchair was singing lullabies to herself in French.

"Mme Broussard," said Beryl, "we have more questions, but your husband can't answer them. There was another detective's name on that report—an Etienne Giguere. How can we get in touch with him?"

"Etienne?" Mme Broussard looked at her in surprise. "You mean you do not know?"

"Know what?"

"He was killed nineteen years ago. Hit by a car while crossing the street." Sadly she shook her head. "They did not find the driver."

Beryl caught Jordan's startled look; she saw in his eyes the same dismay she felt.

"One last question," said Jordan. "When did your husband have his stroke?"

"1974."

"Also nineteen years ago?"

Mme Broussard nodded. "Such a tragedy for the department! First, my husband's stroke. Then three months later, they lose Etienne." Sighing, she turned back to her husband's room. "But that is life, I suppose. And there is nothing we can do to change it...."

Back outside again, the three of them stood for a moment in the sunshine, trying to shake off the gloom of that depressing building.

"A hit and run?" said Jordan. "The driver never caught? I have a bad feeling about this."

Beryl glanced up at the archway. *"Maison de Convalescence,"* she murmured sarcastically. "Hardly a place to recover. More like a place to die." Shivering, she turned to the car. "Please, let's just get out of here."

They drove north, to the Seine. Once again, the blue Peugeot followed them, but none of them paid it much attention; the French agent had become a fact of life— almost a reassuring one.

Suddenly Jordan said, "Hold on, Wolf. Let me off on Boulevard Saint-Germain. In fact, right about here would be fine."

Richard pulled over to the curb. "Why here?"

"We just passed a café—"

"Oh, Jordan," groaned Beryl, "you're not hungry already, are you?"

"I'll meet you back at the hotel," said Jordan, climbing out of the car. "Unless you two care to join me?"

"So we can watch you eat? Thank you, but I'll pass."

Jordan gave his sister an affectionate squeeze of the shoulder and closed the car door. "I'll catch a taxi back. See you later." With a wave, he turned and strolled down the boulevard, his blond hair gleaming in the sunshine.

"Back to the hotel?" asked Richard softly.

She looked at him and thought, *It's always there shimmering between us—the attraction. The temptation. I look in his eyes, and suddenly I remember how safe it feels to be in his arms. How easy it would be to believe in him. And that's where the danger lies.*

"No," she said, looking straight ahead. "Not yet."

"Then where to?"

"Take me to Pigalle. Rue Myrha."

He paused. "Are you certain you want to go there?"

She nodded and stared down at the file in her lap. "I want to see the place where they died."

CAFÉ HUGO. YES, THIS WAS the place, thought Jordan, gazing around at the crowded outdoor tables, the checkered tablecloths, the army of waiters ferrying espresso and cappuccino. Twenty years ago, Bernard had visited this very café. Had sat drinking coffee. And then he had paid the bill and left, to meet his death in a building in

Pigalle. All this Jordan had learned from the police interview with the waiter. But it happened a long time ago, thought Jordan. The man had probably moved on to other jobs. Still, it was worth a shot.

To his surprise, he discovered that Mario Cassini was still employed as a waiter. Well into his forties now, his hair a salt-and-pepper gray, his face creased with the lines of twenty years of smiles, Mario nodded and said, "Yes, yes. Of course I remember. The police, they come to talk to me three, four times. And each time I tell them the same thing. M. Tavistock, he comes for café au lait, every morning. Sometimes, *madame* is with him. Ah, beautiful!"

"But she wasn't with him on that particular day?"

Mario shook his head. "He comes alone. Sits at that table there." He pointed to an empty table near the sidewalk, red-checked cloth fluttering in the breeze. "He waits a long time for *madame*."

"And she didn't come?"

"No. Then she calls. Tells him to meet her at another place. In Pigalle. I take the message and give it to M. Tavistock."

"She spoke to you? On the telephone?"

"*Oui.* I write down address, give to him."

"That would be the address in Pigalle?"

Mario nodded.

"My father—M. Tavistock—did he seem at all upset that day? Angry?"

"Not angry. He seems—how do you say?—worried. He does not understand why *madame* goes to Pigalle. He pays for his coffee, then he leaves. Later I read in the newspaper that he is dead. Ah, *horrible!* The police, they are asking for information. So I call, tell them what I know." Mario shook his head at the tragedy of it all.

At the loss of such a lovely woman as Mme Tavistock and such a generous man as her husband.

No new information here, thought Jordan. He turned to leave, then stopped and turned back.

"Are you certain it was Mme Tavistock who called to leave the message?" he asked.

"She says it is her," said Mario.

"And you recognized her voice?"

Mario paused. It lasted just the blink of an eye, but it was enough to tell Jordan that the man was not absolutely certain. "Yes," said Mario. "Who else would it be?"

Deep in thought, Jordan left the café and walked a few paces along Boulevard Saint-Germain, intending to return on foot to the hotel. But half a block away, he spotted the blue Peugeot. His little blond vampiress, he thought, still following him about. They were headed in the same direction; why not ask her for a ride?

He went to the Peugeot and pulled open the passenger door. "Mind dropping me off at the Ritz?" he asked brightly.

An outraged Colette stared at him from the driver's seat. "What do you think you are doing?" she demanded. "Get out of my car!"

"Oh, come, now. No need for hysterics—"

"Go away!" she cried, loudly enough to make a passerby stop and stare.

Calmly Jordan slid into the front seat. He noted that she was dressed in black again. What was it with these secret agent types? "It's a long walk to the Ritz. Surely it's not *verboten*, is it? To give me a lift back to my hotel?"

"I do not even know who you are," she insisted.

"I know who *you* are. Your name's Colette, you work

for Claude Daumier, and you're supposed to be keeping an eye on me.'' Jordan smiled at her, the sort of smile that usually got him exactly what he wanted. He said, quite reasonably, ''Rather than sneaking around after me all the way up the boulevard, why not be sensible about it? Save us both the inconvenience of this silly cat-and-mouse game.''

A spark of laughter flickered in her eyes. She gripped the steering wheel and stared straight ahead, but he could see the smile tugging at her lips. ''Shut the door,'' she snapped. ''And use the seat belt. It is regulation.''

As they drove up Boulevard Saint-Germain, he kept glancing at her, wondering if she was really as fierce as she appeared. That black leather skirt and the scowl on her face couldn't disguise the fact she was actually quite pretty.

''How long have you worked for Daumier?'' he asked.

''Three years.''

''And is this your usual sort of assignment? Following strange men about town?''

''I follow instructions. Whatever they are.''

''Ah. The obedient type.'' Jordan sat back, grinning. ''What did Daumier tell you about this particular assignment?''

''I am to see you and your sister are not harmed. Since today she is with M. Wolf, I decide to follow you.'' She paused and added under her breath, ''Not as simple as I thought.''

''I'm not all that difficult.''

''But you do the unexpected. You catch me by surprise.'' A car was honking at them. Annoyed, Colette glanced up at the rearview mirror. ''This traffic, it gets worse every—''

At her sudden silence, Jordan glanced at her. "Is something wrong?"

"No," she said after a pause, "I am just imagining things."

Jordan turned and peered through the rear window. All he saw was a line of cars snaking down the boulevard. He looked back at Colette. "Tell me, what's a nice girl like you doing in French Intelligence?"

She smiled—the first real smile he'd seen. It was like watching the sun come out. "I am earning a living."

"Meeting interesting people?"

"Quite."

"Finding romance?"

"Regrettably, no."

"What a shame. Perhaps you should find a new line of work."

"Such as?"

"We could discuss it over supper."

She shook her head. "It is not allowed to fraternize with a subject."

"So that's all I am," he said with a sigh. "A subject."

She dropped him off on a side street, around the corner from the Ritz. He climbed out, then turned and said, "Why not come in for a drink?"

"I am on duty."

"It must get boring, sitting in that car all day. Waiting for me to make another unexpected move."

"Thank you, but no." She smiled—a charmingly impish grin. It carried just a hint of possibility.

Jordan left the car and walked into the hotel.

Upstairs, he paced for a while, pondering what he'd just learned at Café Hugo. That phone call from Madeline—it just didn't fit in. Why on earth would she arrange to meet Bernard in Pigalle? It clearly didn't go along with the theory of a murder-suicide. Could the waiter be lying? Or was he simply mistaken? With all the ambient noise of a busy café, how could he be certain it was really Madeline Tavistock making that phone call?

I have to go back to the café. Ask Mario, specifically, if the voice was an Englishwoman's.

Once again he left the hotel and stepped into the brightness of midday. A taxi sat idling near the front entrance, but the driver was nowhere to be seen. Perhaps Colette was still parked around the corner; he'd ask her to drive him back to Boulevard Saint-Germain. He turned up the side street and spotted the blue Peugeot still parked there. Colette was sitting inside; through the tinted windshield, he saw her silhouette behind the steering wheel.

He went to the car and tapped on the passenger window. "Colette?" he called. "Could you give me another lift?"

She didn't answer.

Jordan swung open the door and slid in beside her. "Colette?"

She sat perfectly still, her eyes staring rigidly ahead. For a moment, he didn't understand. Then he saw the bright trickle of blood that had traced its way down her hairline and vanished into the black fabric of her turtlenecked shirt. In panic, he reached out to her and gave her shoulder a shake. *"Colette?"*

She slid toward him and toppled into his lap.

He stared at her head, now resting in his arms. In her temple was a single, neat bullet hole.

He scarcely remembered scrambling out of the car. What he did remember were the screams of a woman passerby. Then, moments later, he focused on the shocked faces of people who'd been drawn onto this quiet side street by the screams. They were all pointing at the woman's arm hanging limply out of the car. And they were staring at him.

Numbly, Jordan looked down at his own hands.

They were smeared with blood.

5

From the crowd of onlookers standing on the corner, Amiel Foch watched the police handcuff the Englishman and lead him away. An unintended development, he thought. Not at all what he'd expected to happen.

Then again, he hadn't expected to see Colette LaFarge ever again. Or, even worse, to be seen by her. They'd worked together only once, and that was three years ago in Cyprus. He'd hoped, when he walked past her car, with his head down and his shoulders hunched, that she would not notice him. But as he'd headed away, he'd heard her call out his name in astonishment.

He'd had no alternative, he thought as he watched the attendants load her body into the ambulance. French Intelligence thought he was dead. Colette could have told them otherwise.

It hadn't been an easy thing to do. But as he'd turned to face her, his decision was already made. He had walked slowly back to her car. Through the windshield, he'd seen her look of wonder at a dead colleague come back to life. She'd sat frozen, staring at the apparition. She had not moved as he approached the driver's side. Nor did she move as he thrust his silenced automatic into her car window and fired.

Such a waste of a pretty girl, he thought as the ambulance drove away. But she should have known better.

The crowd was dispersing. It was time to leave.

He edged toward the curb. Quietly he dropped his pistol in the gutter and kicked it down the storm drain. The weapon was stolen, untraceable; better to have it found near the scene of the crime. It would cement the case against Jordan Tavistock.

Several blocks away, he found a telephone. He dialed his client.

"Jordan Tavistock has been arrested for murder," said Foch.

"Whose murder?" came the sharp reply.

"One of Daumier's agents. A woman."

"Did Tavistock do it?"

"No. I did."

There was a sudden burst of laughter from his client. "This is priceless! Absolutely priceless! I ask you to follow Jordan, and you have him framed for murder. I can't wait to see what you do with his sister."

"What do you wish me to do?" asked Foch.

There was a pause. "I think it's time to resolve this mess," he said. "Finish it."

"The woman is no problem. But her brother will be difficult to reach, unless I can find a way into the prison."

"You could always get yourself arrested."

"And when they identify my fingerprints?" Foch shook his head. "I need someone else for that job."

"Then I'll find you someone," came the reply. "For now, let's work on one thing at a time. Beryl Tavistock."

A TURKISH MAN NOW OWNED the building on Rue Myrha. He'd tried to improve it. He'd painted the exterior walls, shored up the crumbling balconies, replaced the missing roof slates, but the building, and the street on which it stood, seemed beyond rehabilitation. It was the fault of the tenants, explained Mr. Zamir, as he led them up two flights of stairs to the attic flat. What could one do with tenants who let their children run wild? By all appearances, Mr. Zamir was a successful business-man, a man whose tailored suit and excellent English bespoke prosperous roots. There were four families in the building, he said, all of them reliable enough with the rent. But no one lived in the attic flat—he'd always had difficulty renting that one out. People had come to inspect the place, of course, but when they heard of the murder, they quickly backed out. These silly supersti-tions! Oh, people claim they do not believe in ghosts, but when they visit a room where two people have died...

"How long has the flat been empty?" asked Beryl.

"A year now. Ever since I have owned the building. And before that—" he shrugged "—I do not know. It may have been empty for many years." He unlocked the door. "You may look around if you wish."

A puff of stale air greeted them as they pushed open the door—the smell of a room too long shut away from the world. It was not an unpleasant room. Sunshine washed in through a large, dirt-streaked window. The view looked down over Rue Myrha, and Beryl could see children kicking a soccer ball in the street. The flat was completely empty of furniture; there were only bare walls and floor. Through an open door, she glimpsed the bathroom with its chipped sink and tarnished fixtures.

In silence Beryl circled the flat, her gaze moving across the wood floor. Beside the window, she came to a halt. The stain was barely visible, just a faint brown blot in the oak planks. *Whose blood?* she wondered.

Mum's? Dad's? Or is it both of theirs, eternally mingled?

"I have tried to sand the stain away," said Mr. Zamir. "But it goes very deep into the wood. Even when I think I have erased it, in a few weeks the stain seems to reappear." He sighed. "It frightens them away, you know. The tenants, they do not like to see such reminders on their floor."

Beryl swallowed hard and turned to look out the window. *Why on this street?* she wondered. *In this room? Of all the places in Paris, why did they die here?*

She asked quietly, "Who owned this building, Mr. Zamir? Before you did?"

"There were many owners. Before me, it was a M. Rosenthal. And before him, a M. Dudoit."

"At the time of the murder," said Richard, "the landlord was a man named Jacques Rideau. Did you know him?"

"I am sorry, I do not. That would have been many years ago."

"Twenty."

"Then I would not have met him." Mr. Zamir turned to the door. "I will leave you alone. If you have questions, I will be down in number three for a while."

Beryl heard the man's footsteps creak down the stairs. She looked at Richard and saw that he was standing off in a corner, frowning at the floor. "What are you thinking?" she asked.

"About Inspector Broussard. How he kept trying to point at that photo. The spot he was pointing to would be somewhere around here. Just to the left of the door."

"There's nothing to look at. And there was nothing in the photo, either."

"That's what bothers me. He seemed so troubled by it. And there was something about a briefcase...."

"The NATO file," she said softly.

He looked at her. "How much have you been told about Delphi?"

"I know it wasn't Mum or Dad. They would never have gone to the other side."

"People go over for different reasons."

"But not them. They certainly didn't need the money."

"Communist sympathies?"

"Not the Tavistocks!"

He moved toward her. With every step he took, her pulse seemed to leap faster. He came close enough to make her feel threatened. And tempted. Quietly he said, "There's always blackmail."

"Meaning they had secrets to hide?"

"Everyone does."

"Not everyone turns traitor."

"It depends on the secret, doesn't it? And how much one stands to lose because of it."

In silence they gazed at each other, and she found herself wondering how much he really did know about her parents. How much he wasn't admitting to. She sensed he knew a lot more than he was letting on, and that suspicion loomed like a barrier between them. Those secrets again. Those unspoken truths. She had grown up in a household where certain conversational doors were always kept locked. *I refuse to live my life that way. Ever again.*

She turned away. "They had no reason to be vulnerable to blackmail."

"You were just a child, eight years old. Away at boarding school in England. What did you really know about them? About their marriage, their secrets? What if it was your mother who rented this flat? Met her lover here?''

"I don't believe it. I won't.''

"Is it so difficult to accept? That she was human, that she might have had a lover?'' He took her by the shoulders, willing her to meet his gaze. "She was a beautiful woman, Beryl. If she'd wanted to, she could have had any number of lovers.''

"You're making her out to be a tramp!''

"I'm considering all the possibilities.''

"That she sold out Queen and country? To keep some vile little secret from surfacing?'' Angrily she wrenched away from him. "Sorry, Richard, but my faith runs a little deeper than that. And if you'd known them, really known them, you'd never consider such a thing.'' She pivoted away and walked to the door.

"I did know them,'' he said. "I knew them rather well.''

She stopped, turned to face him. "What do you mean by 'rather well'?''

"We...moved in the same circles. Not the same team, exactly. But we worked at similar purposes.''

"You never told me.''

"I didn't know how much I *should* tell you. How much you should know.'' He began to slowly circle the room, carefully considering each word before he spoke. "It was my first assignment. I'd just completed my training at Langley—''

"CIA?''

He nodded. "I was recruited straight out of the university. Not exactly my first career choice. But somehow they'd gotten hold of my master's thesis, an analysis of Libyan arms capabilities. It turned out to be amazingly close to the mark. They knew I was fluent in a few languages. And that I had taken out quite a large sum in student loans. That was the carrot, you see—the loan payoff. The foreign travel. And, I have to admit, the idea intrigued me, the chance to work as an Intelligence analyst..."

"Is that how you met my parents?"

He nodded. "NATO knew it had a security leak, originating in Paris. Somehow weapons data were slipping through to the East Germans. I'd just arrived in Paris, so there was no question that I was clean. They assigned me to work with Claude Daumier at French Intelligence. I was asked to compose a dummy weapons report, something close to, but not quite, the truth. It was encoded and transmitted to a few select embassy officials in Paris. The idea was to pinpoint the possible source of the leak."

"How were my parents involved?"

"They were attached to the British embassy. Bernard in Communications, Madeline in Protocol. Both were really working for MI6. Bernard was one of a few who had access to classified files."

"So he was a suspect?"

Richard nodded. "Everyone was. British, American, French. Right up to ambassadorial level." Again he began to pace, carefully measuring his words. "So the dummy file went out to the embassies. And we waited to see if it would turn up, like the others, in East German hands. It didn't. It ended up here, in a briefcase. In this very room." He stopped and looked at her. "With your parents."

"And that closed the file on Delphi," she said. Bitterly she added, "How neat and easy. You had your culprit. Lucky for you he was dead and unable to defend himself.''

''I didn't believe it.''

''Yet you dropped the matter.''

''We had no choice.''

''You didn't care enough to learn the truth!''

''No, Beryl. We didn't have the choice. We were instructed to call off the investigation.''

She stared at him in astonishment. ''By whom?''

''My orders came straight from Washington. Claude's from the French prime minister. The matter was dropped.''

''And my parents went on record as traitors,'' she said. ''What a convenient way to close the file.'' In disgust she turned and left the room.

He followed her down the stairs. ''Beryl! I never really believed Bernard was the one!''

''Yet you let him take the blame!''

''I told you, I was ordered to—''

''And of course you always follow orders.''

''I was sent back to Washington soon afterward. I couldn't pursue it.''

They walked out of the building into the bedlam of Rue Myrha. A soccer ball flew past, pursued by a gaggle of tattered-looking children. Beryl paused on the sidewalk, her eyes temporarily dazzled by the sunshine. The street sounds, the shouts of the children, were disorienting. She turned and looked up at the building, at the attic window. The view suddenly blurred through her tears.

''What a place to die,'' she whispered. ''God, what a horrible place to die....''

She climbed into Richard's car and pulled the door closed. It was a blessed relief to shut out the noise and chaos of Rue Myrha.

Richard slid in behind the driver's seat. For a moment, they sat in silence, staring ahead at the ragamuffins playing street soccer.

"I'll take you back to the hotel," he said.

"I want to see Claude Daumier."

"Why?"

"I want to hear his version of what happened. I want to confirm that you're telling me the truth."

"I am, Beryl."

She turned to him. His gaze was steady, unflinching. *An honest look if ever I've seen one,* she thought. *Which only proves how gullible I am.* She wanted to believe him, and there was the danger. It was that blasted attraction between them—the feverish tug of hormones, the memory of his kisses—that clouded her judgment. *What is it about this man? I take one look at his face, inhale a whiff of his scent, and I'm aching to tear off his clothes. And mine, as well.*

She looked straight ahead, trying to ignore all those heated signals passing between them. "I want to talk to Daumier."

After a pause, he said, "All right. If that's what it'll take for you to believe me."

A phone call revealed that Daumier was not in his office; he'd just left to conduct another interview with Marie St. Pierre. So they drove to Cochin Hospital, where Marie was still a patient.

Even from the far end of the hospital corridor, they could tell which room was Marie's; half a dozen policemen were stationed outside her door. Daumier had not yet arrived. Madame St. Pierre, informed that Lord Lovat's niece had arrived, at once had Beryl and Richard escorted into her room.

They discovered they weren't the only visitors Marie

was entertaining that afternoon. Seated in chairs near the patient's bed were Nina Sutherland and Helena Vane. A little tea party was in progress, complete with trays of biscuits and finger sandwiches set on a rolling cart by the window. The patient, however, was not partaking of the refreshments; she sat propped up in bed, a sad and weary-looking French matron dressed in a gray robe to match her gray hair. Her only visible injuries appeared to be a bruised cheek and some scratches on her arms. It was clear from the woman's look of unhappiness that the bomb's most serious damage had been emotional. Any other patient would have been discharged by now; only her status as St. Pierre's wife allowed her such pampering.

Nina poured two cups of tea and handed them to Beryl and Richard. "When did you arrive in Paris?" she said.

"Jordan and I flew in yesterday," said Beryl. "And you?"

"We flew home with Helena and Reggie." Nina sat back down and crossed her silk-stockinged legs. "First thing this morning, I thought to myself, I really should drop in to see how Marie's doing. Poor thing, she does need cheering up."

Judging by the patient's glum face, Nina's visit had not yet achieved the desired result.

"What's the world coming to, I ask you?" said Nina, balancing her cup of tea. "Madness and anarchy! No one's immune, not even the upper class."

"Especially the upper class," said Helena.

"Has there been any progress on the case?" asked Beryl.

Marie St. Pierre sighed. "They insist it is a terrorist attack."

"Well, of course," said Nina. "Who else plants bombs in politicians' houses?"

Marie's gaze quickly dropped to her lap. She looked at her hands, the bony fingers woven together. "I have told Philippe we should leave Paris for a while. Tonight, perhaps, when I am released. We could visit Switzerland...."

"An excellent idea," murmured Helena gently. She reached out to squeeze Marie's hand. "You need to get away, just the two of you."

"But that's turning tail," said Nina. "Letting the criminals know they've won."

"Easy for you to say," muttered Helena. "It wasn't your house that was bombed."

"And if it was my house, I'd stay right in Paris," Nina retorted. "I wouldn't give an inch—"

"You've never had to."

"What?"

Helena looked away. "Nothing."

"What are you muttering about, Helena?"

"I only think," said Helena, "that Marie should do exactly what she wants. Leaving Paris for a while makes perfect sense. Any friend would back her up."

"I *am* her friend."

"Yes," murmured Helena, "of course you are."

"Are you saying I'm not?"

"I didn't say anything of the kind."

"You're muttering again, Helena. Really, it drives me up a wall. Is it so difficult to come right out and say things?"

"Oh, please," moaned Marie.

A knock on the door cut short the argument. Nina's son, Anthony, entered, dressed with his usual offbeat flair in a shirt of electric blue, a leather jacket. "Ready to leave, Mum?" he asked Nina.

At once Nina rose huffily to her feet. "More than ready," she sniffed and followed him to the door. There she stopped and gave Marie one last glance. "I'm only speaking as a friend," she said. "And I, for one, think you should stay in Paris." She took Anthony's arm and walked out of the room.

"Good heavens, Marie," muttered Helena, after a pause. "Why do you put up with the woman?"

Marie, looking small as she huddled in her bed, gave a small shrug. *They are so very much alike,* thought Beryl, comparing Marie St. Pierre and Helena. Neither one blessed with beauty, both on the fading side of middle age, and trapped in marriages to men who no longer adored them.

"I've always thought you were a saint just to let that bitch in your door," said Helena. "If it were up to me..."

"One must keep the peace" was all Marie said.

They tried to carry on a conversation, the four of them, but so many silences intervened. And overshadowing their talk of bomb blasts and ruined furniture, of lost artwork and damaged heirlooms, was the sense that something was being left unsaid. That even beyond the horror of these losses was a deeper loss. One had only to look in Marie St. Pierre's eyes to know that she was reeling from the devastation of her life.

Even when her husband, Philippe, walked into the room, Marie did not perk up. If anything, she seemed to recoil from Philippe's kiss. She averted her face and looked instead at the door, which had just swung open again.

Claude Daumier entered, saw Beryl, and halted in surprise. "You are *here?*"

"We were waiting to see you," said Beryl.

Daumier glanced at Richard, then back at Beryl. "I have been trying to find you both."

"What's wrong?" asked Richard.

"The matter is...delicate." Daumier motioned for them to follow. "It would be best," he said, "to discuss this in private."

They followed him into the hallway, past the nurses' station. In a quiet corner, Daumier stopped and turned to Richard.

"I have just received a call from the police. Colette was found shot to death in her car. Near Place Vendôme."

"Colette?" said Beryl. "The agent who was watching Jordan?"

Grimly Daumier nodded.

"Oh, my God," murmured Beryl. "Jordie—"

"He is safe," Daumier said quickly. "I assure you, he's not in danger."

"But if they killed her, they could—"

"He has been placed under arrest," said Daumier. His gaze, quietly sympathetic, focused on Beryl's shocked face. "For murder."

LONG AFTER EVERYONE ELSE had left the hospital room, Helena remained by Marie's bedside. For a while they said very little; good friends, after all, are comfortable with silence. But then Helena could not hold it in any longer. "It's intolerable," she said. "You simply can't stand for this, Marie."

Marie sighed. "What else am I to do? She has so

many friends, so many people she could turn against me. Against Philippe...."

"But you must do something. Anything. For one, refuse to speak to her!"

"I have no proof. Never do I have proof."

"You don't need proof. Use your eyes! Look at the way they act together. The way she's always around him, smiling at him. He may have told you it was over, but you can see it isn't. And where is he, anyway? You're in the hospital and he scarcely visits you. When he does, it's just a peck on the cheek and he's off again."

"He is preoccupied. The economic summit—"

"Oh, yes," Helena snorted. "Men's business is always so bloody important!"

Marie started to cry, not sobs, but noiseless, pitiful tears. Suffering in silence—that was her way. Never a complaint or a protest, just a heart quietly breaking. *The pain we endure,* thought Helena bitterly, *all for the love of men.*

Marie said in a whisper, "It is even worse than you know."

"How can it possibly be any worse?"

Marie didn't reply. She just looked down at the abrasions on her arms. They were only minor scrapes, the aftermath of flying glass, but she stared at them with what looked like quiet despair.

So that's it, thought Helena, horrified. *She thinks they're trying to kill her. Why doesn't she strike back? Why doesn't she fight?*

But Marie hadn't the will. One could see that, just by the slump of her shoulders.

My poor, dear friend, thought Helena, gazing at Marie

with pity, *how very much alike we are. And yet, how
very different.*

A MAN SAT ON THE BENCH across from him, silently eyeing Jordan's clothes, his shoes, his watch. A well-pickled
fellow by the smell of him, thought Jordan with distaste.
Or did that delightful odor, that unmistakable perfume
of cheap wine and ripe underarms, emanate from the
other occupant of the jail cell? Jordan glanced at the man
snoring blissfully in the far corner. Yes, there was the
likely source.

The man on the bench was still staring at him. Jordan
tried to ignore him, but the man's gaze was so intrusive
that Jordan finally snapped, "What are you looking at?"

"C'est en or?" the man asked.

"Pardon?"

"La montre. C'est en or?" The man pointed at Jordan's watch.

"Yes, of course it's gold!" said Jordan.

The man grinned, revealing a mouthful of rotted teeth.
He rose and shuffled across the cell to sit beside Jordan.
Right beside him. His gaze dropped speculatively to Jor-
dan's shoes. *"C'est italienne?"*

Jordan sighed. "Yes, they're Italian."

The man reached over and fingered Jordan's linen
jacket sleeve.

"All right, that's it," said Jordan. "Hands to yourself,
chap! *Laissez-moi tranquille!*"

The man simply grinned wider and pointed to his own
shoes, a pair of cardboard and plastic creations. "You
like?"

"Very nice," groaned Jordan.

The sound of footsteps and clinking keys approached.

The man sleeping in the corner suddenly woke up and began to yell, *"Je suis innocent! Je suis innocent!"*

"M. Tavistock?" called the guard.

Jordan jumped at once to his feet. "Yes?"

"You are to come with me."

"Where are we going?"

"You have visitors."

The guard led him down a hall, past holding cells jammed full with prisoners. Good grief, thought Jordan, and he'd thought his cell was bad. He followed the guard through a locked door into the booking area. At once his ears were assaulted with the sounds of bedlam. Everywhere phones seemed to be ringing, voices arguing. A ragtag line of prisoners waited to be processed, and one woman kept yelling that it was a mistake, all a mistake. Through the babble of French, Jordan heard his name called.

"Beryl?" he said in relief.

She ran to him, practically knocking him over with the force of her embrace. "Jordie! Oh, my poor Jordie, are you all right?"

"I'm fine, darling."

"You're really all right?"

"Never better, now that you're here." Glancing over her shoulder, he saw Richard and Daumier standing behind her. The cavalry had arrived. Now this terrible business could be cleared up.

Beryl pulled away and frowned at his face. "You look ghastly."

"I probably smell even worse." Turning to Daumier, he said, "Have they found out anything about Colette?"

Daumier shook his head. "A single bullet, nine millimeters, in the temple. Plainly an execution, with no witnesses."

"What about the gun?" asked Jordan. "How can they accuse me without having a murder weapon?"

"They do have one," said Daumier. "It was found in the storm drain, very near the car."

"And no witnesses?" said Beryl. "In broad daylight?"

"It is a side street. Not many passersby."

"But someone must have seen something."

Daumier gave an unhappy nod. "A woman did report seeing a man force his way into Colette's car. But it was on Boulevard Saint-Germain."

Jordan groaned. "Oh, great. That would've been me."

Beryl frowned. "You?"

"I talked her into giving me a ride back to the hotel. My fingerprints will be all over the inside of that car."

"What happened after you got into the car?" Richard asked.

"She let me off at the Ritz. I went up to the room for a few minutes, then came back down to talk to her. That's when I found..." Groaning, he clutched his head. "Lord, this can't be happening."

"Did you see anything?" Richard pressed him.

"Not a thing. But..." Jordan's head slowly lifted. "Colette may have."

"You're not sure?"

"While we were driving to the hotel, she kept frowning at the mirror. Said something about imagining things. I looked, but all I saw was traffic." Miserable, he turned to Daumier. "I blame myself, really. I keep thinking, if only I'd paid more attention, if I hadn't been so wrapped up—"

"She knew how to protect herself," interrupted Daumier. "She should have been prepared."

"That's what I don't understand," said Jordan. "That

she was caught so off guard.'' He glanced at his watch. ''There's still plenty of daylight. We could go back to Boulevard Saint-Germain. Retrace my steps. Something might come back to me.''

His suggestion was met with dead silence.

''Jordie,'' said Beryl, softly, ''you can't.''

''What do you mean, I can't?''

''They won't release you.''

''But they have to release me! I didn't do it!'' He looked at Daumier. To his dismay, the Frenchman regretfully shook his head.

Richard said, ''We'll do whatever it takes, Jordan. Somehow we'll get you out of here.''

''Has anyone called Uncle Hugh?''

''He's not at Chetwynd,'' said Beryl. ''No one knows where he is. It seems he left last night without telling anyone. So we're going to see Reggie and Helena. They've friends in the embassy. Maybe they can pull some strings.''

Dismayed by the news, Jordan could only stand there, surrounded by the chaos of milling prisoners and policemen. *I'm in prison and Uncle Hugh's vanished,* he thought. *This nightmare is getting worse by the second.*

''The police think I'm guilty?'' he ventured.

''I am afraid so,'' said Daumier.

''And you, Claude? What do you think?''

''Of course he knows you're innocent!'' declared Beryl. ''We all do. Just give me time to clear things up.''

Jordan turned to his sister, his beautiful, stubborn sister. The one person he cared most about in the world. He took off his watch and firmly pressed it into her hand.

She frowned. ''Why are you giving me this?''

''Safekeeping. I may be in here a rather long time.

Now, I want you to go home, Beryl. The next plane to London. Do you understand?''

''But I'm not going anywhere.''

''Yes, you are. And Richard is damn well going to see to it.''

''How?'' she retorted. ''By dragging me off by the hair?''

''If that's what it takes.''

''You need me here!''

''Beryl.'' He took her by the shoulders and spoke quietly. Sensibly. ''A woman's been killed. And she was trained to defend herself.''

''It doesn't mean I'm next.''

''It means they're frightened. Ready to strike back. You have to go home.''

''And leave you in this place?''

''Claude will be here. And Reggie—''

''So I fly home and leave you to rot in prison?'' She shook her head in disagreement. ''Do you really think I'd do that?''

''If you love me, you will.''

Her chin came up. ''If I love you,'' she said, ''I'll do no such thing.'' She threw her arms around him in a fierce, uncompromising embrace. Then, brushing away tears, she turned to Richard. ''Let's go. The sooner we talk to Reggie, the sooner we'll clear up this mess.''

Jordan watched his sister walk away. It was just like her, he thought, to steer her own straight and stubborn course through that unruly crowd of pickpockets and prostitutes. ''Beryl!'' he yelled. ''Go home! Don't be a bloody idiot!''

She stopped and looked back at him. ''But I can't help it, Jordie. It runs in the family.'' Then she turned and walked out the door.

6

"**Y**our brother's right," said Richard. "You should go home."

"Don't *you* start now," she snapped over her shoulder.

"I'll drive you to the hotel to pack. Then I'm taking you to the airport."

"You and what regiment?"

"For once will you take some advice?" he yelled.

She spun around on the crowded sidewalk and turned to confront him. "Advice, yes. Orders, no."

"Okay, then just listen for a minute. Your coming to Paris was a crazy move to begin with. Sure, I understand why you did it. I understand that you'd want to know the truth about your parents. But things have changed, Beryl. A woman's been killed. It's a whole new ball game now."

"What am I supposed to do about Jordan? Just leave him there?"

"I'll take care of it. I'll talk to Reggie. We'll get him the best lawyer there is—"

"And I run home? Wash my hands of the whole mess?" She looked down at the watch she was holding. Jordan's watch. Quietly she said, "He's my family. Did you see how wretched he looked? It would kill him to stay in that place. If I left him there, I'd never forgive myself."

"And if something happened to you, Jordan would never forgive himself. And neither would I."

"I'm not your responsibility."

"But you are."

"And who decided that?"

He reached for her then, trapping her face in his hands. "I did," he whispered, and pressed his lips to hers. She was so stunned by the ferocity of his kiss that at first she couldn't react; too many glorious sensations were assaulting her at once. She heard his murmurings of need, felt the hot surge of his tongue into her mouth. Her own body responded, every nerve singing with desire. She was oblivious to the traffic, the passersby on the sidewalk. There were only the two of them and the way their bodies and mouths melted together. All day they'd been fighting this, she thought. And all day she knew it was hopeless. She knew it would come to this— one kiss on a Paris street, and she was lost.

Gently he pulled away and gazed down at her. "*That's* why you have to leave Paris," he murmured.

"Because you command it?"

"No. Because it makes sense."

She stepped back, desperate to put space between them, to regain some control—any control—over her emotions. "Sense to you, perhaps," she said softly. "But not to me." Then she turned and climbed into his car.

He slid in beside her and shut the door. Though they sat in silence, she could feel his frustration radiating throughout the car.

"What can I say that would make you change your mind?" he asked.

"*My* mind?" She looked at him and managed a tight, uncompromising smile. "Absolutely nothing."

"IT's RATHER a sticky situation," said Reggie Vane. "If the charges weren't so serious—theft, perhaps, or even assault—then the embassy might be able to do something. But murder? I'm afraid that's beyond diplomatic intervention."

They were talking in Reggie's private study, a masculine, dark-paneled room very much like her Uncle Hugh's at Chetwynd. The bookshelves were lined with English classics, the walls hung with hunting scenes of foxes and hounds and gentlemen on horseback. The stone fireplace was an exact copy, Reggie had told them, of the hearth in his childhood home in Cornwall. Even the smell of Reggie's pipe tobacco reminded Beryl of home. How comforting to discover that here, on the outskirts of Paris, was a familiar world transplanted straight from England.

"Surely the ambassador can do something?" said Beryl. "This is Jordan we're talking about, not some soccer-club hooligan. Besides, he's innocent."

"Of course he's innocent," said Reggie. "Believe me, if there was anything I could do about it, our Jordan wouldn't stay in that cell a moment longer." He sat down on the couch beside her and clasped her hands, the whole time focusing his mild blue eyes on her face. "Beryl, darling, you have to understand. Even the ambassador himself can't work miracles. I've spoken to him, and he's not optimistic."

"Then there's nothing you or he can do?" Beryl asked miserably.

"I'll arrange for a lawyer—one our embassy recommends. He's an excellent fellow, someone they call in for just this sort of thing. Specializes in English clients."

"And that's all we can hope for? A good attorney?"

Reggie's answer was a regretful nod.

In her disappointment, Beryl didn't hear Richard move to stand close behind her, but she did feel his hands coming to rest protectively on her shoulders. *How I've come to rely on him,* she thought. *A man I shouldn't trust. And yet I do.*

Reggie looked at Richard. "What about the Intelligence angle?" he asked. "Any evidence forthcoming?"

"French Intelligence is working with the police. They'll be running ballistic tests on the gun. No fingerprints were found on it. The fact that he's Lord Lovat's nephew will get him some special consideration. But in the end, it's still a murder charge. And the victim's a Frenchwoman. Once the local papers get hold of the story, it will sound like some spoiled English brat trying to slither out of criminal charges."

"And there's enough ill will toward us British as it is," said Reggie. "After thirty years in this country, I should know. I tell you, as soon as my year's up at the bank, I'm going home." His gaze wandered longingly to the painting over the mantelpiece. It was of a country home, its walls festooned with blue wisteria blossoms. "Helena hated it in Cornwall—thought the house was far too primitive. But it suited my parents. And it suits me." He looked at Beryl. "It's a frightening thing, getting into trouble so far from home. One is always aware that one is vulnerable. And neither class nor money can make things right."

"I've told Beryl she should fly home," said Richard.

Reggie nodded. "My feelings exactly."

"I can't," said Beryl. "I'd feel like a rat jumping ship."

"At least you'd be a live rat," said Richard.

Angrily she shrugged off his touch. "But a rat all the same."

Reggie reached for her hand. "Beryl," he said quietly, "listen to me. I was your mother's oldest friend— we grew up together. So I feel a special responsibility. And you have no idea how painful it is for me to see one of Madeline's children in such a fix. It's awful enough that Jordan's in trouble, but to worry about you, as well…" He gave her hand a squeeze. "Listen to your Mr. Wolf here. He's a sensible fellow. Someone you can trust."

Someone I can trust. Beryl felt Richard's gaze on her back, felt it as acutely as a touch, and her spine stiffened. She focused firmly on Reggie. Dear Reggie, whose shared past with Madeline made him part of her family.

She said, "I know you mean only the best, Reggie, but I can't leave Paris."

The two men looked at each other, exchanging shared expressions of frustration, but not surprise. After all, they had both known Madeline; they could expect nothing less than stubbornness from her daughter.

There was a knock on the study door. Helena poked her head in. "All right for me to come in?"

"Of course," said Beryl.

Helena entered, carrying a tray of tea and biscuits, which she set down on the end table. "I'm always careful to ask first," she said with a smile as she poured out four cups, "before I trespass in Reggie's private abode." She handed Beryl a cup. "Have we made any headway, then?"

From the silence that greeted her question, Helena knew the answer. She looked at once apologetic. "Oh, Beryl. I'm so sorry. Isn't there *something* you can do, Reggie?"

"I'm already doing it," said Reggie, with more than a hint of impatience. Turning his back to her, he took a pipe down from the mantelpiece and lit it. For a moment, there was only the sound of the teacups clinking on saucers and the soft put-put-put of Reggie's lips on the pipe stem.

"Reggie?" ventured Helena again. "It seems to me that calling an attorney is merely being reactive. Isn't there something, well, *active* that could be done?"

"Such as?" asked Richard.

"For instance, the crime itself. We all know Jordan couldn't have done it. So who did?"

Reggie grunted. "You're hardly qualified as a detective."

"Still, it's a question that will have to be answered. That young woman was killed while watching over Jordan. So this may all stem from the reason Jordan's in Paris to begin with. Though I can't quite see how a twenty-year-old case of murder could be so dangerous to someone."

"It was more than murder," Beryl observed. "Espionage was involved."

"That business with the NATO mole," Reggie said to Helena. "You remember. Hugh told us about it."

"Oh, yes. Delphi." Helena glanced at Richard. "MI6 never actually identified him, did they?"

"They had their suspicions," said Richard.

"I myself always wondered," said Helena, reaching for a biscuit, "about Ambassador Sutherland. And why he committed suicide so soon after Madeline and Bernard died."

Richard nodded. "You and I think along the same lines, Lady Helena."

"Though I can't say he didn't have other reasons to jump off that bridge. If I were a man married to Nina, I'd have killed myself long ago." Helena bit sharply into the biscuit; it was a reminder that even mousy women have teeth.

Reggie tapped his pipe and said, "It's not right for us to speculate."

"Still, one can't help it, can one?"

By the time Reggie walked his guests to the front door, darkness had fallen and the night had taken on a damp, unseasonable chill. Even the high walls surrounding the Vanes' private courtyard couldn't seem to shut out the sense of danger that hung in the air that night.

"I promise you," said Reggie, "I'll do everything I can."

"I don't know how to thank you," Beryl murmured.

"Just give me a smile, dear. Yes, that's it." Reggie took her by the shoulders and planted a kiss on her forehead. "You look more and more like your mother every day. And from me, there is no higher compliment." He turned to Richard. "You'll look out for the girl?"

"I promise," said Richard.

"Good. Because she's all we have left." Sadly he touched Beryl's cheek. "All we have left of Madeline."

"WERE THEY ALWAYS that way together?" asked Beryl. "Reggie and Helena?"

Richard kept his eyes on the road as he drove. "What do you mean?"

"The sniping at each other. The put-downs."

He chuckled. "I'm so used to hearing it, I hardly notice it anymore. Yes, I guess it was that way when I met them twenty years ago. I'm sure part of it's due to his resentment of Helena's money. No man likes to feel, well, kept."

"No," she said quietly, looking straight ahead. "I suppose no man would." *Is that how it would be be-*

tween us? she wondered. *Would he hold my money against me? Would his resentment build up over the years, until we ended up like Reggie and Helena, sharing a lifetime of hell together?*

"Part of it, too," said Richard, "is the fact that Reggie never really liked being in Paris, and he never liked being a banker. Helena talked him into taking the post."

"She doesn't seem to like it here much, either."

"No. And so there they are, always sniping at each other. I'd see them at parties with your parents, and I was always struck by the contrast. Bernard and Madeline seemed so much in love. Then again, every man who met your mother couldn't help but fall in love, just a little."

"What was it about her?" asked Beryl. "You said once that she was...enchanting."

"When I met her, she was about forty. Oh, she had a gray hair here and there. A few laugh lines. But she was more fascinating than any twenty-year-old woman I'd ever met. I was surprised to hear that she wasn't born to nobility."

"She was from Cornwall. Old Spanish blood. Dad met her one summer while on holiday." Beryl smiled. "He said she beat him in a footrace. In her bare feet. And that's when he knew she was the one for him."

"They were well matched, in every way. I suppose that's what fascinated me—their happiness. My parents were divorced. It was a pretty nasty split, and it soured me on the whole idea of marriage. But your parents made it look so easy." He shook his head. "I was more shocked than anyone about their deaths. I couldn't believe that Bernard would—"

"He didn't do it. I know he didn't."

After a pause, Richard said, "So do I."

They drove for a moment without speaking, the lights of passing traffic flashing at them through the windshield.

"Is that why you never married?" she asked. "Because of your parents' divorce?"

"It was one reason. The other is that I've never found the right woman." He glanced at her. "Why didn't you marry?"

She shrugged. "Never the right man."

"There must have been someone in your life."

"There was. For a while." She hugged herself and stared out at the darkness rushing past.

"Didn't work out?"

She managed a laugh. "I'm lucky it didn't."

"Do I detect a trace of bitterness?"

"Disillusionment, really. When we first met, I thought he was quite extraordinary. He was a surgeon about to leave on a mercy mission to Nigeria. It's so rare to find a man who really cares about humanity. I visited him, twice, in Africa. He was in his element out there."

"And what happened?"

"We were lovers for a while. And then I came to realize how he saw himself. The great white savior. He'd swoop into a primitive hospital, save a few lives, then fly home to England for a bracing dose of adulation. Which, it turned out, he could never get enough of. One adoring woman wasn't sufficient. He had to have a dozen." Softly she added, "And I wanted to be the only one." She leaned back against the car seat and stared out at the glow of Paris. The City of Light, she thought. Still, there were those shadows, those dark alleys and even darker secrets.

Back at the Place Vendôme, they sat for a moment in the parked car, not speaking, just sitting side by side in the gloom. *We're both exhausted,* she thought. *And the night isn't over yet. I'll have to pack Jordan's things. A toothbrush, a change of clothes. Bring them back to the prison....*

"Then I can't talk you into leaving," he said.

She looked out at the plaza, at the silhouette of two lovers strolling arm in arm through the darkness. "No. Not until he's free. Not until we see this through to the end."

"I was afraid you'd say that. But I'm not surprised. Just the other day you told me you had a hard head."

She looked at his face, saw the gleam of his smile in the shadows. "This isn't hardheadedness, Richard. This is loyalty. To Jordan. To my parents. We're Tavistocks, you see, and we stand by each other."

"Standing by Jordan, I can see. But your parents are dead."

"It's a matter of honor."

He shook his head. "Bernard and Madeline aren't around to care about honor. It's a medieval concept, to march into battle for something as abstract as the family name."

She climbed out of the car. "Obviously the Wolf family name means nothing to you," she said coldly.

He was out of the car and moving right beside her as she walked through the hotel lobby and stepped into the elevator. "Maybe it's my peculiarly American point of view, but my name is what *I* make of it. I don't wear the family crest tattooed on my forehead."

"You couldn't possibly understand."

"Of course not," he retorted as they stepped out of the elevator. "I'm just a dumb Yank."

"I never called you any such thing!"

He followed her into the suite and shut the door with

a thud. "Still, it's clear I'm not up to her Ladyship's standards."

She whirled around and faced him in anger. "You're holding it against me, aren't you? My name. My wealth."

"What's bothering me has nothing to do with your being a Tavistock."

"What *is* bothering you, then?"

"The fact that you won't listen to reason."

"Ah. My hard head."

"Yes, your hard head. And your dumb sense of honor. And your...your..."

She moved right up to him. Tilting up her chin, she stared him straight in the eye. "My what?"

He took her face in his hands and planted a kiss on her mouth, a kiss so long and hard that she had difficulty catching her breath. When at last he pulled back, her legs were wobbly and her pulse was roaring in her ears.

"*That's* what's bothering me," he said. "I can't think straight when you're around. Can't concentrate long enough to tie my own shoelaces. You brush past me, or just look at me, and my mind goes off on certain tangents I'd rather not specify. It's the kind of situation that leads to mistakes. And I don't like to make mistakes."

"You're the one who can't concentrate. And I'm the one who has to fly home?" She turned and started across the room toward the connecting door to Jordan's suite. "Sorry, Richard," she said, moving past the window, "but you'll just have to keep those lusty male hormones under—"

Her words were cut off by the crack of the shattering window.

Reflexes made her pivot away from the sting of flying

glass. In the next instant, Richard lunged at her and sent her sprawling to the shard-littered floor.

Another bullet zinged through the window and thudded into the far wall.

"The light!" shouted Richard. "Got to kill the light!" He began to crawl toward the bedside lamp and had almost reached it when the second window shattered. Broken glass rained on top of him.

"Richard!" screamed Beryl.

"Stay down!" He took a deep breath, then rolled across the floor. He grabbed the lamp cord and yanked the plug from the outlet. Instantly the room was plunged into darkness. The only light came through the windows, shining dimly in from the Place Vendôme. An eerie silence fell over the room, broken only by the hammering of Beryl's heartbeat in her ears.

She started to rise to her knees.

"Don't move!" warned Richard.

"He can't see us."

"He might have an infrared scope. Stay down."

Beryl dropped back to the floor and felt the bite of broken glass through her sleeves. "Where's it coming from?"

"Has to be one of the buildings across the plaza. Long-range rifle."

"What do we do now?"

"We call for reinforcements." She heard him crawling in the darkness, then heard the clang of the telephone hitting the floor. An instant later, he muttered an oath. "Line's dead! Someone's cut the wire."

New panic shot through Beryl. "You mean they've been in the room?"

"Which means—" Suddenly he fell silent.

"Richard?"

"Shh. Listen."

Over her pounding heartbeat, she heard the faint whine of the hotel elevator as it came to a stop at their floor.

"I think we're in trouble," said Richard.

7

"He can't get in," said Beryl. "The door's locked."

"They'll have a passkey. If they managed to get in here earlier..."

"What do we do?"

"Jordan's room. Move!"

At once she was on her knees and crawling toward the connecting door. Only when she'd reached it did she realize Richard wasn't following her.

"Come on!" she whispered.

"You go. I'll hold them off."

She glanced back in disbelief. "What?"

"They'll check this room first to see if we've been hit. I'll slow them down. You get out through Jordan's suite. Head for the stairwell and don't stop running."

Beryl crouched frozen in the connecting doorway. *This is suicide. He has no gun, no weapon at all.* Already he was slipping through the shadows. She could just make out his figure, poised by the door. Waiting for the attack.

The knock on the door made her jerk in panic. "Mlle Tavistock?" called a man's voice. Beryl didn't answer; she didn't dare to. *"Mademoiselle?"* the voice called again.

Richard was gesturing frantically at her through the darkness. *Get out! Now.*

I can't leave him, she thought. *I can't let him fight this alone.*

A key grated in the lock.

There was no time to consider the risks. Beryl grabbed the bedside lamp, scrambled toward Richard, and planted herself right beside him.

"What the hell are you doing?" he whispered.

"Shut up," she hissed back.

They both flattened against the wall as the door swung open in front of them. There was a pause, the span of just a few heartbeats, and then they heard footsteps cross the threshold into the room. The door slowly swung closed, revealing the silhouettes of the intruders—two men, standing in the darkness. Beryl could feel Richard coil up beside her, could almost hear his silent one-two-three countdown. Suddenly he was flying at the nearest man; the force of the impact sent both men slamming to the floor.

Beryl raised the lamp and brought it crashing down on the head of the second intruder. He collapsed at her feet, facedown and groaning. She dropped beside him and began patting his clothes for a gun. Through his jacket, she felt a hard lump under his arm. A holster? She rolled him over onto his back. Only then, as a crack of light through the partially closed door spilled across his face, did she realize their mistake.

"Oh, my God," she said. She glanced at Richard, who'd just grabbed his opponent by the collar and was about to shove him against the wall. "Richard, don't!" she yelled. "Don't hurt him!"

He paused, still clutching the other man's collar in his fists. "Why the hell not?" he muttered.

"Because these are the wrong men, that's why!" She went to the wall switch and flicked on the overhead light.

Richard blinked in the sudden brightness. He stared at the hotel manager, cowering in his grip. Then he turned and looked at the man who lay groaning by the door. It was Claude Daumier.

At once Richard released the manager, who promptly shrank away in terror. "Sorry," said Richard. "My mistake."

"IF I'D KNOWN IT WAS YOU," said Beryl, pressing a bag of ice to Daumier's head, "I wouldn't have whacked you so hard."

"If you had known it was me," muttered Daumier, "I would hope you wouldn't have whacked me at all." He sat up on the couch and caught the bag of ice before it could slide off. "*Zut alors,* what did you use, *chérie?* A brick?"

"A lamp. And not a very big one, either." She glanced at Richard and the hotel manager. Both men were looking slightly the worse for wear—especially the manager. That black eye of his was colorful testimony to the damaging potential of Richard's fist. Now that the crisis was over, and they were safely barricaded in the manager's office, the situation struck Beryl as more than a little hilarious. A senior French Intelligence agent, beaned by a lamp? Richard, still nursing his bruised knuckles. And the poor hotel manager, assiduously maintaining a safe distance from those same knuckles. She could have laughed—if the whole affair hadn't been so frightening.

There was a knock on the door. Instantly Beryl tensed, only to relax again when she saw that it was a policeman. *I'm still high on adrenaline,* she thought as she watched Daumier and the cop converse in French. *Still expecting the worst.*

The policeman withdrew, closing the door behind him.

"What did he say?" Beryl asked.

"The shots were fired from across the plaza," said Daumier. "They have found bullet casings on the roof-top."

"And the gunman?" asked Richard.

Regretfully Daumier shook his head. "Vanished."

"Then he's still on the loose," said Richard. "And we don't know when he'll strike again." He looked at the manager. "What about that telephone wire? Who could've cut it?"

The man shrank back a step, as though expecting another blow. "I do not know, *monsieur!* One of the maids, she says her passkey was misplaced for a few hours today."

"So anyone could have gotten in."

"No one from our staff! They are thoroughly checked. You see, we have many important guests."

"I want your employees revetted. Every last one of them."

The manager nodded meekly. Then, still wincing in pain from the black eye, he left the office.

Richard began to pace, carelessly yanking his tie loose as he moved. "We have an intruder who cuts the phone line. A marksman stationed across the plaza. A high-powered rifle positioned for a shot straight into Beryl's room. Claude, this is sounding worse by the minute."

"Why would they try to kill me?" asked Beryl. "What have I done?"

"You've asked too many questions, that's what." Richard turned to Daumier. "You had it right, Claude. The matter's not dead, not by a long shot."

"We were both in that room, Richard," said Beryl. "How do you know he was aiming at me?"

"I wasn't the one walking past that window."

"You're the one who's CIA."

"The qualifying prefix is *ex,* as in, no longer with the Company. I'm not a threat to anyone."

"And I am?"

"Yes. By virtue of your name—not to mention your curiosity." He glanced at Daumier. "We need a safe house, Claude. Can you arrange it?"

"We keep a flat in Passy for protection of witnesses. It will serve your purpose."

"Who else knows about it?"

"My people. A few ministry officials."

"That's too many."

"It is the best I can offer. It has an alarm system. And I will assign guards."

Richard paused, thinking, weighing the risks. At last he nodded. "It will have to do for tonight. Tomorrow, we'll come up with something else. Maybe a plane ticket." He looked at Beryl.

This time she didn't protest. Already she could feel the adrenaline fading away. A moment ago, every nerve felt wired for action; now a plane home was beginning to sound sensible. All it took was a short flight across the Channel, and she'd be safe in the refuge of Chetwynd. It was all so easy, so tempting.

And she was so very, very tired.

With a numb sense of detachment, Beryl listened as Daumier made the necessary phone calls. He hung up and said, "I will have a car and escort brought around. Beryl's clothes will be delivered to the flat later. Oh, and Richard, you will no doubt want this." He reached under his suit jacket and withdrew a semiautomatic pistol from his shoulder holster. He handed it to Richard. "A loan. Just between us, of course."

"Are you sure you want to part with it?"

"I have another." Daumier slid off his holster, which he also gave to Richard. "You remember how to use one?"

Richard checked the ammunition clip and nodded grimly. "I think it'll come back."

A policeman knocked on the door. The car was waiting.

Richard took Beryl's arm and helped her to her feet. "Time to drop out of sight for a while. Are you ready?"

She looked at the gun he was holding, noted how easily he handled it, how comfortably he slid it into the holster. A professional, she thought. The transformation was almost frightening. *How well do I really know you, Richard Wolf?*

For now, the question was irrelevant. He was the one man she could count on, the one man she had to trust.

She folowed him out the door.

"WE SHOULD BE SAFE HERE. For tonight, at least." Richard double-bolted the apartment door and turned to look at her.

She was standing in the center of the living room, her arms wrapped around her shoulders, a dazed look in her eyes. This was not the brash and stubborn Beryl he knew, he thought. This was a woman who'd faced sheer terror and knew the worst wasn't over yet. He wanted to go to her, to take her in his arms and promise her that nothing would ever hurt her while he was around, but they both knew it was a promise he might not be able to keep. In silence, he circled the flat, checking to see that the windows were secure, the drapes closed. A glance outside told him there were two guards watching the building, one at the front entrance, one at the rear. A safety net, he thought. For when I let my attention slip. And it *would* slip. Sooner or later, he would have to sleep.

Satisfied that all was locked up tight, he went back to the living room. He found Beryl sitting on the couch, very quiet, very still. Almost...defeated.

"Are you all right?" he asked.

She gave a shrug, as though the question was irrelevant—as though they had far more important things to consider.

He took off his jacket and tossed it over a chair. "You haven't eaten. There's some food in the kitchen."

Her gaze focused on his shoulder holster. "Why did you quit the business?" she asked.

"You mean the Company?"

She nodded. "When I saw you holding that gun, it...it suddenly struck me. What you used to be."

He sat down beside her. "I've never killed anyone. If that makes a difference."

"But you're trained to do it."

"Only in self-defense. That's not the same thing as murder."

She nodded, as though trying very hard to agree with him.

He took the Glock from the holster and held it out to her. She regarded it with undisguised abhorrence.

"Yes, I understand how you feel," he said. "This gun's a semiautomatic. Nine millimeter bullets, sixteen cartridges to the magazine. Some people consider it a work of art. I think of it as a tool of last resort. Something I hope to God I never have to use." He set it on the coffee table, where it lay like an evil reminder of violence. "Pick it up if you want to. It's not very heavy."

"I'd rather not." She shuddered and looked away. "I'm not afraid of guns. I mean, I've handled rifles before. I used to go shooting with Uncle Hugh. But those were only clay pigeons."

"Not quite the same thing."

"No. Not quite."

"You asked why I quit the Company." He pointed to the Glock. "That was one of the reasons. I've never killed anyone, and I'm not itching to. For me, the intelligence business was a game. A challenge. The enemy was well-defined—the Russians, the East Germans. But now..." He picked up the gun and held it thoughtfully in his palm. "The world's turned into a crazy place. I can't tell who the enemy is anymore. And I knew that sooner or later, I'd lose my edge. I could already feel it happening."

"Your edge?"

"It's my age, you know. You hit forty and you don't react the way you did as a twenty-year-old. I like to think I've grown smarter, instead, but what I really am is more cautious. And a lot less willing to take risks." He looked at her. "With anyone's life."

She met his gaze. Looking into her eyes, he suddenly found himself wanting to babble all sorts of crazy things. To tell her that the one life he didn't want to risk was hers. When had this stopped being a mere baby-sitting job? he wondered. When had it become something much more? A mission. An obsession.

"You frighten me, Richard," she said.

"It's the gun."

"No, it's you. All the things I don't know about you. All the secrets you're keeping from me."

"From now on, I promise I'll be absolutely honest with you."

"But it started out as half truths. Not telling me you knew my parents. Or how they died. Don't you see, it's my childhood all over again! Uncle Hugh with his head full of classified secrets." She let out a breath of frustration and looked away. "Then I see you with that... thing."

He touched her face and gently turned it toward him. "It's just a temporary evil," he murmured. "Until this is over." She kept looking at him, her eyes bright and moist, her hair tumbling about her shoulders. *She wants to trust me,* he thought. *But she's afraid.*

He couldn't help himself. He kissed her. Once. Twice. The second time, he felt her lips yield under his, felt her whole body seem to turn liquid at his touch. He kissed her a third time and found his hands sliding through her hair, his fingers hopelessly becoming tangled in all that raven silk. She sighed, a delicious sound of surrender, invitation, and she sagged backward onto the couch.

Suddenly he, too, was falling, tumbling on top of her. Their lips met in a touch that instantly turned electric. She reached around his neck and pulled him down hard against her—

And flinched. That blasted gun again. The holster had pushed into her breast, had served as an ugly reminder of all the things that had happened today. All the things that could still happen.

He looked at her face, at her hair flung across the cushions, at the mingling of fear and desire he saw in her eyes. *Not now,* he thought. *Not this way.*

Slowly he pulled away and they both sat up. For a moment, they remained side by side on the couch, not touching, not speaking.

She said, "I'm not ready for this. I'll put my life in your hands, Richard. But my heart, that's a different matter."

"I understand."

"Then you'll also understand that I'm not a fan of James Bond, or anyone remotely like him. I'm not impressed by guns, or by the men who use them." She rose to her feet and moved pointedly away from the couch. Away from him.

"So what does impress you?" he asked. "If not a man's gun?"

She turned to him and he saw a flicker of humor cross her face. *The old Beryl,* he thought. *Thank God she's still there, somewhere.*

"Straight talk," she said. "That's what impresses me."

"Then that's what you'll get. I promise."

She turned and walked to the bedroom. "We'll see."

JORDAN WAS NOT IMPRESSED by this lawyer, no, he was not impressed at all.

The man had greasy hair and a greasy little mustache, and he spoke English with the exaggerated accent of a second-rate actor playing a stereotypical Frenchman. All those "eets" and "zees" and *"Mon Dieus."* Still, Jordan reasoned, since Beryl had hired the man, he must be one of the best attorneys in Paris.

You could have fooled me, thought Jordan, gazing across the prison interview table at the smarmy M. Jarre.

"Not to worry," said the man. "Everything will be taken care of. I am reviewing the papers now, and I believe we will soon reach an agreement to have you released."

"What about the investigation?" asked Jordan. "Any progress?"

"Very slow. You know how it is, M. Tavistock. In a city as large as Paris, the police, they are overworked. You cannot be impatient."

"And my uncle? Have you been able to reach him?"

"He is in complete agreement with my planned course of action."

"Is he coming to Paris?"

"He is detained. Business keeps him at home, I am afraid."

"At home? But I thought..." Jordan paused. Didn't Beryl say Uncle Hugh had left Chetwynd?

M. Jarre rose from the table. "Rest assured that all that can be done, will be done. I have instructed the police to transfer you to a more comfortable cell."

"Thank you," said Jordan, still puzzling over the reference to Uncle Hugh. As the attorney was leaving the room, Jordan called out, "M. Jarre? Did my uncle happen to mention how his...negotiations went in London?"

The attorney glanced back. "They are still in progress, I understand. But I am sure he will tell you himself." He gave a nod of farewell. "Good evening, M. Tavistock. I hope you find your new cell more agreeable." He walked out.

What the dickens is going on? thought Jordan. He wondered about this all the way to his cell—his new cell. One look at the pair of shady characters seated inside and his suspicions about M. Jarre deepened. *This* was more agreeable quarters?

Reluctantly Jordan stepped inside and flinched at the clang of the door shutting behind him. The jailer walked away, his footsteps echoing down the hall.

The two prisoners were staring at his fine Italian shoes, which contrasted dreadfully with the regulation prison garb he was wearing.

"Hello," said Jordan, for want of anything else to say.

"Anglais?" asked one of the men.

Jordan swallowed. *"Oui. Anglais."*

The man grunted and pointed to an empty bunk. "Yours."

Jordan went to the bunk, set his bundle of street clothes on the foot of the bed, and stretched out on the mattress. As the two prisoners babbled away in French, Jordan kept wondering about that greasy attorney and why he had lied about Uncle Hugh. If only he could get in touch with Beryl, ask her what was going on...

He sat up at the sound of footsteps approaching the cell. It was the guard, escorting yet another prisoner— this one a balding, round-cheeked man with a definite waddle and a pleasant enough face. The sort of fellow you'd expect to see standing behind a bakery counter. *Not your typical criminal,* thought Jordan. *But then, neither am I.*

The man entered the cell and was directed to the fourth and last bunk. He sat down, looking stunned by the circumstances in which he found himself. François was his name, and from what Jordan could gather using his elementary command of French, the man's crime had something to do with the fair sex. Solicitation, perhaps? François was not eager to talk about it. He simply sat on his bed and stared at the floor. *We're both new to this,* thought Jordan.

The other two cellmates were still watching him. Sullen young men, obviously sociopathic. He'd have to keep his eye on them.

Supper came—an atrocious goulash accompanied by

French bread. Jordan stared at the muddy brown gravy and thought wistfully of his supper the night before— poached salmon and roast duckling. Ah, well. One had to eat regardless of one's circumstances. What a shame there wasn't a bottle of wine to wash down the meal. A nice Beaujolais, perhaps, or just a common Burgundy. He took a bite of goulash and decided that even a bad bottle of wine would be welcome—anything to dull the taste of this gravy. He forced himself to eat it and made a silent vow that when he got out of here—*if* he got out of here—the first place he'd head for was a decent restaurant.

At midnight, the lights were turned off. Jordan stretched out on the blanket and made every effort to sleep, but found he couldn't. For one thing, his cellmates were snoring to wake the dead. For another, the day's events kept playing and replaying in his mind. That drive with Colette from Boulevard Saint-Germain. The way she had glanced at the rearview mirror. If only he had paid more attention to who might be following them back to the hotel. And then, against his will, he remembered the horror of finding her body in the car, remembered the stickiness of her blood on his hands.

Rage bubbled up inside him—an impotent sense of fury about her death. *It's my fault,* he thought. If she hadn't been watching over him, protecting him.

But that's not why she died, Jordan thought suddenly. He was nowhere nearby when it happened. So why did they kill her? Did she know something, see something...
... or someone?

His thoughts veered in a new direction. Colette must have spotted a face in her rearview mirror, a face in the car that was following them. After she'd dropped Jordan off at the Ritz, maybe she'd seen that someone again. Or he'd seen her and knew she could identify him.

Which made the killer someone Colette knew. Someone she recognized.

He was so intent on piecing together the puzzle, he didn't pay much attention to the creak of the bunk springs somewhere in the cell. Only when he heard the soft rustle of movement did he realize that one of his cellmates was approaching his bed.

It was dark; he could make out only faintly a shadowy figure moving toward him. One of those young hoods, he thought, come to rifle his jacket.

Jordan lay perfectly still and willed his breathing to remain deep and even. *Let the coward think I'm still asleep. When he moves close enough, I'll surprise him.*

The shadow slipped quietly through the darkness. Six feet away, now five. Jordan's heart was pounding, his muscles already tensed for action. *Just a little closer. A little closer. He'll be reaching for the jacket hanging at the foot of the bed....*

But the man moved instead to Jordan's head. There was a faint arc of shadow—an arm being raised to deliver a blow. Jordan's hand shot out just as his assailant attacked.

He caught the other man's wrist and heard a grunt of surprise. His attacker came at him with his free hand. Jordan deflected the blow and scrambled off the bunk. Still gripping his attacker's wrist, he gave it a vicious twist, eliciting a yelp of pain. The man was thrashing to get free now, but Jordan held on. He was not going to get away. Not without learning a lesson. He shoved the man backward and heard the satisfying thud of his opponent's body hitting the cinder-block wall. The man groaned and tried to pull free. Again, Jordan shoved.

This time they both toppled over onto a cot, landing on its sleeping occupant. The man in Jordan's grasp began to writhe, to jerk. At once Jordan realized this was no longer a man fighting to free himself. This was a man in the throes of a convulsion.

He heard the sound of footsteps and then the cell lights flashed on. A guard yelled at him in French.

Jordan released his assailant and backed away in surprise. It was the moon-faced François. The man lay sprawled on the bed, his limbs twitching, his eyes rolled back. The young hood on whom François had landed frantically rolled away from beneath the body and stared in horror at the bizarre display.

François gave a last grunt of agony and fell still.

For a few seconds, everyone watched him, expecting him to move again. He didn't.

The guard gave a shout for assistance. Another guard came running. Yelling at the prisoners to stand back, they rushed into the cell and examined the motionless François. Slowly they straightened and looked at Jordan.

"Est mort," one of them murmured.

"That-that's impossible!" said Jordan. "How can he be dead? I didn't hit him that hard!"

The guards merely stared at him. The other two prisoners regarded Jordan with new respect and backed away to the far side of the cell.

"Let me look at him!" demanded Jordan. He pushed past the guards and knelt by François. One glance at the body and he knew they were right. François was dead.

Jordan shook his head. "I don't understand...."

"Monsieur, you come with us," said one of the guards.

"I couldn't have killed him!"

"But you see for yourself he is dead."

Jordan suddenly focused on a fine line of blood trickling down François's cheek. He bent closer. Only then did he spot the needle-thin dart impaled in the dead man's scalp. It was almost invisible among the salt-and-pepper hairs of his temple.

"What in blazes...?" muttered Jordan. Swiftly he glanced around the floor for a syringe, a dart gun—whatever might have injected that needle point. He saw nothing on the floor or on the bed. Then he looked down at the dead man's hand and saw something clutched in his left fist. He pried open the frozen fingers and the object slid out and landed on the bedcovers.

A ballpoint pen.

At once he was hauled back and shoved toward the cell door. "Go," said the guard. "Walk!"

"Where?"

"Where you can hurt no one." The guard directed Jordan into the corridor and locked the cell door. Jordan caught a fleeting glimpse of his cellmates, watching him in awe, and then he was hustled down the hallway and into a private cell, this one obviously reserved for the most dangerous prisoners. Double-barred, no windows, no furniture, only a concrete slab on which to lie. And a light blazing down relentlessly from the ceiling.

Jordan sank onto the slab and waited. For what? he wondered. Another attack? Another crisis? How could this nightmare possibly get any worse?

An hour passed. He couldn't sleep, not with that light shining overhead. Footsteps and the clank of keys alerted him to a visitor. He looked up to see a guard and a well-dressed gentleman with a briefcase.

"M. Tavistock?" said the gentleman.

"Since there's no one else here," muttered Jordan, rising to his feet, "I'm afraid that must be me."

The door was unlocked, and the man with the briefcase entered. He glanced around in dismay at the Spartan cell. "These conditions... Outrageous," he said.

"Yes. And I owe it all to my wonderful attorney," said Jordan.

"But *I* am your attorney." The man held out his hand in greeting. "Henri Laurent. I would have come sooner, but I was attending the opera. I received M. Vane's message only an hour ago. He said it was an emergency."

Jordan shook his head in confusion. "Vane? Reggie Vane sent you?"

"Yes. Your sister requested my immediate services. And M. Vane—"

"Beryl hired you? Then who the hell was..." Jordan paused as the bizarre events suddenly made sense. Horrifying sense. "M. Laurent," said Jordan, "a few hours ago, there was a lawyer here to see me. A M. Jarre."

Laurent frowned. "But I was not told of another attorney."

"He claimed my sister hired him."

"But I spoke to M. Vane. He told me Mlle Tavistock requested *my* services. What did you say was the other attorney's name?"

"Jarre."

Laurent shook his head. "I am not familiar with any such criminal attorney."

Jordan sat for a moment in stunned silence. Slowly he raised his head and looked at Laurent. "I think you'd better contact Reggie Vane. At once."

"But why?"

"They've already tried to kill me once tonight." Jordan shook his head. "If this keeps up, M. Laurent, by morning I may be quite dead."

8

They were following her again. Black hounds, trotting across the dead leaves of the forest. She heard them rustle through the underbrush and knew they were moving closer.

She gripped Froggie's bridle, struggled to calm her, but the mare panicked. Suddenly Froggie yanked free of Beryl's grasp and reared up.

The hounds attacked.

Instantly they were at the horse's throat, ripping, tearing with their razor teeth. Froggie screamed, a human scream, shrill with terror. *Have to save her,* thought Beryl. *Have to beat them away.* But her feet seemed rooted to the ground. She could only stand and watch in horror as Froggie dropped to her knees and collapsed to the forest floor.

The hounds, mouths bloodied, turned and looked at Beryl.

She awakened, gasping for breath, her hands clawing at the darkness. Only as her panic faded did she hear Richard calling her name.

She turned and saw him standing in the doorway. A lamp was shining in the room behind him, and the light gleamed faintly on his bare shoulders.

"Beryl?" he said again.

She took a deep breath, still trying to shake off the last threads of the nightmare. "I'm awake," she said.

"I think you'd better get up."

"What time is it?"

"Four a.m. Claude just phoned."

"Why?"

"He wants us to meet him at the police station. As soon as possible."

"The police station?" She sat up sharply as a terrible thought came to mind. "Is it Jordan? Has something happened to him?"

Through the shadows, she saw Richard nod. "Someone tried to kill him."

"AN INGENIOUS DEVICE," said Claude Daumier, gingerly laying the ballpoint pen on the table. "A hypodermic needle, a pressurized syringe. One stab, and the drug would be injected into the victim."

"Which drug?" asked Beryl.

"It is still being analyzed. The autopsy will be performed in the morning. But it seems clear that this drug, whatever it was, was the cause of death. There is not enough trauma on the body to explain otherwise."

"Then Jordan won't be blamed for this?" said Beryl in relief.

"Hardly. He will be placed in isolation, no other prisoners, a double guard. There should be no further incidents."

The conference room door opened. Jordan appeared, escorted by two guards. *Dear Lord, he looks terrible,* thought Beryl as she rose from her chair and went to hug him. Never had she seen her brother so disheveled. The beginnings of a thick blond beard had sprouted on his jaw, and his prison clothes were mapped with wrinkles. But as they pulled apart, she gazed in his eyes and saw that the old Jordan was still there, good-humored and ironic as ever.

"You're not hurt?" she asked.

"Not a scratch," he answered. "Well, perhaps a few," he amended, frowning down at his bruised fist. "It's murder on the old manicure."

"Jordan, I swear I never hired any lawyer named Jarre. The man was a fraud."

"I suspected as much."

"The man I did hire, M. Laurent, Reggie swears he's the best there is."

"I'm afraid even the best won't get me out of this fix," Jordan observed disconsolately. "I seem destined to be a long-term resident of this fine establishment. Unless the food kills me first."

"Will you be serious for once?"

"Oh, but you haven't tasted the goulash."

Beryl turned in exasperation to Daumier. "What about the dead man? Who was he?"

"According to the arrest record," said Daumier, "his name was François Parmentier, a janitor. He was charged with disorderly conduct."

"How did he end up in Jordan's cell?" asked Richard.

"It seems that his attorney, Jarre, made a special request for both his clients to be housed in the same cell."

"Not just a request," amended Richard. "It must've been a bribe. Jarre and the dead man were a team."

"Working on whose behalf?" asked Jordan.

"The same party who tried to kill Beryl," said Richard.

"*What?*"

"A few hours ago. It was a high-powered rifle, fired at her hotel window."

"And she's still in Paris?" Jordan turned to his sister.

"That's it. You're going home, Beryl. And you're leaving at once."

"I've been trying to tell her the same thing," said Richard. "She won't listen."

"Of course she won't. My darling little sister never does!" Jordan scowled at Beryl. "This time, though, you don't have a choice."

"You're right, Jordie," said Beryl. "I don't have a choice. That's why I'm staying."

"You could get yourself killed."

"So could you."

They stood facing each other, neither one willing to give ground. *Deadlock,* thought Beryl. *He's worried about me, and I'm worried about him. And we're both Tavistocks, which means neither of us will ever concede defeat.*

But I have the upper hand on this one. He's in jail. I'm not.

In disgust, Jordan turned and flopped into a chair. "For Pete's sake, work on her, Wolf!" he muttered.

"I'm trying to," said Richard. "Meanwhile, we still haven't answered a basic question—who wants you both dead?"

They fell silent for a moment. Through a cloud of fatigue, Beryl looked at her brother, thinking that he was supposed to be the clever one in the family. If he couldn't figure it out, who could?

"The key to all this," said Jordan, "is François, the dead man." He looked at Daumier. "What else do you know about him? Friends, family?"

"Only a sister," said Daumier. "Living in Paris."

"Have your people spoken to her yet?"

"There is no point to it."

"Why not?"

"She is, how do you say...?" Daumier tapped his forehead. "*Retardataire.* She lives at the Sacred Heart Nursing Home. The nuns say she cannot speak, and she is in very poor health."

"What about his job?" said Richard. "You said he worked as a janitor."

"At Galerie Annika. An art gallery, in Auteuil. It is a reputable establishment. Known for its collection of works by contemporary artists."

"What does the gallery say about him?"

"I spoke only briefly to Annika. She says he was a quiet man, very reliable. She will be in later this morning to answer questions." He glanced at his watch. "In the meantime, I suggest we all try to catch some sleep. For a few hours, at least."

"What about Jordan?" asked Beryl. "How do I know he'll be safe here?"

"As I said, he will be kept in a private cell. Strict isolation—"

"That might be a mistake," said Richard. "There'd be no witnesses."

If anything happens to him... Beryl shivered.

Jordan nodded. "Wolf's right. I'd feel a whole lot safer sharing a cell with someone."

"But they could lock you up with another hired killer," said Beryl.

"I know just the fellows to share my cell," said Jordan. "A pair of harmless enough chaps. I hope."

Daumier nodded. "I will arrange it."

It was wrenching to see Jordan marched away. In the doorway, he paused and gave her a farewell wave. That's when Beryl realized she was taking this far harder than he was. But that's old Jordie for you, she mused. Never one to lose his good humor.

Outside, the first streaks of daylight had appeared in the sky, and the sound of traffic had already begun its morning crescendo. Beryl, Richard and Daumier stood on the sidewalk, all of them tottering on the edge of collapse.

"Jordan will be safe," said Daumier. "I will see to it."

"I want him to be more than safe," said Beryl. "I want him out of there."

"For that, we must prove him innocent."

"Then that's exactly what we'll do," she said.

Daumier looked at her with bloodshot eyes. He seemed far older tonight, this kindly Frenchman in whose face the years had etched deep furrows. He said, "What you must do, *chérie*, is stay alert. And out of sight." He turned toward his car. "Tonight, we talk again."

By the time Beryl and Richard had returned to the flat in Passy, Beryl could feel herself nodding off. The latest jolt of tension had worn off, and her energy was on a fast downhill slide. Thank God Richard still seemed to be operating on all cylinders, she thought as they climbed out of the car. If she collapsed, he could drag her up those steps.

He practically did. He put his arm around her and walked her through the door, up the hall and into the bedroom. There, he sat her down on the bed.

"Sleep," he said, "as long as you need to."

"A week should about do it," she murmured.

He smiled. And though sleep was blurring her vision, she saw his face clearly enough to register, once again, that flicker of attraction between them. It was always there, ready to leap into full flame. Even now, exhausted as she was, images of desire were weaving into shape in her mind. She remembered how he'd stood, shirtless, in the bedroom doorway, the lamplight gleaming on his shoulders. She thought how easy it would be to invite him into her bed, to ask for a hug, a kiss. And then, much, much more. *Too much bloody chemistry between us,* she pondered. *It addles my brain, keeps me from concentrating on the important issues. I take one look at him, I inhale one whiff of his scent, and all I can think about is pulling him down on top of me.*

Gently he kissed her forehead. ''I'll be right next door,'' he said, and left the room.

Too tired to undress, she lay down fully clothed on the bed. Daylight brightened outside the window, and the sounds of traffic drifted up from the street. If this nightmare was ever over, she thought, she'd have to stay away from him for a while. Just to get her bearings again. Yes, that's what she'd do. She'd hide out at Chetwynd. Wait for that crazy attraction between them to fade.

But as she closed her eyes, the images returned, more vivid and tempting than ever. They pursued her, right into her dreams.

RICHARD SLEPT FIVE HOURS and rose just before noon. A shower, a quick meal of eggs and toast, and he felt the old engines fire up again. There were too few hours in the day, too many matters to attend to; sleep would have to assume a lower priority.

He peeked in on Beryl and saw that she was still asleep. Good. By the time she woke up, he should be back from making his rounds. Just in case he wasn't, though, he left a note on the nightstand. ''Gone out. Back around three. R.'' Then, as an afterthought, he laid the gun beside the note. If she needed it, he figured, it'd be there for her.

After confirming that the two guards were still on duty, he left the flat, locking the door behind him.

His first stop was 66 Rue Myrha, the building where Madeline and Bernard died.

He had gone over the Paris police report again, had read and reread the landlord's statement. M. Rideau claimed he'd discovered the bodies on the afternoon of July 15, 1973, and had at once notified the police. Upon being questioned, he'd told them that the attic was rented to a Mlle Scarlatti, who used the place only infrequently and paid her rent in cash. On occasion, he had heard moans, whimpers, and a man's voice emanating from the flat. But the only person he ever saw face-to-face was Mlle Scarlatti, whose head scarves and sunglasses made it difficult for him to be specific about her appearance. Nevertheless, M. Rideau was certain that the dead woman in the flat was indeed the lusty Scarlatti woman. And the dead man? The landlord had never seen him before.

Three months after this testimony, M. Rideau had sold the building, packed up his family, and left the country.

That last detail had garnered only a footnote in the police report: "Landlord no longer available for statements. Has left France."

Richard had a hunch that the landlord's departure from the country just might be the most important clue they had. If he could locate Rideau's current whereabouts and question him about those events of twenty years before...

He knocked at each flat in the building, but came up with no leads. Twenty years was a long time; people moved in, moved out. No one remembered any M. Rideau.

Richard went outside and stood for a moment on the sidewalk. A ball hurtled past, pursued by a pack of scruffy kids. The endless soccer match, he mused, watching the tangle of dirty arms and legs.

Over the children's heads, he spotted an elderly woman sitting on her stoop. At least seventy years old, he guessed. Perhaps she'd lived here long enough to know the former residents of this street.

He went over to the woman and spoke to her in French. "Good afternoon."

She smiled a sweet, toothless grin.

"I am trying to find someone who remembers M. Jacques Rideau. The man who used to own that building over there." He pointed to number 66.

Also in French, she answered: "He moved away."

"You knew him, then?"

"His son was all the time visiting in my house."

"I understand the whole family left France."

She nodded. "They went to Greece. And how do you suppose he managed that, eh? Him, with that old car! And the clothes their children wore! But off they go to their villa." She sighed. "And I am here, where I'll always be."

Richard frowned. "Villa?"

"I hear they have a villa, near the sea. Of course, it may not be true—the boy was always making up stories. Why should he start telling the truth? But he claimed it was a villa, with flowers growing up the posts." She laughed. "They must all be dead by now."

"The family?"

"The flowers. They could not even remember to water their pots of geraniums."

"Do you know where in Greece they moved to?"

The woman shrugged. "Somewhere near the sea. But then, isn't all of Greece near the sea?"

"The name of the village?"

"Why should I remember these things? He was not *my* boyfriend."

Frustrated, Richard was about to turn away when he suddenly registered what the woman had just said. "You mean, the landlord's son—he was your daughter's boyfriend?"

"My granddaughter."

"Did he call her? Write her any letters?"

"A few. Then he stopped." She shook her head. "That is how it is with young people. No devotion."

"Did she keep any of those letters?"

The woman laughed. "All of them. To remind her husband what a fine catch he made."

It took a bit of persuasion for Richard to be invited inside the old woman's apartment. It was a dark, cramped flat. Two small children sat at the kitchen table, gnawing fistfuls of bread. Another woman—most likely in her mid-thirties, but with much older eyes—sat spooning cereal into an infant's mouth.

"He wants to see your letters from Gerard," said the grandmother.

The younger woman eyed Richard with suspicion.

"It's important I speak with his father," explained Richard.

"His father doesn't want to be found," she said, and resumed feeding the baby.

"Why not?"

"How should I know? Gerard didn't tell me."

"Does it have to do with the murders? The two English people?"

She paused, the spoon halfway to the baby's mouth. "You are English?"

"No, American." He sat down across from her. "Do you remember the murders?"

"It was a long time ago." She wiped the baby's face. "I was only fifteen."

"Gerard wrote you letters, then stopped. Why?"

The woman gave a bitter laugh. "He lost interest. Men always do."

"Or something could have happened to him. Maybe he couldn't write to you. And he wanted to, very much."

Again, she paused.

"If I go to Greece, I can inquire on your behalf. I only need to know the name of the village."

She sat for a moment, thinking. Wiping up the baby's mess. She looked at her two children, both of them runny nosed and whining. *She's longing to escape,* he imagined. *Wishing her life had turned out some other way. Any other way. And she's thinking about this long-lost boyfriend, and how things might have been, for the two of them, in a villa by the sea....*

She stood up and went into another room. A moment later, she returned and laid a thin bundle of letters down on the table.

There were only four—not exactly a record of devotion. All were still tucked in their envelopes. Richard skimmed their contents, noting an outpouring of adolescent yearnings. "I will come back for you. I will love you always. Do not forget me...." By the fourth letter, the passion was clearly cooling.

There was no return address, either on the letters or on the envelopes. The family's whereabouts were obviously meant to be kept secret. But on one of the envelopes, a postmark was clearly printed: Paros, Greece.

Richard handed the letters back to the woman. She cradled them for a moment, as though savoring the memories. *So many years ago, a lifetime ago, and see what has become of me....*

"If you find Gerard...if he is still alive," she said, "ask him..."

"Yes?" Richard said gently.

She sighed. "Ask him if he remembers me."

"I will."

She held the letters a moment longer. And then, with a sigh, she laid them aside and picked up the spoon. In silence, she began to feed the baby.

HE MADE ONE MORE STOP before returning to the flat, this time at the Sacred Heart Nursing Home.

It was a far grimmer institution than the one Richard had visited the day before. No private rooms here, no sweet-faced nuns gliding down the halls. This was one step above a prison, and a crowded one at that, with three or four patients to a room, many of them restrained in their beds. Julee Parmentier, François's retarded sister, occupied one of the grimmest rooms of all. Barely clothed, she lay on top of a plastic-lined mattress. Protective mitts covered her hands; around her waist was a wide belt, its ends secured to the bed with just enough slack for her to shift from side to side, but not sit up. She barely seemed to register Richard's presence; instead she moaned and stared relentlessly at the ceiling.

"She has been like this for many years," said the nurse. "An accident, when she was twelve. She fell from a tree and hit her head on some stones."

"She can't speak at all? Can't communicate?"

"When her brother François would visit, he said she

would smile. He insisted he saw it. But..." The nurse shrugged. "I saw nothing."

"Did he visit often?"

"Every day. The same time, nine o'clock in the morning. He would stay until lunch, then he would go to his work at the gallery."

"He did this every day?"

"Yes. And on Sunday he would stay later—until four o'clock."

Richard gazed at the woman in the bed and tried to imagine what it must have been like for François to sit for hours in this room with its noise and its smells. To devote every free hour of his life to a sister who could not even recognize his face.

"It is a tragedy," said the nurse. "He was a good man, François."

They left the room and walked away from the sight of that pitiful creature lying on her plastic sheet.

"What will happen to her now?" asked Richard. "Will someone see that she's cared for?"

"It hardly matters now."

"Why do you say that?"

"Her kidneys are failing." The nurse glanced up the hall, toward Julee Parmentier's room, and shook her head sadly. "Another month, two months, and she will be dead."

"BUT YOU MUST KNOW where he went," insisted Beryl.

The French agent merely shrugged. "He did not say, *Mademoiselle*. He only instructed me to watch over the flat. And see that you came to no harm."

"And that's all he said? And then he drove off?"

The man nodded.

In frustration, Beryl turned and went back into the flat,

where she reread Richard's note: "Gone out. Back around three." No explanations, no apologies. She crumpled it up and threw it at the rubbish can. And what was she supposed to do now? Wait around all day for him to return? What about Jordan? What about the investigation?

What about lunch?

Her hunger pangs could no longer be ignored. She went to the kitchen and opened the refrigerator. She stared in dismay at the contents: a carton of eggs, a loaf of bread and a shriveled sausage. No fruit, no vegetables, not even a puny carrot. Stocked, no doubt, by a man.

I'm not going to eat that, she determined, closing the refrigerator door. *But I'm not going to starve, either. I'm going to have a proper meal—with or without him.*

Daumier's men had delivered her belongings to the flat the night before. From the closet, she chose her most nondescript black dress, pinned up her hair under a wide-brimmed hat, and slid on a pair of dark glasses. *Not too hideous,* she decided, glancing at herself in the mirror.

She walked out of the flat into the sunshine.

The guard stationed at the front door confronted her at once. "*Mademoiselle,* you are not allowed to leave."

"But you let *him* leave," she countered.

"Mr. Wolf specifically instructed—"

"I'm hungry," she said. "I get quite cranky when I'm hungry. And I'm not about to live on eggs and toast. So if you can just direct me to the nearest Métro station…"

"You are going *alone?*" he asked in horror.

"Unless you'd care to escort me."

The man glanced uneasily up and down the street. "I have no instructions in this matter."

"Then I'll go alone," she said, and breezily started to walk away.

"Come back!"

She kept walking.

"Mademoiselle!" he called. "I will get the car!"

She turned and flashed him her most brilliant smile. "My treat."

Both guards accompanied her to a restaurant in the nearby neighborhood of Auteuil. She suspected they chose the place not for the quality of its food, but for the intimate dining room and the easily surveyed front entrance. The meal itself was just a shade above mediocre: bland vichyssoise and a cut of lamb that could have doubled for leather. But Beryl was hungry enough to savor every morsel and still have an appetite for the *tarte aux pommes.*

By the time the meal was over, her two companions were in a much more jovial mood. Perhaps this bodyguard business was not such a bad thing, if the lady was willing to spring for a meal every day. They even relented when Beryl asked them to make a stop on the drive back to the flat. It would only take a minute, she said, to look over the latest art exhibit. After all, she might find something to strike her fancy.

And so the men accompanied her to Galerie Annika.

The exhibit area was one vast, soaring gallery—three stories, connected by open walkways and spiral staircases. Sunlight shone down through a skylit dome, illuminating a collection of bronze sculptures displayed on the first floor.

A young woman, her spiky hair a startling shade of red, came forward to greet them. Was there something in particular *Mademoiselle* wished to see?

"May I just look around a bit?" asked Beryl. "Or perhaps you could direct me to some paintings. Nothing too modern—I prefer classical artists."

"But of course," said the woman, and guided Beryl and her escorts up the spiral stairs.

Most of what she saw hanging on the walls was hideous. Landscapes populated by deformed animals. Birds with dog heads. City scenes with starkly cubist buildings. The young woman stopped at one painting and said, "Perhaps this is to your liking?"

Beryl took one look at the nude huntress holding aloft a dead rabbit and said, "I don't think so." She moved on, taking in the eccentric collection of paintings, fabric hangings and clay masks. "Who chooses the work to be displayed here?" she asked.

"Annika does. The gallery owner."

Beryl stopped at a particularly grotesque mask—a man with a forked tongue. "She has a...unique eye for art."

"Quite daring, don't you think? She prefers artists who take risks."

"Is she here today? I'd very much like to meet her."

"Not at the moment." The woman shook her head sadly. "One of our employees died last night, you see. Annika had to speak to the police."

"I'm sorry to hear that."

"Our janitor." The woman sighed. "It was quite unexpected."

They returned to the first-floor gallery. Only then did Beryl spot a work she'd consider purchasing. It was one of the bronze sculptures, a variation on the Madonna-and-child theme. But as she moved closer to inspect it, she realized it wasn't a human infant nursing at the woman's breast. It was a jackal.

"Quite intriguing, don't you think?"

Beryl shuddered and looked at her spiky-haired guide. "What brilliant mind dreamed *this* one up?"

"A new artist. A young man, just building his reputation here in Paris. We are hosting a reception in his honor tonight. Perhaps you will attend?"

"If I can."

The woman reached into a basket and plucked out an elegantly embossed invitation. This she handed to Beryl. "If you are free tonight, please drop in."

Beryl was about to slip the card carelessly into her purse when she suddenly focused on the artist's name. A name she recognized.

Galerie Annika presente:
Les sculptures de Anthony Sutherland
17 juillet 7–9 du soir.

9

"This is crazy," said Richard. "An unacceptable risk."

To his annoyance, Beryl simply waltzed over to the closet and stood surveying her wardrobe. "What do you think would be appropriate tonight? Formal or semi?"

"You'll be out in the open," said Richard. "An art reception! I can't think of a more public place."

Beryl took out a black silk sheath, turned to the mirror, and calmly held the dress to her body. "A public place is the safest place to be," she observed.

"You were supposed to stay here! Instead you go running around town—"

"So did you."

"I had business...."

She turned and walked into the bedroom. "I did, too," she called back cheerfully.

He started to follow her, but halted in the doorway when he saw that she was undressing. At once he turned around and stood with his back pressed against the door-jamb. "A craving for a three-star meal doesn't constitute necessity!" he snapped over his shoulder.

"It wasn't a three-star meal. It wasn't even a half star. But it was better than eggs and moldy bread."

"You're like some finicky kitten, you know that? You'd rather starve than deign to eat canned food like every other cat."

"You're quite right. I'm a spoiled Persian and I want my cream and chicken livers."

"I would've brought you back a meal. Catnip included."

"You weren't here."

And that was his mistake, he realized. He couldn't leave this woman alone for a second. She was too damn unpredictable.

No, actually she *was* predictable. She'd do whatever he *didn't* want her to do.

And what he didn't want her to do was leave the flat tonight.

But he could already hear her stepping into the black dress, could hear the whisper of silk sliding over stockings, the hiss of the zipper closing over her back. He fought to suppress the images those sounds brought to mind—the long legs, the curve of her hips... He found himself clenching his jaw in frustration, at her, at himself, at the way events and passions were spinning out of his control.

"Do me up, will you?" she asked.

He turned and saw that she'd moved right beside him. Her back was turned and the nape of her neck was practically within kissing distance.

"The hook," she said, tossing her hair over one shoulder. He inhaled the flowery scent of shampoo. "I can't seem to fasten it."

He attached the hook and eye and found his gaze lingering on her bare shoulders. "Where did you get that dress?" he asked.

"I brought it from Chetwynd." She breezed over to the dresser and began to slip on earrings. The silk sheath seemed to mold itself to every luscious curve of her body. "Why do you ask?"

"It's Madeline's dress. Isn't it?"

She turned to look at him. "Yes, it is," she said quietly. "Does that bother you?"

"It's just—" he let out a breath "—it's a perfect fit. Curve for curve."

"And you think you're seeing a ghost."

"I remember that dress. I saw her wear it at an embassy reception." He paused. "God, it's really eerie, how that dress seems made for you."

Slowly she moved toward him, her gaze never wavering from his face. "I'm not her, Richard."

"I know."

"No matter how much you may want her back—"

"Her?" He took her wrists and pulled her close to him. "When I look at you, I see only Beryl. Of course, I notice the resemblance. The hair, the eyes. But *you're* the one I'm looking at. The one I want." He bent toward her and gently grazed her lips with a kiss. "That's why I want you to stay here tonight."

"Your prisoner?" she murmured.

"If need be." He kissed her again and heard an answering purr of contentment from her throat. She tilted her head back, and his lips slid to her neck, so smooth, so deliciously perfumed.

"Then you'll have to tie me up..." she whispered.

"Whatever you want."

"...because there's no other way you're going to keep me here tonight." With a maddening laugh, she wriggled free and walked into the bathroom.

Richard suppressed a groan of frustration. From the doorway, he watched as she pinned up her hair. "Exactly what do you expect to get out of this event, anyway?" he demanded.

"One never knows. That's the joy of intelligence

gathering, isn't it? Keep your ears and eyes open and see what turns up. I think we've learned quite a lot already about François. We know he has a sister who's ill. Which means François needed money. Working as a janitor in an art gallery couldn't possibly pay for all the care she needed. Perhaps he was desperate, willing to do anything for money. Even work as a hired assassin.''

"Your logic is unassailable.''

"Thank you.''

"But your plan of action is insane. You don't need to take this risk—''

"But I do.'' She turned to him, her hair now regally swept into a chignon. "Someone wants me and Jordan dead. And there I'll be tonight. A perfectly convenient target.''

What a magnificent creature she is, he thought. *It's that unbeatable bloodline, those Bernard and Madeline genes. She thinks she's invincible.*

"That's the plan, is it?'' he said. "Tempt the killer into making a move?''

"If that's what it takes to save Jordan.''

"And what's to stop the killer from carrying it out?''

"My two bodyguards. And you.''

"I'm not infallible, Beryl.''

"You're close enough.''

"I could make a mistake. Let my attention slip.''

"I trust you.''

"But I don't trust myself!'' Agitated, he began to pace the bedroom floor. "I've been out of the business for years. I'm out of practice, out of condition. I'm forty-two, Beryl, and my reflexes aren't what they used to be.''

"Last night they seemed quick enough to me.''

"Walk out that door, Beryl, and I can't guarantee your safety."

She came toward him, looking him coolly in the eye. "The fact is, Richard, you can't guarantee my safety anywhere. In here, out on the streets, at an artist's reception. Wherever I am, there's a chance things could go wrong. If I stay in this flat, if I stare at these walls any longer, thinking of all the things that could happen, I'll go insane. It's better to be out *there*. Doing something. Jordan isn't able to, so I have to be the one."

"The one to set yourself up as bait?"

"Our only lead is a dead man—François. Someone hired him, Richard. Someone who may have connections to Galerie Annika."

For a moment Richard stood gazing at her, thinking, *She's right, of course. It's the same conclusion I came to. She's clever enough to know exactly what needs to be done. And reckless enough to do it.*

He went to the nightstand and picked up the Glock. A pound and a half of steel and plastic, that's all he had to protect her with. It felt flimsy, insubstantial, against all the dangers lurking beyond the front door.

"You're coming with me?" she said.

He turned and looked at her. "You think I'd let you go alone?"

She smiled, so full of confidence it frightened him. It was Madeline's old smile. Madeline, who'd been every bit as confident.

He slid the Glock into his shoulder holster. "I'll be right beside you, Beryl," he said. "Every step of the way."

ANTHONY SUTHERLAND STOOD posing like a little emperor beside his bronze cast of the Madonna with jackal.

He was wearing a pirate shirt of purple silk, black leather pants and snakeskin boots, and he seemed not in the least bit fazed by all the photographers' flashbulbs that kept popping around him. The art critics were in vapors over the show. "Frightening." "Disturbing." "Images that twist convention." These were some of the comments Beryl overheard being murmured as she wandered through the gallery.

She and Richard stopped to look at another of Anthony's bronzes. At first glance, it had looked like two nude figures entwined in a loving embrace. Closer inspection, however, revealed it to be a man and woman in the process of devouring each other alive.

"Do you suppose that's an allegory for marriage?" said a familiar voice. It was Reggie Vane, balancing a glass of champagne in one hand and two dainty plates of canapés in the other.

He bent forward and gave Beryl an affectionate kiss on the cheek. "You're absolutely stunning tonight, dear. Your mother would be proud of you."

"Reggie, I had no idea you were interested in modern art," said Beryl.

"I'm not. Helena dragged me here." In disgust, he glanced around at the crowd. "Lord, I hate these things. But the St. Pierres were coming, and of course Marie always insists Helena show up as well, just to keep her company." He set his empty champagne glass on top of the bronze couple and laughed at the whimsical effect. "An improvement, wouldn't you say? As long as these two are going to eat each other, they might as well have some bubbly to wash each other down."

An elegantly attired woman swooped in and snatched away the glass. "Please, be more respectful of the work, Mr. Vane," she scolded.

"Oh, I wasn't being disrespectful, Annika," said Reggie. "I just thought it needed a touch of humor."

"It is absolutely perfect as it is." Annika gave the bronze heads a swipe of her napkin and stood back to admire the interwoven figures. "Whimsy would ruin its message."

"What message is that?" asked Richard.

The woman turned to look at him, and her head of boyishly cropped hair suddenly tilted up with interest. "The message," she said, gazing intently at Richard, "is that monogamy is a destructive institution."

"That's marriage, all right," grunted Reggie.

"But free love," the woman continued, "love that has no constraints and is open to all pleasures—that is a positive force."

"Is that Anthony's interpretation of this piece?" asked Beryl.

"It's how *I* interpret it." Annika shifted her gaze to Beryl. "You are a friend of Anthony's?"

"An acquaintance. I know his mother, Nina."

"Where is Nina, by the way?" asked Reggie. "You'd think she'd be front-and-center stage for *darling* Anthony's night of *glory*."

Beryl had to laugh at Reggie's imitation of Nina. Yes, when Queen Nina wanted an audience, all she had to do was throw one of these stylish bashes, and an audience would invariably turn up. Even poor Marie St. Pierre, just out of the hospital, had put in an appearance. Marie stood off in a corner with Helena Vane, the two women huddled together like sparrows in a gathering of peacocks. It was easy to see why they'd be such close friends; both of them were painfully plain, neither one was happily married. That their marriages were not happy was only too clear tonight. The Vanes were avoiding each other, Helena off in her corner darting irritated looks, Reggie standing as far away as possible. And as for Marie St. Pierre—her husband wasn't even in the room at the moment.

"So this is in praise of free love, is it?" said Reggie, eyeing the bronze with new appreciation.

"That is how I see it," said Annika. "How a man and a woman should love."

"I quite agree," said Reggie with a sudden burst of enthusiasm. "Banish marriage entirely."

The woman looked provocatively at Richard. "What do you think, Mr....?"

"Wolf," said Richard. "I'm afraid I don't agree." He took Beryl's arm. "Excuse us, will you? We still have to see the rest of the collection."

As he led Beryl away toward the spiral staircase, she whispered, "There's nothing to see upstairs."

"I want to check out the upper floors."

"Anthony's work is all on the first floor."

"I saw Nina slink up the stairs a few minutes ago. I want to see what she's up to."

They climbed the stairs to the second-floor gallery. From the open walkway, they paused to look over the railing at the crowd on the first floor. It was a flashy gathering, a sea of well-coiffed heads and multicolored silks. Annika had moved into the limelight with Anthony, and as a new round of flashbulbs went off, they embraced and kissed to the sound of applause.

"Ah, free love," sighed Beryl. "She obviously has samples to pass around."

"So I can see."

Beryl gave him a sly smile. "Poor Richard. On duty tonight and can't indulge."

"*Afraid* to indulge. She'd eat me up alive. Like that bronze statue."

"Aren't you tempted? Just a little?"

He looked at her with amusement. "You're baiting me, Beryl."

"Am I?"

"Yes, you are. I know exactly what you're up to. Putting me to the test. Making me prove I'm not like your friend the surgeon. Who, as you implied, also believed in free love."

Beryl's smile faded. "Is that what I'm doing?" she asked softly.

"You have a right to." He gave her hand a squeeze and glanced down again at the crowd. *He's always alert, always watching out for me,* she thought. *I'd trust him with my life. But my heart? I still don't know....*

In the downstairs gallery, a pair of musicians began to play. As the sweet sounds of flute and guitar floated through the building, Beryl suddenly sensed a pair of eyes watching her. She looked down at the cluster of bronze statues and spotted Anthony Sutherland, standing by his Madonna with jackal. He was gazing right at her. And the expression in his eyes was one of cold calculation.

Instinctively she shrank away from the railing.

"What is it?" asked Richard.

"Anthony. It's the way he looks at me."

But by then Anthony had already turned away and was shaking Reggie Vane's hand. An odd young man, thought Beryl. What sort of mind dreams up these nightmarish visions? Women nursing jackals. Couples devouring each other. Had it been so difficult, growing up as Nina Sutherland's son?

She and Richard wandered through the second-floor gallery, but found no sign of Nina.

"Why are you so interested in finding her?" asked Beryl.

"It's not her so much as the way she went up those stairs. Obviously trying not to be noticed."

"And you noticed her."

"It was the dress. Those trademark bugle beads of hers."

They finished their circuit of the second floor and headed up the staircase to the third. Again, no sign of Nina. But as they moved along the walkway, the musicians in the first-floor gallery suddenly ceased playing. In the abrupt silence that followed, Beryl heard Nina's voice—a few loud syllables—just before it dropped to a whisper. Another voice answered—a man's, speaking softly in reply.

The voices came from an alcove, just ahead.

"It's not as if I haven't been patient," said Nina. "Not as if I haven't *tried* to be understanding."

"I know. I know—"

"Do you know what it's been *like* for me? For Anthony? Have you any *idea?* All those years, waiting for you to make up your mind."

"I never let you want for anything."

"Oh, how *fortunate* for us! My goodness, how generous of you!"

"The boy has had the best—everything he's ever wanted. Now he's twenty-one. My responsibility ends."

"Your responsibility," said Nina, "has only just *begun.*"

Richard yanked Beryl around the corner just as Nina emerged from the alcove. She stormed right past them, too angry to notice her audience. They could hear her high heels tapping down the staircase to the lower galleries.

A moment later, a second figure emerged from the alcove, moving like an old man.

It was Philippe St. Pierre.

He went over to the railing and stared down at the crowd in the gallery below. He seemed to be considering the temptation of that two-story drop. Then, sighing deeply, he walked away and followed Nina down the stairs.

Down in the first-floor gallery, the crowd was starting to thin out. Anthony had already left; so had the Vanes. But Marie St. Pierre was still standing in her corner, the abandoned wife waiting to be reclaimed. A full room's length away stood her husband Philippe, nursing a glass of champagne. And standing between them was that macabre sculpture, the bronze man and woman devouring each other alive.

Beryl thought that perhaps Anthony had hit upon the truth with his art. That if people weren't careful, love would consume them, destroy them. As it had destroyed Marie.

The image of Marie St. Pierre, standing alone and forlorn in the corner, stayed with Beryl all the way back to the flat. She thought how hard it must be to play the politician's wife—forever poised and pleasant, always supportive, never the shrew. And all the time knowing that your husband was in love with another woman.

"She must have known about it. For years," said Beryl softly.

Richard kept his gaze on the road as he navigated the streets back to Passy. "Who?" he asked.

"Marie St. Pierre. She must have known about her husband and Nina. Every time she looks at young Anthony, she'd see the resemblance. And how it must hurt her. Yet all these years, she's put up with him."

"And with Nina," said Richard.

Beryl sat back, puzzled. *Yes, she does put up with Nina. And that's the part I don't understand. How she can be so civil, so gracious, to her husband's mistress. To her husband's bastard son....*

"You think Philippe is Anthony's father?"

"That's what Nina meant, of course. All that talk about Philippe's responsibilities. She meant Anthony." She paused. "Art school must be very expensive."

"And Philippe must've paid a pretty bundle over the years, supporting the boy. Not to mention Nina, whose tastes are extravagant, to say the least. Her widow's pension couldn't have been enough to—"

"What is it?" asked Beryl.

"I just had a flash of insight about her husband, Stephen Sutherland. He committed suicide a month after your parents died—jumped off a bridge."

"Yes, you told me that."

"All these years, I've thought his death was related to the Delphi case. I suspected he was the mole, that he killed himself when he thought he was about to be discovered. But what if his reasons for jumping off that bridge were entirely personal?"

"His marriage."

"And young Anthony. The boy he discovered wasn't his son at all."

"But if Stephen Sutherland wasn't Delphi..."

"Then we're back to a person or persons unknown."

Persons unknown. Meaning someone who could still be alive. And afraid of discovery.

Instinctively she glanced over her shoulder, checking to see if they were being followed. Just behind them was the Peugeot with the two French agents; beyond that she saw only a stream of anonymous headlights. Richard was right, she thought. She should have stayed in the flat. She should have kept her head low, her face out of sight. Anyone could have spotted her this afternoon. Or they could be following her right this moment, could be watching her from somewhere in that sea of headlights.

Suddenly she longed to be back in the flat, safely surrounded by four walls. It began to seem endless, this drive to Passy, a journey through a darkness full of perils.

When at last they pulled up in front of the building, she was so anxious to get inside that she quickly started to climb out of the car. Richard pulled her back in.

"Don't get out yet," he said. "Let the men check it first."

"You don't really think—"

"It's a precaution. Standard operating procedure."

Beryl watched the two French agents climb the steps and unlock the front door. While one man stood watch on the steps, the other vanished inside.

"But how could anyone find out about the flat?" she asked.

"Payoffs. Leaks."

"You don't think Claude Daumier—"

"I'm not trying to scare you, Beryl. I just believe in being careful."

She watched as the lights came on inside the flat. First the living room, then the bedroom. At last, the man on the steps gave them the all-clear signal.

"Okay, it must be clean," said Richard, climbing out of the car. "Let's go."

Beryl stepped out onto the curb. She turned toward the building and took one step up the sidewalk—

—and was slammed backward against the car as an explosion rocked the earth. Shattered glass flew from the building and rained onto the street. Seconds later, the sky lit up with the hellish glow of flames shooting through the broken windows. Beryl sank to the ground, her ears still ringing from the blast. She stared numbly as tongues of flame slashed the darkness.

She couldn't hear Richard's shouts, didn't realize he was crouched right beside her until she felt his hands on her face. "Are you all right?" he cried. "Beryl, look at me!"

Weakly she nodded. Then her gaze traveled to the front walkway, to the body of the French agent lying sprawled near the steps.

"Stay put!" yelled Richard as he pivoted away from her. He dashed over to the fallen man and knelt beside him just long enough to feel for a pulse. At once he was back at Beryl's side. "Get in the car," he said.

"But what about the men?"

"That one's dead. The other one didn't stand a chance."

"You don't know that!"

"Just get in the car!" ordered Richard. He opened the door and practically shoved her inside. Then he scrambled around to the driver's side and slid behind the wheel.

"We can't just leave them there!" cried Beryl.

"We'll have to." He started the engine and sent the car screeching away from the curb.

Beryl watched as a succession of streets blurred past. Richard drove like a madman, but she was too stunned to feel afraid, too bewildered to focus on anything but the river of red taillights stretching ahead of them.

"Jordan," she whispered. "What about Jordan?"

"Right now I have to think about you."

"They found the flat. They can get to him!"

"I'll take care of it later. First we get you to a safe place."

"Where?"

He swerved across two lanes and shot onto an off ramp. "I'll come up with one. Somewhere."

Somewhere. She stared out at the night glow of Paris. A sprawling city, an ocean of light. A million different places to hide.

To die.

She shivered and shrank deep into the seat. "And then what?" she whispered. "What happens next?"

He looked at her. "We get out of Paris. Out of the country."

"You mean—go home?"

"No. It won't be safe in England, either." He turned his gaze back to the road. The car seemed to leap through the darkness. "We're going to Greece."

DAUMIER ANSWERED the phone on the second ring. *"Allo?"*

A familiar voice growled at him from the receiver. *"What the hell is going on?"*

"Richard?" said Daumier. "Where are you?"

"A safe place. You'll understand if I don't reveal it to you."

"And Beryl?"

"She's unhurt. Though I can't say the same for your two men. Who knew about the flat, Claude?"

"Only my people."

"Who else?"

"I told no one else. It should have been a safe enough place."

"Apparently you were wrong. Someone found out."

"You were both out of the flat earlier today. One of you could have been followed."

"It wasn't me."

"Beryl, then. You should not have allowed her out of the building. She could've been spotted at Galerie Annika this afternoon and followed back to the flat."

"My mistake. You're right, I shouldn't have left her alone. I can't afford to make any more mistakes."

Daumier sighed. "You and I, Richard, we have known each other too long. This is not the time to stop trusting each other."

There was a brief silence on the other end. Then Richard said, "I'm sorry, but I have no choice, Claude. We're going under."

"Then I will not be able to help you."

"We'll go it alone. Without your help."

"Wait, Richard—"

But the line had already gone dead. Daumier stared at the receiver, then slowly laid it back in the cradle. There was no point in trying to trace the call; Richard would have used a pay phone—and it would be in a different neighborhood from where he'd be staying. The man was once a professional; he knew the tricks of the trade.

Maybe—just maybe—it would keep them both alive.

"Good luck, my friend," murmured Daumier. "I am afraid you will need it."

RICHARD RISKED one more call from the pay phone, this one to Washington, D.C.

His business partner answered with his usual charmless growl. "Sakaroff here."

"Niki, it's me."

"Richard? How is beautiful Paris? Having a good time?"

"A lousy time. Look, I can't talk long. I'm in trouble."

Niki sighed. "Why am I not surprised?"

"It's the old Delphi case. You remember? Paris, '73. The NATO mole."

"Ah, yes."

"Delphi's come back to life. I need your help to identify him."

"I was KGB, Richard. Not Stasi."

"But you had connections to the East Germans."

"Not directly. I had little contact with Stasi agents. The East Germans, you know…they preferred to operate independently."

"Then who *would* know about Delphi? There must be some old contact you can pump for information."

There was a pause. "Perhaps…"

"Yes?"

"Heinrich Leitner," said Sakaroff. "He is the one who could tell you. He oversaw Stasi's Paris operations. Not a field man—he never left East Berlin. But he would be familiar with Delphi's work."

"Okay, he's the man I'll talk to. So how do I get to him?"

"That is the difficult part. He is in Berlin—"

"No problem. We'll go there."

"—in a high-security prison."

Richard groaned. "That *is* a problem." In frustration, he turned and stared through the phone-booth door at the subway platform. "I've got to get in to see him, Niki."

"You'll need approval. That will take days. Papers, signatures…"

"Then that's what I'll have to get. If you could make a few calls, speed things up."

"No guarantees."

"Understood. Oh, and one more thing," said Richard. "We've been trying to get ahold of Hugh Tavistock. It seems he's vanished. Have you heard anything about it?"

"No. But I will check my sources. Anything else?"

"I'll let you know."

Sakaroff grunted. "I was afraid you would say that."

Richard hung up. Stepping away from the pay phone, he glanced around at the subway platform. He saw nothing suspicious, only the usual stream of nighttime commuters—couples holding hands, students with backpacks.

The train for Creteil-Préfecture rolled into the station. Richard stepped onto it, rode it for three stops, then got off. He lingered on the next platform for a few minutes, surveying the faces. No one looked familiar. Satisfied that he hadn't been followed, he boarded the Bobigny-Picasso train and rode it to Gare de l'Est. There he stepped off, walked out of the station, and headed briskly back to the *pension.*

He found Beryl still awake and sitting in an armchair by the window. She'd turned off all the lights, and in the darkness she was little more than a silhouette against the glow of the night sky. He shut and bolted the door. "Beryl?" he said. "Everything all right?"

He thought he saw her nod. Or was it just the quivering of her chin as she took a breath and let out a soft, slow sigh?

"We'll be safe here," he said. "For tonight, at least."

"And tomorrow?" came the murmured question.

"We'll worry about that when the time comes."

She leaned back against the chair cushions and stared straight ahead. "Is this how it was, for you, Richard? Working for Intelligence? Living day to day, not daring to think about tomorrows?"

He moved slowly to her chair. "Sometimes it was like this. Sometimes I wasn't sure there'd be a tomorrow for me."

"Do you miss that life?" She looked at him. He couldn't see her face, but he felt her watching him.

"I left that life behind."

"But do you miss it? The excitement? That lovely promise of violence?"

"Beryl. Beryl, please." He reached for her hand; it was like a lump of ice in his grasp.

"Didn't you enjoy it, just a little?"

"No." He paused. Then softly he said, "Yes. For a short time. When I was very young. Before it turned all too real."

"The way it did tonight. Tonight, it was real for me. When I saw that man lying there..." She swallowed. "This afternoon, you see, we had lunch together, the three of us. They had the veal. And a bottle of wine, and ice cream. And I got them to laugh...." She looked away.

"It seems like a game, at first," said Richard. "A make-believe war. But then you realize that the bullets are real. So are the people." He held her hand in his and wished he could warm it, warm her. "That's what happened to me. All of a sudden, it got too real. And there was a woman...."

She sat very still, waiting, listening. "Someone you loved?" she asked softly.

"No, not someone I loved. But someone I liked, very much. It was in Berlin, before the Wall came down. We were trying to bring over a defector to the West. And my partner, she got trapped on the wrong side. The guard spotted her. Fired.'' He lifted Beryl's hand to his lips and kissed it, held it.

''She...didn't make it?''

He shook his head. ''And it wasn't a game of make-believe any longer. I could see her body lying in the no-man's-zone. And I couldn't reach her. So I had to leave her there, for the other side....'' He released her hand. He moved to the window and looked out at the lights twinkling over Paris. ''That's when I left the business. I didn't want another death on my conscience. I didn't want to feel...responsible.'' He turned to her. In the faint glow from the city, her face looked pale, almost luminous. ''That's what makes this so hard for me, Beryl. Knowing what could happen if I make a mistake. Knowing that your life depends on what I do next.''

For a long time, Beryl sat very still, watching him. Feeling his gaze through the darkness. That spark of attraction crackled like fire between them as it always did. But tonight there was something more, something that went beyond desire.

She rose from the chair. Though he didn't move, she could feel the fever of his gaze as she glided toward him, could hear the sharp intake of his breath as she reached up and touched his beard-roughened face. ''Richard,'' she whispered, ''I want you.''

At once she was swept into his arms. No other embrace, no other kiss, had ever stolen her breath the way this one did. *We are like that couple in bronze,* she thought. *Starved for each other. Devouring each other.*

But this was a feast of love, not destruction.

She whimpered and her head fell back as his mouth slid to her throat. She could feel every stroke of his hands through the silky fabric of her dress. Oh Lord, if he could do this to her with her clothes on, what lovely torment would he unleash on her naked flesh? Already her breasts were tingling under his touch, her nipples turned to tight buds.

He unzipped her dress and slowly eased it off her shoulders.

It hissed past her hips and slid into a silken ripple on the floor. He, too, traced the length of her torso, his lips moving slowly down her throat, her breasts, her belly. Shuddering with pleasure, she gripped his hair and moaned, "No fair..."

"All's fair," he murmured, easing her stockings down her thighs. "In love and war...."

By the time he had her fully undressed, by the time he'd shed his own clothes, she was beyond words, beyond protest. She'd lost all sense of time and space; there was only the darkness, and the warmth of his touch, and the hunger shuddering deep inside her. She scarcely realized how thcy found their way to the bed. Eagerly she sank backward onto the mattress, and heard the squeak of the springs, the quickening duet of their breathing. Then she pulled him down against her, drew him onto and into her.

Starved for each other, she thought as he captured her mouth under his, invaded it, explored it. *Devouring each other.*

And like two who were famished, they feasted.

He reached for her hands, and their fingers entwined in a tighter and tighter knot as their bodies joined, thrusted, exulted. Even as her last shudders of desire faded away, he was still gripping her hands.

Slowly he released them and cradled her face instead. He pressed gentle kisses to her lips, her eyelids. "Next time,'' he whispered, ''we'll take it slower. I won't be in such a hurry, I promise.''

She smiled at him. ''I have no complaints.''

''None?''

''None at all. But next time...''

''Yes?''

She twisted her body beneath him, and they tumbled across the sheets until her body was lying atop his. ''Next time,'' she murmured, lowering her lips to his chest, ''it's my turn to do the tormenting.''

He groaned as her mouth slid hotly down to his belly. ''We're taking turns?''

''You're the one who said it. All's fair...''

''...in love and war.'' He laughed. And he buried his hands in her hair.

THEY MET IN THE usual place, the warehouse behind Galerie Annika. Against the walls were stacked dozens of crates containing the paintings and sculptures of would-be artists, most of them no doubt talentless amateurs hoping for a spot on a gallery wall. *But who can really say which is art and which is rubbish?* thought Amiel Foch, gazing around at the room full of crated dreams. *To me, it is all the same. Pigment and canvas.*

Foch turned as the warehouse door swung open. ''The bomb went off as planned,'' he said. ''The job is done.''

''The job is *not* done,'' came the reply. Anthony Sutherland emerged from the night and stepped into the warehouse. The thud of the door shutting behind him echoed across the bare concrete floor. ''I wanted the woman neutralized. She is still alive. So is Richard Wolf.''

Foch stared at Anthony. ''It was a delayed fuse, set

off two minutes after entry! It could not have ignited on its own."

"Nevertheless, they are still alive. Thus far, your record of success is abysmal. You could not finish off even that stupid creature, Marie St. Pierre."

"I will see to Mme St. Pierre—"

"Forget her! It's the Tavistocks I want dead! Lord, they're like cats! Nine bloody lives."

"Jordan Tavistock is still in custody. I can arrange—"

"Jordan will keep for a while. He's harmless where he is. But Beryl has to be taken care of soon. My guess is that she and Wolf are leaving Paris. Find them."

"How?"

"You're the professional."

"So is Richard Wolf," said Foch. "He will be difficult to trace. I cannot perform miracles."

There was a long silence. Foch watched the other man pace among the crates, and he thought, *This boy is nothing like his mother. This one has the ruthlessness to see things through. And the nerve not to flinch at the consequences.*

"I cannot search blindly," said Foch. "I must have a lead. Will they go to England, perhaps?"

"No, not England." Anthony suddenly stopped pacing. "Greece. The island of Paros."

"You mean...the Rideau family?"

"Wolf will try to contact him. I'm sure of it." Anthony let out a snort of disgust. "My mother should have taken care of Rideau years ago. Well, there's still time to do it."

Foch nodded. "I leave for Paros."

AFTER FOCH HAD LEFT, Anthony Sutherland stood alone in the warehouse, gazing about at the crates. *So many hopes and dreams locked away in here,* he reflected. *But not mine. Mine are on display for all to see and admire. The work of these poor slobs may molder into eternity. But I am the toast of Paris.*

It took more than talent, more than luck. It took the help of Philippe St. Pierre's cold hard cash. Cash that would instantly dry up if his mother was ever exposed.

My father Philippe, thought Anthony with a laugh. *Still unsuspecting after all these years. I have to hand it to my lovely mother—she knows how to keep them under her spell.*

But feminine wiles could take one only so far.

If only Nina had cleaned up this matter years ago. Instead, she'd left a live witness, had even paid the man to leave the country. And as long as that witness lived, he was like a time bomb, ticking away on some lonely Greek island.

Anthony left the warehouse, walked down the alley, and climbed into his car. It was time to go home. Mustn't keep his mother awake; Nina did worry about him so. He tried never to distress her. She was, after all, the only person in this world who really loved him. Understood him.

Like peas in a pod, Mother and I, he thought with a smile. He started his car and roared off into the night.

THEY CAME TO ESCORT HIM from his cell at 9:00 a.m. No explanations, just the clink of keys in the door, and a gruff command in French.

Now what? wondered Jordan as he followed the guard up the corridor to the visitation room. He stepped inside, blinking at the glare of overhead fluorescent lights.

Reggie Vane was waiting in the room. At once he

waved Jordan to a chair. "Sit down. You look bloody awful, my boy."

"I feel bloody awful," said Jordan, and sank into the chair.

Reggie sat down, too. Leaning forward, he whispered conspiratorially, "I brought what you asked for. There's a nice little *charcuterie* around the corner. Lovely duckling terrine. And a few *baguettes.*" He shoved a paper bag under the table. *"Bon appétit."*

Jordan glanced in the bag and gave a sigh of pleasure. "Reggie, old man, you're a saint."

"Had some nice leek tarts to go with it, but the cop at the front desk insisted on helping himself."

"What about wine? Did you manage a decent bottle or two?"

Reggie shoved a second bag under the table, eliciting a musical clink from the contents. "But of course. A Beaujolais and a rather nice Pinot noir. Screw-top caps, I'm afraid—they wouldn't allow a corkscrew. And you'll have to hand over the bottles as soon as they're empty. Glass, you know."

Jordan regarded the Beaujolais with a look of sheer contentment. "How on earth did you manage it, Reggie?"

"Just scratched a few itchy palms. Oh, and those books you wanted—Helena will bring them by this afternoon."

"Capital!" Jordan folded the bag over the bottles. "If one must be in prison, one might as well make it a civilized experience." He looked up at Reggie. "Now, what's the latest news? I've had no word from Beryl since yesterday."

Reggie sighed. "I was dreading that question."

"What's happened?"

"I think she and Wolf have left Paris. After the explosion last night—"

"What?"

"I heard it from Daumier this morning. The flat where Beryl was staying was bombed last night. Two French agents killed. Wolf and your sister are fine, but they're dropping out for a while, leaving the country."

Jordan gave a sigh of relief. Thank God Beryl was out of the picture. It was one less problem to worry about. "What about the explosion?" he asked. "What does Daumier say about it?"

"His people feel there are similarities."

"To what?"

"The bombing of the St. Pierre residence."

Jordan stared at him. "But that was a terrorist attack. Cosmic Solidarity or some crazy group—"

"Apparently bombs are sort of like fingerprints. The way they're put together identifies their maker. And both bombs had identical wiring patterns. Something like that."

Jordan shook his head. "Why would terrorists attack Beryl? Or me? We're civilians."

"Perhaps they think otherwise."

"Or perhaps it wasn't terrorists in the first place," said Jordan, suddenly pushing out of his chair. He paced the room, pumping fresh blood to his legs, his brain. Too many hours in that cell had turned his body to mush; he needed a stiff walk, a slap of fresh air. "What if," he suggested, "that bombing of the St. Pierre place wasn't a terrorist attack at all? What if that Cosmic Solidarity nonsense was just a cover story to hide the real motive?"

"You mean it wasn't a political attack?"

"No."

"But who would want to kill Philippe St. Pierre?"

Jordan suddenly stopped dead as the realization hit him. "Not Philippe," he said softly. "His wife. Marie."

"*Marie* planted the bomb?"

"No! Marie was the *target!* She was the only one home when the bomb went off. Everyone assumes it was a mistake, an error in timing. But the bomber knew exactly what he was doing. He was trying to kill Marie, not her husband." Jordan looked at Reggie with new urgency. "You have to reach Wolf. Tell him what I just said."

"I don't know where he is."

"Ask Daumier."

"He doesn't know, either."

"Then find out where my uncle's gone off to. If ever I needed a family connection, it's right now."

After Reggie had left, the guard escorted Jordan back to his cell. The instant he stepped inside, the familiar smells assaulted him—the odor of sour wine and ripe bodies. Back with old friends, he thought, looking at the two Frenchmen snoring in their cots, the same two men whose cell he'd shared when he was first arrested. A drunk, a thief and him. What a happy little trio they made. He went to his cot and set down the two paper bags with the food and wine. At least he wouldn't have to gag on any more goulash.

Lying down, he stared at the cobwebs in the corner. So many leads to follow, to run down. *A killer's on the loose and here I am, locked up and useless. Unable to test my theories. If I could just get the help of someone I trust, someone I know beyond a doubt is on my side...*

Where the hell is Beryl?

THE GREEK TAVERN KEEPER slid two glasses of retsina onto their table. "Summertime, we have many tourists,"

he said with a shrug. "I cannot keep track of foreigners."

"But this man, Rideau, isn't a tourist," said Richard.
"He's been living on this island twenty years. A Frenchman."

The tavern keeper laughed. "Frenchmen, Dutchmen,
they are all the same to me," he grunted and went back
into the kitchen.

"Another dead end," muttered Beryl. She took a sip
of retsina and grimaced. "People actually *drink* this
brew?"

"And some of them even enjoy it," said Richard.
"It's an acquired taste."

"Then perhaps I'll acquire it another time." She
pushed the glass away and looked around the gloomy
taverna. It was midday, and passengers from the latest
cruise ship had started trickling in from the heat, their
shopping bags filled with the usual tourist purchases:
Grecian urns, fishermen's caps, peasant dresses. Im-
mersed in the babble of half a dozen languages, it was
easy for Beryl to understand why the locals might not
bother to distinguish a Frenchman from any other out-
sider. Foreigners came, they spent money, they left.
What more did one need to know about them?

The tavern keeper reemerged from the kitchen carrying a sizzling platter of calamari. He set it on a table
occupied by a German family and was about to head
back to the kitchen when Richard asked, "Who might
know about this Frenchman?"

"You waste your time," said the tavern keeper. "I
tell you, there is no one on this island named Rideau."

"He brought his family with him," said Richard. "A

wife and a son. The boy would be in his thirties now. His name is Gerard.''

A dish suddenly clattered to the floor behind the counter of the bar. The dark-eyed young woman standing at the tap was frowning at Richard. "Gerard?" she said.

"Gerard Rideau," said Richard. "Do you know him?"

"She doesn't know anything," the tavern keeper insisted, and waved the young woman toward the kitchen.

"But I can see she does," said Richard.

The woman stood staring at him, as though not certain what to do, what to say.

"We've come from Paris," said Beryl. "It's very important we speak to Gerard's father."

"You are not French," said the woman.

"No, I'm English." Beryl nodded toward Richard. "He's American."

"He said...he said it was a Frenchman I should be careful of."

"Who did?"

"Gerard."

"He's right to be careful," said Richard. "But he should know things have gotten even more dangerous. There may be others coming to Paros, looking for his family. He has to talk to us, *now*." He pointed to the tavern keeper. "He'll be your witness. If anything goes wrong."

The woman hesitated, then went into the kitchen. A moment later, she reemerged. "He does not answer the telephone," she said. "I will have to drive you there."

It was a bumpy ride down a lonely stretch of road to Logaras beach. Clouds of dust flew in the open window and coated the jet black hair of their driver. Sofia was her name, and she had been born on the island. Her father managed the hotel near the harbor; now her three brothers ran the business. She could do a better job of it, she thought, but of course no one valued a woman's opinion, so she worked instead at Theo's tavern, frying calamari, rolling dolmas. She spoke four languages; one must, she explained, if one wished to live off the tourist trade.

"How do you know Gerard?" asked Beryl.

"We are friends" was the answer.

Lovers, guessed Beryl, seeing the other woman's cheeks redden.

"His family is French," said Sofia. "His mother died five years ago, but his father is still alive. But their name is not Rideau. Perhaps—" she looked at them hopefully "—it is a different family you are looking for?"

"They might have changed their name," said Beryl.

They parked near the beach and strode out across the rocks and sand. "There," said Sofia, pointing to a distant sailboard skimming the water. "That is Gerard." She waved and called to him in Greek.

At once the board spun around, the multicolored sail snapping about in a neat jibe. With the wind at his back, Gerard surfed to the beach like a bronzed Adonis and dragged the board onto the sand.

"Gerard," said Sofia, "these people are looking for a man named Rideau. Is that your father?"

Instantly Gerard dropped his sailboard. "Our name is not Rideau," he said curtly. Then he turned and walked away.

"Gerard?" called Sofia.

"Let me talk to him," said Richard, and he followed the other man up the beach.

Beryl stood by Sofia and watched the two men confront each other. Gerard was shaking his head, denying any knowledge of any Rideau family. Through the whistle of the wind, Beryl heard Richard's voice and the words "bomb" and "murder." She saw Gerard glance around nervously and knew that he was afraid.

"I hope I have done the right thing," murmured Sofia. "He is worried."

"He should be worried."

"What has his father done?"

"It's not what he's done. It's what he knows."

At the other end of the beach, Gerard was looking more and more agitated. Abruptly he turned and walked back to Sofia. Richard was right behind him.

"What is it?" asked Sofia.

"We go," snapped Gerard. "My father's house."

This time the drive took them along the coast, past groves of struggling olive trees on their left, and the gray-green Aegean on their right. The smell of Gerard's suntan lotion permeated the car. Such a dry and barren land, Beryl observed, looking out across the scrub grass. But to a man from a French slum, this would have seemed like a paradise.

"My father," said Gerard as he drove, "speaks no English. I will have to explain to him what you are asking. He may not remember."

"I'm sure he does remember," said Richard. "It's the reason you left Paris."

"That was twenty years ago. A long time…"

"Do *you* remember anything?" asked Beryl from the back seat. "You were…what? Fifteen, sixteen?"

"Fifteen," said Gerard.

"Then you must remember 66 Rue Myrha. The building where you lived."

Gerard gripped the steering wheel tightly as they

bounced onto a dirt road. "I remember the police coming to see the attic. Asking my father questions. Every day, for a week."

"What about the woman who rented the attic?" asked Richard. "Her name was Scarlatti. Do you remember her?"

"Yes. She had a man," said Gerard. "I used to listen to them through the door. Every Wednesday. All the sounds they made!" Gerard shook his head in amusement. "Very exciting for a boy my age."

"So this Mlle Scarlatti, she used the attic only as a love nest?" asked Beryl.

"She was never there except to make love."

"What did they look like, these two lovers?"

"The man was tall—that's all I remember. The woman, she had dark hair. Always wore a scarf and sunglasses. I do not remember her face very well, but I remember she was quite beautiful."

Like her mother, thought Beryl. Could she be wrong? Had it really been her, meeting her lover in that rundown flat in Pigalle?

She asked softly, "Was the woman English?"

Gerard paused. "She could have been."

"Meaning you're not certain."

"I was young. I thought she was foreign, but I did not know from where. Then, after the murders, I heard she was English."

"Did you see their bodies?"

Gerard shook his head. "My father, he would not allow it."

"So your father was the first to see them?" asked Richard.

"No. It was the man."

Richard glanced at Gerard in surprise. "Which man?"

"Mlle Scarlatti's lover. We saw him climb the steps to the attic. Then he came running back down, quite frantic. That's when we knew something was wrong and called the police."

"What happened to that man?"

"He drove away. I never saw him again. I assumed he was afraid of being accused. And that was why he sent us the money."

"The payoff," said Richard. "I guessed as much."

"For silence?" asked Beryl.

"Or false testimony." He asked Gerard, "How was the money delivered?"

"A man came with a briefcase only hours after the bodies were found. I'd never seen him before—a short, rather stocky Frenchman. He came to our flat, took my father into a back room. I did not hear what they said. Then the short man left."

"Your father never spoke to you about it?"

"No. And he told us we were not to speak of it to the police."

"You're certain that the briefcase contained money?"

"It must have."

"How do you know?"

"Because suddenly we had things. New clothes, a television. And then, soon afterward, we came to Greece. And we bought the house. There, you see?" He pointed. In the distance was a sprawling villa with a red-tiled roof. As they drove closer, Beryl saw bougainvillea trailing up the whitewashed walls and spilling over a covered veranda. Just below the house, waves lapped at a lonely beach.

They parked next to a dusty Citroën and climbed out. The wind whistled in from the sea, stinging their faces with sand. There was no other house in sight, only this solitary building, tucked into the crags of a barren hill.

"Papa?" called Gerard, climbing the stone steps. He swung open the wrought-iron gate. "Papa?"

No one answered.

Gerard pushed through the front door and stepped across the threshold, Beryl and Richard right behind him. Their footsteps echoed through silent rooms.

"I called here from the tavern," said Sofia. "There was no answer."

"His car is outside," said Gerard. "He must be here." He crossed the living room and started toward the dining room. "Papa?" he said, and halted in the doorway. An anguished cry was suddenly wrenched from his throat. He took a step forward and seemed to stumble to his knees. Over his shoulder, Beryl caught a view into the formal dining room beyond.

A wood table stretched the length of the room. At the far end of the table, a gray-haired man had slumped onto his dinner plate, scattering chick-peas and rice across the table's surface.

Richard pushed past Gerard and went to the fallen man. Gently he grasped the head and lifted the face from its pillow of mashed rice.

In the man's forehead was punched a single bullet-hole.

10

Amiel Foch sat at an outdoor café table, sipping espresso and watching the tourists stroll past. Not the usual dentures-and-bifocals crowd, he observed as a shapely redhead wandered by. This must be the week for honeymooners. It was five o'clock, and the last public ferry to Piraeus would be sailing in half an hour. If the Tavistock woman planned to leave the island tonight, she'd have to board that ferry. He'd keep an eye on the gangplank.

He polished off his snack of stuffed grape leaves and started in on dessert, a walnut pastry steeped in syrup. Curious, how the completion of a job always left him ravenous. For other men, the spilling of blood resulted in a surge of libido, a sudden craving for hot, fast sex. Amiel Foch craved food instead; no wonder his weight was such a problem.

Dispatching the old Frenchman Rideau had been easy; killing Wolf and the woman would not be so simple. Earlier today he had considered an ambush, but Rideau's house stood on an empty stretch of shoreline, the only access a five-mile-long dirt road, and there was nowhere to conceal his car. Nowhere to lie in wait without being detected. Foch had a rule he never broke: always leave an escape route. The Rideau house, set in the midst of barren scrub, was too exposed for any such retreat. Richard Wolf was armed and would be watching for danger signs.

Amiel Foch was not a coward. But he was not a fool, either.

Far wiser to wait for another opportunity—perhaps in Piraeus, with its crowded streets and chaotic traffic. Pedestrians were killed all the time. An accident, two dead tourists—it would raise hardly a stir of interest.

Foch's gaze sharpened as the afternoon ferry pulled into port. There was only a brief unloading of passengers; the island of Paros was not, after all, on the usual Mykonos-Rhodes-Crete circuit made by tourists. At the bottom of the gangplank, a few dozen people had already gathered to board. Quickly Foch surveyed the crowd. To his consternation, he saw neither the woman nor Wolf. He knew they'd been on the island today; his contact had spotted the pair in a tavern this morning. Had they slipped away by some other route?

Then he noticed the man in the tattered Windbreaker and black fisherman's cap. Though his shoulders were hunched, there was no disguising the man's height—six feet tall, at least, with a tautly athletic build. The man turned sideways, and Foch caught a glimpse of his face, partly obscured by a few days' worth of stubble. It was, indeed, Richard Wolf. But he appeared to be traveling alone. Where was the woman?

Foch paid his café bill and wandered over to the landing. He mingled with the waiting passengers and studied their faces. There were a number of women, tanned tourists, Greek housewives clad modestly in black, a few hippies in blue jeans. Beryl Tavistock was not among them.

He felt a brief spurt of panic. Had the woman and

Wolf separated? If so, he might never find her. He was tempted to stay on the island, to search her out....

The passengers were moving up the gangplank.

He weighed his choices and decided to follow Wolf. Better to stick with a flesh-and-blood quarry. Sooner or later, Wolf would reunite with the woman. Until then, Foch would have to bide his time, make no moves.

The man in the fisherman's cap walked up the gangplank and into the cabin. After a moment, Foch followed him inside and took a seat two rows behind him, next to an old man with a box of salted fish. It wasn't long before the engines growled to life and the ferry slid away from the dock.

Foch settled back for the ride, his gaze focused on the back of Wolf's head. The smell of fuel and dried fish soon became nauseating. The ferry pitched and heaved on the water, and his lunch of dolmas and espresso was threatening to come back up. Foch rose from his seat and scrambled outside. Standing at the rail, he gulped in a few breaths of fresh air and waited for the nausea to pass. At last it eased, and he reluctantly turned to go back into the cabin. He headed up the aisle, past Wolf—

Or the man he'd *thought* was Wolf.

He was wearing the same ratty Windbreaker, the same black fisherman's cap. But this man was clean shaven, younger. Definitely not the same man!

Foch glanced around the cabin. No Wolf. He hurried outside to the deck. No Wolf. He climbed the stairs to the upper level. Again, no Wolf.

He turned and saw the island of Paros receding behind them, and he let out a strangled curse. It was all a feint! They were still on the island—they had to be.

And I'm trapped on this boat to Piraeus.

Foch slapped the railing and cursed himself for his

own stupidity. Wolf had outsmarted him—again. The old professional using his bag of tricks. There was no point interrogating the man in the cabin; he was probably just some local dupe hired to switch places with Wolf for the ferry ride.

He looked at his watch and calculated how many hours it would take him to get back to the island via a hired boat. With any luck, he could be stalking them tonight. If they were still there. He'd find them, he vowed. Wolf might be a professional. But then, so was he.

FROM INSIDE A NEARBY CAFÉ, Richard watched the ferry glide out of the harbor and heaved a sigh of relief. The old bait and switch had worked; no one had followed him off the boat. He'd been suspicious of one man in particular—a balding fellow in nondescript tourist clothes. Richard had noticed how the man had scanned the boarding passengers, how his gaze had paused momentarily on Richard's face.

Yes, he was the one. The bait was laid out for him.

The switch was a snap.

Once inside the ferry cabin, Richard had tossed his cap and jacket on a seat, walked up the aisle, and exited out the other door. By prior arrangement, Sofia's brother—six foot one and with black hair—had slid into that same seat, donned the cap and jacket, and promptly cradled his face in his arms, as though to sleep.

Richard had waited behind some crates on deck just long enough for all the passengers to board. Then he'd simply walked off the boat.

No one had followed him.

He left the café and climbed into Sofia's car.

It was a six-mile drive to the cove. Sofia and her

brothers had *Melina,* the family fishing boat, ready to go, her engine running, her anchor line set to hoist. Richard scrambled out of the rowboat and up the rope ladder to *Melina*'s deck.

Beryl was waiting for him. He took her in his arms, hugged her, kissed her. "It's all right," he murmured. "I lost him."

"I was afraid I'd lose *you.*"

"Not a chance." He pulled back and smiled at her. With her black hair whipping in the wind, and her eyes the same crystalline green as the Aegean, she reminded him of some Greek goddess. Circe, Aphrodite. A woman who could hold a man forever bewitched.

The anchor thudded on deck. Sofia's brothers guided *Melina*'s bow around to face the open sea.

It started out a rough passage, the summer winds fierce and constant, the sea a rolling carpet of swells. But at sunset, as the sky deepened to a glorious shade of red, the wind suddenly died and the water turned glassy. Beryl and Richard stood on deck and gazed at the darkening silhouettes of the islands.

Sofia said, "We arrive late tonight."

"Piraeus?" asked Richard.

"No. Too busy. We pull in at Monemvassia where no one will see us."

"And then?"

"You go your way. We go ours. It is safer, for all of us." Sofia glanced toward the stern at her two brothers, who were laughing and clapping each other on the back. "Look at them! They think this is a nice little adventure! If they had seen Gerard's father..."

"Will you be all right?" asked Beryl.

Sofia looked at her. "I worry more about Gerard. They may be looking for him."

"I don't think so," said Richard. "He was only a boy when he left Paris. His testimony can't hurt them."

"He remembered enough to tell *you*," countered Sofia.

Richard shook his head. "But I'm not sure what any of it meant."

"Perhaps the killer knows. And he will be looking for Gerard next." Sofia glanced back across the stern, toward the island. Toward Gerard, who had refused to flee. "His stubbornness. It will get him killed," she muttered, and wandered away into the cabin.

"What do you think it meant?" asked Beryl. "That business about the short man with the briefcase? Was it just a payoff to Rideau, to keep him silent?"

"Partly."

"You think there was something else in that briefcase," she said. "Something besides money."

He turned and saw the glow of the sunset on her face, the intensity of her gaze. *She's quick,* he thought. *She knows exactly what I'm thinking.* He said, "I'm sure there was. I think the lover of our mysterious Mlle Scarlatti found himself in a very sticky situation. Two dead bodies in his garret, the police certain to be notified. He sees a way to extricate himself from two crises at once. He sends his man to pay off Rideau, asks him not to identify him to police."

"And the second crisis?"

"His status as a mole."

"Delphi?"

"Maybe he knew Intelligence was about to close in. So he places the NATO documents in a briefcase..."

"And has his hired man plant the briefcase in the garret," finished Beryl. "Near my father's body."

Richard nodded. *"That's* what Inspector Broussard

was trying to tell us—something about a briefcase. Remember that police photo of the murder scene? He kept pointing to an empty spot near the door. What if the briefcase was planted *after* that initial crime photo was taken? The inspector would have realized it was done postmortem.''

''But he couldn't pursue the matter, because French Intelligence confiscated the briefcase.''

''Exactly.''

''They assumed my father was the one who brought the documents into the garret.'' She looked at him, her eyes glittering with determination. ''How do we prove it? Any of it?''

''We identify Mlle Scarlatti's lover.''

''But our only witness was Rideau. And Gerard was just a boy. He scarcely remembers what the man looked like.''

''So we go to another source. A man who would know Delphi's true identity—his East German spymaster. Heinrich Leitner.''

She stared at him in surprise. ''Do you know how to reach him?''

''He's in a high-security prison in Berlin. Trouble is, German Intelligence won't exactly allow us free access to their prisoners.''

''As a diplomatic favor?''

His laugh was plainly skeptical. ''An ex-CIA agent isn't exactly on their most-favored list. Besides, Leitner might not want to see me. Still, it's a chance we'll take.'' He turned to gaze over the bow at the darkening sea.

He felt her move close beside him, felt her nearness as acutely as the warmth of the setting sun. It was enough to drive him crazy, having her so close and being unable to make love to her. He found himself counting the hours until they would be alone again, until he could undress her, make love to her. *And I once considered her too rich for my blood. Maybe she is. Maybe this is just a fever that'll burn itself out, leaving us both sadder and wiser. But for now she's all I think about, all I crave.*

"So that's where we're headed next," she whispered. "Berlin."

"There'll be risks." Their gazes met through the velvet dusk. "Things could go wrong...."

"Not while you're around," she said softly.

I hope you're right, he thought as he pulled her into his arms. *I hope to God you're right.*

THE DICE CLATTERED against the cell wall and came to rest with a five and a six showing.

"Ah-hah!" crowed Jordan, raising a fist in triumph. "What does that make it? Ten thousand francs? *Dix mille?*"

His cellmates, Leroi and Fofo, nodded resignedly.

Jordan held out his hand. "Pay up, gentlemen." Two grubby slips of paper were slapped into his palm. On each was written the number ten thousand. Jordan grinned. "Another round?"

Fofo shook the dice, threw them against the wall, and groaned. A three and a five. Leroi threw a pair of twos.

Jordan threw another five and six. His cellmates handed over two more grubby slips of paper. *Why, I'll be a millionaire by tomorrow,* Jordan rejoiced, looking down at the growing pile of IOUs. On paper, anyway. He picked up the dice and was about to make another toss when he heard footsteps approach.

Reggie Vane was standing outside the cell, holding a basket of smoked salmon and crackers. "Helena sent these over,'' he said as he slid the basket through the small opening at the bottom of the cell door. "Oh, and there's fresh linen, napkins and such. One can't dine properly on paper, can one?''

"Certainly not,'' agreed Jordan, gratefully accepting the basket of goodies. "You are a true friend, indeed, Reggie.''

"Yes, well…'' Reggie grinned and cleared his throat. "Anything for a child of Madeline's.''

"Any word from Uncle Hugh?''

"Still unreachable, according to your people at Chetwynd.''

Jordan set the basket down in frustration. "This is most bizarre! I'm in prison. Beryl's vanished. And Uncle Hugh's probably off on some classified mission for MI6.'' He began to pace the cell, oblivious to the fact that Fofo and Leroi were hungrily raiding the contents of the basket. "What about that bomb investigation? Anything new?''

"The two bombings are definitely linked. The devices were manufactured by the same hand. It appears someone's targeted both Beryl and the St. Pierres.''

"I think the target was Marie St. Pierre, in particular.'' Jordan stopped and looked at Reggie. "Let's say Marie *was* the target. What's the motive?''

Reggie shrugged. "She's not the sort of woman to pick up enemies.''

"You should be able to come up with an answer. She and your wife are best chums, after all. Helena must know who'd want to kill Marie.''

Reggie gave him a troubled look. "It's not as if there's any, well…proof.''

Jordan moved toward him. "What are you thinking?''

"Just rumors. Things Helena might have mentioned.''

"Was it about Philippe?"

Reggie looked down. "I feel a bit...well, ungentle-manly, bringing it up. You see, it happened years ago."

"What did?"

"The affair. Between Philippe and Nina."

Jordan stared at him through the bars. *There it is,* he thought. *There's the motive.* "How long have you known about this?" he asked.

"I heard about it fifteen, twenty years ago. You see, I couldn't understand why Helena disliked Nina so much. It was almost a...a hatred. You know how it is sometimes with females, all those catty looks. I assumed it was jealousy. My Helena's never been comfortable with more...well, attractive women. As a matter of fact, if I so much as glance at a pretty face, she gets down-right nasty about it."

"How did she learn about Philippe and Nina?"

"Marie told her."

"Who else knew about it?"

"I doubt there were many. Poor Marie's not one to advertise her humiliation. To have one's husband dal-lying with a...a piece of baggage like Nina!"

"Yet she stayed married to Philippe all these years."

"Yes, she's loyal that way. And what good would it do to make a public stink of it? Ruin his career? Now he's finance minister. Chances are, he'll go to the top. And Marie will be with him. So in the long run, it was worth it."

"If she lives to see it."

"You're not saying Philippe would kill his own wife? And why now, at this late date?"

"Perhaps she issued an ultimatum. Think about it, Reggie! Here he is, inches away from being prime minister. And Marie says, 'It's your mistress or me. Choose.'"

Reggie looked thoughtful. "If he chooses Nina, he'd have to get rid of his wife."

"Ah, but what if he chooses Marie? And Nina's the one left out in the cold?"

They frowned at each other through the bars.

"Call Daumier," said Jordan. "Tell him what you just told me, about the affair. And ask him to put a tail on Nina."

"You don't really think—"

"I think," said Jordan, "that we've been looking at this from the wrong angle entirely. The bombing wasn't a political act. All that Cosmic Solidarity rubbish was merely a smoke screen, to cover up the real reason for the attack."

"You mean it was personal?"

Jordan nodded. "Murder usually is."

THE FLIGHT TO BERLIN was half-empty, so the only logical reason that disheveled pair of passengers in row two should be sitting in first class was that they must have actually paid the fare, a fact the flight attendant found difficult to believe, considering their appearance. Both wore dark sunglasses, wrinkled clothes and unmistakable expressions of exhaustion. The man had a week's worth of dark stubble on his jaw. The woman was deeply sunburned and her black hair was tangled and powdered with dust. Their only carryon was the woman's purse, a battered straw affair coated with sand. The attendant glanced at the couple's ticket stubs. Athens—Rome—Berlin. With a forced smile, she asked them if they wished to order cocktails.

"Bloody Mary," said the woman in the Queen's perfect English.

"A Rob Roy," said the man. "Hold the bitters."

The woman went to fetch their drinks. When she returned, the man and woman were holding hands and looking at each other with the weary smiles of fellow survivors. They took their drinks from the tray.

"To our health?" the man asked.

"Definitely," the woman answered.

And, grinning, they both tipped back their glasses in a toast.

The meal cart was wheeled out and on it were lobster patties, crown roast of lamb, wild rice and mushroom caps. The couple ate double servings of everything and topped their dinner off with a split of wine. Then, like a pair of exhausted puppies, they curled up against each other and fell asleep.

They slept all the way to Berlin. Only when the plane rolled to a stop at the terminal did they jerk awake, both of them instantly alert and on guard. As the passengers filed out, the flight attendant kept her gaze on that rumpled pair from Athens. There was no telling who they were or what they might be up to. First-class passengers did not usually travel the world dressed like bums.

The couple was the last to disembark.

The attendant followed the pair onto the passenger ramp and stood watching as they walked toward a small crowd of greeters. They made it as far as the waiting area.

Two men stepped into their path. At once the couple halted and pivoted as though to flee back toward the plane. Three more men magically appeared, blocking off their escape. The couple was trapped.

The attendant caught a glimpse of the woman's panicked face, the man's grim expression of defeat. She had been sure there was something wrong about them. They were terrorists, perhaps, or international thieves. And there were the police to make the arrest. She watched as the pair was led away through the murmuring crowd. Definitely not first class, she thought with a sniff of satisfaction. Oh, yes, one could always tell.

RICHARD AND BERYL were shoved forward into a windowless room. "Stay here!" came the barked command, then the door was slammed shut behind them.

"They were waiting for us," said Beryl. "How did they know?"

Richard went to the door and tested the knob. "Dead bolt," he muttered. "We're locked in tight." In frustration, he began to circle the room, searching for another way out. "Somehow they knew we were coming to Berlin...."

"We paid for the tickets in cash. There was no way they could have known. And those were airport guards, Richard. If they want us dead, why bother to arrest us?"

"To keep you from getting your heads shot off," said a familiar voice. "That's why."

Beryl wheeled around in astonishment at the portly man who'd just opened the door. "Uncle *Hugh?*"

Lord Lovat scowled at his niece's wrinkled clothes and tangled hair. "You're a fine mess. Since when did you adopt the gypsy look?"

"Since we hitchhiked halfway across Greece. Credit cards, by the way, are *not* the preferred method of payment in small Greek towns."

"Well, you made it to Berlin." He glanced at Richard. "Good work, Wolf."

"I could've used some assistance," growled Richard.

"And we would've happily provided it. But we had no idea where to find you, until I spoke with your man, Sakaroff. He said you'd be headed for Berlin. We only just found out you'd gone via Athens."

"What are *you* doing in Berlin, Uncle Hugh?" demanded Beryl. "I thought you were off on another one of your secret missions."

"I'm fishing."

"Not for fish, obviously."

"For answers. Which I'm hoping Heinrich Leitner will provide." He took another look at Beryl's clothes and sighed. "Let's get to the hotel and clean you both up. Then we'll pay a visit to Herr Leitner's prison cell."

"You have clearance to speak to him?" said Richard in surprise.

"What do you think I've been doing here these last few days? Wining and dining the necessary officials." He waved them out of the room. "The car's waiting."

In Uncle Hugh's hotel suite, they showered off three days' worth of Greek dust and sand. A fresh set of clothes was delivered to the room, courtesy of the concierge—sober business attire, outfits appropriate for a visit to a high-security prison.

"How do we know Leitner will tell us the truth?" asked Richard as they rode in the limousine to the prison.

"We don't," said Hugh. "We don't even know how much he *can* tell us. He oversaw Paris operations from East Berlin, so he'd be acquainted with code names, but not faces."

"Then we may come away with nothing."

"As I said, Wolf, it's a fishing expedition. Sometimes you reel in an old tire. Sometimes a salmon."

"Or, in this case, a mole."

"If he's cooperative."

"Are you prepared to hear the truth?" asked Richard. The question was directed at Hugh, but his gaze was on Beryl. Delphi could still be Bernard or Madeline, his eyes said.

"Right now, I'd say ignorance is far more dangerous," Hugh observed. "And there's Jordan to consider. I have people watching out for him. But there's always the chance things could go wrong."

Things have already gone wrong, thought Beryl, looking out the car window at the drab and dreary buildings of East Berlin.

The prison was even more forbidding—a massive concrete fortress surrounded by electrified fences. The very best of security, she noted, as they moved through the gauntlet of checkpoints and metal detectors. Uncle Hugh had obviously been expected, and he was greeted with the chilling disdain of an old Cold War enemy. Only when they'd arrived at the commandant's office was any courtesy extended to them. Glasses of hot tea were passed around, cigars offered to the men. Hugh accepted; Richard declined.

"Up until recently, Leitner was most uncooperative," said the commandant, lighting a cigar. "At first, he denied his role entirely. But our files on him are proof positive. He *was* in charge of Paris operations."

"Has Leitner provided any names?" asked Richard.

The commandant peered at Richard through the drifting cloud of cigar smoke. "You were CIA, were you not, Mr. Wolf?"

Richard gave only the briefest nod of acknowledgment. "It was years ago. I've left the business."

"But you understand how it is, to be dogged by one's past associations."

"Yes, I understand."

The commandant rose and went to look out his window at the barbed-wire fence enclosing his prison kingdom. "Berlin is filled with people running from their shadows. Their old lives. Whether it was for money or for ideology, they served a master. And now the master is dead and they hide from the past."

"Leitner's already in prison. He has nothing to lose by talking to us."

"But the people who worked for him—the ones not yet exposed—they have everything to lose. Now the East German files are open. And every day, some curious citizen opens one of those files and discovers the truth. Realizes that a friend or husband or lover was working for the enemy." The commandant turned, his pale blue eyes focused on Richard. "That's why Leitner has been reluctant to give names—to protect his old agents."

"But you say he's more cooperative these days?"

"In recent weeks, yes."

"Why?"

The commandant paused. "A bad heart, the doctors say. It fails, little by little. In two months, three…" He shrugged. "Leitner sees the end coming. And in exchange for a few last comforts, he's sometimes willing to talk."

"Then he may give us answers."

"If he is in the mood." The commandant turned to the door. "So, let us see what sort of mood Herr Leitner is in today."

They followed him down secured corridors, past mounted cameras and grim-faced guards, into the very core of the complex. Here there were no windows; the air itself seemed hermetically sealed from the outside world. *From here there is no escape,* thought Beryl. *Except through death.*

They stopped at cell number five. Two guards, each with his own key, opened separate locks. The door swung open.

Inside, on a wooden chair, sat an old man. Oxygen tubing snaked from his nostrils. His regulation prison garb—tan shirt and pants, no belt—hung loosely on his shrunken frame. The fluorescent lights gave his face a yellowish cast. Beside the man's chair stood an oxygen tank; except for the hiss of the gas flowing through his nasal prongs, the room was silent.

The commandant said, "*Guten Tag,* Heinrich."

Leitner said nothing. Only by a brief flicker of his eyes did he acknowledge the greeting.

"I have brought with me today, Lord Lovat, from England. You are familiar with the name?"

Again, a flicker in the old man's blue eyes. And a whisper, barely audible, "MI6."

"That's right," said Hugh. "Since retired."

"So am I," was the reply, not without a trace of humor. Leitner's gaze shifted to Beryl and Richard.

"My niece," said Hugh. "And a former associate. Richard Wolf."

"CIA?" said Leitner.

Richard nodded. "Also retired."

Leitner managed a faint smile. "How differently we enjoy our retirements." He looked once again at Hugh. "A social call on an old enemy? How thoughtful."

"Not a social call, exactly," said Hugh.

Leitner began to cough, and the effort seemed almost too much for him; when at last he settled back into his chair, his face had a distinctly blue tinge. "What is it you wish to know?"

"The identity of your double agent in Paris. Code name Delphi."

Leitner didn't speak.

"Surely the name is familiar, Herr Leitner. Over the years, Delphi must have passed on invaluable documents. He was your link to NATO operations. Don't you remember?"

"That was twenty years ago," murmured Leitner. "The world has changed."

"We want only his name. That's all."

"So you may put Delphi in a cage like this? Shut away from the sun and air?"

"So we can stop the killing," said Richard.

Leitner frowned. "What killing?"

"It's going on right now. A French agent, murdered in Paris. A man, shot to death in Greece. It's all linked to Delphi."

"That cannot be possible," said Leitner.

"Why?"

"Delphi has been put to sleep."

Hugh frowned at him. "Are you saying he's dead?"

"But that makes no sense," said Richard. "If Delphi's dead, why is the killing still going on?"

"Perhaps," said Leitner, "it has nothing at all to do with Delphi."

"Perhaps you are lying," said Richard.

Leitner smiled. "Always a possibility." Suddenly he began to cough again; it had the gurgling sound of a man drowning in his own secretions. When at last he could speak, it was only between gasps for oxygen. "Delphi was a paid recruit," he said. "Not a true believer. We preferred the believers, you see. They did not cost as much.''

"So he did it for money?'' asked Richard.

"A rather generous sum, over the years.''

"When did it stop?''

"When it became a risk to all involved. So Delphi ended the association. Covered all tracks before your counterintelligence could close in.''

"Is that why my parents were killed?'' asked Beryl. "Because Delphi had to cover his tracks?''

Leitner frowned. "Your parents?''

"Bernard and Madeline Tavistock. They were shot to death in a garret in Pigalle.''

"But that was a murder and suicide. I saw the report.''

"Or were they both murdered? By Delphi?''

Leitner looked at Hugh. "I gave no such order. And that is the truth.''

"Meaning some of what you told us is *not* the truth?'' Richard probed.

Leitner took a deep breath of oxygen and painfully wheezed it out. "Truth, lies,'' he whispered. "What does it matter now?'' He sank back in his chair and looked at the commandant. "I wish to rest. Take these people away.''

"Herr Leitner,'' said Richard, "I'll ask this one last time. Is Delphi really dead?''

Leitner met his gaze with one so steady, so unflinching, it seemed that surely he was about to tell the truth. But the answer he gave was puzzling at best.

"Dormant,'' he said. "That is the word I would use.''

"So he's not dead.''

"For your purposes,'' Leitner said with a smile, "he is.''

11

"A sleeper. That's what Delphi must be," said Richard. They had not dared discuss the matter in the limousine—no telling whom their driver really worked for. But here, in a noisy restaurant, with waiters whisking back and forth, Richard could finally spell out his theories. "I'm sure that's what he meant."

"A sleeper?" asked Beryl.

"Someone they recruit years in advance," said her uncle. "As a young adult. The person may be kept inactive for years. They live a normal life, try to gain influence in some trusted position. And then the signal's sent. And the sleeper's activated."

"So that's what he meant by dormant," said Beryl. "Not dead. But not active, either."

"Precisely."

"For this sleeper to be of any use to them, he'd have to be in a position of influence. Or close to it," said Beryl thoughtfully.

"Which describes Stephen Sutherland to a T," said Richard. "American ambassador. Access to all security data."

"It also describes Philippe St. Pierre," said Hugh. "Minister of Finance. In line for French prime minister—"

"And extremely vulnerable to blackmail," added Beryl, thinking of Nina and Philippe. And of Anthony, the son born of their illicit affair.

"I'll contact Daumier," said Hugh. "Have St. Pierre vetted again."

"While he's at it," said Richard, "ask him to vet Nina."

"Nina?"

"Talk about positions of influence! An ambassador's wife. Mistress to St. Pierre. She could've heard secrets from both sides of the bed."

Hugh shook his head. "Considering her double digit IQ, Nina Sutherland's the last person I'd expect to work for Intelligence."

"And the one person who'd get away with it."

Hugh glanced around impatiently for the waiter. "We have to leave for Paris at once," he said, and slapped enough marks on the table to pay for their coffees. "There's no telling what's happening to Jordan."

"If it is Nina, do you think she could get at Jordan?" asked Beryl.

"All these years, I've overlooked Nina Sutherland," said Hugh. "I'm not about to make the same mistake now."

DAUMIER MET THEM at Orly Airport. "I have reexamined the security files on Philippe and Nina," he said as they rode together in his limousine. "St. Pierre is clean. His record is unblemished. If he is the sleeper, we have no evidence of it."

"And Nina?"

Daumier gave a deep sigh. "Our dear Nina presents a problem. There was an item that was not addressed in her earlier vetting. She was eighteen when she first appeared on the London stage. A small part, quite insignificant, but it launched her acting career. At that time, she had an affair with one of her fellow actors—an East German by the name of Berte Klausner. He claimed he was a defector. But three years later, he vanished from England and was never heard from again.''

''A recruiter?'' asked Richard.

''Possibly.''

''How on earth did this little affair make it past Nina's vetting?'' asked Beryl.

Daumier shrugged. ''It was noted when Nina and Sutherland were married. By then she'd retired from the theater to become a diplomat's wife. She didn't serve in any official capacity. As a rule, security checks on wives—especially if they are American—are not as demanding. So Nina slipped through.''

''Then you have evidence of possible recruitment,'' said Beryl. ''And she could have had access to NATO secrets by way of her husband. But you can't prove she's Delphi. Nor can you prove she's a murderer.''

''True,'' admitted Daumier.

''I doubt you'll get her to confess, either,'' said Richard. ''Nina was once an actress. She could probably brazen her way through anything.''

''That is why I suggest the following action,'' said Daumier. ''A trap. Tempt her into making a move.''

''With what bait?'' asked Richard.

''Jordan.''

''That's out of the question!'' said Beryl.

''He has already agreed to it. This afternoon, he will be released from prison. We move him to a hotel where he will attempt to be conspicuous.''

Hugh laughed. ''Not much of a stretch for our Jordan.''

''My men will be stationed at strategic points in the hotel. If—and when—an attack occurs, we will be prepared.''

''Things could go wrong,'' said Beryl. ''He could be hurt—''

"He could be hurt in prison, as well," said Daumier. "At least this may provide us with answers."

"And possibly a dead body."

"Have you a better suggestion?"

Beryl glanced at Richard, then at her uncle. They were both silent. *I can't believe they're agreeing to this,* she thought.

She looked at Daumier. "What do you want *me* to do?"

"You'd complicate things, Beryl," said Hugh. "It's better for you to stay out of the picture."

"The Vanes' house has excellent security," said Daumier. "Reggie and Helena have already agreed that you should stay with them."

"But I haven't agreed," said Beryl.

"Beryl." It was Richard. He spoke quietly. Unbendingly. "Jordan will be protected from all angles. They'll be ready for the attack. This time, nothing will go wrong."

"Can you guarantee it? Can any of you?"

There was silence.

"Nothing can be guaranteed, Beryl," said Daumier quietly. "We have to take this chance. It may be the only way to catch Delphi."

In frustration, she looked out the window, thinking of the options. Realizing there were none—not if any of this was to be resolved—she said softly, "I'll agree to it on one condition."

"What's that?"

She looked at Richard. "I want you to be with him. I trust you, Richard. If you're watching Jordan, I know he'll be all right."

Richard nodded. "I'll be right by his side."

"Who else knows about this plan?" asked Hugh.

"Just a few of my people," said Daumier. "I was

careful not to let any of this leak out to Philippe St. Pierre.''

"What do Reggie and Helena know?'' asked Beryl.

"Only that you need a safe place to stay. They are doing this as a favor to old friends.''

As an old friend was exactly the way Beryl was greeted upon arrival at the Vanes' residence. As soon as the gates closed behind the limousine, and they were inside the high walls of the compound, she was swept into the comfort of their home. It all seemed so safe, so familiar: the English wallpaper, the tray of tea and biscuits on the end table, the vases of flowers perfuming the rooms. Surely nothing could hurt her here....

There was scarcely time to say goodbye to Richard. While Daumier and Hugh waited outside in the car, Richard pulled Beryl into his arms. They shared a last embrace, a last kiss.

"You'll be perfectly safe here,'' he whispered. "Don't leave the compound for any reason.''

"*You're* the one I worry about. You and Jordan.''

"I won't let anything happen to him.'' He tipped up her chin and pressed his lips to hers. "And that,'' he murmured, "is a promise.'' He touched her face and grinned, a confident grin that made her believe anything was possible.

Then he walked away.

She stood on the doorstep and watched the car drive out of the compound, saw the iron gates close shut behind it. *I'm with you,* she thought. *Whatever happens, Richard, I'm right there beside you.*

"Come, Beryl,'' said Reggie, affectionately draping his arm around her shoulders. "I have an instinct about these things. And I'm positive everything will turn out just fine.''

She looked up at Reggie's smiling face. *Thank God*

for old friends, she thought. And she let him lead her
back into the house.

JORDAN WAS DOWN on all fours in his jail cell, rattling
a pair of dice in his hand. His cellmates, the two shaggy,
ripe-smelling ruffians—or could that odor be Jordan's?—hovered behind him, stamping their feet and
yelling. Jordan threw the dice; they tumbled across the
floor and clattered against the wall. Two fives.

"*Zut alors!*" groaned the cellmates.

Jordan raised his fist in triumph. "*Oh, là là!*" Only
then did he see his visitors staring at him through the
bars. "Uncle Hugh!" he said, jumping to his feet. "Am
I glad to see you!"

Hugh's disbelieving gaze scanned the interior of the
cell. Over the cot was draped a red-checked tablecloth,
laid out with platters of sliced beef, poached salmon, a
bowl of grapes. A bottle of wine sat chilling in a plastic
bucket. And on a chair beside the bed was neatly stacked
a half dozen leather-bound books and a vase of roses.
"This is a prison?" quipped Hugh.

"Oh, I've spruced it up a bit," said Jordan. "The food
was wretched, so I had some delivered. Brought in the
reading material, as well. But," he said with a sigh,
"I'm afraid it's still very much a prison." He tapped the
bars. "As you can see." He looked at Daumier. "So,
are we ready?"

"If you are still willing."

"Haven't much of a choice, have I? Considering the
alternative."

The guard unlocked the door and Jordan stepped out,
carrying his bundle of street clothes. But he couldn't
walk away without a proper goodbye to his cellmates.
He turned and found Fofo and Leroi staring at him
mournfully. "Afraid this is it, fellows," he said. "It's

been—'' he thought a moment, struggling to come up with the right adjective ''—a uniquely fragrant experience.'' On impulse, he tossed his tailored linen jacket to the disbelieving Fofo. ''I think that might fit you,'' he said. ''Wear it in good health.'' Then, with a farewell wave, he followed his companions out of the building and into Daumier's limousine.

They drove him to the Ritz—same floor, different room. A fashionably appropriate place for an assassination, he thought wryly as he came out of the shower and dressed in a fresh suit.

''Bulletproof windows,'' said Daumier. ''Microphones in the front room. And there'll be two men, stationed across the hall. Also, you should have this.'' Daumier reached into his briefcase and pulled out an automatic pistol. He handed it to Jordan, who regarded the weapon with a raised eyebrow.

''Worst-case scenario? I'll actually have to defend myself?''

''A precaution. You know how to use one?''

''I suppose I can muddle through,'' said Jordan, expertly sliding in the ammunition clip. He looked at Richard. ''Now what happens?''

''Have a meal in the restaurant downstairs,'' said Richard. ''Take your time, make sure you're seen by as many employees as possible. Leave a big tip, be conspicuous. And return to your room.''

''And then?''

''We wait and see who comes knocking.''

''What if no one does?''

''They will,'' said Daumier grimly. ''I guarantee it.''

AMIEL FOCH RECEIVED the call a mere thirty minutes later. It was the hotel maid—the same woman who'd been so useful a week before, when he'd needed access to the Tavistocks' suites.

"He is back," she said. "The Englishman."

"Jordan Tavistock? But he's in prison—"

"I have just seen him in the hotel. Room 315. He seems to be alone."

Foch grimaced in amazement. Perhaps those Tavistock family connections had come through. Now he was a free man—and a vulnerable target. "I need to get into his room," said Foch. "Tonight."

"I cannot do it."

"You did it before. I'll pay double."

The maid gave a snort of disgust. "It's still not enough. I could lose my job."

"I'll pay more than enough. Just get me the passkey again."

There was a silence. Then the woman said, "First, you leave the envelope. Then, I get you the key."

"Agreed," said Foch, and hung up.

He immediately made a call to Anthony Sutherland. "Jordan Tavistock is out of prison," he said. "He's taken a room at the Ritz. Do you still wish me to proceed?"

"This time, I want it done right. Even if I have to supervise it myself. When do we move?"

"I do not think it is wise—"

"When do we move?"

Foch swallowed his angry response. It was a mistake letting Sutherland take part. The boy was just a voyeur, eager to experience the ultimate power—the taking of a life. Foch had sensed it years ago, from the day they'd first met. He'd known just by looking at him that he'd be addicted to thrills, to intensity, be it sexual or otherwise.

Now the young man wished to experience something novel. Murder. This was a mistake, surely, a mistake....

"Remember who's paying your fees, M. Foch," said Sutherland. "And outrageous fees, too. I'm the one who makes the decisions, not you."

Even if they are stupid, dangerous decisions? wondered Foch. At last he said, "It will be tonight. We wait for him to sleep."

"Tonight," agreed Sutherland. "I'll be there."

AT ELEVEN-THIRTY, JORDAN turned off the lights in his hotel room, stuffed three pillows under the bedspread, and fluffed it all up so that it vaguely resembled a human shape. Then he took his position by the door, next to Richard. In the darkness they sat and waited for something to happen. Anything to happen. So far, the evening had been a screaming bore. Daumier had made him a prisoner of his own hotel room. He'd watched two hours of telly, glanced through *Paris Match,* and completed five crossword puzzles. *What must I do to attract this assassin?* he wondered. *Send him an engraved invitation?*

Sighing, he leaned back against the wall. "Is this the sort of thing you used to do, Wolf?" he murmured.

"A lot of waiting around. A lot of boredom," said Richard. "And every so often, a moment of abject terror."

"What made you leave the business? The boredom or the terror?"

Richard paused. "The rootlessness."

"Ah. The man longs for home and hearth." Jordan smiled. "So tell me, does my sister figure into the equation?"

"Beryl is...one of a kind."

"You didn't answer the question."

"The answer is, I don't know," Richard admitted. He squared his shoulders to ease the tension in his muscles. "Sometimes, it seems like the world's worst possible match. Sure, I can put on a tuxedo, stand around swirling a snifter of brandy. But I don't fool anyone, least of all myself. And certainly not Beryl."

"You really think that's what she needs? A fop in black tie?"

"I don't know what she needs. Or what she wants. I know she probably thinks she's in love. But how the devil can anyone know for certain, when things are so crazy?"

"You wait till things *aren't* so crazy. Then you decide."

"And live with the consequences."

"You're already lovers, aren't you?"

Richard looked at him in surprise. "Are you always so inquisitive about your sister's love life?"

"I'm her closest male relative. And therefore responsible for defending her honor." Jordan laughed softly. "Someday, Wolf, I may have to shoot you. That is, if I survive the night."

They both laughed. And they settled back to wait.

At 1:00 a.m., they heard the faint click of a door closing in the hallway. Had someone just stepped out of the stairwell? Instantly Jordan snapped fully alert, his adrenaline kicking into overdrive. He whispered, "Did you hear—"

Richard was already rising to a crouch. Through the darkness, Jordan could sense the other man tensing for action. Where were Daumier's agents? he wondered frantically. Were the two of them on their own?

A key grated slowly in the lock. Jordan froze, heart thundering, the sweat breaking out on his palms. The gun felt slippery in his grasp.

The door swung open; two figures slowly edged into the room. The first took aim at the bed. A single bullet was all the gunman managed to squeeze off before Richard flew at him sideways. The force of his assault sent both men thudding to the floor.

Jordan shoved his gun into the ribs of the second intruder and barked, "Freeze!"

To Jordan's astonishment, the man didn't freeze, but turned and fled from the room.

Jordan dashed after him into the hall, just in time to see the two French agents tackle the fugitive to the floor. They yanked him, kicking and squirming, back to his feet. In amazement, Jordan stared at the man. *"Anthony?"*

"I'm bleeding!" spat Anthony Sutherland. "They broke my nose! I think they broke my nose!"

"Keep squealing, and they'll break a lot more," growled Richard.

Jordan turned and saw Richard haul the gunman out of the room. He yanked his head back, so Jordan could see his face. "Take a good look. Recognize him?"

"Why, it's my bogus attorney," said Jordan. "M. Jarre."

Richard nodded and forced the balding Frenchman to the floor. "Now let's find out his real name."

"IT'S EXTRAORDINARY," mused Reggie, "how very much you look like your mother."

The butler had long since cleared away the coffee cups, and Helena had vanished upstairs to see to the guest room. Beryl and Reggie sat alone together, enjoying a nip of brandy in his wood-paneled library. A fire crackled in the hearth—not for warmth on this July night, but for reassurance, the ancestral comfort of flames against the night, against the world's evils.

Beryl cradled the brandy snifter in her hands and watched the reflection of firelight in the golden liquid. She said, "When I remember her, it's from a child's point of view. So I remember only the things a child finds important. Her smile. The softness of her hands."

"Yes, yes. That was Madeline."

"I've been told she was quite enchanting."

"She was," said Reggie softly. "She was the loveliest, most extraordinary woman I've ever known...."

Beryl looked up and saw that he was staring at the fire as though seeing, in its flames, the faces of old ghosts. She gave him a fond look. "Mother told me once that you were her oldest and dearest friend."

"Did she?" Reggie smiled. "Yes, I suppose that's true. Did you know we played together, as children. In Cornwall..." He blinked and she thought she saw the faint gleam of tears on his lashes. "I was the first, you know," he murmured. "Before Bernard. Before..." Sighing, he sank back in his chair. "But that was a long time ago."

"You still think of her a great deal."

"It's difficult not to." He drained his brandy glass. Unsteadily he poured another—his third. "Every time I look at you, I think, 'There's Madeline, come back to life.' And I remember how much, how very much I miss her—" Suddenly he stiffened and glanced at the doorway. Helena was standing there, wearily shaking her head. "You've had more than enough for tonight, Reggie."

"It's only my third."

"And how many more will come after that one?"

"Bloody few, if you have your way."

Helena came into the room and took his arm. "Come, darling. You've kept Beryl up long enough. It's time for bed."

"It's only one o'clock."

"Beryl's tired. And you should be considerate."

Reggie looked at their guest. "Oh. Oh, yes, perhaps you're right." He rose to his feet and moved on unsteady legs toward Beryl. She turned her face as he bent over to plant a kiss on her cheek. It was a wet, sloppy kiss, heavy with the smell of brandy, and she had to suppress the urge to pull away. He straightened, and once again she saw the sheen of tears in his eyes. "Good night, dear," he murmured. "You'll be perfectly safe with us."

With a sense of pity, Beryl watched the old man shuffle out of the library.

"He's simply not able to tolerate spirits the way he used to," said Helena, sighing. "The years pass, you know, and he forgets that things change. Including his capacity for liquor." She gave Beryl a rueful smile. "I do hope he didn't bore you too much."

"Not at all. We talked about Mother. He said I remind him of her."

Helena nodded. "Yes, you do resemble her. Of course, I didn't know her nearly as well as Reggie did." She sat down on the armrest of a chair. "I remember the first time I met her. It was at my wedding. Madeline and Bernard were there, practically newlyweds themselves. You could see it, just by the way they looked at each other. Quite a lovely couple..." Helena picked up Reggie's brandy snifter, tidied the table. "When we met again in Paris, it was fifteen years later, and she hadn't aged a bit. It was eerie how unchanged she was. When all the rest of us felt so acutely the passage of time."

There was a long pause. Then Beryl asked, "Did she have a lover?" The question was asked softly, so softly it was almost swallowed in the gloom of that library.

The silence that followed stretched on so long, she thought perhaps her words had gone unnoticed. But then

Helena said, "It shouldn't surprise you, should it? Madeline had that magic about her. That certain something the rest of us seem to lack. It's a matter of luck, you know. It's not something one achieves through effort or study. It's in one's genes. An inheritance, like a silver spoon in one's mouth."

"My mother wasn't born with a silver spoon."

"She didn't need one. She had that magic, instead." Abruptly Helena turned to leave. But in the doorway she caught herself and looked back at Beryl with a smile. "I'll see you in the morning. Good night."

Beryl nodded. "Good night, Helena."

For a long time, Beryl frowned at the empty doorway and listened to Helena ascend the stairs. She went to the hearth and stared at the dying embers. She thought of her mother, wondered if Madeline had ever stood here, in this library, in this house. Yes, of course she would have. Reggie was her oldest friend. They would have visited back and forth, the two couples, as they had in England years before....

Before Helena had insisted Reggie accept the Paris post.

The question suddenly came to her: *Why?* Was there some unspoken reason the Vanes had suddenly left England? Helena had grown up in Buckinghamshire; her ancestral home was a mere two miles from Chetwynd. Surely it must have been difficult to pack up her household, to leave behind all that was familiar, and move to a city where she couldn't even speak the language. One didn't blithely make such a move.

Unless one was fleeing *from* something.

Beryl's head lifted. She found herself staring at a ridiculous statuette on the mantelpiece—a fat little man holding a rifle. It had the inscription: "Reggie Vane—most likely to shoot his own foot. Tremont Gun Club."

Lined up beside it were various knickknacks from Reggie's past—a soccer medal, an old photo of a cricket team, a petrified frog. Judging by the items on display, this must be Reggie's private abode, the room to which he retreated from the world. The room that would hold his secrets.

She scanned the photos, and nowhere did she see a picture of Helena. Nor was there one on the desk or on the bookshelves—a fact she thought odd, for she remembered her father's library and all the snapshots of Madeline he kept so conspicuously in view. She moved to Reggie's cherry desk and quietly began to open the drawers. The first revealed the expected clutter of pens and paper clips. She opened the second and saw only a sheaf of cream-colored stationery and an address book. She closed the drawers and began to circle the room, thinking, *This is where you keep your most private treasures. The memories you hide, even from your wife....*

Her gaze came to rest on the leather footstool. It appeared to be a matched set with the easy chair, but it had been moved out of position, and instead sat at the side of the chair where it served no purpose...except to stand on.

She glanced directly up at the mahogany breakfront that stood against the wall. The shelves were filled with antique books, protected behind glass doors. The cabinet was at least eight feet tall, and on top was a matched pair of china bowls.

Beryl pushed the footstool over to the breakfront, climbed onto the stool, and reached up to retrieve the first bowl. It was empty and coated in dust. So was the second bowl. But as she slid the bowl back onto the cabinet, she met resistance. She reached back as far as she could, and her fingers met something flat and leathery. She grasped the edge and pulled it off the cabinet.

It was a photo album.

She took it over to the hearth and sat down by the dying fire. There she opened the cover to the first picture in the album. It was of a laughing, black-haired girl. The girl was twelve years old perhaps, and sitting on a swing, her skirt bunched up hoydenishly around her thighs, her bare legs dangling. On the next page was another photo—the same girl, a bit older now, dressed in May Day finery, flowers woven into her tangled hair. More photos, all of the black-haired girl: clad in waders and fishing in a stream, waving from a car, hanging upside down from a tree branch. And last—a wedding photo. It had been torn jaggedly in two, so that the groom was missing, and only the bride remained.

For an eternity, Beryl stared at the face she knew from her childhood—the face so very much like her own. She touched the smiling lips, traced the upswept tendrils of black hair. She thought about how it must be for a man to so desperately love a woman. To lose her to another man. To flee from those memories of her to a foreign city, only to have her reappear in that same city. And to find that, even fifteen years later, the feelings remain, and there is nothing you can do to ease your anguish, nothing at all...so long as she is alive.

Beryl shut the album and went to the telephone. She didn't know how to reach Richard, so she dialed Daumier's number instead and was greeted by a recorded message, intoned in businesslike French.

After the beep, she said, "Claude, it's Beryl. I have to speak to you at once. I think I've found some new evidence. Please, come get me! As soon as you—" She stopped, her hand suddenly frozen on the receiver. What was that click on the line?

She listened for other sounds, but heard only the pounding of her own heart—and silence. She hung up.

The extension, she thought. Someone had been listening on the extension.

Quickly she rose to her feet. *I can't stay here, not in this house. Not under this roof. Not when I know he could have been the one.*

Clutching the album firmly in her arms, she left Reggie's library and hurried across the foyer. After disarming the security system, she stepped out the front door.

Outside, it was a cool night, the sky clear, the stars faintly twinkling against the distant haze of city light. She looked across the stone courtyard and saw that the iron gates were closed—no doubt locked, as well. As a bank executive in Paris, Reggie was a prime target for terrorists; he would install the very best security for his home.

I have to get out of here, she determined. *Without anyone knowing.*

And then what? Thumb a ride to the nearest police station? Daumier's flat? *Anywhere but here.*

She traced the perimeter of the courtyard, scarching the high wall for a doorway, an exit. She spotted another gate, but it, too, was locked. No way around it, she thought. She'd have to climb over. Quickly she scanned the trees and spotted an apple tree with a branch overhanging the wall. Clutching the photo album in one hand, she scrambled up onto the lowest branch. It was an easy climb to the next branch, and the next, but every movement made the tree sway and sent apples thudding noisily to the ground. At the top of the wall, she tossed the album down on the other side and dropped to the ground beside it. At once she scooped up the album and turned toward the road.

The blinding beam of a flashlight made her freeze.

"So it's not a burglar after all," said a voice. "What on earth are you doing, Beryl?"

Squinting against the light, Beryl could barely make
out Helena's silhouette standing before her. "I...I
wanted to take a walk. But the gate was locked."

"I would have opened it for you."

"I didn't want to wake you." She turned her gaze
from the flashlight. "Please, could you drop the torch?
It hurts my eyes."

The beam slowly fell, and stopped at the photo album
in Beryl's arms. Beryl had clasped the album to her
chest, hoping Helena hadn't recognized it, but it was too
late. She had already seen it.

"Where was it?" asked Helena softly. "Where did
you find it?"

"The library," said Beryl. No point in lying now; the
evidence was there, plainly in her grasp.

"All these years," murmured Helena. "He kept it all
these years. And he swore to me—"

"What, Helena? What did he swear to?"

There was silence. "That he no longer loved her,"
came the whispered answer. Then a laugh, full of self-
mockery. "I've lost out to a ghost. It was hopeless
enough when she was alive. But now she's dead, and I
can't fight back. The dead, you see, don't grow old.
They stay young and beautiful. And perfect."

Beryl took a step forward, her arms extended in sympathy. "They weren't lovers, Helena. I know they
weren't."

"I was never perfect enough."

"But he married you. There must have been love involved—"

Helena stepped away, angrily brushing off Beryl's offer of comfort. "Not love! It was spite. Some stupid,
masculine gesture to show her he couldn't be hurt. We
were married a month after she was. I was his conso-
lation prize, you see. I gave him all the right connec-

tions. And the money. He happily accepted those. But he never really wanted my love."

Again, Beryl tried to reach out to her; again, Helena rebuffed the gesture. Beryl said softly, "It's time to move on, Helena. Make your own life, without him. While you're still young…"

"He *is* my life."

"But all these years, you must have known! You must have suspected that Reggie was the one who—"

"Not Reggie."

"Helena, please think about it!"

"Not Reggie."

"He was obsessed, unable to let her go! To let another man have her—"

"It was me."

Those three words, uttered so quietly, chilled Beryl's blood to ice. She stared at the silhouette standing before her, her thoughts instantly shifting to ones of escape. She could flee down the road, pound at the nearest door…. She shifted onto the balls of her feet and was about to make a dash past Helena, when she heard the click of the pistol hammer.

"You look so very much like her," whispered Helena. "When I first saw you, years ago at Chetwynd, it was almost as if she'd come back. And now, I have to kill her all over again."

"But I'm not Madeline—"

"It makes no difference now who you are. Because you know." Helena raised her arm and Beryl saw, through the shadows, the faint gleam of the gun in her hand. "The garage, Beryl," she said. "We're going for a drive."

12

"Amiel Foch," said Daumier, flipping through a file folder. "Age forty-six, formerly with French Intelligence. Presumed dead three years ago, after a helicopter crash off Cyprus—"

"He faked his own death?" asked Richard.

Daumier nodded. "It is not an easy matter to resign from Intelligence and simply start work as a mercenary. One would be subject to constraints."

"But if one is declared dead—"

"Precisely." Daumier skimmed the next page and stopped. "Here it is," he said. "The link we have been searching for. In 1972, M. Foch served as our liaison to the American mission. It seems there was a telephone threat against Ambassador Sutherland's family. For several years, Amiel Foch remained in contact with the Sutherland household. He was later reassigned to other duties, until his...death."

"When he became available for private clients. To perform any service," said Hugh.

"Including assassination." Daumier closed the folder and said to his assistant, "Bring in Mrs. Sutherland."

The woman who walked through the door was the same brash and confident Nina Sutherland that Richard had always known. She swept into the room, glanced around with disdain at her audience, then gracefully settled into a chair. "A bit late in the day for a command performance, don't you think?" she asked.

And a performance was just what they were going to get, thought Richard. Unless they shook her up. He pulled up a chair and sat down, facing her. "You know that Anthony's been taken into custody?"

A flicker of fear—just a flicker—rippled through her eyes. "It's a mistake, of course. He's never done anything wrong in his life."

"Murder through hire? Contracts with assassins?" Richard raised an eyebrow. "Ironclad charges, multiple witnesses. I'd say this is serious enough to warrant a very long stay behind bars."

"But he's only a boy and not—"

"He's of age. And fully responsible for his crimes." Richard glanced at Daumier. "Claude and I were just discussing what a shame it was. To be locked up so young. He'll be, how old when he's released, Claude? Fifty, do you think?"

"I would guess closer to sixty," said Daumier.

"Sixty." Richard shook his head and sighed. "His whole life behind him. No wife. No children." Richard looked Nina sympathetically in the eyes. "No grandchildren..."

Nina's face had turned ashen. She said in a whisper, "What do you want from me?"

"Cooperation."

"And what's my payback?"

"We can be lenient," said Daumier. "After all, he *is* just a boy."

Swallowing hard, Nina looked away. "It's not his fault. He doesn't deserve to be—"

"He's responsible for the deaths of two French agents. And the attempted murders of Marie St. Pierre and Jordan."

"He didn't do anything!"

"But he hired Amiel Foch to do his dirty work. What kind of a monster did you raise, Nina?"

"He was only trying to protect *me!*"

"From what?"

Nina's head drooped. "The past," she whispered. "It never goes away. Everything else changes, but the past..."

The past, thought Richard, remembering Heinrich Leitner's words. *We're always in its shadow.* "You were Delphi," he said. "Weren't you?"

Nina said nothing.

He leaned forward, and his voice dropped to a quiet, almost intimate murmur. "Perhaps it started out as a bit of a lark," he suggested. "An amusing game of spies and counterspies. Perhaps you liked the excitement. Or was it the money that tempted you? Whatever the reason, you passed a secret or two to the other side. Then it was classified documents. And suddenly you were in their pocket."

"It was only for a short time!"

"But by then it was too late. NATO intelligence got wind of it. And they were closing in. So you worked out a way to shift the blame. Somehow you lured Bernard and Madeline to your little love nest in Rue Myrha. There you shot them both."

"No."

"You planted the documents near Bernard's body."

"No."

Richard grabbed Nina by the shoulders and forced her to look at him. "And then you walked away and went on with your merry life. Isn't that how it went?"

Nina gave a pitiful sob. "I didn't kill them!"

"Isn't it?"

"I swear I didn't kill them! They were already dead!"

Richard released her. Nina sank back into the chair, her whole body shuddering with sobs.

"Who killed them?" demanded Richard. "Amiel Foch?"

"No, I never asked him to."

"Philippe?"

She looked up sharply. "No! He was the one who *found* them. He was frantic when he called me. Afraid he'd be accused of it. That's when I called in Foch. Asked him to make arrangements with Rideau, the landlord. A cash payment to change his testimony."

"And the documents? Who planted them?"

"Foch did. By then, the police had already been called. Foch had to slip the briefcase into the garret."

Jordan cut in, "She's just admitted she's Delphi. Now we're supposed to believe some other mysterious culprit did the killing?"

"It's the truth!" insisted Nina.

"Oh, right!" sneered Jordan. "And the killer just happened to choose the very flat where you and Philippe met every week?"

Nina shook her head in bewilderment. "I don't know why he chose our flat."

"It had to be you. Or Philippe," said Jordan.

"I would never...he would never..."

"Who else knew about the garret?" asked Richard.

"No one."

"Marie St. Pierre?"

"No." She paused, then whispered, "Yes, perhaps..."

"So Philippe's wife knew."

Nina nodded miserably. "But no one else."

"Wait," Jordan suddenly interjected. "Someone else *did* know about it."

Everyone looked at him.

"What?" said Richard.

"I heard it from Reggie. Helena knew about the affair—Marie told her. And if Marie knew about the garret on Rue Myrha, then—"

"So did Helena." Richard stared at Jordan. With that one look, they both knew what the other was thinking.

Beryl.

Instantly they both turned to leave. "Get us some backup!" Richard snapped to Daumier. "Have them meet us there!"

"The Vanes' residence?"

Richard didn't answer; he was already running out the door.

"Get in the car," said Helena.

Beryl halted, her hand frozen on the door handle of the Mercedes. "There'll be questions, Helena."

"And I'll have the answers. I was asleep, you see. I slept all night. And when I woke up, you were gone. Left the compound on your own, never to be seen again."

"Reggie will remember—"

"Reggie won't remember a thing. He's stone drunk. As far as he knows, I never left the bed."

"They'll suspect you—"

"It's been twenty years, Beryl. And they still don't suspect." She raised the gun. "Get in. The driver's seat. Or do I have to change my story? Tell them I thought I was shooting a burglar?"

Beryl stared at the gun barrel pointed squarely at her chest. She had no choice. Helena really would shoot her. She climbed into the car.

Helena slid in beside her and tossed the keys into Beryl's lap. "Start the engine."

Beryl turned the key; the Mercedes purred to life like

a contented cat. "My mother never meant to hurt you," said Beryl softly. "She was never interested in Reggie. She never wanted him."

"But he wanted *her*. Oh, I saw how he used to look at her! Do you know, he used to say her name in his sleep. There I'd be, lying next to him, and he'd be thinking of her. I never knew, I never really knew, if they were..." She swallowed. "Drive."

"Where?"

"Just go out the gate. Go!"

Beryl eased the Mercedes out of the garage and across the cobblestoned courtyard. Helena pressed a remote control and the iron gate automatically swung open. It closed again behind them as they drove through. Ahead stretched the tree-lined road. No other cars, no other witnesses.

The steering wheel felt slick with her sweat. Beryl gripped it tightly, just to keep her hands from shaking. "My father never hurt you," she whispered. "Why did you have to kill him?"

"Someone had to be blamed. Why not make it a dead man? And the fact it was Nina's secret flat—that made it all the more convenient." She laughed. "You should have seen how Nina and Philippe scrambled to cover things up."

"And Delphi?"

Helena shook her head in bewilderment. "What about Delphi?"

So she knows nothing about it, thought Beryl. *All this time, we've been chasing the wrong clues. Richard will never know—will never suspect—what really happened.*

The road began to curve and wind through the trees. They were headed into the depths of the Bois de Boulogne. *Is this where they'll find me?* she wondered, dismayed. *In some lonely copse of trees? At the muddy bottom of a pond?*

She peered ahead to the road beyond their headlights. They were approaching another curve.

It may be my only chance. I can let her shoot me. Or I can go down fighting. She pointed the car on a straight course. Then she hit the accelerator pedal. The engine roared and tires screamed. Beryl was thrust back against the seat as the Mercedes lurched forward.

Helena cried out, "No!" and clawed for control of the wheel. A split-second before they hit the trees, Helena managed to swerve them sideways. Suddenly they were tumbling like helpless riders in an out-of-control carnival ride. The Mercedes toppled over and over, windows shattered, and the two passengers were flung against the dashboard.

The car came to rest on its roof.

It was the blare of the horn that dragged Beryl back to consciousness. And the pain. Excruciating pain, tearing at her leg. She tried to move and realized that her chest was wedged against the steering wheel, and that her head was somehow cradled in the small space between the windshield and the upside-down dashboard. She pushed away from the steering wheel. The effort made her cry out in pain, but she managed to slide her body a few precious inches across the crumpled roof. For a moment, she rested, gasping for breath, waiting for the pain in her leg to ease. Then, gritting her teeth, she pushed again and managed to slide through into a larger pocket of space. The front seat? Everything seemed so mangled, so confusing in the darkness. The tumble had left her disoriented.

But she was not so dazed that she didn't smell the odor of gasoline growing stronger every second. *I have to get to a window—have to squeeze through before it explodes.* Blindly she reached out to feel her surroundings, and her hand shoved up against something warm. Something wet. She twisted her head around and came face-to-face with Helena's corpse.

Beryl screamed. Suddenly frantic to get out, to escape those sightless eyes, she squirmed away, clawing for the window. New pain, even more excruciating, ripped through her shattered leg and flooded her eyes with tears. She touched window frame, bits of glass and then...a branch! *I'm almost there. Almost there.*

Half crawling, half dragging herself, she managed to squeeze through the opening. Just as her body rolled onto the ground, the dirt beneath her seemed to give way and she began to slide down a leafy embankment. She landed in a ditch near some trees.

A burst of light suddenly shot into the sky. Through eyes blurred with agony, she looked up and saw the first flicker of the inferno. Seconds later, she heard the popping of glass, then a terrifying whoosh as a fountain of flames engulfed the vehicle.

Why, Helena? Why? The flames blurred, faded into a gathering darkness. She closed her eyes and shivered among the fallen leaves.

THREE MILES FROM the Vanes' residence, they spotted the fire. It was a car, upended, stretched diagonally across the road. A Mercedes.

''It's Helena's,'' shouted Richard. ''My God, it's Helena's!'' He leaped out and ran toward the burning car. He almost tripped over a shoe lying in the road. To his horror he saw it was a woman's pump. *''Beryl!''* he screamed. He was about to make a desperate lunge for the car door when the flames suddenly shot higher. A window burst out, scattering glass across the pavement. The searing heat sent him stumbling backward, his nostrils stinging with the stench of his own singed hair. He recovered his balance and was about to make another lunge through the flames when Jordan grabbed his arm.

"Wait!" cried Jordan.

Richard wrenched away. "Have to get her out!"

"No, *listen!*"

That's when he heard it—a moan, almost inaudible. It came not from the car, but from somewhere in the trees.

At once he and Jordan were scrambling along the roadside, yelling Beryl's name. Again, Richard heard the moan, closer now, coming from the shadows just below the road. He clambered down the dirt bank and stumbled into a drainage ditch.

That's where he found her, sprawled among the leaves. Barely conscious.

He gathered her up and was terrified by how limp, how cold her body felt in his arms. *She's in shock,* he realized. *We have precious little time....*

"Have to get her to a hospital!" he yelled.

Jordan ran ahead and yanked open the car door. Richard, clutching Beryl in his arms, slid into the back seat.

"Go!" he barked.

"Hang on," muttered Jordan, scrambling into the driver's seat. "It's going to be a wild ride."

With a screech of tires, their car shot off down the road. *Stay with me, Beryl,* Richard begged silently as he cradled her body in his arms. *Please, darling. Stay with me....*

But as the car sped through the darkness, she seemed to grow ever colder to his touch.

THROUGH THE HAZE of anesthesia, she heard him call her name, but the sound of his voice seemed so very far away, seemed to come from a distant place she could not possibly reach. Then she felt his hand close tightly over hers, and she knew he was right beside her. She could not see his face; she could not muster enough strength to open her eyes. Yet she knew he was there, that he would still be there when she awoke the next morning.

But it was Jordan whom she saw sitting by her bed. The late-morning sunlight streamed over his fair hair and a leather-bound book of poetry lay in his lap. He was reading Milton. *Dear Jordan,* she thought. *Ever reliable, ever serene. If only I had inherited such peace of mind.*

Jordan glanced up from the page and saw that she was awake. "Welcome back to the world, little sister," he said with a smile.

She groaned. "I'm not so sure I want to be back."

"The leg?"

"Killing me."

He reached for the call button. "Time to indulge in the miracle of morphine."

But even miracles take time. After the nurse delivered the injection, Beryl closed her eyes and waited for the pain to ease, for the blessed numbness to descend.

"Better?" asked Jordan.

"Not yet." She took a deep breath. "God, I hate being an invalid. Talk to me. Please."

"About what?"

Richard, she thought. *Please tell me about Richard. Why he isn't here. Why he's not the one sitting in that chair....*

Jordan said, quietly, "You know, he was here. Earlier this morning. But then Daumier called."

She lay still, not speaking. Waiting to hear more.

"He cares about you, Beryl. I'm sure he does." Jordan closed his book and set it on the bedside table. "Really, he seems an agreeable fellow. Quite capable."

"Capable," she murmured. "Yes, he is that."

"He didn't turn tail and run. He did look after you."

"As a favor," she amended. "To Uncle Hugh."

He didn't answer. And she thought that Jordie, too, had his doubts about their odds for happiness. And so did she. From the very beginning.

The morphine began to take effect. Little by little, she felt herself drift toward sleep. Only vaguely did she hear Richard enter the room and speak softly to Jordan. They murmured something about Helena and her body being burned beyond recognition. As the drug swept her brain toward unconsciousness, a memory suddenly flashed with horrifying vividness into her mind—the flames engulfing the car, engulfing Helena.

For loving too deeply, too fiercely, this was Helena's punishment.

She felt Richard take her hand and press it to his lips.

And what punishment, she wondered, would be hers?

Epilogue

Buckinghamshire, England
Six weeks later

Froggie was restless, stamping about in her stall, whinnying for escape.

"Look at her, the poor thing," Beryl said and sighed. "She hasn't been run nearly enough, and I think she's going quite insane. You'll have to exercise her for me."

"Me? On the back of that...that maniac?" Jordan snorted. "I'm much too fond of my own neck."

Beryl hobbled over to the stall on her crutches. At once Froggie poked her head over the door and gave Beryl an insistent want-to-go-running nudge. "Oh, but she's such a pussycat."

"A pussycat with a foul temper."

"And she so badly needs a good, hard gallop."

Jordan looked at his sister, who was wobbling unsteadily on leg cast and crutches. She seemed so pale and thin these days. As if those long weeks in the hospital had drained something vital from her spirit. A bit of pallor was to be expected, of course, considering all the blood she'd lost, all the days of pain she'd suffered after the operation to pin her shattered femur. Now the leg was healing well, and the pain was only a memory, but she still seemed only a ghost of herself.

It was Richard Wolf's fault.

At least the fellow had been decent enough to hang around during Beryl's hospitalization. In fact, he'd practically haunted her room, spending every daylight hour by her bed. And all the flowers! Every morning, a fresh bouquet.

Then, one day, he was gone. Jordan hadn't heard the explanation. He'd walked into his sister's hospital room that morning and found her staring out the window, all packed and ready to go home to Chetwynd.

Three weeks ago, they'd flown back. And she's been brooding ever since, he thought, looking at her wan face.

"Go on, Jordie," she said. "Give her a bit of a run. It'll be another month before I can ride her again."

Resignedly, Jordan swung open the stall door and led Froggie out to be saddled. "You'd better behave, young lady," he muttered to the beast. "No rearing. No bucking. And definitely no trampling your poor, defenseless rider."

Froggie gave him a look that could only be interpreted as the equine equivalent of *we'll see about that.*

Jordan mounted and gave Beryl a wave.

"Take care of her!" Beryl called out. "See she doesn't hurt herself!"

"Your concern is most touching!" he managed to blurt out just before Froggie took off at a mad gallop for the fields. Jordan managed a last backward glance at Beryl standing forlornly by the stable. How small she looked, how fragile. Not at all the Beryl he knew. Would she ever be herself again?

Froggie was bearing him toward the woods. He concentrated on hanging on for dear life as the beast made a beeline for the stone wall. "You just have to take that bloody hurdle, don't you?" he muttered as Froggie's mane whipped his face. "Which means *I* have to take the bloody hurdle—"

Together they flew over the wall, clearing it neatly. *Still in the saddle,* thought Jordan with a grin of triumph. *Not so easy to get rid of me, is it?*

It was the last thought in his head before Froggie tossed him off her back.

Jordan landed, fortunately enough, on a large clump of moss. As he sprawled beneath the wildly spinning treetops, he was vaguely aware of the sound of tires grinding across the dirt road, and then he heard someone call his name. Groggily he sat up.

Froggie was standing over him, looking not in the least bit apologetic. And behind her, climbing out of a red M.G., was Richard Wolf.

"Are you all right?" Richard called out, running toward him.

"Tell me, Wolf," Jordan groaned. "Are you out to kill all the Tavistocks? Or are you after one of us in particular?"

Laughing, Richard helped him to his feet. "I'd lay the blame where it belongs. On the horse."

Both men looked at Froggie. She answered with what sounded suspiciously like a laugh.

Richard asked quietly, "How's Beryl doing these days?"

Jordan began to clap the dirt from his trousers. "Her leg's healing fine."

"Besides the leg?"

"Not so fine." Jordan straightened and looked the other man in the eye. "Why did you walk out?"

Sighing, Richard looked off in the direction of Chetwynd. "She asked me to."

"What?" Jordan stared at him in bewilderment. "She never told me—"

"She's a Tavistock, like you. Doesn't believe in whining or complaining. Or losing face. It's that pride of hers.''

"Ah, so it was like that, was it?" Jordan said. "An argument?"

"Not even that. It just seemed, with all those differences between us…" He shook his head and laughed. "Face it, Jordan. She's tea and crumpets, I'm coffee and doughnuts. She'd hate it in Washington. And I'm not sure I could adjust to…this." He gestured to the rolling fields of Chetwynd.

But you will adjust, foresaw Jordan. *And so will she. Because it's plain for any idiot to see that you two belong together.*

"Anyway," said Richard, "when Niki called and reminded me we had a job in New Delhi, Beryl told me to go. She thought it would be a good test for us to be apart for a while. Said the Royal Family does it that way. To see if absence makes the heart—and hormones—forget."

"And does it?"

Richard grinned. "Not a chance," he said, and climbed back into his car. "I may be signing up with your wild and crazy family, after all. Any objections?"

"None," said Jordan. "But I *will* offer a bit of advice. That is, if you two expect to share a long and healthy life together."

"What's the advice?"

"Shoot the horse."

Laughing, Richard let out the brake and sped away toward Chetwynd.

Toward Beryl.

As Jordan watched the M.G. vanish around the bend, he thought, *Good luck to you, little sister. I'm glad one of us has finally found someone to love. Now if only I could be so fortunate…*

He turned to Froggie. "And as for you," he said aloud, "I am about to teach you exactly who's boss around here."

Froggie gave a snort. Then, with a triumphant toss of her mane, she turned and galloped away, riderless, toward Chetwynd.

"IT'S QUITE UNLIKE YOU to be brooding this way," said Uncle Hugh as he picked another tomato and set it in his basket. He looked faintly ridiculous in his floppy gardening hat. More like the groundskeeper than the lord of the manor. Crouching on his knees, he uncovered another bright red globe and carefully plucked the treasure. "Don't know why you're so gloomy these days. After all, the leg's almost healed."

"It's not the leg," said Beryl.

"One would think you were permanently crippled."

"It's not the leg."

"Well, what is it, then?" asked Hugh, moving on to the row of pole beans. Suddenly he stopped and glanced back at her. "Oh, it's him, isn't it?"

Sighing, Beryl reached for her crutches and rose from the garden bench. "I don't wish to discuss it."

"You never do."

"I still don't," she said, and stubbornly headed down the brick path toward the maze. She brushed past the edging of lavender, stirring the scents of the late summer garden. Once they'd walked this path together, she thought. And now she was walking it alone.

She entered the maze and, using her crutches, maneuvered around all the secret twists and turns. At last she emerged at the center and sat down on the stone bench. *Yes, I'm brooding again,* she realized. *Uncle Hugh's right. Have to stop this and get on with my life.*

But first, she would have to stop thinking of him. Had

he stopped thinking of her? All the doubts, the fears, came back to assail her. She'd put him to the test, she thought. And he'd failed it.

From a distance, she heard someone call her name. It was so faint at first, she thought she might have imagined it. But there it was again—moving closer now!

She lurched to her feet, wobbling on the crutches. *"Richard?"*

"Beryl?" came the answering shout. "Where are you?"

"In the maze!"

His footsteps moved closer along the path. "Where?"

"The center!"

Through the high hedge walls, she heard his sheepish laughter. "And now I'm expected to find my way to the cheese?"

"Just think of it," she challenged him, "as a test of true love."

"Or true insanity," he muttered, rustling into the maze.

"I'm quite annoyed with you, you know," she called.

"I think I've noticed."

"You didn't write. You didn't call, not once!"

"I was too busy trying to catch planes back to London. And besides, I wanted you to miss me. Did you?"

"No, I didn't."

"You didn't?"

"Not at all." She bit her lip. "Oh, perhaps a bit..."

"Ah, so you *did* miss me—"

"But not much."

"I missed *you.*"

She paused. "Did you?" she asked softly.

"So much, in fact, that if I don't find the bloody center of this bloody maze pretty damn quick, I'm going to—"

"Going to what?" she asked breathlessly.

A rustle of branches made her turn. Suddenly he was

there beside her, pulling her into his arms, covering her mouth with a kiss so deep, so insistent, she felt herself swaying dizzily. The crutches slipped away and fell to the ground. She didn't need them—not when he was there to hold her.

He drew away and smiled at her. "Hello again, Miss Tavistock," he whispered.

"You came back," she murmured. "You really came back."

"Did you think I wouldn't?"

"Does that mean you've thought about it? About us?"

He laughed. "I could scarcely concentrate on anything else. On the job, the client. Finally I had to call in Niki to pinch-hit for me, while I straighten out this mess with you."

She asked softly, "You think it *can* be straightened out?"

Gently he framed her face with his hands. "I don't know. Some folks would probably call us a long shot."

"And they'd be right. There are so many things that could pull us apart...."

"And just as many things that will keep us together." He lowered his face to hers, gently brushed her lips with his. "I confess, I'll never make a proper gentleman. Cricket's not my bag. And you'll have to put a gun to my head to get me up on a horse. But if you're willing to overlook those terrible flaws..."

She threw her arms around his neck. "What flaws?" she whispered, and their lips met again.

From the distance came the peal of the ancient church bells. Six o'clock. The coming of twilight and shadows, sweetly scented. *And love,* thought Beryl as he pulled her, laughing, into his arms.

Quite definitely, love.

Stolen

In memory of Jum Heacock

'In thy face I see the map
of honour, truth and loyalty.'

—*Henry VI, Part III*
William Shakespeare

Prologue

Simon Trott stood on the rolling deck of the *Cosima,* and through the velvety blackness of night he saw the flames. They burned just offshore, not a steady fire, but a series of violent bursts of light that cast the distant swells in a hellish glow.

"That's her," the *Cosima*'s captain said to Trott as both men peered across the bow. "The *Max Havelaar.* Judging by those fireworks, she'll be going down fast." He turned and yelled to the helmsman, "Full ahead!"

"Not much chance of survivors," said Trott.

"They're sending off a distress call. So someone's alive."

"Or was alive."

As they neared the sinking vessel, the flames suddenly shot up like a fountain, sending out sparks that seemed to ignite the ocean in puddles of liquid fire.

The captain shouted over the roar of the *Cosima*'s engines, "Slow up! There's fuel in the water!"

"Throttling down," said the helmsman.

"Ahead slowly. Watch for survivors."

Trott moved to the forward rail and stared across the watery inferno. Already the *Max Havelaar* was sliding backward, her stern nearly submerged, her bow tipping toward the moonless sky. A few minutes more and she'd sink forever into the swells. The water was deep, and salvage impractical. Here, two miles off the Spanish coast, was where the *Havelaar* would sink to her eternal rest.

Another explosion spewed out a shower of embers, leafing the ripples with gold. In those few seconds before the sunlike brilliance faded, Trott spotted a hint of movement off in the darkness. A good two hundred yards away from the *Havelaar,* safely beyond the ring of fire, Trott saw a long, low silhouette bobbing in the water. Then he heard the sound of men's voices, calling.

"Here! We are here!"

"It's the lifeboat," said the captain, aiming the searchlight toward the voices. "There, at two o'clock!"

"I see it," said the helmsman, at once adjusting course. He throttled up, guiding the bow through drifts of burning fuel. As they drew closer, Trott could hear the joyous shouts of the survivors, a confusing babble of Italian. How many in the boat? he wondered, straining to see through the murk. Five. Perhaps six. He could almost count them now, their arms waving in the searchlight's beam, their heads bobbing in every direction. They were thrilled to be alive. To be in sight of rescue.

"Looks like most of the *Havelaar*'s crew," said the captain.

"We'll need all hands up here."

The captain turned and barked out the order. Seconds later the *Cosima*'s crew had assembled on deck. As the bow knifed across the remaining expanse of water, the men stood in silence near the bow rail, all eyes focused on the lifeboat just ahead.

By the searchlight's glare Trott could now make out the number of survivors: six. He knew the *Max Havelaar* had sailed from Naples with a crew of eight. Were there two still in the water?

He turned and glanced toward the distant silhouette

of shore. With luck and endurance, a man could swim that distance.

The lifeboat was adrift off their starboard side.

Trott shouted, "This is the *Cosima!* Identify yourselves!"

"Max Havelaar!" shouted one of the men in the lifeboat.

"Is this your entire crew?"

"Two are dead!"

"You're certain?"

"The engine, she explodes! One man, he is trapped below."

"And your eighth man?"

"He falls in. Cannot swim!"

Which made the eighth man as good as dead, thought Trott. He glanced at *Cosima*'s crew. They stood watching, waiting for the order.

The lifeboat was gliding almost alongside now.

"A little closer," Trott called down, "and we'll throw you a line."

One of the men in the lifeboat reached up to catch the rope.

Trott turned and gave his men the signal.

The first hail of bullets caught its victim in midreach, arms extended toward his would-be saviors. He had no chance to scream. As the bullets rained down from the *Cosima,* the men fell, helpless before the onslaught. Their cries, the splash of a falling body, were drowned out by the relentless spatter of automatic gunfire.

When it was finished, when the bullets finally ceased, the bodies lay in a coiled embrace in the lifeboat. A silence fell, broken only by the slap of water against the *Cosima*'s hull.

One last explosion spewed a finale of sparks into the air. The bow of the *Max Havelaar*—what remained of her—tilted crazily toward the sky. Then, gently, she slid backward into the deep.

The lifeboat, its hull riddled with bullet holes, was already half submerged. A *Cosima* crewman heaved a loose anchor over the side. It landed with a thud among the bodies. The lifeboat tipped, emptying its cargo of corpses into the sea.

"Our work is done here, Captain," said Trott. Matter-of-factly he turned toward the helm. "I suggest we return to—"

He suddenly halted, his gaze focused on a patch of water a dozen yards away. What was that splash? He could still see the ripples of reflected firelight worrying the water's surface. There it was again. Something silvery gliding out of the swells, then slipping back under the water.

"Over there!" shouted Trott. "Fire!"

His men looked at him, puzzled.

"What did you see?" asked the captain.

"Four o'clock. Something broke the surface."

"I don't see anything."

"Fire at it, anyway."

One of the gunmen obligingly squeezed off a clip. The bullets sprayed into the water, their deadly rain splashing a line across the surface.

They watched for a moment. Nothing appeared. The water smoothed once again into undulating glass.

"I know I saw something," said Trott.

The captain shrugged. "Well, it's not there now." He called to the helmsman, "Return to port!"

Cosima came about, leaving in her wake a spreading circle of ripples.

Trott moved to the stern, his gaze still focused on the suspicious patch of water. As they roared away he thought he spotted another flash of silver bob to the surface. It was there only for an instant. Then, in a twinkling, it was gone.

A fish, he thought. And, satisfied, he turned away.

Yes, that must be what it was. A fish.

Chapter One

"A small burglary. That's all I'm asking for." Veronica Cairncross gazed up at him, tears shimmering in her sapphire eyes. She was dressed in a fetching off-the-shoulder silk gown, the skirt arranged in lustrous ripples across the Queen Anne love seat. Her hair, a rich russet brown, had been braided with strands of seed pearls and was coiled artfully atop her aristocratic head. At thirty-three she was far more stunning, far more chic than she'd been at the age of twenty-five, when he'd first met her. Through the years she'd acquired, along with her title, an unerring sense of style, poise and a reputation for witty repartee that made her a sought-after guest at the most glittering parties in London. But one thing about her had not changed, would never change.

Veronica Cairncross was still an idiot.

How else could one explain the predicament into which she'd dug herself?

And once again, he thought wearily, it's faithful old chum Jordan Tavistock to the rescue. Not that Veronica didn't need rescuing. Not that he didn't want to help her. It was simply that this request of hers was so bizarre, so fraught with dire possibilities, that his first instinct was to turn her down flat.

He did. "It's out of the question, Veronica," said Jordan. "I won't do it."

"For me, Jordie!" she pleaded. "Think what will happen if you don't. If he shows those letters to Oliver—"

"Poor old Ollie will have a fit. You two will row for a few days, and then he'll forgive you. That's what will happen."

"What if Ollie doesn't forgive me? What if he—what if he wants a…" She swallowed and looked down. "A divorce," she whispered.

"Really, Veronica." Jordan sighed. "You should have thought about this before you had the affair."

She stared down in misery at the folds of her silk gown. "I didn't think. That's the whole problem."

"No, it's obvious you didn't."

"I had no idea Guy would be so difficult. You'd think I broke his heart! It's not as if we were in love or anything. And now he's being such a bastard about it. Threatening to tell all! What gentleman would sink so low?"

"No gentleman would."

"If it weren't for those letters I wrote, I could deny the whole thing. It would be my word against Guy's then. I'm sure Ollie would give me the benefit of the doubt."

"What, exactly, did you write in those letters?"

Veronica's head drooped unhappily. "Things I shouldn't have."

"Confessions of love? Sweet nothings?"

She groaned. "Much worse."

"More explicit, you mean?"

"Far more explicit."

Jordan gazed at her bent head, at the seed pearls and russet hair glimmering in the lamplight. And he thought, *It's hard to believe I was once attracted to this woman.* But that was years ago, and he'd been only twenty-two and a bit gullible—a condition he sincerely hoped he'd outgrown.

Veronica Dooley had entered his social circle on the arm of an old chum from Cambridge. After the chum bowed out, Jordan had inherited the girl's attentions, and for a few dizzy weeks he'd thought he might be in love. Better sense prevailed. Their parting was amicable, and they'd remained friends over the years. She'd gone on to marry Oliver Cairncross, and although *Sir* Oliver was a good twenty years older than his bride, theirs had been a classic match between money on his side and beauty on hers. Jordan had thought them a contented pair.

How wrong he'd been.

"My advice to you," he said, "is to come clean. Tell Ollie about the affair. He'll most likely forgive you."

"Even if he does, there's still the letters. Guy's just upset enough to send them to all the wrong people. If Fleet Street ever got hold of them, Ollie would be publicly humiliated."

"You think Guy would really stoop so low?"

"I don't doubt it for a minute. I'd offer to pay him off if I thought it would work. But after all that money I lost in Monte Carlo, Ollie's keeping a tight rein on my spending. And I couldn't borrow any money from you. I mean, there are some things one simply *can't* ask of one's friends."

"Burglary, I'd say, lies in that category," noted Jordan dryly.

"But it's not burglary! I wrote those letters. Which makes them *mine*. I'm only retrieving what belongs to me." She leaned forward, her eyes suddenly glittering like blue diamonds. "It wouldn't be difficult, Jordie. I know exactly which drawer he keeps them in. Your sister's engagement party is Saturday night. If you could invite him here—"

"Beryl detests Guy Delancey."

"Invite him anyway! While he's here at Chetwynd, guzzling champagne—"

"I'm burgling his house?" Jordan shook his head. "What if I'm caught?"

"Guy's staff takes Saturday nights off. His house will be empty. Even if you *are* caught, just tell them it's a prank. Bring a—a blow-up doll or something, for insurance. Tell them you're planting it in his bed. They'll believe you. Who'd doubt the word of a Tavistock?"

He frowned. "Is that why you're asking *me* to do this? Because I'm a Tavistock?"

"No. I'm asking you because you're the cleverest man I know. Because you've never, ever betrayed any of my secrets." She raised her chin and met his gaze. It was a look of utter trust. "And because you're the only one in the world I can count on."

Drat. She would have to say that.

"Will you do it for me, Jordie?" she asked softly. Pitifully. "Tell me you will."

Wearily he rubbed his head. "I'll think about it," he said. Then he sank back in the armchair and gazed resignedly at the far wall, at the paintings of his Tavistock ancestors. Distinguished gentlemen, every one of them, he thought. Not a cat burglar in the lot.

Until now.

AT 11:05, THE lights went out in the servants' quarters. Good old Whitmore was right on schedule as usual. At 9:00 he'd made his rounds of the house, checking to see that the windows and doors were locked. At 9:30 he'd tidied up downstairs, fussed a bit in the kitchen, perhaps brewed himself a pot of tea. At 10:00 he'd retired upstairs, to the blue glow of his private telly. At 11:05 he turned off his light.

This had been Whitmore's routine for the past week, and Clea Rice, who'd been watching Guy Delancey's house since the previous Saturday, assumed that this would be his routine until the day he died. Menservants, after all, strived to maintain order in their employers' lives. It wasn't surprising they'd maintain order in their own lives, as well.

Now the question was, how long before he'd fall asleep?

Safely concealed behind the yew hedge, Clea rose to her feet and began to rock from foot to foot, trying to keep the blood moving through her limbs. The grass had been wet, and her stirrup pants were clinging to her thighs. Though the night was warm, she was feeling chilled. It wasn't just the dampness in her clothes; it was the excitement, the anticipation. And, yes, the fear. Not a great deal of fear—she had enough confidence in her own ability to feel certain she wouldn't be caught. Still, there was always that chance.

She danced from foot to foot to keep the adrenaline pumping. She'd give the manservant twenty minutes to fall asleep, no longer. With every minute that passed, her window of opportunity was shrinking. Guy Delancey could return home early from the party tonight, and she wanted to be well away from here when he walked in that front door.

Surely the butler was asleep now.

Clea slipped around the yew hedge and took off at a sprint. She didn't stop running until she'd reached the cover of shrubbery. There she paused to catch her breath, to reevaluate her situation. There was no hue and cry from the house, no signs of movement anywhere in the darkness. Lucky for her, Guy Delancey abhorred dogs; the last thing she needed tonight was some blasted hound baying at her heels.

She slipped around the house and crossed the flagstone terrace to the French doors. As expected, they were locked. Also as expected, it would be an elementary job. A quick glance under her penlight told her this was an antique warded lock, a bit rusty, probably as old as the house itself. When it came to home security, the English had light years of catching up to do. She fished the set of five skeleton keys out of her fanny pack and began trying them, one by one. The first three keys didn't fit. She inserted the fourth, turned it slowly and felt the tooth slide into the bolt notch.

A piece of cake.

She let herself in the door and stepped into the library. By the glow of moonlight through the windows she could see books gleaming in shelves. Now came the hard part— where was the Eye of Kashmir? Surely not in this room, she thought as the beam of her penlight skimmed the walls. It was too accessible to visitors, pathetically unsecured against thieves. Nevertheless, she gave the room a quick search.

No Eye of Kashmir.

She slipped out of the library and into the hallway. Her light traced across burnished wood and antique vases. She prowled through the first-floor parlor and solarium. No Eye of Kashmir. She didn't bother with the kitchen or dining areas—Delancey would never choose a hiding place so accessible to his servants.

That left the upstairs rooms.

Clea ascended the curving stairway, her footsteps silent as a cat's. At the landing she paused, listening for any sounds of discovery. Nothing. To the left she knew was the servants' wing. To the right would be Delancey's bedroom. She turned right and went straight to the room at the end of the hall.

The door was unlocked. She slipped through and closed it softly behind her.

Through the balcony windows moonlight spilled in, illuminating a room of grand proportions. The twelve-foot-high walls were covered with paintings. The bed was a massive four-poster, its mattress broad enough to sleep an entire harem. There was an equally massive chest of drawers, a double wardrobe, nightstands and a gentleman's writing desk. Near the balcony doors was a sitting area— two chairs and a tea table arranged around a Persian carpet, probably antique.

Clea let out an audible groan. It would take hours to search this room.

Fully aware of the minutes ticking by, she started with the writing desk. She searched the drawers, checked for hidden niches. No Eye of Kashmir. She moved to the dresser, where she probed through layers of underwear and hankies. No Eye of Kashmir. She turned next to the wardrobe, which loomed like a monstrous monolith against the wall. She was just about to swing open the wardrobe door when she heard a noise and she froze.

It was a faint rustling, coming from somewhere outside the house. There it was again, louder.

She swiveled around to face the balcony windows. Something bizarre was going on. Outside, on the railing, the wisteria vines quaked violently. A silhouette suddenly popped up above the tangle of leaves. Clea caught one glimpse of the man's head, of his blond hair gleaming in the moonlight, and she ducked back behind the wardrobe.

This was just wonderful. They'd have to take numbers to see whose turn it was to break in next. This was one hazard she hadn't anticipated—an encounter with a rival thief. An incompetent one, too, she thought in disgust as she heard the sharp clatter of outdoor pottery, quickly stilled. There was an intervening silence. The burglar was listening for sounds of discovery. Old Whitmore must be deaf, thought Clea, if he didn't hear *that* racket.

The balcony door squealed open.

Clea retreated farther behind the wardrobe. What if he

discovered her? Would he attack? She'd brought nothing with which to defend herself.

She winced as she heard a thump, followed by an irritated mutter of "*Damn* it all!"

Oh, Lord. This guy was more dangerous to himself than to her.

Footsteps creaked closer.

Clea shrank back, pressing hard against the wall. The wardrobe door swung open, coming to a stop just inches from her face. She heard the clink of hangers as clothes were shoved aside, then the hiss of a drawer sliding out. A flashlight flicked on, its glow spilling through the crack of the wardrobe door. The man muttered to himself as he rifled through the drawer, irritated grumblings in the queen's best English.

"Must be mad. That's what I am, stark raving. Don't know how she talked me into this...."

Clea couldn't help it; curiosity got the better of her. She eased forward and peered through the crack between the hinges of the door. The man was frowning down at an open drawer. His profile was sharply cut, cleanly aristocratic. His hair was wheat blond and still a bit ruffled from all that wrestling with the wisteria vine. He wasn't dressed at all like a burglar. In his tuxedo jacket and black bow tie, he looked more like some cocktail-party refugee.

He dug deeper into the drawer and suddenly gave a murmur of satisfaction. She couldn't see what he was removing from the drawer. *Please,* she thought. *Let it not be the Eye of Kashmir.* To have come so close and then to lose it....

She leaned even closer to the crack and strained to see over his shoulder, to find out what he was now sliding into his jacket pocket. So intently was she staring, she scarcely had time to react when he unexpectedly grasped the wardrobe door and swung it shut. She jerked back into the shadows and her shoulder thudded against the wall.

There was a silence. A very long silence.

Slowly the beam of the flashlight slid around the edge of the wardrobe, followed cautiously by the silhouette of the man's head.

Clea blinked as the light focused fully on her face. Against the glare she couldn't see him, but he could see *her*. For an eternity neither of them moved, neither of them made a sound.

Then he said, "Who the hell are *you?*"

THE FIGURE COILED up against the wardrobe didn't answer. Slowly Jordan played his torchlight down the length of the intruder, noting the stocking cap pulled low to the eyebrows, the face obscured by camouflage paint, the black turtleneck shirt and pants.

"I'm going to ask you one last time," Jordan said. "Who are you?"

He was answered with a mysterious smile. The sight of it surprised him. That's when the figure in black sprang like a cat. The impact sent Jordan staggering backward against the bedpost. At once the figure scrambled toward the balcony. Jordan lunged and managed to grab a handful of pant leg. They both tumbled to the floor and collided with the writing desk, letting loose a cascade of pens and pencils. His opponent squirmed beneath him and rammed a knee into Jordan's groin. In the onrush of pain and nausea, Jordan almost let go. His opponent got one hand free and was scrabbling about on the floor. Almost too late Jordan saw the pointed tip of a letter opener stabbing toward him.

He grabbed his opponent's wrist and savagely wrestled away the letter opener. The other man struck back just as savagely, arms flailing, body twisting like an eel. As Jordan fought to control those pummeling fists, he snagged his opponent's stocking cap.

A luxurious fountain of blond hair suddenly tumbled out across the floor, to ripple in a shimmering pool under the moonlight. Jordan stared in astonishment.

A woman.

For an endless moment they stared at each other, their breaths coming hard and fast, their hearts thudding against each other's chests.

A woman.

Without warning his body responded in a way that was both automatic and unsuppressibly male. She was too warm, too close. And very, very female. Even through their clothes, those soft curves were all too apparent. Just as the state of his arousal must be firmly apparent to her.

"Get off me," she whispered.

"First tell me who you are."

"Or *what?*"

"Or I'll—I'll—"

She smiled up at him, her mouth so close, so tempting he completely lost his train of thought.

It was the creak of approaching footsteps that made his brain snap back into function. Light suddenly spilled under the doorway and a man's voice called, "What's this, now? Who's in there?"

In a flash both Jordan and the woman were on their feet and dashing to the balcony. The woman was first over the railing. She scrambled like a monkey down the wisteria vine. By the time Jordan hit the ground, she was already sprinting across the lawn.

At the yew hedge he finally caught up with her and pulled her to a halt. "What were you doing in there?" he demanded.

"What were *you* doing in there?" she countered.

Back at the house the bedroom lights came on, and a voice yelled from the balcony, "Thieves! Don't you come back! I've called the police!"

"I'm not hanging around *here,*" said the woman, and made a beeline for the woods.

Jordan sighed. "She does have a point." And he took off after her.

For a mile they slogged it out together, dodging brambles, ducking beneath branches. It was rough terrain, but she seemed tireless, moving at the steady pace of someone in superb condition. Only when they'd reached the far edge of the woods did he notice that her breathing had turned ragged.

He was ready to collapse.

They stopped to rest at the edge of a field. The sky was cloudless, the moonlight thick as milk. Wind blew, warm and fragrant with the smell of fallen leaves.

"So tell me," he managed to say between gulps of air, "do you do this sort of thing for a living?"

"I'm not a thief. If that's what you're asking."

"You act like a thief. You dress like a thief."

"I'm not a thief." She sagged back wearily against a tree trunk. "Are you?"

"Of course not!" he snapped.

"What do you mean, *of course not?* Is it beneath your precious dignity or something?"

"Not at all. That is— I mean—" He stopped and shook his head in confusion. "What *do* I mean?"

"I haven't the faintest," she said innocently.

"I'm *not* a thief," he said, more sure of himself now. "I was…playing a bit of a practical joke. That's all."

"I see." She tilted her head up to look at him, and her expression was plainly skeptical in the moonlight. Now that they weren't grappling like savages, he realized she was quite petite. And, without a doubt, female. He remembered how snugly her sweet curves had fit beneath him, and suddenly desire flooded through his body, a desire so intense it left him aching. All he had to do was step close to this woman and those blasted hormones kicked in.

He stepped back and forced himself to focus on her face. He couldn't quite make it out under all that camouflage paint, but it would be easy to remember her voice. It was low and throaty, almost like a cat's growl. Definitely not English, he thought. American?

She was still eyeing him with a skeptical look. "What did you take out of the wardrobe?" she asked. "Was that part of the practical joke?"

"You...saw that?"

"I did." Her chin came up squarely in challenge. "*Now* convince me it was all a prank."

Sighing, he reached under his jacket. At once she jerked back and pivoted around to flee. "No, it's all right!" he assured her. "It's not a gun or anything. It's just this pouch I'm wearing. Sort of a hidden backpack." He unzipped the pouch. She stood a few feet away, watching him warily, ready to sprint off at the first whiff of danger. "It's a bit sophomoric, really," he said, tugging at the pouch. "But it's good for a laugh." The contents suddenly flopped out and the woman gave a little squeak of fright. "See? It's not a weapon." He held it out to her. "It's an inflatable doll. When you blow it up, it turns into a naked woman."

She moved forward, eyeing the limp rubber doll. "Anatomically correct?" she inquired dryly.

"I'm not sure, really. I mean, er..." He glanced at her, and his mind suddenly veered toward *her* anatomy. He cleared his throat. "I haven't checked."

She regarded him the way one might look at an object of pity.

"But it *does* prove I was there on a prank," he said, struggling to stuff the deflated doll back in the pouch.

"All it proves," she said, "is that you had the foresight to bring an excuse should you be caught. Which, in your case, was a distinct possibility."

"And what excuse did *you* bring? Should you be caught?"

"I wasn't planning on getting caught," she said, and started across the field. "Everything was going quite well, as a matter of fact. Until you bumbled in."

"What was going quite well? The burglary?"

"I told you, I'm not a thief."

He followed her through the grass. "So why did *you* break in?"

"To prove a point."

"And that point was?"

"That it could be done. I've just proven to Mr. Delancey that he needs a security system. And my company's the one to install it."

"You work for a *security* company?" He laughed. "Which one?"

"Why do you ask?"

"My future brother-in-law's in that line of work. He might know your firm."

She smiled back at him, her lips immensely kissable, her teeth a bright arc in the night. "I work for Nimrod Associates," she said. Then, turning, she walked away.

"Wait. Miss—"

She waved a gloved hand in farewell, but didn't look back.

"I didn't catch your name!" he said.

"And I didn't catch yours," she said over her shoulder. "Let's keep it that way."

He saw her blond hair gleam faintly in the darkness. And then, in a twinkling, she was gone. Her absence seemed to leave the night colder, the darkness deeper. The only hint that she'd even been there was his residual ache of desire.

I shouldn't have let her go, he thought. *I know bloody well she's a thief.* But what could he have done? Hauled her to the police? Explained that he'd caught her in Guy Delancey's bedroom, where neither one of them belonged?

With a weary shake of his head, he turned and began the long tramp to his car, parked a half mile away. He'd have to hurry back to Chetwynd. It was getting late and he'd be missed at the party.

At least his mission was accomplished; he'd stolen Veronica's letters back. He'd hand them over to her, let her lavish him with thanks for saving her precious hide. After all, he *had* saved her hide, and he was bloody well going to tell her so.

And then he was going to strangle her.

Chapter Two

The party at Chetwynd was still in full swing. Through the ballroom windows came the sounds of laughter and violin music and the cheery clink of champagne glasses. Jordan stood in the driveway and considered his best mode of entry. The back stairs? No, he'd have to walk through the kitchen, and the staff would certainly find that suspicious. Up the trellis to Uncle Hugh's bedroom? Definitely not; he'd done enough tangling with vines for the night. He'd simply waltz in the front door and hope the guests were too deep in their cups to notice his disheveled state.

He straightened his bow tie and brushed the twigs off his jacket. Then he let himself in the front door.

To his relief, no one was in the entrance hall. He tiptoed past the ballroom doorway and started up the curving staircase. He was almost to the second-floor landing when a voice called from below.

"Jordie, where on earth have you been?"

Suppressing a groan, Jordan turned and saw his sister, Beryl, standing at the bottom of the stairs. She was looking flushed and lovelier than ever, her black hair swirled elegantly atop her head, her bared shoulders lustrous above the green velvet gown. Being in love certainly agreed with her. Since her engagement to Richard Wolf a month ago, Jordan had seldom seen her without a smile on her face.

At the moment she was not smiling.

She stared at his wrinkled jacket, his soiled trouser legs and muddy shoes. She shook her head. "I'm afraid to ask."

"Then don't."

"I'll ask anyway. What happened to you?"

He turned and continued up the stairs. "I went out for a walk."

"That's all?" She bounded up the steps after him in a rustle of skirts and stockings. "First you make me invite that horrid Guy Delancey—who, by the way, is drinking like a fish and going 'round pinching ladies' bottoms. Then you simply vanish from the party. And you reappear looking like that."

He went into his bedroom.

She followed him.

"It was a long walk," he said.

"It's been a long party."

"Beryl." He sighed, turning to face her. "I really *am* sorry about Guy Delancey. But I can't talk about it right now. I'd be betraying a confidence."

"I see." She went to the door, then glanced back. "I *can* keep a secret, you know."

"So can I." Jordan smiled. "That's why I'm not saying a thing."

"Well, you'd best change your clothes, then. Or someone's going to ask why you've been climbing wisteria vines." She left, shutting the door behind her.

Jordan looked down at his jacket. Only then did he notice the leaf, poking like a green flag from his buttonhole.

He changed into a fresh tuxedo, combed the twigs from his hair and went downstairs to rejoin the party.

Though it was past midnight, the champagne was still flowing and the scene in the ballroom was as jolly as when he'd left it an hour and a half earlier. He swept up a glass from a passing tray and eased back into circulation. No one mentioned his absence; perhaps no one had noticed it. He worked his way across the room to the buffet table, where a magnificent array of hors d'oeuvres had been laid out, and he helped himself to the Scottish salmon. Breaking and entering was hard work, and he was famished.

A whiff of perfume, a hand brushing his arm, made him turn. It was Veronica Cairncross. "Well?" she whispered anxiously. "How did it go?"

"Not exactly clockwork. You were wrong about the butler's night off. There was a manservant in the house. I could have been caught."

"Oh, no," she moaned softly. "Then you didn't get them…."

"I got them. They're upstairs."

"You *did?*" A smile of utter happiness burst across her face. "Oh, Jordie!" She leaned forward and threw her arms around him, smearing salmon on his tuxedo. "You saved my life."

"I know, I know." He suddenly spotted Veronica's husband, Oliver, moving toward them. At once Jordan extricated himself from her embrace. "Ollie's coming this way," he whispered.

"Is he?" Veronica turned and automatically beamed her thousand-watt smile at Sir Oliver. "Darling, there you are! I lost track of you."

"You don't seem to be missing me much," grunted Sir Oliver. He frowned at Jordan, as though trying to divine his real intentions.

Poor fellow, thought Jordan. Any man married to Veronica was deserving of pity. Sir Oliver was a decent enough fellow, a descendant of the excellent Cairncross family, manufacturers of tea biscuits. Though twenty years older than his wife, and bald as a cue ball, he'd managed to win Veronica's hand—and to keep that hand well studded with diamonds.

"It's getting late," said Oliver. "Really, Veronica, shouldn't we be going home?"

"So soon? It's just past midnight."

"I have that meeting in the morning. And I'm quite tired."

"Well, I suppose we'll have to be going, then," Veronica said with a sigh. She smiled slyly at Jordan. "I think I'll sleep well tonight."

Just see that it's with your husband, thought Jordan with a shake of his head.

After the Cairncrosses had departed, Jordan glanced down and saw the greasy sliver of salmon clinging to his lapel. Drat, another tuxedo bites the dust. He wiped away the mess as best he could, picked up his glass of champagne and waded back into the crowd.

He cornered his future brother-in-law, Richard Wolf, near the musicians. Wolf was looking happy and dazed— just the way one expected a prospective bridegroom to look.

"So how's our guest of honor holding up?" asked Jordan.

Richard grinned. "Giving the old handshake a rest."

"Good idea to pace oneself." Jordan's gaze shifted toward the source of particularly raucous laughter. It was Guy Delancey, clearly well soused and leaning close to a buxom young thing. "Unfortunately," Jordan observed, "not everyone here believes in pacing himself."

"No kidding," said Wolf, also looking at Delancey. "You know, that fellow tried to put the make on Beryl tonight. Right under my nose."

"And did you defend her honor?"

"Didn't have to," said Richard with a laugh. "She does a pretty good job of defending herself."

Delancey's hand was now on Miss Buxom's lower back. Slowly that hand began to slide down toward dangerous terrain.

"What do women see in a guy like that, anyway?" asked Richard.

"Sex appeal?" said Jordan. Delancey did, after all, have rather dashing Spanish looks. "Who knows what attracts women to certain men?" Lord only knew what had attracted Veronica Cairncross to Guy. But she was rid of him now. If she was sensible, she'd damn well stay on the straight and narrow.

Jordan looked at Richard. "Tell me, have you ever heard of a security firm called Nimrod Associates?"

"Is that based here or abroad?"

"I don't know. Here, I imagine."

"I haven't heard of it. But I could check for you."

"Would you? I'd appreciate it."

"Why are you interested in this firm?"

"Oh…" Jordan shrugged. "The name came up in the course of the evening."

Richard was looking at him thoughtfully. Damn, it was that intelligence background of his, an aspect of Richard Wolf that could be either a help or a nuisance. Richard's antennae were out now, the questions forming in his head. Jordan would have to be careful.

Luckily, Beryl sauntered up at that moment to bestow a kiss on her intended. Any questions Richard may have entertained were quickly forgotten as he bent to press his lips to his fiancée's upturned mouth. Another kiss, a hungry twining of arms, and poor old Richard was oblivious to the rest of the world.

Ah, young lovers, sizzling in hormones, thought Jordan and polished off his drink. His own hormones were simmering tonight as well, helped along by the pleasant buzz of champagne.

And by thoughts of that woman.

He couldn't seem to get her out of his thick head. Not her voice, nor her laugh, nor the catlike litheness of her body twisting beneath his....

Quickly he set his glass down. No more champagne tonight. The memories were intoxicating enough. He glanced around for the tray of soda water and spotted his uncle Hugh entering the ballroom.

All evening Hugh had played genial host and proud uncle to the future bride. He'd happily guzzled champagne and flirted with ladies young enough to be his granddaughters. But at this particular moment Uncle Hugh was looking vexed.

He crossed the room, straight toward Guy Delancey. The two men exchanged a few words and Delancey's chin shot up. An instant later an obviously upset Delancey strode out of the ballroom, calling loudly for his car.

"Now what's going on?" said Jordan.

Beryl, her cheeks flushed and pretty from Richard's kissing, turned to look as Uncle Hugh wandered in their direction. "He's obviously not happy."

"Dreadful way to finish off the evening," Hugh was muttering.

"What happened?" asked Beryl.

"Guy Delancey's man called to report a burglary at the house. Seems someone climbed up the balcony and walked straight into the master bedroom. Imagine the cheek! And with the butler at home, too."

"Was anything stolen?" asked Richard.

"Don't know yet." Hugh shook his head. "Almost makes one feel a bit guilty, doesn't it?"

"Guilty?" Jordan forced a laugh from his throat. "Why?"

"If we hadn't invited Delancey here tonight, the burglar wouldn't have had his chance."

"That's ridiculous," said Jordan. "The burglar—I mean, if it *was* a burglar—"

"Why wouldn't it be a burglar?" asked Beryl.

"It's just—one shouldn't draw conclusions."

"Of course it's a burglar," said Hugh. "Why else would one break into Guy's house?"

"There could be other…explanations. Couldn't there?"

No one answered.

Smiling, Jordan took a sip of soda water. But the whole time he felt his sister's gaze, watching him closely.

Suspiciously.

THE PHONE WAS ringing when Clea returned to her hotel room. Before she could answer it, the ringing stopped, but she knew it would start up again. Tony must be anxious. She wasn't ready to talk to him yet. Eventually she would have to, of course, but first she needed a chance to recover from the night's near catastrophe, a chance to figure out what she should do next. What Tony should do next.

She rooted around in her suitcase and found the miniature bottle of brandy she'd picked up on the airplane. She went into the bathroom, poured out a splash into a water glass and stood sipping the drink, staring dejectedly at her reflection in the mirror. In the car she'd managed to wipe away most of the camouflage paint, but there were still smudges of it on her temples and down one side of her nose. She turned on the faucet, wet a facecloth and scrubbed away the rest of the paint.

The phone was ringing again.

Carrying her glass, she went into the bedroom and picked up the receiver. "Hello?"

"Clea?" said Tony. "What happened?"

She sank onto the bed. "I didn't get it."

"Did you get in the house?"

"Of course I got in!" Then, more softly, she said, "I was close. So close. I searched the downstairs, but it wasn't there. I'd just gotten upstairs when I was rudely interrupted."

"By Delancey?"

"No. By another burglar. Believe it or not." She managed a tired laugh. "Delancey's house seems to be quite the popular place to rob."

There was a long silence on the other end of the line. Then Tony asked a question that instantly chilled her. "Are you sure it was just a burglar? Are you sure it wasn't one of Van Weldon's men?"

At the mention of that name, Clea's fingers froze around the glass of brandy. "No," she murmured.

"It's possible, isn't it? They may have figured out what you're up to. Now *they'll* be after the Eye of Kashmir."

"They couldn't have followed me! I was so careful."

"Clea, you don't know these people—"

"The hell I don't!" she retorted. "I know *exactly* who I'm dealing with!"

After a pause Tony said softly, "I'm sorry. Of course you know. You know better than anyone. But I've had my ear to the ground. I've been hearing things."

"What things?"

"Van Weldon's got friends in London. Friends in high places."

"He has friends everywhere."

"I've also heard…" Tony's voice dropped. "They've upped the ante. You're worth a million dollars to them, Clea. Dead."

Her hands were shaking. She took a desperate gulp of

brandy. At once her eyes watered, tears of rage and despair. She blinked them away.

"I think you should try the police again," Tony said.

"I'm not repeating that mistake."

"What's the alternative? Running for the rest of your life?"

"The evidence is *there.* All I have to do is get my hands on it. Then they'll *have* to believe me."

"You can't do it on your own, Clea!"

"I can do it. I'm sure I can."

"Delancey will know someone's broken in. Within twenty-four hours he'll have his house burglarproof."

"Then I'll get in some other way."

"How?"

"By walking in his front door. He has a weakness, you know. For women."

Tony groaned. "Clea, no."

"I can handle him."

"You *think* you can—"

"I'm a big girl, Tony. I can deal with a man like Delancey."

"This makes me sick. To think of you and…" He made a sound of disgust. "I'm going to the police."

Firmly Clea set down her glass. "Tony," she said. "There's no other way. I have some breathing space now. A week, maybe more before Van Weldon figures out where I am. I have to make the most of it."

"Delancey may not be so easy."

"To him I'll just be another dimwitted bimbo. A rich one, I think. That should get his attention."

"And if he gives you too much attention?"

Clea paused. The thought of actually making love to that oily Guy Delancey was enough to nauseate her. With any luck, it would never get that far.

She'd see to it it never got that far.

"I'll handle it," she said. "You just keep your ear to the ground. Find out if anything else has come up for sale. And stay out of sight."

After she'd hung up, Clea sat on the bed, thinking about the last time she'd seen Tony. It had been in Brussels. They'd both been happy, so very happy! Tony had had a brand-new wheelchair, a sporty edition, he called it, for upper-body athletes. He had just received a fabulous commission for the sale of four medieval tapestries to an Italian industrialist. Clea had been about to leave for Naples, to finalize the purchase. Together they had celebrated not just their good fortune but the fact they'd finally found their way out of the darkness of their youth. The darkness of their shared past. They'd laughed and drunk wine and talked about the men in her life, the women in his, and about the peculiar hazards of courting from a wheelchair. Then they'd parted.

What a difference a month made.

She reached for her glass and drained the last of the brandy. Then she went to her suitcase and dug around in her clothes until she found what she was looking for: the box of Miss Clairol. She stared at the model's hair on the box, wondering if perhaps she should have chosen something more subtle. No, Guy Delancey wasn't the type to go for subtle. Brazen was more his style.

And "cinnamon red" should do the trick.

"I'VE CHECKED THE name Nimrod Associates," said Richard. "There's no such security firm. At least, not in England."

The three of them were sitting on the terrace, enjoying a late breakfast. As usual, Beryl and Richard were snuggling cheek to cheek, laughing and darting amorous glances at each other. In short, behaving precisely as one would expect a newly engaged couple to behave. Some of that snuggling might be due to the unexpected chill in the air. Summer was definitely over, Jordan thought with regret. But the sun was shining, the gardens still clung stubbornly to their blossoms and a bracing breakfast on the terrace was just the thing to clear the fog of last night's champagne from his head.

Now, after two cups of coffee, Jordan's brain was finally starting to function. It wasn't just the champagne that had left him feeling muddled this morning; it was the lack of sleep. Several times in the night he'd awakened, sweating, from the same dream.

About the woman. Though her face had been obscured by darkness, her hair was a vivid halo of silvery ripples. She had reached up to him, her fingers caressing his face, her flesh hot and welcoming. As their lips had met, as his hands had slid into those silvery coils of hair, he'd felt her body move against his in that sweet and ancient dance. He'd gazed into her eyes. The eyes of a panther.

Now, by the light of morning, the symbolism of that nightmare was all too clear. Panthers. Dangerous women.

He shook off the image and poured himself another cup of coffee.

Beryl took a nibble of toast and marmalade, the whole time watching him. "Tell me, Jordie," she said. "Where did you hear about Nimrod Associates?"

"What?" Jordan glanced guiltily at his sister. "Oh, I don't know. A while ago."

"I thought it came up last night," said Richard.

Jordan reached automatically for a slice of toast. "Yes, I suppose that's when I heard it. Veronica must have mentioned the name."

Beryl was still watching him. This was the downside

of being so close to one's sister; she could tell when he was being evasive.

"I notice you're rather chummy with Veronica Cairncross these days," she observed.

"Oh, well." He laughed. "We try to keep up the friendship."

"At one time, I recall, it was more than friendship."

"That was ages ago."

"Yes. Before she was married."

Jordan looked at her with feigned astonishment. "You're not thinking...good Lord, you can't possibly imagine..."

"You've been acting so *odd* lately. I'm just trying to figure out what's wrong with you."

"Nothing. There's nothing wrong with me." *Save for the fact I've recently taken up a life of crime,* he thought.

He took a sip of tepid coffee and almost choked on it when Richard said, "Look. It's the police."

An official car had turned onto Chetwynd's private road. It pulled into the gravel driveway and out stepped Constable Glenn, looking trim and snappy in uniform. He waved to the trio on the terrace.

As the policeman came up the steps, Jordan thought, *This is it, then. I'll be ignominiously hauled off to prison. My face in the papers, my name disgraced...*

"Good morning to you all," said Constable Glenn cheerily. "May I inquire if Lord Lovat's about?"

"You've just missed him," said Beryl. "Uncle Hugh's gone off to London for the week."

"Oh. Well, perhaps I should speak with you, then."

"Do sit down." Beryl smiled and indicated a chair. "Join us for some breakfast."

Oh, lovely, thought Jordan. What would she offer him next? *Tea? Coffee? My brother, the thief?*

Constable Glenn sat down and smiled primly at the

cup of coffee set before him. He took a sip, careful not to let his mustache get wet. "I suppose," he said, setting his cup down, "that you know about the robbery at Mr. Delancey's residence."

"We heard about it last night," said Beryl. "Have you any leads?"

"Yes, as a matter of fact. We have a pretty good idea what we're dealing with here." Constable Glenn looked at Jordan and smiled.

Weakly, Jordan smiled back.

"A matter of excellent police work, I'm sure," said Beryl.

"Well, not exactly," admitted the constable. "More a case of carelessness on the burglar's part. You see, she dropped her stocking cap. We found it in Mr. Delancey's bedroom."

"She?" said Richard. "You mean the burglar's a woman?"

"We're going on that assumption, though we could be wrong. There was a very long strand of hair in the cap. Blond. It would've reached well below her—or his—shoulders. Does that sound like anyone you might know?" Again he looked at Jordan.

"No one I can think of," Jordan said quickly. "That is— there *are* some blondes in our circle of acquaintances. But not a burglar among them."

"It could be anyone. Anyone at all. It's not the first break-in we've had in this neighborhood. Three just this year. And the culprit might even be someone you know. You'd be surprised, Mr. Tavistock, what sort of misbehavior occurs, even in your social circle."

Jordan cleared his throat. "I can't imagine."

"This woman, whoever she is, is quite bold. She entered through a downstairs locked door. Got upstairs without

alarming the butler. Only then did she get careless—
caused a bit of a racket. That's when she was chased out."

"Was anything taken?" asked Beryl.

"Not so far as Mr. Delancey knows."

So Guy Delancey didn't report the stolen letters,
thought Jordan. Or perhaps he never even noticed they
were missing.

"This time she slipped up," said Constable Glenn. "But
there's always the chance she'll strike again. That's what I
came to warn you about. These things come in waves, you
see. A certain neighborhood will be chosen. Delancey's
house isn't that far from here, so Chetwynd could be in
her target zone." He said it with the authority of one who
had expert knowledge of the criminal mind. "A residence
as grand as yours would be quite a temptation." Again he
looked directly at Jordan.

Again Jordan had that sinking feeling that the good
Constable Glenn knew more than he was letting on. *Or is
it just my guilty conscience?*

Constable Glenn rose and addressed Beryl. "You'll let
Lord Lovat know of my concerns?"

"Of course," said Beryl. "I'm sure we'll be perfectly all
right. After all, we do have a security expert on the prem-
ises." She beamed at Richard. "And he's *quite* trustworthy."

"I'll look over the household arrangements," said Richard. "We'll beef up security as necessary."

Constable Glenn nodded in satisfaction. "Good day,
then. I'll let you know how things develop."

They watched the constable march smartly back to his
car. As it drove away, up the tree-lined road, Richard said,
"I wonder why he felt the need to warn us personally."

"As a special favor to Uncle Hugh, I'm sure," said Beryl.
"Constable Glenn was employed by MI6 years ago as a

'watcher'—domestic surveillance. I think he still feels like part of the team."

"Still, I get the feeling there's something else going on."

"A woman burglar," said Beryl thoughtfully. "My, we *have* come a long way." Suddenly she burst out laughing. "Lord, what a relief to hear it's a *she!*"

"Why?" asked Richard.

"Oh, it's just too ridiculous to mention."

"Tell me, anyway."

"You see, after last night, I thought—I mean, it occurred to me that—" She laughed harder. She sat back, flush with merriment, and pressed her hand to her mouth. Between giggles she managed to choke out the words. "I thought *Jordie* might be the cat burglar!"

Richard burst out laughing, as well. Like two giddy school kids, he and Beryl collapsed against each other in a fit of the sillies.

Jordan's response was to calmly bite off a corner of his toast. Though his throat had gone dry as chalk, he managed to swallow down a mouthful of crumbs. "I fail to see the humor in all this," he said.

They only laughed harder as he bore the abuse with a look of injured dignity.

CLEA SPOTTED GUY Delancey walking toward the refreshment tent. It was the three-minute time-out between the third and fourth chukkers, and a general exodus was under way from the polo viewing stands. Briefly she lost sight of him in the press of people, and she felt a momentary panic that all her detective work would be for nothing. She'd made a few discreet inquiries in the village that morning, had learned that most of the local gentry would almost certainly be headed for the polo field that afternoon. Armed with that tip, she'd called Delancey's house,

introduced herself as Lady So-and-So, and asked the butler if Mr. Delancey was still meeting her at the polo game
as he'd promised.

The butler assured her that Mr. Delancey would be at
the field.

It had taken her the past hour to track him down in the
crowd. She wasn't about to lose him now.

She pressed ahead, plunging determinedly into the
Savile-Row-and-silk-scarf set. The smell of the polo field,
of wet grass and horseflesh, was quickly overpowered by
the scent of expensive perfumes. With an air of regal as-
suredness—pure acting on her part—Clea swept into the
green-and-white-striped tent and glanced around at the
well-heeled crowd. There were dozens of tables draped
in linen, silver buckets overflowing with ice and champagne, fresh-faced girls in starched aprons whisking about
with trays and glasses. And the ladies—what hats they
wore! What elegant vowels tripped from their tongues!
Clea paused, her confidence suddenly wavering. Lord,
she'd never pull this off….

She glimpsed Delancey by the bar. He was standing
alone, nursing a drink. *Now or never,* she thought.

She swayed over to the counter and edged in close to
Delancey. She didn't look at him, but kept her attention
strictly focused on the young fellow manning the bar.

"A glass of champagne," she said.

"Champagne, coming up," said the bartender.

As she waited for the drink, she sensed Delancey's gaze.
Casually she shifted around so that she was almost, but not
quite, looking at him. He was indeed facing her.

The bartender slid across her drink. She took a sip and
gave a weary sigh. Then she drew her fingers slowly, sen-
suously, through her mane of red hair.

"Been a long day, has it?"

Clea glanced sideways at Delancey. He was fashionably tanned and impeccably dressed in autumn-weight cashmere. Though tall and broad shouldered, his once striking good looks had gone soft and a bit jowly, and the hand clutching the whiskey glass had a faint tremor. *What a waste,* she thought, and smiled at him prettily.

"It has been rather a long day." She sighed, and took another sip. "Afraid I'm not very good in airplanes. And now my friends haven't shown up as promised."

"You've just flown in? From where?"

"Paris. Went on holiday for a few weeks, but decided to cut it short. Dreadfully unfriendly there."

"I was there just last month. Didn't feel welcome at all. I recommend you try Provence. Much friendlier."

"Provence? I'll keep that in mind."

He sidled closer. "You're not English, are you?"

She smiled at him coyly. "You can tell?"

"The accent—what, American?"

"My, you're quick," she said, and noted how he puffed up with the compliment. "You're right, I'm American. But I've been living in London for some time. Ever since my husband died."

"Oh." He shook his head sympathetically. "I'm so sorry."

"He was eighty-two." She sipped again, gazing at him over the rim of her glass. "It was his time."

She could read the thoughts going through his transparent little head. *Filthy rich old man, no doubt. Why else would a lovely young thing marry him? Which makes her a rich widow....*

He moved closer. "Did you say your friends were supposed to meet you here?"

"They never showed." Sighing, she gave him a helpless look. "I took the train up from London. We were supposed to drive back together. Now I suppose I'll just have to take the train home."

"There's no need to do that!" Smiling, he edged closer to her. "I know this may sound a bit forward. But if you're at loose ends, I'd be delighted to show you 'round. It's a lovely village we have here."

"I couldn't impose—"

"No imposition at all. I'm at loose ends myself today. Thought I'd watch a little polo, and then go off to the club. But this is a far pleasanter prospect."

She looked him up and down, as though trying to decide if he could be trusted. "I don't even know your name," she protested weakly.

He thrust out his hand in greeting. "Guy Delancey. Delighted to make your acquaintance. And you are..."

"Diana," she said. Smiling warmly, she shook his hand. "Diana Lamb."

Chapter Three

It was three minutes into the fourth chukker. Oliver Cairn-cross, mounted on his white-footed roan, swung his mallet on a dead run. The thwock sent the ball flying between the goalposts. Another score for the Bucking'shire Boys! Enthusiastic applause broke out in the viewing stands, and Sir Oliver responded by sweeping off his helmet and dipping his bald head in a dramatic bow.

"Just look at him," murmured Veronica. "They're like children out there, swinging their sticks at balls. Will they never grow up?"

Out on the field Sir Oliver strapped his helmet back in place and turned to wave to his wife in the stands. He frowned when he saw that she was leaning toward Jordan.

"Oh, no." Veronica sighed. "He's seen you." At once she rose to her feet, waving and beaming a smile of wifely pride. Sitting back down, she muttered, "He's so bloody suspicious."

Jordan looked at her in astonishment. "Surely he doesn't think that you and I—"

"You *are* my old chum. Naturally he wonders."

Yes, of course he does, thought Jordan. Any man married to Veronica would probably spend his lifetime in a perpetual state of doubt.

The ball was tossed. The thunder of hoofbeats, the whack of a mallet announced the resumption of play.

Veronica leaned close to Jordan. "Did you bring them?" she whispered.

"As requested." He reached into his jacket and withdrew the bundle of letters.

At once she snatched them out of his hand. "You didn't read them, did you?"

"Of course not."

"Such a gentleman!" Playfully she reached up and pinched his cheek. "You promise you won't tell anyone?"

"Not a soul. But this is absolutely the last time, Veronica. From now on, be discreet. Or better yet, honor those marriage vows."

"Oh, I will, I will!" she declared fervently. She stood and moved toward the aisle.

"Where are you going?" he called.

"To flush these down the loo, of course!" She gave him a gay wave of farewell. "I'll call you, Jordie!" As she turned to make her way up the aisle, she brushed past a broad-shouldered man. At once she halted, her gaze slanting up with interest at this new specimen of masculinity.

Jordan shook his head in disgust and turned his attention back to the polo game. Men and horses thundered past, chasing that ridiculous rubber ball across the field. Back and forth they flew, mallets swinging, a tangle of sweating men and horseflesh. Jordan had never been much of a polo fan. The few times he'd played the game he'd come away with more than his share of bruises. He didn't trust horses and horses didn't trust him and in the inevitable struggle for authority, the beasts had a seven-hundred-pound advantage.

There were still four chukkers left to go, but Jordan had

had his fill. He left the viewing stands and headed for the refreshment tent.

In the shade of green-and-white-striped awning, he strolled over to the wine bar and ordered a glass of soda water. With so much celebrating this past week, he'd been waking up every morning feeling a bit pickled.

Sipping his glass of soda, Jordan wandered about looking for an unoccupied table. He spotted one off in a corner. As he approached it, he recognized the occupant of the neighboring table. It was Guy Delancey. Seated across from Delancey, her back to Jordan, was a woman with a magnificent mane of red hair. The couple seemed to be intently engaged in intimate conversation. Jordan thought it best not to disturb them. He walked straight past them and was just sitting down at the neighboring table when he caught a snatch of their dialogue.

"Just the spot to forget one's troubles," Guy was saying. "Sun. Sugary beaches. Waiters catering to your every whim. Do consider joining me there."

The woman laughed. The sound had a throaty, hauntingly familiar ring to it. "It's rather a leap, don't you think, Guy?" she said. "I mean, we've only just met. To run off with you to the Caribbean…"

Slowly Jordan turned in his chair and stared at the woman. Lustrous cinnamon red hair framed her face, softening its angles. She had fair, almost translucent skin with a hint of rouge. Though she was not precisely beautiful, there was a hypnotic quality to those dark eyes, which slanted like a cat's above finely carved cheekbones. *Cat's eyes,* he thought. *Panther's eyes.*

It was her. It had to be her.

As though aware that someone was watching her, she raised her head and looked at Jordan. The instant their gazes met she froze. Even the rouge couldn't conceal the sudden blanching of her skin. He sat staring at her, and she at him, both of them caught in the same shock of mutual recognition.

What now? wondered Jordan. Should he warn Guy Delancey? Confront the woman on the spot? And what would he say? *Guy, old chap, this is the woman I bumped into while burgling your bedroom....*

Guy Delancey swiveled around and said cheerily, "Why, hello, Jordan! Didn't know you were right behind me."

"I...didn't want to intrude." Jordan glanced in the woman's direction. Still white-faced, she reached for her drink and took a desperate swallow.

Guy noted the direction of Jordan's gaze. "Have you two met?" he asked.

Their answer came out in a simultaneous rush.

"Yes," said Jordan.

"No," said the woman.

Guy frowned. "Aren't you two sure?"

"What he means," the woman cut in before Jordan could say a word, "is that we've *seen* each other before. Last week's auction at Sotheby's, wasn't it? But we've never actually been introduced." She looked Jordan straight in the eye, silently daring him to contradict her.

What a brazen hussy, he thought.

"Let me properly introduce you two," said Guy. "This is Lord Lovat's nephew, Jordan Tavistock. And this—" Guy swept his hand proudly toward the woman "—is Diana Lamb."

The woman extended a slender hand across the table as Jordan turned his chair to join them. "Delighted to make your acquaintance, Mr. Tavistock."

"So you two met at Sotheby's," said Guy.

"Yes. Terribly disappointing collection," she said. "The St. Augustine estate. One would think there'd be *something*

worth bidding on, but no. I didn't make a single offer."
Again she looked straight at Jordan. "Did you?"

He saw the challenge in her gaze. He saw something else as well: a warning. *You spill the beans,* said those cheerful brown eyes, *and so will I.*

"Well, did you, Jordie?" asked Guy.

"No," muttered Jordan, staring fiercely at the woman. "Not a one."

At his capitulation, the woman's smile broadened to dazzling. He had to concede she'd beaten him this round; next round she'd not be so lucky. He'd have the right words ready, his strategy figured out....

"...dreadful shambles. Pitiful, really. Don't you agree?" said Guy.

Suddenly aware that he was being addressed, Jordan looked at Guy. "Pardon?"

"All the estates that have fallen on hard times. Did you know the Middletons have decided to open Greystones to public tours?"

"I hadn't heard," said Jordan.

"Lord, can you imagine how humiliating that must be? To have all those strangers tramping through one's house, snapping photos of your loo. I'd never sink so low."

"Sometimes one has no choice," said Jordan.

"Certainly one has the choice! You're not saying you'd ever let the tourists into Chetwynd, would you?"

"No, of course not."

"Neither would I let them into Underhill. Plus, there's the problem of security, something I'm acutely tuned in to after that robbery attempt last night. People may *claim* they're tourists. But what if they're really thieves, come to check the layout of the place?"

"I agree with you on that point," said Jordan, looking straight at the woman. "One can't be too careful."

The little thief didn't bat an eyelash. She merely smiled back, those brown eyes wide and innocent.

"One certainly can't," said Guy. "And that goes triply for you. When I think of the fortune in art hanging on your walls…"

"Fortune?" said the woman, her gaze narrowing.

"I wouldn't call it a fortune," Jordan said quickly.

"He's being modest," said Guy. "Chetwynd has a collection any museum would kill for."

"All of it under tight security," said Jordan. "And I mean, *extremely* tight."

The hussy laughed. "I believe you, Mr. Tavistock."

"I certainly hope you do."

"I'd like to see Chetwynd some day."

"Hang around with me, darling," said Guy, "and we might wangle an invitation."

With a last squeeze of the woman's hand, Guy rose to his feet. "I'll have the car sent 'round, how about it? If we leave now, we'll avoid the jam in the parking lot."

"I'll come with you," she offered.

"No, no. Do stay and finish your drink. I'll be back as soon as the car's ready." He turned and disappeared into the crowd.

The woman sat back down. No shrinking violet, this one; brazenly she faced Jordan. And she smiled.

FROM ACROSS THE refreshment tent Charles Ogilvie spotted the woman. He knew it had to be her; there was no mistaking the hair color. "Cinnamon red" was precisely how one would describe that glorious mane of hers. A superb job, courtesy of Clairol. Ogilvie had found the discarded hair-color box in the bathroom rubbish can when he'd searched her hotel room this morning, had confirmed its effect when he'd pulled a few silky strands from her hairbrush. Miss Clea Rice, it appeared, had done another quick-change job. She was getting better at this. Twice she'd metamorphosed into a different woman. Twice he'd almost lost her.

But she wasn't good enough to shake him entirely. He still had the advantage of experience. And she had the disadvantage of not knowing what *he* looked like.

Casually he strolled a few feet along the tent perimeter, to get a better look at her profile, to confirm it was indeed Clea Rice. She'd gone heavy with the lipstick and rouge, but he still recognized those superb cheekbones, that ivory skin. He also had no trouble recognizing Guy Delancey, who had just risen to his feet and was now moving away through the crowd, leaving Clea at the table.

It was the other man he didn't recognize.

He was a blond chap, long and lean as a whippet, impeccably attired. The man slid into the chair where Delancey had been sitting and faced the Rice woman across the table. It was apparent, just by the intensity of their gazes, that they were not strangers to each other. This was troubling. Where did this blond man fit in? No mention of him had appeared in the woman's dossier, yet there they were, deep in conversation.

Ogilvie took the lens cap off his telephoto. Moving behind the wine bar, he found a convenient vantage point from which to shoot his photos, unobserved. He focused on the blond man's profile and clicked off a few shots, then took a few shots of Clea Rice, as well. A new partner? he wondered. My, she was resourceful. Three weeks of tailing the woman had left him with a grudging sense of admiration for her cleverness.

But was she clever enough to stay alive?

He reloaded his camera and began to shoot a second roll.

"I LIKE THE hair," said Jordan.

"Thank you," the woman answered.

"A bit flashy, though, don't you think? Attracts an awful lot of attention."

"That was the whole idea."

"Ah, I see. Guy Delancey."

She inclined her head. "Some men are *so* predictable."

"It's almost unfair, isn't it? The advantage you have over the poor dumb beasts."

"Why shouldn't I capitalize on my God-given talents?"

"I don't think you're putting those talents quite to the use He intended." Jordan sat back in his chair and returned her steady gaze. "There's no such company as Nimrod Associates. I've checked. Who are you? Is Diana Lamb your real name?"

"Is Jordan Tavistock yours?"

"Yes, and you didn't answer my question."

"Because I find you so much more interesting." She leaned forward, and he couldn't help but glance down at the deeply cut neckline of her flowered dress.

"So you own Chetwynd," she said.

He forced himself to focus on her face. "My uncle Hugh does."

"And that fabulous art collection? Also your uncle's?"

"The family's. Collected over the years."

"Collected?" She smiled. "Obviously I've underestimated you, Mr. Tavistock. Not the rank amateur I thought you were."

"What?"

"Quite the professional. A thief *and* a gentleman."

"I'm nothing of the kind!" He shot forward in his chair and inhaled such an intoxicating whiff of her perfume he felt dizzy. "The art has been in my family for generations!"

"Ah. One in a long line of professionals?"

"This is absurd—"

"Or are you the first in the family?"

Gripping the table in frustration, he counted slowly to five and let out a breath. "I am not, and have never been, a thief."

"But I saw you, remember? Rooting around in the wardrobe. You took something out—papers, I believe. So you *are* a thief."

"Not in the same sense *you* are."

"If your conscience is so clear, why didn't you go to the police?"

"Perhaps I will."

"I don't think so." She flashed him that maddening grin of triumph. "I think when it comes to thievery, *you're* the more despicable one. Because you make victims of your friends."

"Whereas you make friends of your victims?"

"Guy Delancey's not a friend."

"Astonishing how I misinterpreted that scene between you two! So what's the plan, little Miss Lamb? Seduction followed by a bit of larceny?"

"Trade secrets," she answered calmly.

"And why on earth are you so fixated on Delancey? Isn't it a bit risky to stick with the same victim?"

"Who said *he's* the victim?" She lifted the glass to her lips and took a delicate sip. He found her every movement oddly fascinating. The way her lips parted, the way the liquid slid into that moist, red mouth. He found himself swallowing as well, felt his own throat suddenly go parched.

"What is it Delancey has that you want so very badly?" he asked.

"What were those papers you took?" she countered.

"It won't work, you know."

"What won't work?"

"Trying to lump me in your category. *You're* the thief."

"And you're not?"

"What I lifted from that wardrobe has no intrinsic value. It was a personal matter."

"So is this for me," she answered tightly. "A personal matter."

Jordan frowned as a thought suddenly struck him. Guy Delancey had romanced Veronica Cairncross, and then had threatened to use her letters against her. Had he done the same to other women? Was Diana Lamb, or someone close to her, also a victim of Guy's?

Or am I trying to talk myself out of the obvious? he thought. The obvious being, this woman was a garden-variety burglar, out for loot. She'd already proven herself adept at housebreaking. What else could she be?

Such a pity, he thought, eyeing that face with its alabaster cheeks and nut brown eyes. Sooner or later those intelligent eyes would be gazing out of a jail cell.

"Is there any way I can talk you out of this?" he asked.

"Why would you?"

"I just think it's a waste of your apparent...talents. Plus there's the matter of it being morally wrong, to boot."

"Right, wrong." She gave an unconcerned wave of her hand. "Sometimes it isn't clear which is which."

This woman was beyond reform! And the fact he knew she was a thief, knew what she had planned, made him almost as guilty if she succeeded.

Which, he decided, she would not.

He said, "I won't let you, you know. While I'm not particularly fond of Guy Delancey, I won't let him be robbed blind."

"I suppose you're going to tell him how we met?" she asked. Not a flicker of anxiety was in her eyes.

"No. But I'm going to warn him."

"Based on what evidence?"

"Suspicions."

"I'd be careful if I were you." She took another sip of her drink and placidly set the glass down. "Suspicions can go in more than one direction."

She had him there, and they both knew it. He couldn't warn Delancey without implicating himself as a thief. If Delancey chose to raise a fuss about it to the police, not only would Jordan's reputation be irreparably tarnished, Veronica's, too, would suffer.

No, he'd prefer not to take that risk.

He met Diana's calm gaze with one just as steady. "An ounce of prevention is worth a pound of cure," he said, and smiled.

"Meaning what, pray tell?"

"Meaning I plan to make it bloody difficult for you to so much as lift a teaspoon from the man and get away with it."

For the first time he saw a ripple of anxiety in her eyes. Her brightly painted red lips drew tight. "You don't understand. This is not your concern—"

"Of course it is. I plan to watch you like a hawk. I'm going to follow you and Delancey everywhere. Pop up when you least expect it. Make a royal nuisance of myself. In short, Miss Lamb, I've adopted you as my crusade. And if you make one false move, I'm going to cry wolf." He sat back, smiling. "Think about it."

She *was* thinking about it, and none too happily, judging by her expression.

"You can't do this," she whispered.

"I can. I have to."

"There's too much at stake! I won't let you ruin it—"

"Ruin *what*?"

She was about to answer when a hand closed over her

shoulder. She glanced up sharply at Guy Delancey, who'd just returned and now stood behind her.

"Sorry if I startled you," he said cheerily. "Is everything all right?"

"Yes. Yes, everything's fine." Though the color had drained from her face, she still managed to smile, to flash Delancey a look of coquettish promise. "Is the car ready?"

"Waiting at the gate, my lady." Guy helped her from her chair. Then he gave Jordan a careless nod of farewell. "See you around, Jordan."

Jordan caught a last glimpse of the woman's face, looking back at him in smothered anger. Then, with shoulders squared, she followed Delancey into the crowd.

You've been warned, Diana Lamb, thought Jordan. Now he'd see if she heeded that warning. And just in case she didn't...

Jordan pulled a handkerchief out of his jacket pocket. Gingerly he picked up the woman's champagne glass by the lower stem and peered at the smudge of ruby red lipstick. He smiled. There, crystal clear on the surface of the glass, was what he'd been looking for.

Fingerprints.

OGILVIE FINISHED SHOOTING his third roll of film and clipped the lens cap back on his telephoto. He had more than enough shots of the blond man. By tonight he'd have the images transmitted to London and, with any luck, an ID would be forthcoming. The fact Clea Rice had apparently picked up an unknown associate disturbed him, if only because he'd had no inkling of it. As far as he knew, the woman traveled alone, and always had.

He'd have to find out more about the blond chap.

The woman rose from her chair and departed with Guy Delancey. Ogilvie tucked his camera in his bag and left the tent to follow them. He kept a discreet distance, far enough back so that he would blend in with the crowd. She was an easy subject to tail, with all that red hair shimmering in the sunlight. The worst possible choice for anyone trying to avoid detection. But that was Clea Rice, always doing the unexpected.

The couple headed for the gate.

Ogilvie picked up his pace. He slipped through the gates just in time to see that head of red hair duck into a waiting Bentley.

Frantically Ogilvie glanced around the parking lot and spotted his black MG socked in three rows deep. By the time he could extricate it from that sea of Jaguars and Mercedes, Delancey and the woman could be miles away.

In frustration he watched Delancey's Bentley drive off. So much for following them; he'd have to catch up with her later. No problem. He knew which hotel she was staying at, knew that she'd paid for the next three nights in advance.

He decided to shift his efforts to the blond man.

Fifteen minutes later he spotted the man leaving through the gates. By that time Ogilvie had his car ready and waiting near the parking-lot exit. He saw the man step into a champagne gold Jaguar, and he took note of the license number. The Jaguar pulled out of the parking lot.

So did Ogilvie's MG.

His quarry led him on a long and winding route through rolling fields and trees, leaves already tinted with the fiery glow of autumn. Blueblood country, thought Ogilvie, noting the sleek horses in the pasture. Whoever *was* this fellow, anyway?

The gold Jaguar finally turned off the main road, onto a private roadway flanked by towering elms. From the main road Ogilvie could just glimpse the house that lay beyond those elms. It was magnificent, a stone-and-turret manor surrounded by acres of gardens.

He glanced at the manor name. It was mounted in bronze on the stone pillars marking the roadway entrance.

Chetwynd.

"You've come up in the world, Clea Rice," murmured Ogilvie.

Then he turned the car around. It was four o'clock. He'd have just enough time to call in his report to London.

VICTOR VAN WELDON had had a bad day. The congestion in his lungs was worse, his doctors said, and it was time for the oxygen again. He thought he'd weaned himself from that green tank. But now the tank was back, hooked onto his wheelchair, and the tubes were back in his nostrils. And once again he was feeling his mortality.

What a time for Simon Trott to insist on a meeting.

Van Weldon hated to be seen in such a weak and vulnerable condition. Through the years he had prided himself on his strength. His ruthlessness. Now, to be revealed for what he was—an old and dying man—would grant Simon Trott too much of an advantage. Although Van Weldon had already named Trott his successor, he was not yet ready to hand over the company reins. *Until I draw my last breath,* he thought, *the company is mine to control.*

There was a knock on the door. Van Weldon turned his wheelchair around to face his younger associate as he walked into the room. It was apparent, by the look on Trott's face, that the news he brought was not good.

Trott, as usual, was dressed in a handsomely tailored suit that showed his athletic frame to excellent advantage. He had it all—youth, blond good looks, all the women he could possibly hope to bed. *But he does not yet have the company,* thought Van Weldon. *He is still afraid of me. Afraid of telling me this latest news.*

"What have you learned?" asked Van Weldon.

"I think I know why Clea Rice headed for England," said Trott. "There have been rumors...on the black market..." He paused and cleared his throat.

"What rumors?"

"They say an Englishman has been boasting about a secret purchase he made. He claims he recently acquired..." Trott looked down. Reluctantly he finished. "The Eye of Kashmir."

"*Our* Eye of Kashmir? That is impossible."

"That is the rumor."

"The Eye has not been placed on the market! There is no way anyone could acquire it."

"We have not inventoried the collection since it was moved. There is a possibility..."

The two men exchanged looks. And Van Weldon understood. They both understood. *We have a thief among our ranks. A traitor who has dared to go against us.*

"If Clea Rice has also heard rumors of this sale, it could be disastrous for us," said Van Weldon.

"I'm quite aware of that."

"Who is this Englishman?"

"His name is Guy Delancey. We're trying to locate his residence now."

Van Weldon nodded. He sank back in his wheelchair and for a moment let the oxygen wash through his lungs. "Find Delancey," he said softly. "I have a feeling that when you do, you will also find Clea Rice."

Chapter Four

"To new friends," said Guy as he handed Clea a glass brimming with champagne.

"To new friends," she murmured and took a sip. The champagne was excellent. It would go to her head if she wasn't careful, and now, more than ever, she needed to keep her head. Such a sticky situation! How on earth was she to case the joint while this slobbery Casanova was all over her? She'd planned to let him make only a few preliminary moves, but it was clear Delancey had far more than just a harmless flirtation in mind.

He sat down beside her on the flowered settee, close enough for her to get a good look at his face. For a man in his late forties, he was still reasonably attractive, his skin relatively unlined, his hair still jet black. But the watery eyes and the sagging jowls were testimony to a dissipated life.

He leaned closer, and she had to force herself not to pull back in repulsion as those eyes swam toward her. To her relief, he didn't kiss her—yet. The trick was to hold him off while she dragged as much information as she could out of him.

She smiled coyly. "I love your house."

"Thank you."

"And the art! Quite a collection. All originals, I take it?"

"Naturally." Guy waved proudly at the paintings on the walls. "I haunt the auction houses. At Sotheby's, if they see me coming, they rub their hands together in glee. Of course, this isn't the best of my collection."

"It isn't?"

"No, I keep the finer pieces in my London town house. That's where I do most of my entertaining. Plus, it has far better security."

Clea felt her heart sink. Darn, was that where he kept it, then? His London town house? Then she'd wasted the week here in Buckinghamshire.

"It's a major concern of mine these days," he murmured, leaning even closer toward her. "Security."

"Against theft, you mean?" she inquired innocently.

"I mean security in general. The wolf at the door. The chill of a lonely bed." He bent toward her and pressed his sodden lips to hers. She shuddered. "I've been searching so long for the right woman," he whispered. "A soul mate..."

Do women actually fall for this line? she wondered.

"And when I looked in your eyes today—in that tent— I thought perhaps I'd found her."

Clea fought the urge to burst out laughing and managed—barely—to return his gaze with one just as steady. Just as smoldering. "But one must be careful," she murmured.

"I agree."

"Hearts are so very fragile. Especially mine."

"Yes, yes! I know." He kissed her again, more deeply. This was more than she could bear.

She pulled back, rage making her breath come hard and fast. Guy didn't seem at all disturbed by it; if anything, he took her heavy breathing as a sign of passion.

"It's too soon, too fast," she panted.

"It's the way it was meant to be."

"I'm not ready—"

"I'll *make* you ready." Without warning he grasped her breast and began to knead it vigorously like a lump of bread dough.

Clea sprang to her feet and moved away. It was either that or slug him in the mouth. At the moment she was all in favor of the latter. In a shaky voice she said, "Please, Guy. Maybe later. When we know each other better. When I feel I know *you*. As a person, I mean."

"A person?" He shook his head in frustration. "What, exactly, do you need to know?"

"Just the small things that tell me about you. For instance…" She turned and gestured to the paintings. "I know you collect art. But all I know is what I see on these walls. I have no idea what moves you, what appeals to you. Whether you collect other things. Besides paintings, I mean." She gave him a questioning look.

He shrugged. "I collect antique weapons."

"There now, you see?" Smiling, she came toward him. "I find that fascinating! It tells me you have a masculine streak of adventure."

"It does?" He looked pleased. "Yes, I suppose it does."

"What sort of weapons?"

"Antique swords. Pistols. A few daggers."

Her heart gave an extra thump at that last word. *Daggers*. She moved closer to him. "Ancient weaponry," she murmured, "is wonderfully erotic, I think."

"You do?"

"Yes, it—it conjures up knights in armor, ladies in castle towers." She clasped her hands and gave a visible shiver of excitement. "It gives me goose bumps just to think of it."

"I had no idea it had that effect on women," he said in wonder. With sudden enthusiasm he rose from the couch. "Come with me, my lady," he said, taking her hand. "And

I'll show you a collection that'll send shivers down your spine. I've just picked up a new treasure—something I purchased on the sly from a very private source."

"You mean the black market?"

"Even more private than that."

She let him guide her into the hallway and up the stairs. *So he keeps it on the second floor,* she thought. Probably the bedroom. To think she had gotten so close to it that night.

Somewhere, a phone was ringing. Guy ignored it.

They reached the top of the stairs. He turned right, toward the east wing—the bedroom—and suddenly halted.

"Master Delancey?" called a voice. "You've a telephone call."

Guy glanced back down the stairs at the gray-haired butler who stood on the lower landing. "Take a message," he snapped.

"But it—it's—"

"Yes?"

The butler cleared his throat. "It's Lady Cairncross."

Guy winced. "What does she want?"

"She wishes to see you immediately."

"You mean *now?*"

Guy hurried down the stairs to take the receiver. From the upper landing Clea listened to the conversation below.

"Not a good time, Veronica," Guy said. "Couldn't you... look, I have other things to do right now. You're being unreasonable. No. Veronica, you mustn't! We'll talk about this some other— Hello? Hello?" He frowned at the receiver in dismay, then dropped it back in the cradle.

"Sir?" inquired the butler. "Might I be of service?"

Guy glanced up, suddenly aware of his predicament. "Yes! Yes, you'll have to see that Miss Lamb's brought home."

"Home?"

"Take her to a hotel! In the village."

"You mean—now?"

"Yes, bring the car 'round. Go!"

Guy scampered up the steps, snatched Clea by the arm and began to hustle her down to the front door. "Dreadfully sorry, darling, but something's come up. Business, you understand."

Clea planted her heels stubbornly into the carpet. "Business?"

"Yes, an emergency—client of mine—"

"Client? But I don't even know what you *do* for a living!"

"My chauffeur will find you a hotel room. I'll pick you up at five tomorrow, how about it? We'll make it an evening."

He gave her a quick kiss, then Clea was practically pushed out the front door. The car was already waiting, the chauffeur standing beside the open door. Clea had no choice but to climb in.

"I'll call you tomorrow!" yelled Guy, and waved.

As the chauffeur drove her out through the gates, Clea clutched the leather armrest in frustration. *I was so damn close, too,* she thought. He'd been about to show her the dagger. She could have had her hands on it, were it not for the phone call from that woman.

Just who the hell *was* Veronica?

VERONICA CAIRNCROSS TURNED from the telephone and looked inquiringly at Jordan. "Well? Do you think that call did the trick?"

"If it didn't," he said, "then your visit will."

"Oh, must I really go see him? I told you, I want nothing to do with the man."

"It's one sure way to flush that woman out of the house before she does any damage."

"There must be some other way to stop her! We could call the police—"

"And have it all come out? My late-night foray into Guy's house? Those stolen letters?" He paused. "Your affair with Delancey?"

Veronica gave a vigorous shake of her head. "We certainly can't tell them *that*."

"That's what I thought you'd say."

Resignedly, Veronica picked up her purse and started for the door. "Oh, all right. I got you into this. I suppose I owe you the favor."

"Plus, it's your civic duty," observed Jordan. "The woman's a thief. No matter what bitter feelings you have for Guy, you can't let him be robbed blind."

"Guy?" Veronica laughed. "I don't give a damn what happens to *him*. It's your lady burglar I'm thinking of. If she gets caught and talks to the police..."

"Then my reputation is mud," admitted Jordan.

Veronica nodded. "And so, I'm afraid, is mine."

CLEA KICKED OFF her high heels, tossed her purse in a chair and flung herself with a groan across the hotel bed. What a ghastly day. She hated polo, she despised Guy Delancey and she detested this red hair. All she wanted to do was go to sleep, to forget the Eye of Kashmir, to forget everything. But whenever she closed her eyes, whenever she tried to sleep, the old nightmares would return, the sights and sounds of terror so vivid she thought she was reliving it.

She fought the memories, tried to push them aside with more pleasant images. She thought of the summer of '72, when she was eight and Tony was ten, and they'd posed together for that photo that later graced Uncle Walter's mantelpiece. They'd been dressed in identical tans and bib overalls, and Tony had draped his skinny arm over her scrawny shoulder. They'd grinned at the camera like a pair of shysters in training, which they were. They had the world's best teacher, too: Uncle Walter, con man *extraordinaire,* damn his larcenous heart of gold. How was the old fellow faring in prison these days? she wondered. Uncle Walter would be up for parole soon. Maybe—just maybe—prison had changed him, the way it had changed Tony.

The way it had changed her.

Maybe Uncle Walter would walk out of those prison gates and into a straight life, sans con games and grifters.

Maybe pigs could fly.

She jerked as the phone rang. At once she reached for the receiver. "Hello?"

"Diana, darling! It's me!"

She rolled her eyes. "Hello, Guy."

"Dreadfully sorry about what happened this afternoon. Forgive me?"

"I'm thinking about it."

"My chauffeur said you're planning to stay in the village for a few days. Perhaps you'll give me a chance to make it up to you? Tomorrow night, say? Supper and a musicale at an old friend's house. And the rest of the evening at mine."

"I don't know."

"I'll show you my collection of antique weapons." His voice dropped to an intimate murmur. "Think of all those knights in shining armor. Damsels in distress…"

She sighed. "Oh, all right."

"I'll be by at five. Pick you up at the Village Inn."

"Right. See you at five." She hung up and realized she

had a splitting headache. Ha! It was her just punishment for playing Mata Hari.

No, her *real* punishment would come if she actually had to bed that dissolute wretch.

Moaning, she rose to her feet and headed toward the bathroom to wash off the smell of polo ponies and the greasy touch of Guy Delancey.

DELANCEY WAS SCARCELY sober when he came to fetch her the next evening. She debated the wisdom of climbing into the car with him behind the wheel, but decided she had no choice—not if she wanted to see this through. All things considered, the dangers of riding with a tipsy driver seemed almost insignificant. Risk was a relative thing and this was the night for taking risks.

"Should be a jolly bunch tonight," said Guy, dodging traffic along the winding road. High hedgerows obscured the view of the road ahead; Clea could only hope that some car wasn't zooming toward them from the opposite direction. "I don't go for the music, really. It's more for the conversation afterward. The laughs."

And the drinks, she thought, clutching the armrest as they whizzed past a tree with inches to spare.

"Thought it'd be my chance to introduce you," said Guy. "Show you off to my friends."

"Will Veronica be there?"

He shot her a startled glance. "What?"

"Veronica. The one who called yesterday. You know, your client."

"Oh. Oh, *her.*" His laugh was patently forced. "No, she's not a music fan. I mean, she's fond of rock and roll, that sort of rubbish, but not classical music. No, she won't be there." He paused, then added under his breath, "Lord, I hope not, anyway."

Twenty minutes later his hopes were dashed when they walked into the Forresters' music room. Clea heard Guy suck in a startled breath and mutter, "I don't believe it" as a russet-haired woman approached them from across the room. She was dressed in a stunning gown of cream lawn, and around her neck hung a magnificent strand of pearls. But it wasn't the woman whom Clea focused on.

It was the woman's companion, a man who was now regarding Clea with a look of calm amusement. Or was it triumph she saw in Jordan Tavistock's sherry brown eyes?

Guy cleared his throat. "Hello, Veronica," he managed to say.

"I'd heard there was a new lady in your life."

"Yes, well…" Guy managed a weak smile.

Veronica turned her gaze to Clea, and offered an outstretched hand. "I'm Veronica Cairncross."

Clea returned the handshake. "Diana Lamb."

"We're old friends, Guy and I," Veronica explained. "*Very* old friends. And yet he does manage to surprise me sometimes."

"I surprise *you?*" Guy snorted. "Since when did you become a fan of musicales?"

"Since Jordan invited me."

"Oliver is so trusting."

"Who's Oliver?" Clea ventured to ask.

Guy laughed. "Oh, no one. Just her husband. A minor inconvenience."

"You are an *ass,*" hissed Veronica, and she turned and stalked away.

"Takes one to know one!" Guy retorted and followed her out of the room.

Jordan and Clea, equally cast adrift, looked at each other.

Jordan sighed. "Isn't love grand?"

"*Are* they in love?"

"I think it's obvious they still are."

"Is that why you brought her here? To sabotage my evening?"

Jordan picked up two glasses of white wine from a passing butler and handed a glass to Clea. "As I once said to you, Miss Lamb—or is it Miss Lamb?—I've taken on your reformation as my personal crusade. I'm going to save you from a life of crime. At least, while you're in my neighborhood."

"Territorial, aren't you?"

"Very."

"What if I gave you my solemn oath not to cut into your territory? I'll let you keep your hunting grounds."

"And you'll quietly leave the area?"

"Provided you carry out your side of the bargain."

He eyed her suspiciously. "What are you proposing?"

Clea paused, studying him, wondering what made him tick. She'd thought Jordan Tavistock attractive from the very beginning. Now she realized he was far more than just a pretty face and a pair of broad shoulders. It was what she saw in his eyes that held her interest. Intelligence. Humor. And more than a touch of determination. He might be an incompetent burglar, but he had class, he had contacts and he had an insider's familiarity with this neighborhood. By the looks of him, he was an independent, not a man who'd work for someone else. But she might be able to work *with* him.

She might even enjoy it.

She glanced around at the crowded room and motioned Jordan into a quiet corner. "Here's my proposition," she said. "I help you, you help me."

"Help you do what?"

"One itty-bitty job. Nothing, really."

"Just a small burglary?" He rolled his eyes. "Where have I heard that line before?"

"What?"

"Never mind." He sighed and took a sip of wine. "What, may I ask, would I get in return?"

"What would you like?"

His gaze focused with instant clarity on hers. And she knew by the sudden ruddiness of his cheeks that the same lascivious thought had flickered in both their brains.

"I'm not going to answer that," he said.

"Actually, I was thinking of offering up my expert advice in exchange," she said. "I think you could use it."

"Private tutelage in the art of burglary? That *is* a difficult offer to turn down."

"I won't actually help you do it, of course. But I'll give you tips."

"From personal experience?"

She smiled at him blandly over the wineglass. *Time to inflate the old résumé,* she thought. While burgling had never actually been her occupation, she did have a knack for it, and she'd rubbed shoulders with the best in the business, Uncle Walter among them. "I'm good enough to make a decent living," she said simply.

"A tempting proposition. But I'll have to decline."

"I can do wonders for your career."

"I'm not in your line of work."

"Well, what line of work *are* you in?" she blurted in frustration.

There was a long silence. "I'm a gentleman," he said.

"And what else?"

"Just a gentleman."

"That's an occupation?"

"Yes." He smiled sheepishly. "Full time, as a matter of

fact. Still, it leaves me enough leisure for other pursuits. Such as local crime prevention."

"All right." She sighed. "What *can* I offer you just to stay out of my way? And not pop up at inconvenient times?"

"So that you can finish the job on poor old Guy Delancey?"

"Then I'll be out of here for good. Promise."

"What does he own that's so tempting to you, anyway?"

She stared down at her wineglass, refusing to meet his gaze. No, she wouldn't tell him. She couldn't tell him. For one thing, she didn't trust him. If he heard about the Eye of Kashmir, he might want it for himself, and then where would that leave her? No evidence, no proof. She'd be left twisting in the wind.

And Victor Van Weldon would go unpunished.

"It must be quite a valuable item," he said.

"No, its value is rather more..." She hesitated, searching for a believable note. "Sentimental."

He frowned. "I don't understand."

"Guy has something that belongs to my family. Something that's been ours for generations. It was stolen from us a month ago. We want it back."

"If it's stolen property, why not go to the police?"

"Delancey knew it was hot when he purchased it. You think he'd admit to its ownership?"

"So you're going to steal it back?"

"I haven't any choice." Meekly she met his gaze, and she saw a flicker of uncertainty in his eyes. Just a flicker. Was he actually buying this story? She was surprised how rotten that made her feel. She'd been telling a lot of lies lately, had justified each and every one of them by reminding herself this was what she had to do to stay alive. But lying to Jordan Tavistock felt somehow, well...*criminal*.

Which made no sense at all, because that's exactly what *he* was. A thief and a gentleman, she thought, gazing up at him. He had the most penetrating brown eyes she'd ever seen. A face made up of intriguing angles. And a smile that could make her knees weak.

In wonder she glanced down at her drink. What was *in* this wine, anyway? The room was starting to feel warm and she was having trouble catching her breath.

The return of Guy Delancey was like an unwelcome slap of cold air. "It's starting," said Guy.

"What is?" murmured Clea.

"The music. Come on, let's sit down."

She focused at last on Guy and saw that he was looking positively grim. "What about Veronica?"

"Don't mention the name to me," he growled.

Now Veronica entered the room, and she came toward them, her gaze pointedly avoiding Guy. "Jordie, *darling,*" she purred, snatching Jordan's arm with ruthless possession. "Let's sit down, shall we?"

With a look of resignation, Jordan allowed himself to be led away to the performance room.

The musicians, a visiting string quartet from London, were already tuning up, and the audience was settled in their seats. Clea and Guy sat on the opposite end of the room from Jordan and Veronica, but the two couples might as well have been seated side by side, for all the barbed looks flying between Guy and Veronica. All during the performance Clea could almost hear the zing of arrows soaring back and forth.

Dvorak was followed by Bartok, Quartet no. 6, and then Debussy. Through it all, Clea was busy plotting out the evening, wondering how close she could get to the Eye of Kashmir. Hoping that this would be the last evening she'd have to put up with Guy Delancey, with the lies, and with this hideous red hair. She scarcely heard the music. It was only when applause broke out that she realized the program had come to an end.

Refreshments followed, an elegant display of cakes and canapés and wine. A lot of wine. Guy, who'd been barely on the edge of sobriety when he entered the house, now proceeded to drink himself into outright intoxication. It was Veronica's presence that did it. The sight of a lost love flirting with her new escort was just too much for Guy.

Clea watched him reach for yet another glass of wine and decided that things had gone far enough. But how to stop him without making a scene? He was already talking too loudly, laughing too heartily.

That's when Jordan stepped in. She hadn't asked him to, but she'd seen him frowning at Guy, counting the glasses of wine he'd consumed. Now he slipped in beside Guy and said quietly, "Perhaps you should slow down a bit, chap?"

"Slow down what?" demanded Guy.

"That's your sixth, I believe. And you'll be driving the lady home."

"I can handle it."

"Come on, Delancey," Jordan urged. "A little self-control."

"Self-*control?* Who the hell're you to be talking about self-control?" Guy's voice had risen to a bellow, and all around them, conversations ceased. "You take up with another man's wife and you point at *me?*"

"No one's taken up with anyone's wife—"

"At least when I did it, I had the decency to be discreet about it!"

Veronica gave a startled gasp of dismay and ran out of the room.

"Coward!" Guy yelled after her.

"Delancey, please," murmured Jordan. "This isn't the time or place—"

"Veronica!" Guy broke away and pushed his way toward the door. "Why don't you face the bloody music for once! Veronica!"

Jordan looked at Clea. "He's pickled. You can't drive home with him tonight."

"I'll handle him."

"Well, take his keys, at least. Insist on driving yourself."

That was exactly what she'd planned to do. But when she followed Guy outside, she found that he and Veronica were still wrangling away, and loudly, too. Guy was so drunk he was weaving, barely able to stay on his feet. Lying bitch, he kept saying, couldn't trust her, could never trust her. She'd rip your heart in pieces, that's what she'd do, damn her, and he didn't need that. He could find another woman with just the snap of his fingers.

"Then why don't you?" Veronica lashed back.

"I will! I have." Guy swiveled around and focused, bleary-eyed, on Clea. He grabbed her hand. "Come on, let's go!"

"Not in your condition," Clea said, pulling back.

"There's nothing wrong with my condition!"

"Give me the car keys, Guy."

"I can drive."

"No, you can't." She pulled out of his grasp. "Give me the keys."

In disgust he waved her off. "Go on, then. Find your own way home! To hell with both of you! To hell with women!" He stumbled away to his car. With difficulty he managed to open the door and climb in.

"Bloody idiot," muttered Veronica. "He's going to get himself killed."

She's right, thought Clea. She ran to Guy's car and yanked open the door. "Come on, get out."

"Go away."

"You're not driving. I am."

"Go away!"

Clea grabbed his arm. "I'll take you home. You get into the back seat and lie down."

"I don't take orders from any bloody *woman!*" he roared and viciously shoved her away.

Tottering on high heels, Clea stumbled backward and landed in the shrubbery. Stupid man, he was too damn drunk to listen to reason. Even as she struggled to disentangle her necklace from the branches, she could hear him cranking the engine, could hear him muttering about parasitic women. He cursed and slapped the steering wheel as the motor died. Again he cranked the ignition. Just as Clea managed to free her necklace from the shrub, just as she started to sit up, the car's engine roared to life. Without even a farewell glance at her, Guy pulled away.

Idiot, she thought, and rose to her feet.

The explosion slammed her backward. She flew clear over the shrub and landed flat on her back under a tree. She was too stunned to feel the pain of the impact. What she registered first were the sounds: the screams and shouts, the clatter of flying metal hitting the road and then the crackle of flames. Still she felt no pain, just a vague awareness that it was surely to come. She got to her knees and began to crawl like a baby—toward what, she didn't know. Just away from the tree, from the damn bushes. Her brain was starting to work now and it was telling her things she didn't want to know. Her head was starting to hurt, too. Pain and awareness in a simultaneous rush. She thought she was crying, but she wasn't sure; she couldn't even hear her own voice through the roar of noises. She couldn't tell if the warmth streaming down her cheek was blood or tears or both. She kept crawling, thinking, *I'm dead if I don't get away. I'm dead.*

A pair of shoes stood in her way. She looked up and saw a man staring down at her. A man who seemed vaguely familiar, only she couldn't quite figure out why.

He smiled and said, "Let me get you to a hospital."

"No—"

"Come on, you're hurt." He grabbed her arm. "You need to see a doctor."

"No!"

Suddenly the man's hand evaporated and he was gone.

Clea huddled on the ground, the night twirling around her in a carousel of flames and darkness. She heard another voice now—this one familiar. Hands grasped her by the shoulders.

"Diana? *Diana?*"

Why was he calling her that? It wasn't her name. She squinted up into the face of Jordan Tavistock.

And she fainted.

Chapter Five

The doctor switched off the ophthalmoscope and turned on the hospital room light. "Everything appears neurologically intact. But she has had a concussion, and that brief loss of consciousness concerns me. I recommend at least one night in hospital. For observation."

Jordan looked at the pitiful creature lying in bed. Her red hair was tangled with grass and leaves, and her face was caked with dried blood. He said, "I wholeheartedly agree, Doctor."

"Very good. I don't expect there'll be any problems, but we'll watch for danger signs. In the meantime, we'll keep her comfortable and—"

"I can't stay," the woman said.

"Of course you're staying," said Jordan.

"No, I have to get out of here!" She sat up and swung her legs over the side of the bed.

Jordan quickly moved to restrain her. "What the blazes are you doing, Diana?"

"Have to... Have to..." She paused, obviously dizzy, and gave her head a shake.

"You can't leave. Not after a concussion. Now then, let's get back into bed, all right?" Gently but firmly he urged her back under the covers. That attempt to sit up had drained all the color from her face. She seemed as fragile as tissue paper, and so insubstantial she might float away without the weight of the blankets to hold her down. Yet her eyes were bright and alive and feverish with...what? Fear? Grief? Surely she didn't harbor any real feelings for Guy Delancey?

"I'll have a nurse in to help you straightaway," said the doctor. "You just rest, Miss Lamb. Everything will be fine."

Jordan gave her hand a squeeze. It felt like a lump of ice in his grasp. Then, reluctantly, he followed the doctor out of the room.

Down the hall, out of the woman's earshot, Jordan asked, "What about Mr. Delancey? Do you know his condition?"

"Still in surgery. You'd have to inquire upstairs. I'm afraid it doesn't sound hopeful."

"I'm surprised he's alive at all, considering the force of that blast."

"You really think it was a bomb?"

"I'm sure it was."

The doctor glanced at the nurses' station, where a policeman stood waiting for a chance to question the woman. Two cops had grilled her already, and they hadn't been very considerate of her condition. The doctor shook his head. "God, what's the world coming to? Terrorist bombs going off in *our* corner of the world now...."

Terrorists? thought Jordan. Yes, of course it *would* be blamed on some shadowy villain, some ill-defined evil. Who but a terrorist would plant a bomb in a gentleman's car? It was a miracle that only one person had been seriously hurt tonight. A half dozen other musicale guests had suffered minor injuries—glass cuts, abrasions—and the police were calling this a lucky escape.

For everyone but Delancey.

Jordan rode the lift upstairs to the surgical floor. The waiting room was aswarm with police, none of whom would tell him a thing. He hung around for a while, hoping to hear some news, any news, but all he could learn was that Delancey was still alive and on the operating table. As for whether he would live, that was a matter for God and the surgeons.

He returned to the woman's floor. The policeman was still standing in the nurses' station, sipping coffee and chatting up the pretty clerk. Jordan walked right past them and opened the door to Diana's room.

Her bed was empty.

At once he felt a flicker of alarm. He crossed to the bathroom door and knocked. "Diana?" he called. There was no answer. Cautiously he opened the door and peeked inside.

She wasn't there, either, but her hospital gown was. It lay in a heap on the linoleum.

He yanked open the closet door. The shelves were empty; the woman's street clothes and purse had vanished.

What the hell are you thinking? he wondered. Why would she crawl out of her hospital bed, get dressed and steal away like a thief into the night?

Because she is a thief, you bloody fool.

He ran out of the room and glanced up and down the hall. No sign of her. The idiot cop was still flirting with the clerk and was oblivious to anything but the buzz of his own hormones. Jordan hurried down the hall, toward the emergency stairs. If the woman was running from the police, then she'd probably avoid the lift, which opened into the lobby. She'd go for the side exit, which led straight to the parking lot.

He pushed into the stairwell. He was on the third floor. When last he'd seen Diana, she'd looked scarcely strong enough to stand, much less run down two flights of stairs. Could she make it? Was she even now lying in a dead faint on some lower landing?

Terrified of what he might find, Jordan started down the stairs.

HER HEAD WAS pounding mercilessly, the high heels were killing her, but she kept marching like a good soldier down the road. That was how she managed to keep going, left-right-left, some inner drill sergeant screaming commands in her brain. Don't stop, don't stop. The enemy approaches. March or die.

And so she marched, stumbling along on her high heels, her head aching so badly she could scream. Twice she heard a car approaching and had to scramble off the road to hide in the bushes. Both times the cars passed without seeing her, and she crawled back to the road and resumed her painful march. She had only a vague plan of what came next. The nearest village couldn't be more than a few miles away. If she could just get to a train station, she could get out of Buckinghamshire. Out of England.

And then where do I go?

No, she couldn't think that far ahead. All she knew was that she'd failed miserably, that there'd be no more chances and that she was at the very top of Van Weldon's hit list. With new desperation she pushed on, but her feet didn't seem to be working, and the road was weaving before her eyes. *Can't stop,* she thought. *Have to keep going.* But shadows were puddling her vision now, creeping in from the sides. Suddenly nauseated, she dropped to her knees and lowered her head, waiting for the dizziness to pass. Crouching there in the darkness, she vaguely sensed the vibrations through the asphalt. Little by little the sound penetrated the fog clouding her brain.

It was a car, approaching from behind.

Her gaze shot back up the road and she saw the headlights gliding toward her. With a spurt of panic she stumbled to her feet, ready to dash into the bushes, but the dizziness at once assailed her. The headlights danced, blurred into a haze. She discovered she was on her knees, and that the asphalt was biting into her palms. The slam of a car door, the hurried crunch of shoes over gravel told her it was too late. She'd been spotted.

"No," she said as arms closed around her body. "Please, no!"

"It's all right—"

"No!" she screamed. Or thought she had. Her face was wedged against someone's chest, and her cry came out no louder than a strangled whisper. She began to flail at her captor, her fists connecting with his back, his shoulders. The arms only closed in tighter.

"Stop it, Diana! I won't hurt you. *Stop it!*"

Sobbing, she raised her head, and through a mist of tears and confusion she saw Jordan gazing down at her. Her fists melted as her hands reached out to clutch at his jacket. The wool felt so warm, so substantial. Like the man. They stared at each other, her face upturned to his, her body feeling numb and weightless in his arms.

All at once his mouth was on hers, and the numbness gave way to a flood of glorious sensations. With that one kiss he offered his warmth, his strength, and she drank from it, felt its nourishment revive her battered soul. She wanted more, more, and she returned his kiss with the desperate need of a woman who's finally found, in a man's arms, what she'd long been seeking. Not desire, not passion, but comfort. Protection. She clung to him, relinquishing all control of her fate to the only man who'd ever made her feel safe.

Neither of them heard the sound of the approaching car.

It was the distant glare of headlights that forced them to pull apart. Clea turned to look up the road and registered the twin lights burning closer. Instantly she panicked. She jerked out of Jordan's arms and plunged headlong into the bushes.

"Wait!" called Jordan. "Diana?"

Blindly she thrashed through the branches, desperate to flee, but her legs still weren't working right. She heard Jordan right behind her, his footsteps snapping across twigs as he ran to catch up. He snagged her arm.

"Diana—"

"They'll see me!"

"Who?"

"Let me go!"

On the road, the car braked to a stop. They heard the door swing open. At once Clea dropped to the ground and cowered in the shadows.

"Halloa!" called a man's voice. "Everything all right?"

Please, Jordan, Clea prayed. *Cover for me! Don't tell him I'm here....*

There was a pause, then she heard Jordan call back, "Everything's fine!"

"Saw your car had pulled off. Just wanted to check," said the man.

"I'm, er..." Jordan gave a convincingly sheepish laugh. "Answering the call of nature."

"Oh. Well. Carry on, then." The car door slammed shut, and the taillights glided away down the road.

Clea, still shaking, gave a sob of relief. "Thank you," she whispered.

For a moment he stood watching her in silence. Then he reached down and pulled her to her feet. She swayed unsteadily against him.

"Come on," he said gently. "I'll take you back to the hospital."

"No."

"Now see here, Diana. You're in no condition to be wandering around at night."

"I can't go back."

"What are you afraid of, anyway? The police?"

"Just let me *go!*"

"They won't arrest you. You haven't done anything." He paused. Softly he asked, "Have you?"

She wrenched herself free. That one effort cost her what little strength she had left. Suddenly her head was swimming and the darkness seemed to whirl around her like black water. She didn't remember sinking to the ground, didn't remember how she got into his arms, but suddenly she was there, and he was carrying her to the car. She was too tired to struggle, too weak to care anymore what happened to her. She was thrust into the front seat, where she sagged with her head against the door, trying not to faint, fighting the nausea that was beginning to roil her stomach again. *Can't throw up in this nice car,* she thought. *What a shame it would be to ruin his leather upholstery.* She vaguely registered the fact that he was sitting beside her, that the car was now moving. That was enough to nudge fear back into her addled brain.

She reached for his arm, her fingers clutching at his jacket sleeve. "Please," she begged. "Don't take me back to the hospital."

"Relax. I won't force you to go back."

She struggled to focus. Through the darkness of the car, she saw his profile, lean and tense as he stared ahead at the road.

"If you insist, I'll take you to your hotel," he offered. "But you need someone to look after you."

"I can't go there, either."

He frowned at her. Her fear, her desperation, must have registered on her face. "All right, Diana." He sighed. "Just tell me where you want to go."

"The train station."

He shook his head. "You're in no condition to travel."

"I can do it."

"You can scarcely stand up on your own two feet!"

"I have no choice!" she cried. Then, with a desperate sob, she whispered, "I have no choice."

He studied her in silence. "You're not getting on the train," he said at last. "I won't allow it."

"Won't *allow* it?" Sudden rage made her raise her head in defiance. "You have no right. You don't have any idea what I'm facing—"

"Listen to me! I'm taking you to a safe place. You have to trust me on this." He looked at her, a gaze so direct it defied her not to believe him. How simple it would be to hand over her fate to this man, and hope for the best. She wanted to trust him. She *did* trust him. Which meant it was all over for her, because no one who made a mistake that stupid would live long enough to regret it.

I don't have a choice, she thought as another wave of dizziness sent her head lolling to her knees. She might as well wave the white flag. Her future was now out of her hands.

And firmly in the grasp of Jordan Tavistock.

"How is she doing?" asked Richard.

Drained and exhausted, Jordan joined Richard in the library and poured himself a generous shot of brandy. "Obviously scared out of her wits," he said. "But otherwise she seems all right. Beryl's putting her to bed now. Maybe we'll get more out of her in the morning." He drained the brandy in a few gulps, then proceeded to pour himself a well-deserved second shot. He could feel Richard's doubtful gaze on him as he took another sip and sank into the easy chair by the fireplace. Sobriety was normally one of Jordan's virtues. It was unlike him to guzzle a triple brandy in one sitting.

It was certainly not like him to drag home stray females.

Yet that's exactly what he had upstairs at this moment, bundled away in the guest bedroom. Thank God Beryl hadn't bombarded him right off with questions. His sister was good that way; in a crisis she simply did what needed to be done. For the moment the bruised little waif would be well taken care of.

Questions, however, were sure to follow, and Jordan didn't know how to answer them because he himself didn't have the answers. He didn't even know why he'd brought Diana home. All he knew was that she was terrified, and that he couldn't turn his back on her. For some insane reason he felt responsible for the woman.

Even more insane, he *wanted* to feel responsible for her.

He leaned back and rubbed his face with both hands. "What a night," he groaned.

"You've been a very busy fellow," Richard observed. "Car bombs. Runaway females. Why didn't you tell us all this was cooking?"

"I had no idea bombs *would* be going off! I thought all I was dealing with was a cat burglar. Or is it burglaress?" He gave his head a shake to clear away the pleasant fog of brandy. "Theft is one thing. But she never mentioned anything about mad bombers."

Richard moved closer. "My question is," he said quietly, "who was the intended victim?"

"What?" Jordan looked up. He had great respect for his future brother-in-law. Years of working in the intelligence business had taught Richard that one should never accept evidence at face value. One had to examine around it, under it, looking for the twists and turns that might lead to completely different conclusions. Richard was doing that now.

"The bomb was planted in Guy Delancey's car," said Richard. "It could have been a random attack. It could have been aimed specifically at Delancey. Or..."

Jordan frowned at Richard. He saw that they were both considering the same possibility. "Or the target wasn't Delancey at all," Jordan finished softly.

"She was supposed to be riding in the car with him," said Richard. "She would have been killed, as well."

"There's no doubt Diana's terrified. But she hasn't told me what she's afraid of."

"What *do* you know about the woman?"

Jordan shook his head. "All I know is her name is Diana Lamb. Other than that I can't tell you much. I'm not even sure what her real hair color is! One day she's blond, then the next day she transforms into a redhead."

"What about the fingerprints? The ones you got off her glass?"

"I had Uncle Hugh's friend run them through the Scotland Yard computer. No match. Not a surprise, really. Since I'm sure she's a Yank."

"You *have* been busy, haven't you? Why the hell didn't you let me in on this earlier? I could've sent the fingerprints off to American authorities by now."

"I wasn't at liberty to say a thing. I'd promised Veronica, you see."

Richard laughed. "And a gentleman always keeps his promises."

"Well, yes. Except under certain circumstances. Such as car bombs." Jordan stared at his empty brandy snifter and considered pouring another. No, better not. Just look at what drink had done to Guy Delancey. Drink and women—the sole purpose of Delancey's life. And now he lay deprived of both.

Jordan set down the glass. "Motive," he said. "That's what I don't know. Why would someone kill Diana?"

"Or Delancey."

"That," said Jordan, "isn't too difficult to answer. God only knows how many women he's gone through in the past year. Add to that a few angry husbands, and you've probably got a slew of people who'd love to knock him off."

"Including your friend Veronica and her husband."

That possibility made Jordan pause. "I hardly think either one of them would ever—"

"Nevertheless, we have to consider them. Everyone's a suspect."

The sound of footsteps made both men turn. Beryl walked into the library and frowned at her brother and her fiancé. "Who's a suspect?" she demanded.

"Richard wants to include anyone who's had an affair with Guy Delancey," said Jordan.

Beryl laughed. "It'd be easier to start off with who *hasn't* had an affair with the man." She caught Richard's inquiring glance and she snapped, "No, I never have."

"Did I say anything?" asked Richard.

"I saw the look in your eye."

"On that note," cut in Jordan, rising to his feet, "I think I'll make my escape. Good night all."

"Jordan!" called Beryl. "What about Diana?"

"What about her?"

"Aren't you going to tell me what's going on?"

"No."

"Why not?"

"Because," he said wearily, "I haven't the faintest idea."

He walked out of the library. He knew he owed Beryl an explanation, but he was too exhausted to repeat the story a second time. Richard would fill her in on the details.

Jordan climbed the stairs and started up the hall toward his bedroom. Halfway there, he stopped. Some compulsion made him turn around and walk, instead, to the bedroom where Diana was staying. He lingered outside the closed door, debating whether he should walk away.

He couldn't help himself; he tapped on the door. "Diana?" he called.

There was no answer. Quietly he entered the room.

A corner lamp had been left on, and the glow spilled softly over the bed, illuminating its sleeping occupant. She lay curled up on her side, her arms wrapped protectively around her chest, her hair rippling in red-gold waves across the pillow. The linen nightgown she wore was Beryl's, and a few sizes too big; the billowing sleeves almost engulfed her hands. He knew he should leave, but he found himself sinking into the chair beside the bed. There he watched her sleep and thought how very small she looked, how defenseless she truly was.

"My little thief," he murmured.

A sigh suddenly escaped her throat and she stirred awake. She looked at him with unfocused eyes, then slowly seemed to comprehend where she was.

"I'm sorry," he said, and rose from the chair. "I didn't mean to wake you. Go back to sleep." He turned to leave.

"Jordan?"

He glanced back at her. She seemed to be lost in a sea of white sheets and goose-down pillows and puffy nightgown linen, and he had the ridiculous urge to pull her out of there before she drowned.

"I...have to tell you something," she whispered.

"It can wait till tomorrow."

"No, I have to tell you now. It's not fair of me, pulling you into this. When you could get hurt."

Frowning, he moved back to the bed. "The bomb. In the car. *Was* it meant for Guy?"

"I don't know." She blinked, and he saw the sparkle of tears on her lashes. "Maybe. Or maybe it was meant for me. I can't be sure. That—that's what makes this so confusing. Not knowing if I'm the one who was supposed to die. I keep thinking..." She looked at him, her eyes full of torment. "I keep thinking it's my fault, what happened to Guy. He never really did anything wrong. I mean, not *seriously* wrong. He just got caught up in a bit of greed. But he didn't deserve..." She swallowed and looked down at the sheets. "He didn't deserve to die," she whispered.

"There's a chance he might live."

"You saw the explosion! Do you really think anyone could survive it?"

After a pause Jordan admitted, "No. To be honest, I don't think he'll survive."

They fell silent for a moment. *Had she cared at all for Delancey?* he wondered. *Or are her tears purely from guilt?* He couldn't help but feel a little guilty himself. After all, he'd invaded the man's house. He'd never really liked Delancey, had thought him laughable. But now the man was at death's door. No one, not even Guy Delancey, deserved such a terrible end.

"Why do you think *you* might have been the target?" he asked.

"Because..." She let out a deep breath. "Because it's happened before."

"Bombs?"

"No. Other things. Accidents."

"When?"

"A few weeks ago, in London, I was almost run down by a taxi."

"In London," he noted dryly, "that could happen to anyone."

"It wasn't the only time."

"You mean there was another accident?"

She nodded. "In the Underground. I was standing on the train platform. And someone pushed me."

He stared at her skeptically. "Are you positive, Diana? Isn't it more likely that someone just bumped into you?"

"Do you think I'm *stupid?*" she cried. "Wouldn't I know it if someone *pushed* me?" With a sob of frustration she buried her face in her hands.

Her unexpected outburst left him stunned. For a moment he could think of nothing to say. Then, gently, he reached for her shoulder. With that one touch, something seemed to leap between them. A longing. Through the flimsy nightgown fabric he felt the warmth of her skin, and with sudden vividness he remembered the taste of her mouth, the sweetness of her kisses earlier that night.

Ruthlessly he suppressed all those inconvenient urges now threatening to overwhelm his sense of reason. He sat beside her on the bed. "Tell me," he said. "Tell me again what happened in the Underground."

"You won't believe me."

"Give me a chance. Please."

She raised her head and looked at him, her gaze moist and uncertain. "I—I fell onto the tracks. The train was just pulling in. If it hadn't been for a man who saw me..."

"A man? Then someone pulled you out?"

She nodded. "I never even learned his name. All I remember is that he reached down and yanked me back onto the platform. I tried to thank him, but he just—just told me to be more careful. And then he was gone." She shook her head in bewilderment. "My guardian angel."

He looked into those glistening brown eyes and wondered if any of this was possible. Wondered how anyone could be cold-blooded enough to push this woman under a train.

"Why would anyone want you dead?" he asked. "Is it something you've done?"

Instantly she stiffened, as though he'd struck her. "What do you mean, is it something I've done?"

"I'm just trying to understand—"

"Do you think I deserve this somehow? That I must be guilty of something?"

"Diana, I'm not accusing you of anything. It's just that murder—attempted murder—generally involves a motive. And you haven't told me what it is."

He waited for an answer, but he realized that he'd somehow lost her. She was huddled in a self-protective embrace, as though to ward off any further attacks he might launch against her.

"Diana," he said gently, "you have to trust me."

"I don't have to trust anyone."

"It would make it easier. If I'm to help you at all—"

"You've already helped me. I can't really ask you for anything more."

"The least you can do is tell me what I've gotten involved in. If bombs are going to be blowing up around here, I'd like to know why."

She sat stubbornly huddled, not responding. In frustration he rose from the bed, paced to the door, then paced back. Damn it all, she *was* going to tell him. Even if he had to use the threat of last resort.

"If you don't tell me," he said, "I really shall have to call the police."

She looked up in astonishment and gave a disbelieving laugh. "The *police?* I'd think they're the last people you'd want to call. Considering."

"Considering what?"

"Delancey's bedroom. The minor matter of a little burglary."

Sighing, he clawed his hair back. "The time has come to set you straight on that. The truth is, I broke into Guy's house as a favor to a lady."

"What favor?"

"She'd written a few…indiscreet letters to him. She wanted the letters back."

"You're saying it was all a gentleman's errand?"

"You could call it that."

"You didn't mention any lady before."

"That's because I'd promised her I'd stay silent. For the sake of her rather tenuous marriage. But now Delancey's been hurt and bombs are exploding. I think it's time to start telling the truth." He gave her a pointed look. "Don't you agree?"

She thought it over for a moment. Then her gaze slid away from his and she said, "All right. I guess it's confession time." She took a deep breath. "I'm not a thief, either."

"Why were you in Delancey's bedroom?"

"I was doing my job. We're trying to collect evidence. An insurance fraud case."

This time Jordan burst out laughing. "You're claiming to be with the police?"

Red faced, she looked up defiantly. "Why is that funny?"

"Which branch do you work for? The local constabulary? Scotland Yard? Interpol, perhaps?"

"I…I work for a private investigator. Not the police."

"Which investigator?"

"You wouldn't know the company."

"I see. And who, may I ask, is the subject of your investigation?"

"He's not English. His name's not important to you."

"How does Guy Delancey fit in?"

Wearily she ran her hand through her hair. In a voice drained of emotion, she said, "A few weeks ago Guy purchased an antique dagger known as the Eye of Kashmir. It was one of several art pieces reportedly carried aboard the *Max Havelaar* last month. That ship later sank off the coast of Spain. Nothing was recovered. The man who owned the vessel—a Belgian—filed a thirty-two-million-dollar insurance claim for the loss of the ship. And for the artwork. He owned it all."

Jordan frowned. "But you say Delancey recently acquired this dagger. When?"

"Three weeks ago. *After* the boat sank."

"Then…the dagger was never aboard the vessel."

"Obviously not. Since Delancey was able to buy it from some private seller."

"And that's the case you're trying to build? Against the owner of the boat? This Belgian fellow?"

She nodded. "He gets reimbursed by the insurance company for the losses. And he keeps the art to resell. It works out as a sort of double indemnity."

"How did you know Delancey'd acquired the dagger?"

Drained, she sank back against the pillows. "People brag." She sighed. "Delancey did, anyway. He told friends about a seventeenth-century dagger he'd bought from a private source. A dagger with a star corundum—a sapphire—mounted in the hilt. Word got around in the antiques community. From the description, we knew it was the Eye of Kashmir."

"And that's what you were trying to steal from Delancey?"

"Not steal. Confirm its whereabouts. So it can later be confiscated as evidence."

Silently he mulled over this rush of new information. Or was it new fabrication? "You told me earlier tonight that you were stealing something once owned by your family."

She gave a regretful shrug. "I lied."

"Really?"

"I didn't know if I could trust you."

"And you trust me now?"

"You've given me no reason not to." She studied his face, as though looking for some betraying sign that he was not to be trusted, that she'd made a fatal mistake. Slowly she smiled. A coy, almost seductive smile. "And you've been so awfully kind to me. A true gentleman."

Kind? he thought with a silent groan. Was there anything that could dash a man's hopes more brutally than to be called *kind?*

"I *can* trust you," she asked, "can't I?"

He began to pace again, feeling irritated at her, at himself, at how much he wanted to believe this latest outlandish story. He'd been gazing too long into those doe eyes of hers. It was turning his brain into gullible mush. "Why not trust me?" he muttered in exasperation. "Since I've been so awfully *kind.*"

"Why are you angry? Is it because I lied to you before?"

"Shouldn't I be angry?"

"Well, yes. I suppose so. But now that I've come clean—"

"Have you?"

Her jaw squared. It made her even prettier, damn it. He could kick himself for being so susceptible to this creature.

"Yes," she said, her gaze steady. "The Belgian, the *Max*

Havelaar, the dagger—it's all *completely* on the level." She paused, then added quietly, "So is the danger."

The bomb is proof enough of that, he thought.

That, and the sight of her curled up in that bed, gazing at him with those liquid brown eyes, was enough to make him accept everything she'd told him. Which meant he was either going out of his mind or he was too exhausted to think straight.

They both needed to sleep.

He knew he should simply say good-night and walk out of the room. But some irresistible compulsion made him lean down and place a kiss on her forehead. The scent of her hair, the sweetness of soap, was intoxicating.

At once he backed away. "You'll be absolutely safe here," he said.

"I believe you," she said. "And I don't know why I should."

"Of course you should. It's the solemn word of a gentleman." Smiling, he turned off the lamp and left the room.

An hour later he still lay awake in bed, thinking about what she'd told him. All that babbling about insurance fraud and undercover investigations was rubbish and he knew it. But he did believe she was in danger. That much he could see in her eyes: the fear.

He considered just how safe she was here. He knew the house was up-to-date when it came to locks and alarm systems. During the years Uncle Hugh had worked with British Intelligence, security had been a priority here at Chetwynd. The grounds had been monitored, the personnel screened, the rooms regularly swept for listening devices. But since his uncle's retirement a few months ago, those precautions had gradually fallen by the wayside. Civilians, after all, did not need the trappings of a fortress.

While Chetwynd was still fairly secure, anyone determined to break in could probably find a way.

But first they'd have to learn that the woman was here.

That last thought eased Jordan's fears. No one outside this house could possibly know the woman's location. As long as that fact remained a secret, she was safe.

Chapter Six

Clea waited until the house had fallen completely silent before she climbed out of bed. Her head still pounded, and the floor seemed to wobble under her bare feet, but she forced herself to cross the room and crack open the door.

The hallway was deserted. At the far end a small lamp burned, casting its glow across the carpet runner. Next to the lamp was a telephone.

Noiselessly Clea crept down the hall and picked up the receiver. Shaking off a twinge of guilt, she punched in Tony's number in Brussels. All right, so it was a long-distance call. This was an emergency, and the Tavistocks could surely afford the phone bill.

Four rings and Tony answered. "Clea?"

"I'm in trouble," she whispered. "Somehow they've tracked me down."

"Where are you?"

"Safe for the moment. Tony, Delancey's been hurt. He's in a hospital, not expected to live."

"What? How…"

"A bomb went off in his car. Look, I don't think I can reach the Eye. Not for a while. There'll be hordes of police watching his house."

He didn't answer. She thought for a moment the call had been cut off. Then Tony said, "What do you plan to do?"

"I don't know." She glanced around at the sound of a creak, but saw no one. Just old house noises, she thought, her heart still hammering. She said softly, "If they found me, they could find you, too. Get out of Brussels. Go somewhere else."

"Clea, there's something I have to tell you—"

She spun around at another noise. It came from one of the bedrooms. Someone was awake! She hung up the phone and scurried away up the hall.

Back in her room she stood by the door, listening. To her relief, she heard nothing more. At least she'd had a chance to warn Tony. Now it was time to think about herself. She locked the door and wedged a chair against it for good measure. Then she climbed back into bed.

Her headache was starting to fade; perhaps by morning she'd be as good as new. In which case she'd leave Chetwynd and get the hell away before Van Weldon's people tracked her down again. She'd been lucky up till now, but luck couldn't hold, not against the sort of people she was facing. Another change of appearance was called for. A haircut and a reincarnation as a brunette. Glasses. Yes, that might do it, might allow her to slip unnoticed into the London crowd. Once she got out of England, Van Weldon might lose interest in her. She might have a chance of surviving to a ripe old age.

Might.

Tony dropped the receiver back in the cradle. "She hung up on me," he said, and turned to the other man. "I couldn't keep her on the line."

"It may have been long enough."

"Christ, she sounded scared out of her wits. Can't you people call this off?"

"Not yet. We don't have enough. But we're getting close."

"How do you know?"

"Because Van Weldon's getting close to her. He'll be making another move soon."

Tony watched the other man pull out a cigarette and tap it against his lighter. *Why do people do that, tap their cigarettes?* Just another annoying habit of this fellow. In the past week Tony had gotten to know Archie MacLeod's every tic, every quirk, and he was well-nigh sick of the man. If only there was some other way.

But there wasn't. MacLeod knew all about Tony's past, knew about the years he'd spent in prison. If Tony didn't cooperate, MacLeod and Interpol would have that information broadcast to every antiques buyer in Europe. They'd ruin him. Tony had no choice but to go along with this crazy scheme. And pray that Clea didn't get killed in the process.

"You let Van Weldon get too close this time," Tony observed. "Clea could've been blown up in that car."

"But she wasn't."

"Your man slipped up. Admit it!"

MacLeod exhaled a puff of cigarette smoke. "All right, so we were taken by surprise. But your cousin's alive, isn't she? We're keeping an eye on her."

Tony laughed. "You don't even know where she is!"

MacLeod's cellular phone rang. He picked it up, listened a moment, then hung up. He looked at Tony. "We know exactly where she is."

"The phone call?"

"Traced to a private residence. A Hugh Tavistock in Buckinghamshire."

Tony shook his head. "Who's that?"

"We're running the check now. In the meantime, she'll be safe. Our field man's been notified of her whereabouts."

Tony sat on the bed and clutched his head. "When Clea finds out about this, she's bloody well going to kill me."

"From what we've seen of your cousin," said MacLeod with a laugh, "she very likely will."

"THEY HAVE LOST her," said Simon Trott.

Victor Van Weldon allowed no trace of alarm to show on his face as he received the news, but he could feel the rage tightening its grip on his chest. In a moment it would pass. In a moment he'd let his displeasure be known. But he must not lose control, not in front of Simon Trott.

"How did it happen?" asked Van Weldon, his voice icy calm.

"It happened at the hospital. She was taken there after the bombing. Somehow she slipped away from our man."

"She was injured?"

"A concussion."

"Then she can't have gotten very far. Track her down."

"They're trying to. They're afraid, though, that..."

"What?"

"She may have enlisted the help of authorities."

Again, that giant fist seemed to close around Van Weldon's chest. He paused for a moment, struggling for air, counting the seconds for the spell to pass. This was a bad one, he thought, and all because of that woman. She'd be the death of him. He took out his bottle of nitroglycerin and slipped two tablets under his tongue. Slowly the discomfort began to fade. I'm not ready to die, he thought. Not yet.

He looked at Trott. "Have we any proof she's contacted the authorities?"

"She's escaped too many times. She must be getting help. From the police. Or Interpol."

"Not Clea Rice. She'd never trust the police." He slipped the nitroglycerin bottle back in his pocket and took a deep breath. The pain was gone.

"She has been lucky, that's all," said Van Weldon. He gave a careless wave of his hand. "Her luck will run out."

SHE HAD NOT meant to sleep so late, but the concussion had left her groggy and the bed was so comfortable and she felt safe in this house—the safest she'd felt in weeks. By the time she finally crawled out of bed, the sun was shining straight through her window and her headache had faded to only a dull soreness.

I'm still alive, she thought in wonder.

From various parts of the house came the sounds of morning stirrings: creaking floorboards, water running through the pipes. Too late to make an escape unnoticed. She would simply have to play the guest for a few hours. Later she'd slip away, make it on foot to the village train station. How far was it, a few miles? She could do it. After all, she'd once trudged ten miles along the Spanish coast. And that was in the dead of night, while sopping wet. But then, she hadn't been wearing high heels.

She surveyed her clothes. Her dress, torn and dirt stained, was draped over a chair. Her stockings were in shreds. Her shoes, those wretched instruments of torture, sat mocking her with their three-inch spike heels. No, she'd rather go barefoot. Or perhaps in bedroom slippers? She spied a pair by the dresser, comfy-looking pink slippers edged with fluff. Wouldn't *that* blend in with the crowd?

She pulled on a silk bathrobe she found in the closet, slid her feet into the pink slippers and pulled away the chair she'd wedged against the door. Then she ventured out of the room.

The rest of the household was already up and about. She went downstairs and spied them through the French doors. They were outside, assembled around a breakfast table on the terrace. It looked like a photo straight from the pages of some stylish magazine, the iron railings traced by climbing roses, the dew-kissed autumn garden, the table with its linen and china. And the people sitting around that table! There was Beryl with her model's cheekbones and glossy black hair. There was Richard Wolf, lean and relaxed, his arm slung possessively around Beryl's shoulders.

And there was Jordan.

If last night had been a trial for him, it certainly didn't show this morning. He was looking unruffled and elegant as ever, his fair hair almost silvery in the morning light, his tweed jacket perfectly molded to his shoulders. As Clea watched them through the glass, she thought how perfect they looked, like thoroughbreds reared on bluegrass. It wasn't envy she felt, but a sense of wonder, as though she were observing some alien species. She could move among them, could even act the part, but the wrong blood would always run in her veins. Tainted blood. Like Uncle Walter's blood.

Too timid to intrude on that perfect tableau, she turned to retreat upstairs. But as she backed away from the French doors she heard Jordan call her name and she knew she'd been spotted. He was waving to her, beckoning her to join them. No chance of escape now; she'd simply have to brazen it out.

She smoothed out the silk robe, ran her fingers through her hair and stepped out onto the terrace. Only then did she remember the pink slippers. The soles made painfully distinct scuffing sounds across the flagstones.

Jordan rose and pulled out a chair for her. "I was about to check on you. Feeling better this morning?"

Uneasily she tugged the edges of the robe together. "I'm really not dressed for breakfast. My clothes are a mess and I didn't know what else—"

"Don't give it a thought. We're a casual bunch here."

Clea glanced at Beryl, flawlessly pulled together in cashmere and jodhpurs, at Jordan in his wool tweed. A casual bunch. Right. Resignedly she sat down in the offered chair and felt like some sort of zoo specimen with fluffy pink feet. While Jordan poured her coffee and dished out a serving of eggs and sausages, she found herself focusing on his hands, on his long fingers, on the golden hairs glittering on the backs of his wrists. An aristocrat's hands, she thought, and remembered with sudden clarity the gentle strength with which those hands had reached for her in the road last night.

"Don't you care for eggs?"

She blinked at her plate. Eggs. Yes. Automatically she picked up the fork and felt all eyes watching her as she took her first bite.

"I did try to leave you some fresh clothes this morning," Beryl explained. "But I couldn't seem to get in your door."

"I had a chair in front of it," said Clea.

"Oh." Beryl gave a sheepish smile, as though to say, *Well, of course. Doesn't everybody barricade their door?*

No one seemed to know how to respond, so they simply watched Clea eat. Their gazes were not unfriendly, merely...puzzled.

"It's just a habit I picked up," Clea said as she poured cream in her coffee. "I don't trust locks, you see. It's so easy to get past them."

"Is it?" said Beryl.

"Especially bedroom doors. One can bypass your typical bedroom lock in five seconds. Even the newer ones with the disk tumblers."

"How very useful to know that," Beryl murmured.

Clea looked up and saw that everyone was watching her with fascination. Face flushing, she quickly dropped her gaze back to the eggs. *I'm babbling like an idiot,* she thought.

She flinched when Jordan reached for her hand.

"Diana, I've told them."

She stared at him. "Told them? You mean…about…"

"Everything. The way we met. The attempts on your life. I *had* to tell them. If they're to help you, then they need to know it all."

"Believe me, we *do* want to help," said Beryl. "You can trust us. Every bit as much as you trust Jordie."

Clea's hands were unsteady. She dropped them to her lap. *They're asking me to trust them,* she thought in misery. *But I'm the one who hasn't been telling the truth.*

"We have resources that might prove useful," said Jordan. "Connections with Intelligence. And Richard's firm specializes in security. If you need any help at all…"

The offer was almost too tempting to resist. For weeks she'd been on her own, had hopscotched from hotel to hotel, never sure whom she could trust, or where she would go next. She was so very tired of running.

And yet she wasn't ready to put her life in anyone's hands. Not even Jordan's.

"The only favor I ask," she said quietly, "is a ride to the train station. And perhaps…" She glanced down at the pink slippers and gave a laugh. "A change of clothes?"

Beryl rose to her feet. "That I can certainly arrange." She tugged on her fiancé's arm. "Come on, Richard. Let's go rummage around in my closet."

Clea was left sitting alone with Jordan. For a moment

they sat in silence. Up in the trees, doves cooed a lament to the passing of summer. The clouds drifted across the sun, tarnishing the morning to gray.

"Then you'll be leaving us," said Jordan.

"Yes." She folded her napkin and carefully laid it on the table. Though she remained focused on that small square of cream linen, she couldn't shut out her awareness of the man. She could almost feel the warmth of his gaze. All her senses were conspiring against her efforts at indifference. Last night, with that first kiss, they'd crossed some invisible threshold, had wandered into territory with no boundaries, where the possibilities seemed limitless.

That's all they are, she reminded herself. *Possibilities.* Fantasies winking in the murk of half-truths. She had told him so many lies, had changed her story so many times. She still hadn't told him the worst truth of all. Who she was, what she was.

What she had been.

Better to leave him with the fantasy, she thought. Let him assume the best about me. And not know the worst.

She looked up and found he was watching her with a gaze both puzzled and thoughtful. "Where will you go next?" he asked.

"London. It's clear I can't handle this alone. My...associates at the agency will carry on the investigation."

"And what will you do?"

She gave a shrug, a smile. "Take an easier case. Something that doesn't involve exploding cars."

"Diana, if you ever need my help—anything at all—"

Their gazes met and she saw in his eyes the offer of more than just assistance. She had to fight off the temptation to confess everything, to draw him into this dangerous mess.

She shook her head. "I have some very capable colleagues. They'll see I'm taken care of. But thanks for the offer."

He gave a curt nod of the head and said no more about it.

SEATED ON A bench on the train platform, a gray-suited man read his newspapers and watched the passengers gather for the twelve-fifteen to London. It was the fourth train of the day, and so far he hadn't spotted Clea Rice. The bench was occupied by three other women and a bouncy child who kept knocking at the newspaper, and the man was ready to give the brat a whack out of frustration. He'd been so sure Clea Rice would choose the train; now it looked as if she'd managed to sneak out of town some other way. Yes, she was definitely getting better at the game—a quick study at doing the unexpected. He still didn't know how she'd managed to slip away from the hospital last night. That would have been a far easier place to finish it, a private room, the patient under sedation. He had passed for a doctor once before, on a previous job. He certainly could have repeated the ruse.

A pity she hadn't cooperated.

Now he'd have to track her down again, before she vanished into the teeming masses of London.

"Other people 'ere could use the bench, y'know," said a woman.

He looked sideways and saw a steel-haired lady toting a shopping bag. "It's occupied," he said, and snapped his newspaper taut.

"Decent man'd leave it to folks wi' difficulties," said the woman.

He kept reading his newspaper, his fingers suddenly itching for the automatic in his shoulder holster. A hole right between the old biddy's eyes, that's what he'd like to do, just to shut her up. She was nattering on and on now about the dearth of gentlemen in this world, saying it to no one in particular, but loudly enough to draw the attention of people standing nearby. This was not good.

He stood, shot a poisonous look at the old hag, and surrendered his spot on the bench. She claimed it with a grunt of satisfaction. Folding up his newspaper, he wandered to the other end of the platform.

That's when he spotted Clea Rice.

She'd just emerged from the loo. She was wearing a houndstooth skirt and jacket, both a few sizes too large. Her hair was almost completely concealed by a scarf, but a few tendrils of red bangs peeked out. That, plus the way she moved—her gaze darting around, her circuitous route keeping her well away from the platform's edge— told him it was her.

This was not the place to do it.

He decided he'd let her board and would follow her onto the train. There he could keep an eye on her. Perhaps when she got off again...

He had his ticket ready. He stepped forward and joined the crowd of passengers waiting to board.

So CLEA RICE was taking the twelve-fifteen to London. Not the wisest move she could make, thought Charles Ogilvie as he stood in line behind her at the ticket office. He'd had no trouble tailing her from Chetwynd. Jordan Tavistock's champagne gold Jaguar wasn't exactly easy to miss. If he had been able to stay on their trail, surely someone else could do it, as well.

And now the woman was about to board a train in broad daylight.

Ogilvie reached the head of the line and quickly purchased his ticket. Then he followed the woman onto the platform. She vanished into the women's loo. He waited.

Only as the train approached the station did she reemerge. There were about two dozen people standing on the platform, a mingling of business types and housewives, any one of whom could prove lethal. Ogilvie allowed his gaze to drift casually across the faces, trying to match one of them with a face he might have seen before.

At the far edge of the crowd he spotted someone who seemed familiar, a man in a gray suit and carrying a newspaper. His face, while not in any way distinctive, still struck a memory chord. Where had he seen him before?

The hospital. Last night, in the lobby. The man had been buying a paper from the hall newsstand.

Now he was boarding the twelve fifteen to London. Right behind Clea Rice.

A surge of adrenaline pumped through Ogilvie's veins. If something was going to happen, it'd be soon. Perhaps not here in the crowd, but on the train, or at the next stop. All it took was a gun barrel to the back of the head. Clea Rice would never see it coming.

The man in the gray suit was edging closer to the woman.

Ogilvie pushed forward. Already he had his jacket unbuttoned, his shoulder holster within easy reach. His gaze stayed focused on Mr. Gray Suit. At the first sign of attack, he'd bloody well better be ready. He was Clea Rice's only lifeline.

And there'd be no second chances.

ALMOST THERE. ALMOST there.

Clea clutched the ticket like a good-luck charm as she waited for the train to glide to a stop. She hung back a bit, allowing everyone else to press forward first. The memory of that incident in the London Underground was still too fresh; never again would she stand at any platform edge while a train pulled in. All it took was one push from behind. No, it was better to hang back where she could see trouble coming.

The train had pulled to a stop. Passengers were starting to board.

Clea eased into the gathering. Her headache had come throbbing back with a vengeance, and she longed for the relative privacy of a train compartment. A few more steps, and she'd be on her way back to London. To anonymity. It was the best choice, after all—to simply drop out of sight. She'd been insane to think she could match wits with Van Weldon, an opponent who'd met her every thrust with a deadlier parry, who had every reason, and every resource, to crush her. Call it surrender, but she was ready to yield. Anything to stay alive.

She was so focused on getting aboard that she didn't notice the disturbance behind her. Just as she climbed onto the first step, a hand gripped her by the arm and tugged her back onto the platform.

She spun around, every nerve instantly wired for attack, her fingers arcing to claw across her assailant's face. An instant before striking flesh, she froze.

"Jordan?" she said in astonishment.

He grabbed her wrist. "Let's get out of here."

"What are you doing?"

"I'll explain later. Come on."

"But I'm leaving—"

He tugged her away, out of the line of passengers. She tried to yank free but he caught her by the shoulders and pulled her close to him. "Listen to me," he whispered. "Someone's followed us here, from Chetwynd. You can't get on the train."

Instantly she stiffened. His breath felt hot in her hair, and her awareness of his scent, his warmth, had never been more acute. Even through the tweed jacket she could feel the thudding of his heart, the tension in his arms. Without a word she nodded, and the arms encircling her relaxed their hold. Together they turned away from the train and took a step back up the platform.

A man seemed to appear from nowhere. He materialized directly in their path, a man in a gray suit. His face was scarcely worth noting; it was the gun in his hand that drew Clea's stunned gaze.

She was already pivoting away to the left when the first shot rang out. Something slammed into her shoulder, shoving her away. Jordan. In what seemed like slow motion she caught a flash of Jordan's tweed jacket as he lunged against her, and then she was stumbling sideways, falling to her knees onto the platform. The impact of the pavement sent a shock wave straight up her spine. The pain in her head was almost blinding.

Screams erupted all around her. She scrambled back to her feet, at the same time twisting around to locate the attacker. The platform was a melee of panicked bodies scattering in every direction. Jordan still shielded her from a clear view, but over his shoulder she caught a glimpse of the gunman.

Just as he caught a glimpse of her. He raised his pistol.

The shot was like a thunderclap. Clea flinched, but she felt no pain, no impact, nothing but astonishment that she was still alive.

On the gunman's face was registered equal astonishment. He stared down at his chest, where the crimson stain of blood was rapidly blossoming across his shirt. He wobbled, dropped to his knees.

"Get out of here!" barked a voice somewhere off to the side.

Clea turned and saw a second man with a gun standing a few yards away. Frantically he waved at her to get moving.

The man in the gray suit was crawling on hands and knees now, gurgling, cursing, still refusing to drop his pistol. It took a firm push from Jordan to propel Clea forward. Suddenly her legs were working again. She began to run along the edge of the platform, every pounding footstep like another nail being driven into her aching head. She could hear Jordan right behind her, could hear the shouts of confusion echoing in their wake. They reached the rear of the train, leapt off onto the tracks and dashed across to the opposite platform.

Clea scrambled up first. Jordan seemed to be lagging behind. She paused to grab his hand and haul him up from the tracks.

"Don't wait for me," he gasped as they sprinted for the steps. "Just go—the parking lot—"

"I have to wait for you! You have the bloody car keys!"

The Jaguar was double-parked near the station gate. Jordan tossed Clea his keys. "You'd better drive," he said.

She didn't stop to argue. She slid in behind the wheel and threw the car into gear. They screeched out of the lot.

Farther up the road the sound of sirens drew close. The police were headed for the station, thought Clea; they weren't interested in *her*.

She was right. Two police cars sped right past them and kept going.

Clea glanced in the rearview mirror and saw that the road behind them was empty. "No one seems to be following us. I think we're all right."

"For now."

"You said we were tailed from Chetwynd. How did you know?"

"I wasn't sure at first. I kept seeing a black MG on the

road behind us. Then it dropped out of sight. That's why I didn't mention it. I thought it was gone."

"But you came back to get me."

"On the way out of the gate I saw the MG again. It was pulling in to a parking space. That's when I realized..." Grimacing, he shifted in his seat. "Are you going to tell me what the hell's going on?"

"Someone just tried to kill us."

"That I think I knew. Who was the gunman?"

"You mean his name?" She shook her head. Just that movement brought the throbbing back to her skull. "No idea."

"And the other man? The one who just saved our lives?"

"I don't know his name, either. But..." She paused. "I think I've seen him before. In London. The Underground."

"Your guardian angel?"

"But this time *you* saw him. So I guess he's not an angel at all." She glanced in the mirror. Still no one following them. Breathing more easily, she thought ahead to what came next. Chetwynd?

As if he'd read her mind, he said, "We can't go back to Chetwynd. They'll be expecting that."

"*You* could go back."

"I'm not so sure."

"You're not the one they want."

"Are you going to tell me who *they* are?"

"The same people who blew up Guy Delancey's car."

"These people—are they connected with this mysterious Belgian? Or was that just another fable?"

"It's the truth. Sort of."

He groaned. "Sort of?"

She glanced sideways and she noticed that his jaw was tightly squared. *He must be as terrified as I am,* she thought.

"I think I have the right to know the whole truth," he said.

"Later. When I've carved us out some breathing space." She nudged the accelerator. The Jaguar responded with a quiet purr and a burst of speed. "Right now, I just want to get the hell out of this county. When we hit London—"

"London?" He shook his head. "You think it'll be that easy? Just cruise down the highway? If they're as dangerous as you say, they'll have the main roads covered."

And a pale gold Jaguar wasn't a car they'd be likely to miss, she realized. She'd have to ditch the Jag. And maybe the man, as well. He'd be better off without her. Trouble seemed to attach itself to her like iron filings to a magnet, and when the next crisis hit, she didn't want Jordan caught in the cross fire. She owed him that much.

"There's a turnoff coming up," he said. "Take it."

"Where does it go?"

"Back road."

"To London?"

"No. It'll take us to an inn. I know the proprietors. There's a barn where we can hide the car."

"And how do I get to London?"

"We don't. We stay put for a while and get our bearings. Then we figure out our next move."

"I say our next move is to keep going! On foot if we have to! I won't hang around this neighborhood any longer than—"

"But I'm afraid I'll have to," he murmured.

She glanced sideways again. What she saw almost made her swerve off the road in horror.

He had pulled back the edge of his jacket and was staring down at his shirt. Bright splotches of blood stained the fine linen.

Chapter Seven

"Oh, my god," said Clea. "Why didn't you tell me?"

"It's not serious."

"How the hell can you tell?"

"I'm still breathing, aren't I?"

"Oh, that's just *wonderful*." She spun the wheel and sent the Jag in a dizzying U-turn. "We're going to a hospital."

"No." He reached over and grabbed her hand. "They'd be on you in a flash."

"What am I supposed to do? Let you bleed to death?"

"I'm all right. I think it's stopped." He looked down again at his shirt. The stains didn't seem to be spreading. "What's the cliché? 'It's only a flesh wound'?"

"What if it isn't? What if you're bleeding internally?"

"I'll be the first to beg for help. Believe me," he added with a pained smile, "I'm truly a coward at heart."

A coward? she thought. Not this man. He was the least cowardly man she knew.

"Go to the inn," he insisted. "If this is really serious, I can call for help."

Reluctantly she made another U-turn and headed back the way they'd been going. The turnoff brought them onto a narrow road lined by hedgerows. Through gaps in the foliage she spied a patchwork of fields and stone walls. The hedgerows gave way to a graveled driveway, and they pulled up at last in front of the Munstead Inn. A cottage garden, its blossoms fading into autumn, lined the front walk.

Clea scrambled out of the car to help Jordan to his feet.

"Let me walk on my own," he said. "Best to pretend nothing's wrong."

"You might faint."

"I'd never do anything so embarrassing." Grunting, he managed to slide out of the car and stand without her assistance. He made it on his own power through the garden and up the front steps.

Their knock on the door was answered by an elderly gentleman whose peat-colored trousers hung limp on his bony frame. He peered at them through bifocals, then exclaimed in pleasure, "Why, if it isn't young Mr. Tavistock!"

Jordan smiled. "Hello, Munstead. Any rooms available?"

"For friends o' yours, anytime!" The old man stepped aside and waved them into the front hall. "Chetwynd's full up, then?" he asked. "No room for guests?"

"Actually, this room would be for me and the lady."

"You and…" Munstead turned and regarded Jordan with surprise. A sly grin spread across his face. "Ah, it's a bit of a hush thing, is it?"

"Just between us."

Munstead winked. "Gotcha, sir."

Clea didn't know how Jordan managed to hold up his end of the banter. As the old man rummaged for a key, Jordan politely inquired as to Mrs. Munstead's health, asked how the garden was this summer and were the children coming to visit at Christmas? At last they were led upstairs to the second floor. Under better circumstances Clea might have appreciated the romantic touches to the place, the flocked wallpaper, the lace curtains. Now her only focus was to get Jordan into a bed and his wound checked.

When they were safely behind closed doors, Clea practically forced Jordan down onto the mattress. He sat there, his face screwed up in discomfort, as she pulled off the tweed jacket. The droplets of blood staining his shirt led a trail under his right arm.

She unbuttoned the shirt. The blood had dried, adhering the fabric to his skin. Slowly, gently she peeled the shirt off, revealing a broad chest with tawny hair, some of it caked with blood. What she saw looked more like a slash than a bullet wound, as though a knife blade had caught him just in front of the armpit and sliced straight back along his right side.

She gave a sigh of relief. "It looks like just a graze. Caught you in passing. It could just as easily have gone straight through your chest. You're lucky."

He stared down at his wound and frowned. "Maybe it's more a case of divine intervention than luck."

"What?"

"Hand me my coat."

Perplexed, she passed him the tweed jacket. The bullet's entry was easy to locate. It cut a hole through the fabric over the right chest. Jordan reached inside the inner pocket and pulled out a handsome watch attached to a chain. Clearly stamped on the gold watch cover was an ugly dent.

"A helping hand from beyond the grave," he said, and handed Clea the watch.

She flipped open the dented cover. Inside was engraved the name Bernard Tavistock.

"My father's," said Jordan. "I inherited it on his death. It seems he's still watching out for me."

"Then you'd better keep it close by," she said, handing it back. "So it can ward off the next bullet."

"I sincerely hope there won't *be* a next bullet. This one's bloody uncomfortable as it is."

She went into the bathroom, soaked a towel in warm water and wrung it out. When she came back to the bed, he was looking almost sheepish about all the fuss. As she bent to clean the wound, their heads brushed, and she inhaled a disturbingly primal mingling of scents. Blood and sweat and after-shave. His breath warmed her hair, and that warmth seemed to seep into her cheeks. Desperately trying to ignore his effect on her, she kept her gaze focused on his wound.

"I had no idea you'd been hurt," she said softly.

"It was the first shot. I sort of stumbled into it."

"Stumbled, hell! You pushed me away, you idiot."

He laughed. "Chivalry goes unappreciated."

Without warning she planted both hands on either side of his face and lowered her mouth to his in a fierce kiss. She knew at once it was a mistake. Her stomach seemed to drop away inside her. She felt his lips press hard against hers, heard his growl of both longing and satisfaction. Before he could tug her against him, she pulled away.

"You see, you're wrong," she whispered. "Chivalry is most definitely appreciated."

"If that's my reward, I may just do it again."

"Well, don't. Once is chivalry. Twice is stupidity."

Breathing hard, she focused her attention back on his wound. She could feel him watching her, could still taste the tang of his lips on hers, but she stubbornly refused to meet his gaze. If she did, they'd only kiss again.

She wiped up the last dried flecks of blood and straightened. "How are we going to dress it?"

"I've a first aid kit in the car. Bandages and such."

"I'll get it."

"Park the car in the barn, while you're at it. Get it out of sight."

With almost a sense of relief, she fled the room and hurried down the stairs. Once outside, she felt she could breathe again, felt she was back in control.

She walked deliberately to the Jaguar, started the engine and parked it inside the barn. After fetching the first aid kit out of the trunk, she stood by the car for a moment, taking deep, calming breaths of hay-scented air. At last her headache was all but gone and she could think clearly again. *Must concentrate,* she thought. *Remember what it is I'm facing. I can't afford to be distracted. Even by someone as distracting as Jordan.*

With first aid kit in hand, she returned to the room. The instant she stepped inside she felt her hard-won composure begin to crack around the edges. Jordan was standing at the window, his broad back turned to her, his gaze focused somewhere on the garden outside. She suppressed the impulse to go to him, to slide her hands down that expanse of naked skin.

"I hid the car," she said.

She thought he nodded, but he didn't answer.

After a pause she asked, "Is something wrong?"

He turned to look at her. "I called Chetwynd."

She frowned, trying to understand why, with that one call, his whole demeanor should change. "You called? Why?"

"To tell them what's happened. We're going to need help."

"It's better if they don't know. Safer if we don't—"

"Safer for whom?"

"For everyone. They might talk to the wrong people. Reveal things they shouldn't—"

She couldn't read his expression against the glare of

the window. But she could hear the anger in his voice. "If I can't count on my own family, who *can* I count on?"

Stung by his tone, she sat on the bed and stared dully at the first aid kit in her lap. "I envy you your blind faith," she said softly. She opened the kit. Inside were bandages, adhesive tape, a bottle of antiseptic. "Come here. I'd better dress that wound."

He came to the bed and sat beside her. Neither of them spoke as she opened packets of gauze and snipped off lengths of tape. She heard him suck in a startled gasp of air when she dabbed on the antiseptic, but he said nothing. His silence frightened her. Something had changed between them since she'd left the room, something about that phone call to Chetwynd. She was afraid to ask about it, afraid to cut what few threads of connection still remained between them. So she said nothing, but simply finished the task, the whole time fighting off a sense of panic that she'd lost him. Or even worse, that he'd turned against her.

Her worst suspicions seemed confirmed when he said, as she was pressing the last strip of tape to his chest, "Richard's on his way."

She sat back and stared at him. "You told him where we are?"

"I had to."

"Couldn't you just say you're alive and well? Leave it at that?"

"He has something to tell me."

"He could have said everything over the phone."

"It has to be face-to-face." Jordan paused, then he added quietly, "It has to do with you."

She sat clutching the roll of tape, her gaze frozen on his face. *He knows,* she thought. She felt sick to her stomach, sick of herself and her sorry past. Whatever attraction Jordan had felt for her was obviously gone now, destroyed by some revelation gleaned from a phone call.

She swallowed and looked away. "What did he tell you?"

"Only that you haven't been entirely honest about who you are."

"And…" She cleared her throat. "How did he find out?"

"Your fingerprints."

"What fingerprints?"

"The polo field. You left them on your glass in the refreshment tent."

It took her a moment for the implications to sink in. "Then you—*you're* the one who—"

He nodded. "I picked up your glass. Your fingerprints weren't on record at Scotland Yard. So I asked Richard to check with American authorities. And they had the prints on file."

She shot to her feet and backed away from the bed. "I trusted you!"

"I never meant to hurt you."

"No, you just prowled around behind my back."

"I knew you weren't being straight with me. How else could I find out? I had to know."

"Why? What difference would it make to you?" she cried.

"I wanted to believe you. I wanted to be absolutely sure of you."

"So you set out to prove I'm a fraud."

"Is that what I've proved?"

She shook her head and laughed. "What else would I be but a fraud? It's what you looked for. It's what you expected to find."

"I don't know what I expected to find."

"Maybe that I'd be some—some princess in disguise?

Instead you learn the truth. A frog instead of a princess. Oh, but you must be *so* disappointed! *I* find it disappointing that I can't ever outrun my past. No matter how hard I try, it follows me around like one of those little cartoon rain clouds over my head." She looked down at the flowered rug. For a moment she studied the pattern of its weave. Then, wearily, she sighed. "Well, I do thank you for your help. You've been more of a gentleman than any man has ever been to me. I wish...I'd hoped..." She shook her head and turned to the door.

"Where are you going?"

"It's a long walk to London. I think I'll get started."

In an instant he was on his feet and crossing toward her. "You can't go."

"I have a life to get on with."

"And how long will it last? What happens at the next train station?"

"Are you volunteering to take another bullet?"

He caught her arm and pulled her against him. As she collided with his chest, she felt her whole body turn liquid against his heat.

"I'm not sure what I'm volunteering for," he murmured. "But I think I've already signed up..."

The kiss caught them both off-balance. The instant their lips met, Clea felt herself swaying, tilting. He pressed her to the wall, his lips on hers, his body a warm and breathing barrier to escape. Their breaths were coming so loud and fast, their sighs so needy, that she didn't hear the footsteps creaking on the stairs, didn't hear them approach their room.

The knock on the door made them both jerk apart. They stared at each other, faces flushed with passion, hair equally tousled.

"Who is it?" Jordan called.

"It's me."

Jordan opened the door.

Richard Wolf stood in the hall. He glanced at Clea's red-dened cheeks, then looked at Jordan's bare chest. Without comment he stepped into the room and locked the door behind him. Clea noticed he had a file folder stuffed with papers.

"You weren't followed?" asked Jordan.

"No." Richard looked at Clea, and she almost felt like slinking away, so cool was that gaze of his. *So now the truth will be spilled. He knows all, of course.* That must be what he had in that folder—the proof of her identity. Who and what she'd been. He would lay it all out for Jordan, and she wouldn't be able to deny it. And how would Jordan react? With anger, disgust?

Feeling defeated beyond words, she went to the bed and sat down. She wouldn't look at either one of the men; she didn't want to see their faces as they shared the facts about Clea Rice. She would just sit here and passively confirm it all. Then she would leave. Surely Jordan wouldn't bother to stop her this time. Surely he'd be happy to see her go.

She waited on the bed and listened as the truth was finally told.

"Her name isn't Diana Lamb," said Richard. "It's Clea Rice."

Jordan looked at the woman, half expecting a protest, a denial, *some* sort of response, but she said nothing. She only sat with her shoulders hunched forward, her head drooping with what looked like profound weariness. It was almost painful to look at her. This was not at all the brash Diana—correction, Clea—he knew. But then, he'd never really known her, had he?

Richard handed the folder to Jordan. "That was faxed to me just an hour ago from Washington."

"From Niki?"

Richard nodded. Nikolai Sakaroff was his partner in Sakaroff and Wolf, Security Consultants. Formerly a colonel with the KGB and now an enthusiastic advocate of capitalism, Sakaroff had turned his talents for intelligence gathering to more profitable uses. If anyone could dig up obscure information, it was Niki.

"Her fingerprints were on file with the Massachusetts police," said Richard. "Once that fact was established, the rest of it came easy."

Jordan opened the folder. The first page he saw was a grainy reproduction of a mug shot, a frontal and two profiles. The faxing process had blurred the details, but he could still tell it was a younger version of Clea. The subject gazed unsmiling at the camera, her dark eyes wide and bewildered, her lips pressed tightly together. Her hair, free flowing about her shoulders, appeared to be blond. Jordan glanced once again at the live woman. She hadn't moved.

He turned to the next page.

"Three years ago she was convicted of harboring a felon and destruction of evidence," said Richard. "She served ten months in the Massachusetts State Penitentiary, with time off for good behavior."

Jordan turned to Clea. "Is this true?"

She gave a low and bitter laugh. "Yes. In prison I was *very* well behaved."

"And the rest of it? The conviction? The ten months served?"

"You have it all there. Why are you asking me?"

"Because I want to know if it's true."

"It's true," she whispered, and her head seemed to droop even lower.

She seemed in no mood to elaborate, so Jordan turned back to Richard. "Who was the felon? The one she aided?"

"His name's Walter Rice. He's still serving time in Massachusetts."

"Rice? Is he a relative?"

"He's my uncle Walter," said Clea dully.

"What crime did this uncle Walter commit?"

"Burglary. Fraud. Trafficking in stolen goods." She shrugged. "Take your pick. Uncle Walter had a long and varied career."

"Of which Clea was a part," said Richard.

Clea's chin shot up. It was the first spark of anger she'd displayed. "That's not true!"

"No? What about your juvenile record?"

"Those were supposed to be sealed!"

"Sealed doesn't mean nonexistent. At age twelve, you were caught trying to pawn stolen jewelry. At age fourteen, you and your cousin burglarized half a dozen homes on Beacon Hill."

"I was only a child! I didn't know what I was doing!"

"What did you *think* you were doing?"

"Whatever Uncle Walter told us to do!"

"Did Uncle Walter have such power over you that you didn't know right from wrong?"

She looked away. "Uncle Walter was…he was the one I looked up to. You see, I grew up in his house. It was just the three of us. My cousin Tony and my uncle and me. I know what we did was wrong. But the burglaries—they didn't seem real to me, you know. It was more of a…a game. Uncle Walter used to dare us. He'd say, 'Who's clever enough to beat *that* house?' And we'd feel cowardly if we didn't take him up on the dare. It wasn't the money. It was never the money." She looked up. "It was the challenge."

"And what about that issue of right and wrong?"

"That's why I stopped. I was eighteen when I moved

out of Uncle Walter's house. For eight years I stayed on the straight and narrow. I swear it."

"In the meantime, your uncle went right on robbing houses. The police say he was responsible for dozens of burglaries in Boston's wealthiest neighborhoods. Luckily, no one was ever hurt."

"He'd never hurt anyone! Uncle Walter didn't even own a gun."

"No, he was just a virtuous thief."

"He swore he never took from people who couldn't afford it."

"Of course not. He went where the money was. Like any smart burglar."

She stared down again at her knotted hands. A convicted criminal, thought Jordan. She hardly looked the part. But she had managed to deceive him from the start, and he knew now he couldn't trust his own eyes, his own instincts. Not where she was concerned.

He refocused his attention on the file. There were a few pages of notes written in Niki Sakaroff's precise hand, dates of arrest, conviction, imprisonment. There was a copy of a news article about the career of Walter Rice, whose exploits had earned legendary status in the Boston area. As Clea had said, old Walter never actually hurt anyone. He just robbed and he did it with style. He was known as the Red Rose Thief, for his habit of always leaving behind his calling card: a single rose, his gesture of apology to the victims.

Even the most skillful thief, however, eventually meets with bad luck. In Walter's case it took the form of an alert homeowner with a loaded pistol. Caught in the act, with a bullet in his arm, Walter found himself scrambling out the window for his life.

Two days later he was arrested in his niece's apartment, where he'd sought refuge and first aid.

No wonder she did such a good job of dressing my wound, thought Jordan. *She's had practice.*

"It seems to be a Rice family trait," observed Richard. "Trouble with the law."

Clea didn't refute the statement.

"What about this cousin Tony?" asked Jordan.

"He served six years. Burglary," said Richard. "Niki hears through the grapevine that Tony Rice is somewhere in Europe, working as a fence in black market antiques. Am I right, Miss Rice?"

Clea looked up. "Leave Tony out of this. He's clean now."

"Is he the one you're working with?"

"I'm not working with anyone."

"Then how were you planning to fence the loot?"

"What loot?"

"The items you planned to steal from Guy Delancey?"

She reacted with a look of hopeless frustration. "Why do I bother to answer your questions?" she said. "You've already tried and convicted me. There's nothing left to say."

"There's plenty left for you to say," said Jordan. "Who's trying to kill you? And maybe pop me off in the process?"

"He won't bother with you, once I'm gone."

"*Who* won't?"

"The man I told you about." She sighed. "The Belgian."

"You mean that part of the story was true?"

"Yes. Absolutely true. So was the part about the *Max Havelaar.*"

"What Belgian?" asked Richard.

"His name is Van Weldon," said Clea. "He has people

working for him everywhere. Guy was just an accidental victim. *I'm* the one Van Weldon wants dead."

There was a long silence. Richard said slowly, "Victor Van Weldon?"

A glint of fear suddenly appeared in Clea's eyes. She was staring at Richard. "You...know him?"

"No. I just heard the name. A short time ago, in fact." He was frowning at Clea, as though seeing some new aspect to her face. "I spoke to one of the constables about the man shot at the railway station."

"The one who tried to kill us?" said Jordan.

Richard nodded. "He's been identified as a George Fraser. English, with a London address. They tried to track down his next of kin, but all they came up with was the name of his employer. He's a service rep for the Van Weldon Shipping Company."

At the mention of the company's name, Jordan saw Clea give an involuntary shudder, as though she'd just been touched by the chill hand of evil. Nervously she rose to her feet and went to the window, where she stood hugging herself, staring out at the afternoon sunlight.

"What about the other gunman?" asked Jordan.

"No sign of him. It seems he managed to slip away."

"My guardian angel," murmured Clea. "Why?"

"You tell us," said Richard.

"I know why someone's trying to kill me. But not why anyone wants to keep me *alive*."

"Let's start with what you do know," said Jordan. He went to her, placed his hand gently on her shoulder. She felt so small, so insubstantial to his touch. "Why does Victor Van Weldon want you dead?"

"Because I know what happened to the *Max Havelaar*."

"Why it sank, you mean?"

She nodded. "There was nothing valuable aboard that

boat. Those insurance claims were false. And the crew was considered expendable."

"How do you know all this?"

"Because I was there." She turned and looked at him, her eyes haunted by some vision of horror only she could see. "I was aboard the *Max Havelaar* the night it went down."

Chapter Eight

"It was my first trip to Naples," she said. "My first year ever in Europe. I was desperate to escape all those bad memories from prison. So when Tony wrote, inviting me to Brussels, I leapt at the chance."

"That's your cousin?" asked Richard.

Clea nodded. "He's been in a wheelchair since his accident on the autobahn last year. He needed someone he could trust to serve as his business representative. Someone who'd round up buyers for the antiques he sells. It's a completely legitimate business. Tony's no longer dealing in the black market."

"And that's why you were in Naples? On your cousin's behalf?"

"Yes. And that's where I met my two Italian sailors." She looked away again, out the window. "Carlo and Giovanni..."

They were the first mate and navigator aboard a boat docked in the harbor. Both men had liquid brown eyes and ridiculously long lashes and a penchant for innocent mischief. Both adored blondes. And although they'd flirted and made eyes at her, Clea had known on some instinctive level that they were absolutely harmless. Besides, Giovanni was a good friend of Tony's, and in Italy the bond of trust between male friends overrode even the Ital-

ian's finely honed mating instinct. Much as they might be
tempted, neither man would dream of crossing the line
with Clea.

"We spent seven evenings together, the three of us,"
murmured Clea. "Eating in cafés. Splashing in fountains.
They were so sweet to me. So polite." She gave a soft
laugh. "I thought of them as younger brothers. And when
they came up with this wild idea of taking me to Brussels
aboard their ship, I never thought to be afraid."

"You mean as a passenger?" asked Jordan.

"More as an honored stowaway. It was a little escapade
we hatched over Campari and pasta. Their ship was sailing in a few days, and they thought, wouldn't it be fun if
I came along? Their captain had no objections, as long as
I stayed below and out of sight until they left the harbor.
He didn't want any flack from the ship's owner. I could
come out on deck once we were at sea. And in Brussels
they'd sneak me off again."

"You trusted them?"

"Yes. It sounds crazy now, but I did. They were so…
harmless." Clea smiled at the memory. "Maybe it was all
that Campari. Maybe I was just hungry for a bit of adventure. We had it all planned out, you see. The wine we'd
bring aboard. The meals I'd whip up for everyone. They
told me it was a large boat, and the only cargo was a few
crates of artwork bound for an auction house in Brussels.
There'd be plenty of room for a crew of eight. And me.

"So that night I was brought aboard. While the men got
ready to leave, I waited below in the cargo hold. Giovanni
brought me hot tea and chocolate biscuits. He was such
a nice boy…."

"It was the *Max Havelaar* you boarded?" asked Richard softly.

She swallowed. "Yes. It was the *Max Havelaar*." She

took a deep breath, mustering the strength to continue. "She was an old boat. Everything was rusted. Everything seemed to creak. I thought it odd that a vessel that large would carry as its only cargo a few crates of artwork.

"I saw a manifest sheet hanging on one of the crates in the hold. I looked it over. And that's when I realized there was a fortune's worth of antique art in those crates."

"Was the owner listed?"

"Yes. It was the Van Weldon company. They were the shipping agent, as well."

"What did you do then?"

"I was curious, of course. I wanted to take a peek, but all the crates were nailed shut. I looked around for a bit, and finally found a knothole in one of the boards. It was big enough to shine a penlight through. What I saw inside didn't make sense."

"What was there?"

"Stones. The bottom of the crate was lined with stones."

She turned from the window. The two men were staring at her in bewilderment. No wonder. She, too, had been just as bewildered.

"Did you speak to the crew about this?" asked Richard.

"I waited until we'd left the dock. Then I found Giovanni. I asked him if he realized they were carrying crates of rocks. He only laughed. Said I must be seeing things. He'd been told the crates were valuable. He'd seen them loaded aboard himself."

"Who loaded them?"

"The Van Weldon company. They came in a truck directly from their warehouse."

"What did you do then?"

"I insisted we speak to Vicenzo. The captain. He laughed at me, too. Why would a company ship rocks, he kept asking me. And he had other concerns at the time.

The southern coast of Sardinia was coming up, and he had to keep a watch out for other ships. He told me he'd check the cargo later.

"It wasn't until we'd passed Sardinia that I was able to drag them below decks to look. They finally pried open one of the crates. There was a layer of wood shavings on top. Typical packing material. I told them to keep digging. They went through the shavings, then through a layer of newspapers. They kept going deeper and deeper, expecting to find the artwork that was on the manifest. All they found were stones."

"The captain must have believed you then?"

"Of course. He had no choice. He decided to radio Naples, to find out what was going on. So we climbed up the steps to the bridge. Just as we got there, the engine room exploded."

Richard and Jordan said nothing. They only watched her in grim silence as she told them about the last moments of the *Max Havelaar.*

In the panic that followed the explosion, as Giovanni radioed his last SOS, as the crew—what remained of the crew—scrambled to lower the lifeboat, the rocks in the cargo hold were forgotten. Survival was all that mattered. The flames were spreading rapidly; the *Max Havelaar* would be a floating inferno.

They lowered the lifeboat onto the swells. There was no time to climb down the ladder; with the flames licking at their backs, they leapt into the dark Mediterranean.

"The water was so cold," she said. "When I surfaced, I could see the *Havelaar* was all in flames. The lifeboat was drifting about a dozen yards away. Carlo and the second mate had already managed to crawl in, and they were leaning over the gunwale, trying to haul aboard Vicenzo.

Giovanni was still in the water, struggling just to keep his head up.

"I've always been a strong swimmer. I can stay afloat for hours if I have to. So I yelled to the men that they should get the others to climb aboard first. And I treaded water...." She'd felt strangely calm, she remembered. Almost detached from the crisis. Perhaps it was the rhythmic motion of her limbs stroking the liquid darkness. Perhaps it was the sense of dreamlike unreality. She hadn't been afraid. Not yet.

"I knew the Spanish coast was only two miles or so to the north. By morning we could've paddled the lifeboat to land. Finally, all the men were hauled aboard. I was the only one left in the water. I swam over to the lifeboat and had just reached up for a hand when we all heard the sound of an engine."

"Another boat?" asked Jordan.

"Yes. A speedboat of some kind. Suddenly the men all were shouting, waving like crazy. The lifeboat was rocking back and forth. I was behind the gunwale and couldn't see the other boat as it came toward us. They had a searchlight. And I heard a voice calling to us in English. Some sort of accent—I'm not sure what kind. He identified their boat as the *Cosima*.

"Giovanni reached down to help me climb aboard. He'd just grabbed my hand when..." She paused. "When the *Cosima* began to fire on us."

"On the *lifeboat?*" asked Jordan, appalled.

"At first I didn't understand what was happening. I could hear the men crying out. And my hand slid away from Giovanni's. I saw that he was crumpled against the gunwale, staring down at me. I didn't understand that the sound was gunfire. Until a body fell into the water. It was Vicenzo's," she whispered, and looked away.

"How did you escape?" asked Jordan, gently.

Clea took an unsteady breath. "I dove," she said softly. "I swam underwater as far as my lungs would carry me. As fast as I could stroke away from that searchlight. I came up for air, then dove again and kept swimming. I thought I heard bullets hitting the water around me, but *Cosima* didn't chase after me. I just kept swimming and swimming. All night. Until I reached the coast of Spain."

She stood for a moment with bowed head. Neither man spoke. Neither man broke the silence.

"They killed them all," she whispered. "Giovanni. The captain. Six helpless men in a lifeboat. They never knew there was a witness."

Jordan and Richard stood watching her. They were both too shocked by her story to say a word. She didn't know if they believed any of it; all she knew was that it felt good to finally tell it, to share the burden of horror.

"I reached the coast around dawn," she continued. "I was cold. Exhausted. But mostly I was desperate to reach the police." She shook her head. "That was my mistake, of course. Going to the police."

"Why?" asked Jordan gently.

"I ended up in some village police station, trying to explain what had happened. They made me wait in a back room while they checked the story. It turns out they called the Van Weldon company, to confirm their boat was missing. It made sense, I suppose. I can't blame the police for checking. So I waited three hours in that room for some representative from Van Weldon to arrive. Finally he did. I heard his voice through the door. I recognized it." She trembled at the memory. "It was the voice from the *Cosima*."

"You mean the killers were working for Van Weldon?" said Jordan.

Clea nodded. "I was climbing out that window so fast I must have left scorch marks. I've been running ever since. I found out later that *Cosima*'s registered owner is the Van Weldon Shipping Company. They sabotaged the *Havelaar*. They murdered its crew."

"And then claimed it as a giant loss," said Richard. "Artwork and all."

"Only there *wasn't* any artwork aboard," said Clea. "It was a dummy shipment, meant to go down on a boat they didn't need anymore. The real art's being stored somewhere. I'm sure it will be sold, piece by piece, on the black market. A double profit, counting the insurance."

"Who carried the policy?"

"Lloyd's of London."

"Have you contacted them?"

"Yes. They were skeptical of my story. Kept asking me what I wanted out of this, whether I had a grudge against the Van Weldon company. Then they learned about my prison record. After that, they didn't believe anything I said." Sighing, she went to the bed and sat down. "I told my cousin Tony to drop out of sight—he's the obvious person they'd use to track me down. He's in a wheelchair. Vulnerable. He's hiding out somewhere in Brussels. I can't really expect much help from him. So I'm floundering around on my own."

A long silence passed. When at last she found the courage to look up, she saw that Jordan was frowning at the wall, and that Richard Wolf was obviously not convinced of her story.

"You don't believe me, do you, Mr. Wolf?" she said.

"I'll reserve judgment for later. When I've had a chance to check the facts." He turned to Jordan. "Can we talk outside?"

Jordan nodded and followed Richard out of the room.

From the window Clea watched the two men standing in the garden below. She couldn't hear what they were saying, but she could read their body language—the nods, the grim set of Jordan's face. After a few moments Richard climbed in his car and drove away. Jordan reentered the building.

Clea stood waiting for him. She was afraid to face him, afraid to confront his skepticism. Why should he believe her? She was an ex-con. In the past month she had told so many lies she could scarcely keep them all straight. It was too much to ask that he would take her word for it this time.

The door opened and Jordan entered, his expression unreadable. He studied her for a moment, as though not certain just what to do with her. Then he let out a deep breath.

"You certainly know how to throw a fellow for a loop," he said.

"I'm sorry" was all she could think of saying.

"Sorry?"

"I never meant to drag you into this. Or your family either. It would be easier all around if you just go home. Somehow I'll get to London."

"It's a little late in the game, isn't it? To be casting me off?"

"You'll have no problems. Van Weldon isn't interested in *you*."

"But he is."

"What?"

"That's what Richard wanted to tell me. On his way to meet us, he was followed. Someone's watching Chetwynd, monitoring everyone's comings and goings."

Clea stiffened with alarm. "They followed him here?"

"No, he lost them."

"How can he be sure?"

"Believe me, Richard's an old hand at this. He'd know if he was followed."

Heart racing, she began to pace the room. She didn't care how skilled Richard Wolf might be—the chances were, he would underestimate Van Weldon's power, his resources. She'd spent the past month fighting for her life. She'd made it her business to learn everything she could about Van Weldon, and she knew, better than anyone, how far his tentacles reached. He had already discovered the link between her and the Tavistocks. It was just a matter of time before he used that knowledge to track her down.

She stopped pacing and looked at Jordan. "What next? What does your Mr. Wolf have in mind?"

"A fact-finding mission. Some discreet inquiries, a chat with Lloyd's of London."

"What do we do in the meantime?"

"We sit tight and wait right here. He'll call us in the morning."

She nodded and turned away. *In the morning,* she thought, *I'll be gone.*

VICTOR VAN WELDON was having another attack, and this was a severe one, judging by the pallor of his face and the tinge of blue around his lips. Van Weldon was not long for this world, thought Simon Trott—a few months at the most. And then he'd be gone and the path would be clear for his appointed successor—Trott himself.

If Van Weldon didn't sack him first, a possibility that was beginning to seem likely since the latest news had broken.

"How can this be?" Van Weldon wheezed. "You said it was under control. You said the woman was ours."

"A third party stepped in at the last moment. He ruined everything. And we lost a man."

"What about this family you mentioned—the Tavistocks?"

"The Tavistocks are a distraction, nothing more. It's not them I'm worried about."

"Who, then?"

Trott paused, reluctant to broach the possibility. "Interpol," he said at last. "It seems the woman has attracted their attention."

Van Weldon reacted with a violent spasm of coughing. When at last he'd caught his breath again, he turned his malevolent gaze to Trott. "You have brought us to disaster."

"I'm sure it can be remedied."

"You left the task to fools. And so," he added ironically, "did I."

"The police have nothing. Our man is dead. He can't talk."

"Clea Rice can."

"We'll find her again."

"How? Every day she grows more and more clever. Every day we seem to grow more and more stupid."

"Eventually we'll have a lead. Our contact in Buckinghamshire—"

Van Weldon gave a snort. "That contact is a liability! I want the connection severed. And there must be a consequence. I will not tolerate such treachery."

Trott nodded. Consequences. Penalties. Yes, he understood their necessity.

He only hoped that he would not someday be on the receiving end.

IT WAS WELL after dark when Richard Wolf finally drove in through the gates of Chetwynd. As he passed between the stone pillars his gaze swept the road, searching for a telltale silhouette, a movement in the bushes. He knew he was being watched, just as he knew he'd been followed earlier today. Even if he didn't quite believe Clea Rice's story, he did believe that she was in real danger. Her fear had infected him as well, had notched up his alertness to the point he was watching every shadow. He was glad Beryl had gone off to London for a few days. He'd call her later and suggest she stay longer—anything to keep her well away from this Clea Rice mess.

A car he didn't recognize was parked in the driveway.

Richard pulled up beside it. Cautiously he got out and circled around the Saab, glanced through the window at the interior. Inside were a few folded newspapers, nothing to identify the driver.

He went up the steps to the house.

Davis greeted him at the front door and helped him off with his raincoat. "You have a visitor, Mr. Wolf."

"So I've noticed. Who is it?"

"A Mr. Archibald MacLeod. He's in the library."

"Did he mention the purpose of his visit?"

"Some sort of police business."

At once Richard crossed the hall to the library. A man—brown haired, short but athletic build—stood beside the far bookcase, examining a leather-bound volume. He looked up as Richard entered.

"Mr. MacLeod? I'm Richard Wolf."

"Yes, I know. I've made inquiries. I've just spoken to an old colleague of yours—Claude Daumier, French Intelligence. He assures me I can have complete confidence in you." MacLeod closed the book and slid it back on the shelf. "I'm from Interpol."

"And I'm afraid I'm quite in the dark."

"We believe you and Mr. Tavistock have stumbled into a somewhat hazardous situation. I'm anxious to see that no one gets hurt. That's why I'm here to ask for your co-operation."

"In what matter?"

"Tell me where I can find Clea Rice."

Richard hoped his alarm didn't show on his face. "Clea Rice?" he asked blankly.

"I know you're familiar with the name. Since you requested an ID of her fingerprints. And a copy of her criminal record. The American authorities alerted us to that fact."

The man really must be with the police, Richard concluded. Nevertheless, he decided to proceed cautiously. Just because MacLeod was a cop didn't mean he could be trusted.

Richard crossed to the fireplace and sat down. "Before I tell you anything," he said, "I'd like to hear the facts."

"You mean about Clea Rice?"

"No. About Victor Van Weldon."

"Then will you tell me how to find Miss Rice?"

"Why do you want her?"

"We've decided it's time to move on her. As soon as possible."

Richard frowned. "You mean—you're arresting her?"

"Not at all." MacLeod faced him squarely. "We've used Miss Rice long enough. It's time to bring her into protective custody."

A SOFT DRIZZLE was falling as Clea stepped out the front door of the Munstead Inn. It was past midnight and all was dark inside, the other occupants having long since retired. For a full hour she had lain awake beside Jordan, waiting until she was certain he was asleep. Since the revelations of that afternoon, mistrust seemed to loom between them, and they had staked out opposite sides of the bed. They'd scarcely spoken to each other, much less touched.

Now she was leaving, and it was all for the better. The break was cleaner this way—no sloppy emotions, no uneasy farewells. He was the gentleman. She was the ex-con. Never the twain could meet.

The back gate squealed as she opened it. She froze, listening, but all she heard was the whisper of drizzle on tree leaves and, in the distance, the barking of a dog. She pulled her jacket tightly against the moist chill and began to trudge down the road.

It would be an all-night walk; by daybreak she could be miles from here. If her feet held out. If she wasn't spotted by the enemy.

Ahead stretched the twin hedgerows lining both sides of the road. She debated whether or not to walk on the far side of the hedge, where she would be hidden from the road, but after a few steps in the mud she decided the pavement was worth the risk. She wouldn't get far in this sucking mire. Chances were, no one would be driving this late at night, anyway. She slogged back around the hedge and clambered onto the road. There she froze.

The silhouette of a man was standing before her.

"You could have told me you were leaving," said Jordan.

Relieved it was him, she found her breath again. "I could have."

"Why didn't you?"

"You would have stopped me. And I can't afford any more delays. Not when I know they're one step behind."

"You'll be safer with me than without me."

"No, I'm safer on my own. I'm getting good at this, you know. I may actually survive to see the ripe old age of thirty-one."

"As what, a fugitive? What kind of life is that?"

"At least it's a life."

"What about Van Weldon? He gets off with murder?"

"I can't do anything about that. I've tried. All it's earned me is a bunch of thugs on my tail and a head of peroxide-damaged hair. I give up, okay? He wins. And I'm out of here." She turned and began to walk away, down the road.

"Why did you come to England, anyway? Was it really the dagger you were after?"

"Yes. I thought, if I could steal it back, I'd have my evidence. I could prove to everyone that Van Weldon was lying. That he'd filed a false claim. And maybe—maybe someone would believe me."

"If what you're saying is true—"

"*If* it's true?" She turned in disgust and continued walking up the road. Away from him. "I suppose I made up the guy with the gun, too."

He followed her. "You can't keep running. You're the only witness to what happened to the *Havelaar*. The only one who can nail Van Weldon in court."

"If he doesn't nail me first."

"The police need your testimony."

"They don't believe me. And they won't without solid evidence. I wouldn't trust the police, anyway. You think Van Weldon got rich playing by the rules? Hell, no. I've checked into him. He has a hundred lawyers who'll pull strings to get him off. And probably a hundred cops in his pocket. He owns a dozen ships, fourteen hotels and three casinos in Monaco. Okay, so last year he didn't do so well. He got overextended and lost a bundle. That's why he ditched the *Havelaar* to—pardon the pun—keep his head above water. He's a little desperate and a little paranoid. And he'll squash anyone who gets in his way."

"I'll get you help, Clea."

"You have a nice mansion and a CIA-in-law. That's not enough."

"My uncle worked for MI6. British Intelligence."

"I suppose your uncle's chummy with a few members of Parliament?"

"Yes, he is."

"So is Van Weldon. He makes friends everywhere. Or he buys them."

He grabbed her arm and pulled her around to face him. "Clea, eight men died on the *Havelaar*. You saw it happen. How can you walk away from that?"

"You think it's easy?" she cried. "I try to sleep at night, and all I see is poor Giovanni slumping over the lifeboat. I hear gunfire. And Vicenzo moaning. And I hear the voice of that man. The one on the *Cosima*. The one who ordered them all killed…." She swallowed back an unexpected swell of tears. Angrily she wiped them away. "So, no, it ain't easy. But it's what I have to do if I want—"

Jordan cut her off with a sharp tug on her arm. Only at that instant did Clea notice the flicker of light reflected in his face. She spun around to face the road.

In the distance a car was approaching. As it rounded a curve, its headlights flitted through the hedgerow branches.

At once Jordan and Clea were dashing back the way they'd come. The hedges were too high and thick to cross; their only escape route was along the road. Rain had left the pavement slippery, and Clea's every step was bogged down by the mud still clinging to her shoes. Any second they'd be spotted.

Jordan yanked her sideways, through a gap in the hedge.

They tumbled through and landed together in a bed of wet grass. Seconds later the car drove past and continued on, toward the Munstead Inn. Through the stillness of the night they heard the engine's growl fade away. Then there was nothing. No car doors slamming, no voices.

"Do you think they've gone on?" whispered Clea.

"No. It's a dead-end road. There's only the inn."

"Then what are they doing?"

"Watching. Waiting for something."

For us, she thought.

Suddenly she was frantic to get away, to escape the threat of that car and its faceless occupants. This time she didn't dare use the road. Instead she headed across the field, not knowing where she was going, knowing only that she had to get as far away from the Munstead Inn as she could. The mud sucked at her shoes, slowing every step, making her stumble again and again, until she felt as if she was trapped in that familiar nightmare of pursuit, her legs refusing to work. She was panting so hard she didn't hear Jordan following at her heels. Only when she fell to her knees and he reached down for her did she realize he was right beside her.

He pulled her back to her feet. She stood swaying, her legs shaky, her breath coming in gasps. Around them stretched the dark vastness of the field. Overhead the sky was silvery with mist and rain.

"We're all right," he panted, struggling to catch his breath, as well. "They're not following us."

"How did they know where to look for us?"

"It couldn't have been the Munsteads."

"Then it was Richard Wolf."

"No," said Jordan firmly. "It wasn't Richard."

"They could've followed him—"

"He said he wasn't followed."

"Then he was wrong!" She pulled away. "I should never have trusted you. Any of you. Now it's going to get me killed." She turned and struggled on through the mire.

"Clea, wait."

"Go home, Jordan. Go back to being a gentleman."

"Can you keep on running?"

"Damn right I can! I'm getting as far away as possible. I yanked on the tiger's tail. I was lucky to live through it."

"You think Van Weldon will let you go? He'll hunt you down, Clea. Wherever you run, you'll be looking over your shoulder. You're a constant threat to him. The one person who could destroy him. Unless he destroys you first."

She turned. In the darkness of the field his face was a black oval against the silver of the night clouds. "What do you want me to do? Fight back? Surrender?" She gave a sob of desperation. "Either way, Jordan, I'm lost. And I'm scared." She hugged herself in the rain. "And I'm freezing to death."

At once his arms came around her, pulling her into his embrace. They were both damp and shivering, yet even through their soaked clothes she felt his warmth seep toward her. He took her face in his hands, and the kiss he pressed to her lips was enough to sweep away, just for a moment, her discomfort. Her fear. As the rain began to beat down on the fields and the clouds swept across the moon, she was aware only of him, the salty heat of his mouth, the way his body molded itself around hers.

When at last she'd caught her breath again, and they stood gazing at each other in the darkness, she found she was no longer shaking from fear, but from longing.

For him.

He said softly, "I know a place we can go tonight. It's a long walk. But it will be warm there, and dry."

"And safe?"

"And safe." Again he framed her face in his hands and kissed her. "Trust me."

I have no choice, she thought. *I'm too tired to think of what I should do. Where I should go.*

He took her hand. "We cross this field, then follow the roads," he said. "On pavement, so they won't be able to track our footprints."

"And then?"

"It's a three-, four-mile walk. Think you can make it?"

She thought about the men in the car, waiting outside the Munstead Inn. She wondered if somewhere, in the cylinder of one of their guns, there lurked a bullet with her name on it.

"I can make it," she said, her pace quickening. "I'll do anything," she added under her breath, "to stay alive."

Chapter Nine

A few taps of a rock and the window shattered.

Jordan broke away the jagged edges and climbed in. A moment later he reappeared at the cottage's front door and motioned for Clea to enter.

She stepped inside and found herself standing in a quaint room furnished with rough-hewn antiques and pewter lamps. Massive ceiling beams, centuries old, ran the length of the room, and all around her, burnished wainscoting gleamed against the whitewashed walls. It would have been a cozy room were it not so cold and drafty. The English, thought Clea, must have thermally insulated hides.

Jordan, soaked as he was, looked scarcely discomfited as he moved about the room, closing shutters. "I'll have to make it up to old Monty, that broken window. He'll understand. Doesn't much use this cottage except in the summer. In fact, I believe he's in Moritz at the moment. Trying to land the next Mrs. Montgomery Dearborn."

How many Mrs. Dearborns are there? Clea wanted to ask, but she couldn't get out the question; her teeth were chattering too hard. What feeling she had left in her limbs was quickly fading to numbness. She knew she should strip off her wet clothes, should try to start a fire in the hearth, but she couldn't seem to make her body move. She could only stand there, water dripping from her clothes onto the wood floor.

Jordan turned on a lamp. By the light's glow he caught his first real look at her. "Good Lord," he said, touching her face. "You're like an ice cube."

"Fire," she whispered. "Please, start a fire."

"That'll take too long. You need to get warmed up now." He pulled her down a hall and into the bathroom. Quickly he turned on the shower spigot. As water hissed out in a sputtering stream he began to peel off her sopping wool jacket.

"Electric coil heater," said Jordan. "It'll warm up in a minute." He tossed her jacket aside and unzipped her skirt. She was too cold to care about anything so trivial as modesty; she let him pull her skirt off, let the fabric drop in a pile on the floor. The water was steaming now; he tested the temperature, then thrust her, underwear and all, into the shower.

Even with hot water streaming over her body, it seemed to take forever for her to stop shaking. She huddled, dazed, under the spigot. Slowly the heat penetrated her numbness and she could feel her blood start to circulate again, could feel the flush of warmth at last seeping toward her core.

"Clea?" she heard Jordan say.

She didn't answer. She was too caught up in the pleasure of being warm again. Sighing, she shifted around to let the stream roll down her back. Vaguely, through the rattle of water, she heard Jordan call.

"Are you all right?"

Before she could answer, the shower curtain was abruptly pushed aside. She found herself gazing up at Jordan's face.

As he was gazing at hers.

For a moment they said nothing. The only sound was

the pounding of the shower. And the pulsing of her heart-beat in her ears. Though she was barely clothed, though her transparent undergarments clung to her skin, Jordan's gaze never wavered from her face. He seemed mesmer-ized by what he saw there. Drawn by the longing he surely recognized in her eyes.

She reached out and touched his face. His cheek felt rough and chilled under her hot fingertips. Just that one contact, that brush of her skin against his, seemed to melt all the barriers between them. She felt another kind of heat ignite within her. She pulled his face down to hers and met his lips in a kiss.

At once they were both clinging to each other. Whim-pering. Hot water streamed across their shoulders, hers bare, his still clothed in the shirt. Through the curls of steam, she saw in his face the long-suppressed desire that had been throbbing between them since the night they'd met.

She pressed even more eagerly against him and gave a soft sigh of pleasure, of triumph, at the burgeoning re-sponse of his body.

"Your clothes," she murmured, and reached up fever-ishly to pull off his shirt. He shrugged it off onto the bath-room floor, baring his chest, so recently bandaged. The golden hairs were damp and matted from the shower. They were both breathing in gasps now, both working franti-cally at his belt.

Somehow they got the water shut off. Somehow they managed to find their way out of the shower, out of the bathroom with its obstacle course of wet clothes littering the tiles. They left a trail of still more wet clothes, lying where they'd dropped, his trousers near the bathroom door, her bra in the hallway, his undershorts at the threshold of the bedroom. By the time they reached the bed, there were no more clothes to shed. There was only damp flesh and murmurs and the yearning to be joined.

The bedroom was cold and they slid, shivering, beneath the goose-down duvet. As they lay with limbs intertwined, mouths exploring, tasting, the heat of their bodies warmed the bed. Her shivering ceased. The room's chill was forgotten in the rush of sensations now flooding through her, the sweet ache between her thighs, the sharp darts of pleasure as his mouth found her breasts, drawing her nipples to almost agonizing tautness.

She rose above him and returned the torment with a vengeance. Her mouth traced down the plane of his chest, grazed his belly, seeking ever more sensitive flesh. Groaning, he gripped her shoulders, and his body twisted off the mattress, rolling her onto the pillow. Suddenly she was lying beneath him, his body hard atop hers, his hands cupping her face.

Their gazes met, held. They never stopped looking at each other, even as he slid inside her, filled her. Even as she cried out with the pleasure of his penetration.

He moved slowly, gently. Their gazes held.

His breaths came faster, his hands clutching more tightly at her face. Still they looked at each other, joined in a bond that went deeper than flesh.

Only when she felt that exquisite ache build to the first ripples of release did she close her eyes and surrender to the sensations flooding through her. A soft cry floated from her throat, a sound both foreign and wonderful. It was matched, seconds later, by his groan. Through the ebbing waves of her own pleasure she felt his last frantic thrusts, and then he pulsed deep within her. With a shuddering sigh his spent body came to rest and fell still.

She cradled his head against her shoulder. As she

pressed a kiss to his damp hair, she felt a wave of tenderness so overpowering it frightened her.

We made love. What does it mean?

They'd enjoyed each other's bodies. They'd given each other satisfaction and, for a few moments, even happiness.

But what does it mean?

She pressed another kiss to the damp tendrils and felt again that twinge of affection, so intense this time it brought tears to her eyes. Blinking them away, she turned her face from him, only to feel his hand cradle her cheek and nudge her gaze back to his.

"You are the most surprising woman I've ever met," he said.

She swallowed. And laughed. "That's me. Full of surprises."

"And delights. I never know what to expect from you. And it's starting to drive me quite mad." He lowered his mouth and tenderly brushed his lips against hers, tasting, nibbling. Enjoying. Already she could feel the rekindling of his arousal, could feel his heaviness stirring against her thigh.

She slid her hand between their hips and with a few silken strokes she had him hard and throbbing again. "You're full of surprises yourself," she murmured.

"No, I'm quite…" he gave a sigh of delight "—conventional."

"Are you?" She lowered her mouth to his nipple and traced a circle of wetness with her tongue.

"Some would even call me—" he dropped his head back and groaned "—damned predictable."

"Sometimes," she whispered, "predictable is good."

With her tongue she began to trace a wet line across his chest to his other nipple. He was breathing hard, struggling to check his rising tide of passion.

"Wait. Clea…" He caught her face. Gently he tilted it up toward him and looked at her. "I have to know. Why were you crying?"

"I wasn't."

"You were. A moment ago."

She studied him, hungrily devouring every detail. The way the light played on his ruffled hair. The crescent shadows cast by his eyelashes. The way he looked at *her,* so quietly, intently. As though she was some strange, unknowable creature.

"I was thinking," she said, "how different you are from any man I've known."

"Ah. No wonder you were crying."

She laughed and gave him a playful slap. "No, silly. What I meant was, the men I've known were always… after something. Wanting something. Planning the next take."

"You mean, like your uncle Walter?"

"Yes. Like my uncle Walter."

The mention of her past, her flawed childhood, suddenly dampened her desire. She pulled away from him. Sitting up, she hugged her knees. If only she could make that part of her life drop away. If only she could be born anew. Without shame.

"I'm embarrassed to admit he's my relative," she said.

He laughed. "I'm embarrassed by my relatives all the time."

"But none of yours are in prison…are they?"

"Not as of this moment, no."

"Uncle Walter is. So was my cousin Tony." She paused and added softly, "So was I."

He reached for her hand. He didn't say anything. He just watched her, and listened.

"It was so ironic, really. For eight years I went perfectly

straight. And suddenly Uncle Walter pops up outside my apartment. Bleeding all over my front porch. I couldn't turn him in. And he wouldn't let me take him to the hospital. So there I was, stuck with him. I burned his clothes. Tossed his lock picks in a Dumpster across town. And then the police showed up." She gave a shrug, as though that last detail was scarcely worth mentioning. "The funny thing is," she said, "I don't hate him for it. Not a bit. You can't hate Uncle Walter. He's so damn…" She gave a sheepish shrug. "Lovable."

Laughing, he pressed her palm to his lips. "You have a most unique take on life. Like no other woman I've known."

"How many ex-cons have you slept with?"

"You, I must admit, are my first."

"Yes, I imagine you'd normally prefer a proper lady."

He frowned at her. "What's this rubbish about *proper* ladies, anyway?"

"Well, I don't exactly qualify."

"*Proper* is dull. And you, my dear Miss Rice, are not dull."

She tossed her head back and laughed. "Thank you, Mr. Tavistock, for the compliment."

He tugged her toward him. "And as for your notorious uncle Walter," he whispered, pulling her down on top of him, "if he's related to you, he must have some redeeming features."

She smiled down at him. "He *is* charming."

He cupped her face and kissed her. "I'm sure."

"And clever."

"I can imagine."

"And the ladies say he's quite irresistible…."

Again Jordan's mouth found hers. His kiss, deeper, harder, swept all thoughts of Uncle Walter from her mind.

"Quite irresistible," murmured Jordan, and he slid his hand between her thighs.

At once she was lost, needing him, crying out for him. She bared her warmth and he took it tenderly. And when it was over, when exhaustion finally claimed him, he fell asleep with his head on her breast.

She smiled down at his tousled hair. "You will remember me fondly some day, won't you, Jordan?" she whispered.

And she knew it was the best she could hope for.

It was all she dared hope for.

HE AWAKENED TO the subtle perfume of a woman's scent, to the tickle of hair against his face. He opened his eyes and by the gray light slanting in through the shutters he saw Clea asleep beside him. Without a trace of makeup, and her hair lushly tangled across the pillow, she looked like some fairy princess over whom a spell of deathless repose had been cast. Unarousable, untouchable. Not altogether real.

How real she'd felt to him last night! Not a princess at all, but a temptress, full of sweet mischief and even sweeter fire.

Even now he couldn't resist her. He reached for her and kissed her on the mouth.

Her reaction was abrupt and startling. She gave a shudder of alarm and jerked up from the pillow.

"It's all right," he soothed. "It's only me."

She stared for a moment, as though not recognizing him. Then she gave a soft gasp and shook her head. "I—I haven't been sleeping very well. Needless to say."

He watched her huddle beneath the duvet and wondered how she had maintained her sanity through these weeks of running and hiding. He couldn't help but feel a rush of pity for her. It was mingled with admiration for her strength. Her will to live.

She glanced at the window and saw daylight gleaming through the closed shutters. "They'll be searching for us. We can't stay here much longer."

"We can't exactly stroll away, either. Not without help."

"Oh, no. No more calling on friends and family. I'm sure that's how they found us last night. Your Richard Wolf must have told someone."

"He'd never do that."

"Then they followed him. Or they've tapped your phone. Something." Abruptly she climbed out of bed and snatched up her underwear. Finding it still damp, she tossed it in disgust onto a chair. "I'm going to have to leave naked."

"Then you'll most certainly catch someone's eye."

"You're not much help. Can't you get out of bed, at least?"

"I'm thinking. I think best in bed."

"Bed is where most men don't think at all." She picked up her bra. It, too, was damp. She looped it over the door-knob and glanced around the room in frustration. "You say the man who owns this place is a bachelor?"

"In between states of wedded bliss."

"Does he have any women's clothes?"

"I've never thought to ask Monty such a personal question."

"You know what I mean."

He rose from the bed and went to open the wardrobe door. Inside hung two summer suits, a raincoat and a few neatly pressed shirts. On Jordan they'd all fit nicely. On Clea they'd look ridiculous. He took out a bathrobe and tossed it to her.

"Unless we can turn you into a six-foot man," he said, "this wardrobe won't work. And even if we did find women's clothes in here, there's still the matter of your hair. That flaming red isn't the most subtle color."

She snatched a lock of her hair and frowned at it. "I hate it, anyway. Let's cut it off."

He eyed those lustrous waves and was forced to give a regretful nod. "Monty always keeps a bottle of hair dye around to touch up his graying temples. We could darken what's left of your hair."

"I'll find some scissors."

"Wait. Clea," he said. "We have to talk."

She turned to him, her jaw set with the determination of what had to be done. "About what?"

"Even if we do change your appearance, running may not be your best option."

"I think it's my only option."

"There's still the authorities."

"They didn't believe me before. Why should they believe me now? My word's nothing against Van Weldon's."

"The Eye of Kashmir would change that."

"I don't have it."

"Delancey does."

She shook her head. "By now, Van Weldon must have realized what a mistake it was to sell the Eye so soon. His people will be trying to get it back."

"What if they haven't? It may still be in Delancey's house, waiting to be snatched. By us."

She went very still. "Us?" she asked quietly.

"Yes, us." He smiled at her, a smile that did not seem to inspire much confidence, judging by her expression. "Congratulations. Meet your new partner in crime," he said.

"That's supposed to make me feel better?"

"Doesn't it?"

"I'm just thinking about your last burglary attempt. And how close you came to getting us both handcuffed."

"That was inexperience. I'm now fully seasoned."

"Right. And ready for the frying pan."

"What is this, a crisis of confidence? You told me you used to burglarize houses just for the challenge of it."

"I didn't know better then. I was a kid."

"And now you're experienced. Better at the art."

Letting out a breath, she began to pace a line back and forth in the carpet. "I know I could break in again. I'm *sure* I could. But I don't know where to look. The dagger could be anywhere upstairs. The bedroom, the guest rooms. I'd need time."

"Together, we could do it in half the time."

"Or get caught twice as fast," she muttered. And she left the room.

He followed her into the kitchen, where he found her rummaging through drawers for the scissors. "There's always the other option," he said. "The logical one. The reasonable one. We go to the police."

"Where they'll laugh in my face, the way they did before. And Van Weldon will know exactly where to find me."

"You'll be under protection. I promise."

"The safest place for me, Jordan, is out where I can run. A moving target's not so easy to hit." She found the scissors and handed them to him. "Especially when the target keeps changing its appearance. Go ahead, do it."

He looked down at the scissors, then looked at that beautiful mane of hair. The task was almost too painful, but he had no choice. Regretfully he took a handful of cinnamon red hair. Just the scent of those silky strands was enough to reawaken all the memories of last night. The way her body had fitted against his. The way she'd moved beneath him, not a docile release but the joyous shudders of a wild creature.

That's what she was. A wild thing. Sensuous. Unpredictable. In time she would drive him crazy.

Already he was losing his long-practiced sense of self-control. All it took was a few whiffs of her hair, the touch of silk in his palm, and he was ready to drag her back to bed.

He gave his head a shake to clear away those inconvenient images. Then he lifted the scissors and calmly, deliberately, began to snip off her hair.

BY THE GRAY morning light, they followed the footprints in the mud—a pair of them, one large set, one smaller set, veering away from the road. The prints headed west across the field. It had rained heavily last night, and the tracks were easy to follow for about three hundred yards or so, until they connected up with another road. Then, after a few muddy imprints on the pavement, the footprints faded.

They could be anywhere by now.

Archie MacLeod gazed out over the field and cursed. "I should've known she'd do this. Probably got one inkling we were on her trail and off she goes. Like a bloody she-fox, that one."

"You can hardly blame her," said Richard. "Of course she'd expect the worst. How did your people fumble this one? They were supposed to bring her into custody. Instead they managed to chase her underground."

"Their orders were to do it quietly. Somehow she got wind of them."

"Or Jordan did," said Richard. "I should have contacted him last night. Told him what was coming down. Now he'll wonder."

"You don't think he doubts *you?*"

"No. But he'll be cautious now. He'll assume Van Weldon's got me covered, that it won't be safe to contact me. That's what I'd assume in his place."

"So how do we find them now?"

"We don't." Richard turned to his car and slid in behind the wheel. "And we hope Van Weldon doesn't, either."

"I'm not so confident of that."

"Jordan's clever. So is Clea Rice. Together they may do all right."

MacLeod leaned in the car window. "Guy Delancey died this morning."

"I know," said Richard.

"And we've just heard rumors that Victor Van Weldon's upped the price on Clea Rice to two million. Within twenty-four hours this area will be swarming with contract men. If they get anywhere near Clea Rice, she won't stand a chance. Neither will Tavistock."

Richard stared at him. "Why the hell did you wait so long to bring her into custody? You should have locked her under guard weeks ago."

"We didn't know whether to believe her."

"So you waited for Van Weldon to make a move, was that the strategy? If he tried to kill her, she must be telling the truth?"

MacLeod slapped the car door in frustration. "I'm not defending what we've done. I'm just saying we're now convinced she's told the truth." He leaned forward. "Jordan Tavistock is your friend. You must have an idea where he'd go."

"I'm not even sure he's the one calling the shots right now. It might be the woman."

"You let me know if you come up with any ideas. Anything at all about where they might go next."

Richard started the car. "I know where *I'd* go if I were

them. I'd get away from here. I'd run as fast as I could. And I'd damn well get lost in a crowd."

"London?"

Richard nodded. "Can you think of a better place to hide?"

"THAT WOMAN MUST have nine lives. And she's used up only three of them," said Victor Van Weldon. He was wheezing again. His breathing, which was normally labored even on the best of days, had the moist rattle of hopelessly congested lungs.

Soon, thought Simon Trott. Victor was a dying man. What a relief it would be when it was over. No more of these distasteful audiences, these grotesque scenes of a virtual corpse fighting to hang on. If only the old man would just get it over with and die. Until then, he'd have to stay in the old man's good graces. And for that, he'd have to take care of this Clea Rice problem.

"You should have seen to this yourself," said Victor. "Now we've lost our chance."

"We'll find her again. We know she's still with Tavis-tock."

"Has he surfaced yet?"

"No. But eventually he'll turn to his family. And we'll be ready."

Van Weldon exhaled a deep sigh. His breathing seemed clearer, as though the assurances had eased the congestion in his lungs. "I want you to see to it personally."

Trott nodded. "I'll leave for London this evening."

CROUCHED BEHIND THE yew hedge of Guy Delancey's yard, Jordan and Clea waited in the darkness for the house lights to go out. Whitmore's nightly habit was as it had always been, the checking of the windows and doors at nine o'clock, the pause in the kitchen to brew a pot of tea, then the retreat upstairs to his room in the servants' wing. How many years has the fellow clung to that petrified routine of his? Clea wondered. What a shock it must be to him, to know that all would soon change.

Clea and Jordan had heard it on the radio that morning: Guy Delancey was dead.

Soon others would come to claim this house. And old Whitmore, a relic from the dinosaur age, would be forced to evolve.

The lights in the servants' wing went out.

"Give him half an hour," whispered Jordan. "Just to make sure he's asleep."

Half an hour, thought Clea, shivering. She'd freeze by then. She was dressed in Monty's black turtleneck and a baggy pair of jeans, which she'd shortened with a few snips of the scissors. It wasn't enough protection against this chill autumn night.

"Which way do we enter?" asked Jordan.

Clea scanned the house. The French door leading from the terrace was how she'd broken in the last time. No doubt that particular lock had since been replaced. So, undoubtedly, had the locks on all the ground-floor doors and windows.

"The second floor," she said. "Balcony off the master bedroom."

"That's how I got in the last time."

"And if *you* managed to do it," she said dryly, "it must have been a piece of cake."

"Oh, right, insult your partner. See where it gets you."

She glanced at him. His blond hair was concealed under a watch cap, and his face was blackened with grease. In the darkness only the white arc of his teeth showed in a Cheshire-cat grin.

"You're sure you're up to this?" she asked. "It could get sticky in there."

"Clea, if things do go wrong, promise me."

"Promise you what?"

"You'll run. Don't wait for me. And don't look back."

"Trying to be chivalrous again? Something silly like that?"

"I just want to get things straight now. Before things go awry."

"Don't say that. It's bad luck."

"Then this is for good luck." He took her arm, pulled her against him and kissed her. She floundered in his embrace, torn between wanting desperately to get kissed again, and wanting to stay focused on the task that lay ahead. When he finally released her, they stared at each other for a moment. Only the gleam of his eyes and teeth were visible in the darkness.

That was a farewell kiss, she realized. In case things went wrong. In case they got separated and never saw each other again. A chill wind blew and the trees creaked overhead. As the moments passed, and the night grew colder, she tried to commit every detail to memory. Because she knew, as he did, that every step they took could end in disaster. She had not counted on this complication, had not wanted this attraction. But here it was, shimmering between them. The fact it couldn't last, that any feelings they had for each other were doomed by who she was, and who he was, only made those feelings all the sweeter. *Will you miss me someday, Jordan Tavistock?* she wondered. *As much as I'll miss you?*

At last he turned and looked at the house. "I think it's time," he said softly.

She, too, turned to face the house. The wind swept the lawn, bringing with it the smell of dead leaves and chill earth. The scent of autumn, she thought. Too soon, winter would be upon them....

She eased away from the hedge and began to move through the shadows. Jordan was right behind her.

They crossed the lawn, their shoes sinking into wet grass. Beneath the bedroom balcony they crouched to reassess the situation. They heard only the wind and the rustle of leaves.

"I'll go first," he said.

Before she could protest, he was scrambling up the wisteria vine. She winced at the rattle of branches, expecting at any moment that the balcony doors would fly open, that Whitmore would appear waving a shotgun. Lucky for them, old Whitmore still seemed to be a sound sleeper. Jordan made it all the way up without a hitch.

Clea followed and dropped noiselessly onto the balcony.

"Locked," said Jordan, trying the doorknob.

"Expected as much," she whispered. "Move away."

He stepped aside and watched in respectful silence as she shone a penlight on the lock. "This should be even easier than the one downstairs," she whispered and gently inserted the makeshift L-pick she'd fashioned that afternoon using a wire hanger and a pair of pliers. "Circa 1920. Probably came with the house. Let's hope it's not so rusty that it bends my..." She gave a soft chuckle of satisfaction as the lock clicked open. Glancing at Jordan she said wryly, "There's nothing like a good stiff tool."

He answered, just as wryly, "I'll remember to keep one on me."

The room was as she'd remembered it, the medieval curtained bed, the wardrobe and antique dresser, the desk and tea table near the balcony doors. She'd searched the desk and dresser before; now she'd take up where she had left off.

"You search the wardrobe," she whispered. "I'll do the nightstands."

They set to work. By the thin beam of her penlight she examined the contents of the first nightstand. In the drawers she found magazines, cigarettes and various other items that told her Guy Delancey had used this bed for activities beyond mere sleeping. A flicker of movement overhead made her aim the penlight at the ceiling. There was a mirror mounted above the bed. To think she had actually considered a romp in this bachelor playpen! Turning her attention back to the nightstand, she saw that the magazines featured naked ladies galore, and not very attractive ones. Entertainment, no doubt, for the nights Guy couldn't find female companionship.

She searched the second nightstand and found a similar collection of reading material. So intent was she on poking for hidden drawers, she didn't notice the creak of floorboards in the hallway. Her only warning was a sharp hiss from Jordan, and then the bedroom door flew open.

The lights sprang on overhead.

Clea, caught in midcrouch beside the bed, could only blink in surprise at the shotgun barrel pointed at her head.

Chapter Ten

The gun was wavering ominously in Whitmore's unsteady grasp. The old butler looked most undignified in his ratty pajamas, but there was no mistaking the glint of triumph in his eyes.

"Gotcha!" he barked. "Thinkin' to rob a dead man, are you? Think you can get away with it again? Well, I'm not such an old fool!"

"Apparently not," said Clea. She didn't dare glance in Jordan's direction, but off in her peripheral field of vision she spied him crouched beside the wardrobe, out of Whitmore's view. The old man hadn't yet realized there were two burglars in the room.

"Come on, come on! Out from behind that bed! Where I can see you!" ordered Whitmore.

Slowly Clea rose to her feet, praying that the man's trigger finger wasn't as unsteady as his grip. As she straightened to her full height, Whitmore's gaze widened. He focused on her chest, on the unmistakable swell of breasts.

"Ye're only a woman," he marveled.

"Only?" She gave him a wounded look. "How insulting."

At the sound of her voice, his eyes narrowed. He scanned her grease-blackened face. "You sound familiar. Do I know you?"

She shook her head.

"Of course! You come to the house with poor Master Delancey! One of his lady friends!" The grip on the shotgun steadied. "Come 'ere, then! Away from the bed, you!"

"You're not going to shoot me, are you?"

"We're going to wait for the police. They'll be here any minute."

The police. There wasn't much time. Somehow they had to get that gun away from the old fool.

She caught a glimpse of Jordan, signaling to her, urging her to shift the butler's gaze toward the left.

"Come on, move out from behind the bed!" ordered Whitmore. "Out where I can get a clear shot if I have to!"

Obediently she crawled across the mattress and climbed off. Then she took a sideways step, causing Whitmore to turn leftward. His back was now squarely turned to Jordan.

"I'm not what you think," she said.

"Denying you're a common thief, are you?"

"Certainly not a *common* one, anyway."

Jordan was approaching from the rear. Clea forced herself not to stare at him, not to give Whitmore any clue of what was about to happen….

What *was* about to happen? Surely Jordan wouldn't bop the old codger on the head? It might kill him.

Jordan raised his arms. He was clutching a pair of Guy Delancey's boxer shorts, was going to pull them like a hood over old Whitmore's head. Somehow Clea had to get that gun pointed in another direction. If startled, Whitmore might automatically let fly a round.

She gave a pitiful sob and fell to her knees on the floor. "You can't let them arrest me!" she wailed. "I'm afraid of prison!"

"Should've thought of that before you broke in," said Whitmore.

"I was desperate! I had to feed my children. There was no other way…." She began to sob wretchedly.

Whitmore was staring down at her, astonished by this bizarre display. The shotgun barrel was no longer pointed at her head.

That's when Jordan yanked the boxer shorts over Whitmore's face.

Clea dived sideways, just as the gun exploded. Pellets whizzed past. She scrambled frantically back to her feet and saw that Jordan already had Whitmore's arms restrained, and that the gun had fallen from the old man's grasp. Clea scooped it up and shoved it in the wardrobe.

"Don't hurt me!" pleaded Whitmore, his voice muffled by the makeshift hood. The boxer shorts had little red hearts. Had Delancey really pranced around in little red hearts? "Please!" moaned Whitmore.

"We're just going to keep you out of trouble," said Clea. Quickly she bound the butler's hands and feet with Delancey's silk ties and left him trussed on the bed. "Now you lie there and be a good boy."

"I promise!"

"And maybe we'll let you live."

There was a pause. Then Whitmore asked fearfully, "What do you mean by *maybe?*"

"Tell us where Delancey keeps his weapons collection."

"What weapons?"

"Antique swords. Knives. Where are they?"

"There's not much time!" hissed Jordan. "Let's get out of here."

Clea ignored him. *"Where are they?"* she repeated.

The butler whimpered. "Under the bed. That's where he keeps them!"

Clea and Jordan dropped to their knees. They saw nothing beneath the rosewood frame but carpet and a few dust balls.

Somewhere in the night, a siren was wailing.

"Time to go," muttered Jordan.

"No. Wait!" Clea focused on an almost imperceptible crack running the length of the bed frame. A seam in the wood. She reached underneath and tugged.

A hidden drawer glided out.

At her first glimpse of the contents, she gave an involuntary gasp of wonder. Jewels glittered in hammered-gold scabbards. Sword blades of finely tempered Spanish steel lay in gleaming display. In the deepest corner were stored the daggers. There were six of them, all exquisitely crafted. She knew at once which dagger was the Eye of Kashmir. The star sapphire mounted in the hilt gave it away.

"They were his pride and joy," moaned Whitmore. "And now you're stealing them."

"I'm only taking one," said Clea, snatching up the Eye of Kashmir. "And it didn't belong to him, anyway."

The siren was louder now and closing in.

"Let's *go!*" said Jordan.

Clea jumped to her feet and started toward the balcony. "Cheerio!" she called over her shoulder. "No hard feelings, right?"

"Bloody unlikely!" came the growl from under the boxer shorts.

She and Jordan scrambled down the wisteria vine and took off across the lawn, headed at a mad dash for the woods fringing the property. Just as they reached the cover of trees, a police car careened around the bend, siren screaming. Any second now the police would find Whitmore tied up on the bed and then all hell would break loose. The threat of pursuit was enough to send Jordan and Clea scrambling deep into the woods. Replay of the night we met, thought Clea. Hanging around Jordan Tavistock must be bad luck; it always seemed to bring the police on her tail.

The sting of branches whipping her face, the ache of her muscles, didn't slow her pace. She kept running, listening for sounds of pursuit. A moment later she heard distant shouting, and she knew the chase had begun.

"Damn," she muttered, stumbling over a tree root.

"Can you make it?"

"Do I have a choice?"

He glanced back toward the house, toward their pursuers. "I have an idea." He grabbed her hand and tugged her through a thinning copse of trees. They stumbled into a clearing. Just ahead, they could see the lights of a cottage.

"Let's hope they don't keep any dogs about," he said and started toward the cottage.

"What are you doing?" she whispered.

"Just a small theft. Which, I'm sorry to say, seems to be getting routine for me."

"What are you stealing? A car?"

"Not exactly." Through the darkness his teeth gleamed at her in a smile. "Bicycles."

IN THE LAUGHING Man Pub, Simon Trott stood alone at the bar, nursing a mug of Guinness. No one bothered him, and he bothered no one, and that was the way he liked it. None of the usual poking and prodding of a stranger by the curious locals. The villagers here, it seemed, valued a man's privacy, which was all to the better, as Trott had no tolerance tonight for even minor annoyances. He was not in a good mood. That meant he was dangerous.

He took another sip of stout and glanced at his watch. Almost midnight. The pub owner, anxious to close up, was already stacking up glasses and darting impatient looks at his customers. Trott was about to call it a night when the pub door opened.

A young policeman walked in. He sauntered to the bar where Trott stood and called for an ale. A few moments went by, no one saying a word. Then the policeman spoke.

"Been some excitement around 'ere tonight," he said to no one in particular.

"What sort?" asked the bartender.

"'Nother robbery, over at Under'ill. Guy Delancey's."

"Thieves gettin' bloody cheeky these days, if you ask me," the bartender said. "Goin' for the same 'ouse twice."

"Aren't they, though?" The policeman shook his head. "Makes you wonder what's become of society these days." He drained his mug. "Well, I best be gettin' 'ome. 'Fore the missus gets to worryin'." He paid the tab and walked out of the pub.

Trott left, as well.

Outside, in the road, the two men met. They walked across the village green, stepping in and out of shadows.

"Anything stolen from Underhill tonight?" asked Trott.

"The butler says just one item was taken. Antique weapon of some sort."

Trott's head lifted in sudden interest. "A dagger?"

"That's right. Part of a collection. Other things weren't touched."

"And the thieves?"

"There were two of them. Butler only saw the woman."

"What did she look like?"

"Couldn't really tell us. Had some sort of black grease on 'er face. No fingerprints, either."

"Where were they last seen?"

"Escaped through the trees. Could've gone in any direction. I'm afraid we lost 'em."

Then Clea Rice had not left Buckinghamshire, thought Trott. Perhaps she was right now in this very village.

"If I 'ear more, I'll let you know," said the policeman.

Their conversation had come to an end. Trott reached into his jacket and produced an envelope stuffed with five-pound notes. Not a lot of money, but enough to help keep a young cop's family clothed and fed.

The policeman took the envelope with an odd reluctance. "It's only information you'll be wantin', right? You won't be expecting more?"

"Only information," Trott reassured him.

"Times are…difficult, you see. Still, there are things I don't—won't—do."

"I understand." And Trott did. He understood that even upright cops could be tempted. And that for this one, the downhill slide had already begun.

After the two men parted, Trott returned to his room in the inn and called Victor Van Weldon.

"As of a few hours ago, they were still in the area," said Trott. "They broke into Delancey's house."

"Did they get the dagger?"

"Yes. Which means they've no reason to hang around here any longer. They'll probably be heading for London next."

Even now, he thought, Clea Rice must be wending her way along the back roads to the city. She'll be feeling a touch of triumph tonight. Perhaps she's thinking her ordeal will soon end. She'll sense hope, even victory whenever she looks at that dagger. The dagger she calls the Eye of Kashmir.

How wrong she will be.

THE SOUNDS OF London traffic awakened Clea from a sleep so heavy she felt drugged. She rolled onto her back and peered through slitted lids at the daylight shining in through the ratty curtains. How long had they slept? Judging by her grogginess it might have been days.

They'd checked in to this seedy hotel around six in the morning. Both of them had stripped off their clothes and collapsed on the bed, and that was the last she remembered. Now, as her brain began to function again, the events of last night came back to her. The endless wait at the station for the 4:00 a.m. train out of Wolverton. The fear that, lurking among the shadows on the platform, was someone who'd been watching for them. And then, during the train ride to London, the anxiety that they'd be robbed, that they'd lose their precious cargo.

She reached under the bed and felt the wrapped bundle. The Eye of Kashmir was still there. With a sigh of relief she settled back on the bed, next to Jordan.

He was asleep. He lay with his face turned toward her, his bare shoulder tanned a warm gold against the linen, his wheat-colored hair boyishly tousled. Even in sleep he looked every inch the aristocrat. Smiling, she stroked his hair. *My darling gentleman,* she thought. *How lucky I am to have known you. Someday, when you're married to some proper young lady, when your life has settled in according to plan, will you still remember your Clea Rice?*

Sitting up, she stared at her own reflection in the dresser mirror. Right, she thought.

Suddenly depressed, she left the bed and went to take a shower. Later, as she inspected her latest hair color—this time a nut brown, courtesy of Monty's bottle of hair dye—she felt resentment knot up in her stomach. She was not a lady, nor was she proper, but she damn well had her assets. She was bright, she could think fast on her feet and, most important, she could take care of herself. What possible use did *she* have for a gentleman? He'd be a nuisance, really, dragging her off all the time to soirees. Whatever those were. She'd never fit into his world. He'd never fit into hers.

But here, in this room with the mangy carpet and mildewed towels, they could share a temporary world. A world of their own making. She was going to enjoy it while it lasted.

She went back to the bed and climbed in next to Jordan.

At the touch of her damp body, he stirred and murmured, "Is this my wake-up call?"

She answered his question by sliding her hand under the covers and stroking slowly down the length of his torso. He sucked in a startled gasp as she found exquisitely tender flesh and evoked the hoped-for response.

"If that was my wake-up call," he groaned, "I think it worked."

"Maybe now you'll get up, sleepyhead," she said, laughing, and rolled away.

He caught her arm and hauled her right back. "What about this?"

"What about what?"

"This."

Her gaze traveled to the distinct bulge under the sheets. "Shall I take care of that for you?" she whispered.

"Seeing as you're the reason it's there in the first place…"

She rolled on top of him, fitting her hips to his. He was at her mercy now, and she intended to make him beg for his pleasure. But as their bodies moved together, as she felt him grasp her hips in both hands and pull her down against him, it was she who was at his mercy, she who was begging for release. He gave it to her, in wave after glorious wave, and through the roar of her pulse in her ears she heard him say her name aloud. Once, twice, in a murmur of delight.

Yes, I'm the one he's making love to, she thought. *Me. Only me.*

For these few sweet moments, it was enough.

ANTHONY VAUXHALL WAS a starched little prig of a man with a nose that always seemed to be tilted up in distaste of mere mortals. Jordan had met him several times before, on matters relating to his late parents' estate. Their conversations had been cordial, and he hadn't formed much of an opinion of the man either way.

He was forming an opinion of Anthony Vauxhall now, and it wasn't a good one.

It was nearly 4:00 p.m., and they were seated in Vauxhall's office in the Lloyd's of London building on Leadenhall Street. In the past hour and a half Jordan and Clea had managed to purchase decent clothes, grab a bite to eat and scurry downtown to Lloyd's before the offices closed. Now it appeared that their efforts might prove futile. Vauxhall's response to Clea's story was one of obvious skepticism.

"You must understand, Miss Rice," said Vauxhall, "Van Weldon Shipping is one of our most distinguished clients. One of our oldest clients. Our relationship goes back three generations. For us to accuse Mr. Van Weldon of fraud is, well…" He cleared his throat.

"Perhaps you weren't listening to Miss Rice's story," said Jordan. "She was *there.* She was a witness. The loss of the *Max Havelaar* wasn't an accidental sinking. It was sabotage."

"Even so, how can we assume Van Weldon is responsible? It could have been another party. Pirates of some kind."

"Doesn't a multimillion-dollar claim concern your firm?"

"Well, naturally."

"Wouldn't your underwriters want to know if they've paid out to a company that staged its own losses?"

"Of course, but—"

"Then why aren't you taking these accusations seriously?"

"Because—" Vauxhall took a deep breath. "I spoke to Colin Hammersmith about this very matter. Right after I got your call earlier today. He's in charge of our investigations branch. He'd heard this rumor a few weeks back and his advice was, well…" Vauxhall shifted uneasily. "To consider the source," he said at last.

The source. Meaning Clea Rice, ex-con.

Jordan didn't need to look at her; he could feel her pain, as surely as if the blow had landed on his own shoulders. But when he did look at her, he was impressed by how well she was taking it, her chin held high, her expression calm and focused.

Ever since that long red hair had been cut away, her face had seemed even more striking to him, her sculpted cheeks feathered by wisps of brown hair, the dark eyes wide and gamine. He had known Clea Rice as a blonde, then a redhead and now a brunette. Though he'd found each and every version of her fascinating, of all her incarnations, this one he liked the best. Perhaps it was the fact he could actually focus on her face now, without the distraction of all that hair. Perhaps it matched her personality, those elfin tendrils wisping around her forehead.

Perhaps he was beyond caring about details as inconsequential as hair because he was falling in love with her.

That's why this insult by Vauxhall so enraged him.

He said, none too civilly, "Are you questioning Miss Rice's integrity?"

"Not…not exactly," said Vauxhall. "That is—"

"What *are* you questioning, then?"

Vauxhall looked miserable. "The story, it just appears— Oh, let's be frank, Mr. Tavistock. A slaughter at sea? Sabotage of one's own vessel? It's so shocking as to be—"

"Unbelievable."

"Yes. And when the accused is Victor Van Weldon, the story seems even more farfetched."

"But I saw it," insisted Clea. "I was there. Why won't you believe me?"

"We've already looked into it. Or rather, Mr. Hammersmith's department did. They spoke to the Spanish police, who assert that it was most probably an accident. An engine explosion. No bodies were ever found. Nor did they find evidence of murder."

"They wouldn't," said Clea. "Van Weldon's people are too clever."

"And as for the wreckage of the *Havelaar,* it went down in deep water. It's not easily salvageable. So we have nothing on which to base an accusation of sabotage."

Throughout Vauxhall's almost disdainful rebuttal, Clea had maintained her composure. She had regarded the man with almost regal calm. Jordan had watched in fascination as she took it all without batting an eyelash. Now he recognized the glimmer of triumph in her eyes. She was going to unveil the evidence.

Clea reached into her purse and withdrew the cloth-wrapped bundle that she'd so carefully guarded for the past sixteen hours. "You may find it difficult to take my word," she said, laying the bundle on his desk. "I understand that. After all, who am I to walk in off the street and tell you some fantastic tale? But perhaps this will change your mind."

Vauxhall frowned at the bundle. "What is that?"

"Evidence." Clea removed the cloth wrapping. As the

last layer fell away, Vauxhall sucked in an audible gasp of wonder. A jeweled scabbard lay gleaming in its undistinguished bed of muslin cloth.

Clea slid the dagger out of the scabbard and laid it down, razor tip pointed toward Vauxhall. "It's called the Eye of Kashmir. Seventeenth century. The jewel in the hilt is a blue star sapphire from India. You'll find a description of it in your files. It was part of Victor Van Weldon's collection, insured by your company. A month ago it was being transported from Naples to Brussels aboard a vessel which, coincidentally, was also insured by your company. The *Max Havelaar*."

Vauxhall glanced at Jordan, then back at Clea. "But that would mean…"

"This dagger should be on the ocean floor right now. But it isn't. Because it was never aboard the *Havelaar*. It was kept safely in storage somewhere, then sold on the black market to an Englishman."

"How did *you* get it?"

"I stole it."

Vauxhall stared at her for a moment, as though not certain she was being serious. Slowly he reached for his intercom button. "Miss Barrows," he murmured, "could you ring Mr. Jacobs, down in appraisals? Tell him to come up to my office. And have him bring his loupe or whatever it is he uses to examine gems."

"I'll ring him at once."

"Also, could you fetch the Van Weldon company's file for me? I want the papers for an antique dagger known as the Eye of Kashmir." Vauxhall sat back in his chair and regarded Clea with a troubled look. "This puts a new complexion on things. Mr. Van Weldon's claims, if I recall correctly, were in the neighborhood of fifteen million pounds for the art collection alone. This—" he waved at the dagger "—would call his claims into question."

Jordan looked at Clea and recognized her look of relief. *It's over,* he read in her eyes. *This nightmare is finally over.*

He took her hand. It was clammy, shaking, as though in fear. Of all the frightening events this past week, this moment must have been one of the most harrowing, because she had traveled so long and hard to reach it. She was too tense to smile at him, but he felt her fingers tighten around his. When this is over, he thought, well and truly over, we're going to celebrate. We're going to check in to a hotel suite and have all our meals delivered. And we're going to make love day and night until we're too exhausted to move. Then we'll sleep and start all over again....

They continued to cast knowing looks back and forth even as Vauxhall's secretary entered to deliver Van Weldon's files, even as Mr. Jacobs arrived from appraisals to examine the dagger. He was a distinguished-looking gentleman with a full mane of silver hair. He studied the Eye for what seemed like an eternity. At last he looked up and said to Vauxhall, "May I see the policy appraisal?"

Vauxhall handed it over. "There's a photo, as well. It seems to be identical."

"Yes. It does." Mr. Jacobs squinted at the photo, then regarded the dagger again. This time he focused his attention on the star sapphire. "Quite excellent work," he murmured, peering through the jeweler's loupe. "Exquisite craftsmanship."

"Don't you think it's time to call the authorities?" asked Jordan.

Vauxhall nodded and reached for the telephone. "Even Victor Van Weldon can't argue away the Eye of Kashmir, can he?"

Mr. Jacobs looked up. "But this isn't the Eye of Kashmir," he said.

The room went absolutely silent. Three pairs of eyes stared at the elderly appraiser.

"What do you mean, it's not?" demanded Vauxhall.

"It's a reproduction. A synthetic corundum. An excellent one, probably made using the Verneuil method. But as you'll see, the star is rather more pronounced than you'd find in a natural stone. It's worth perhaps two, three hundred pounds, so it's not entirely without value. But it's not a true star sapphire, either." Mr. Jacobs regarded them with a calm, bespectacled gaze. "This is not the Eye of Kashmir."

Clea's face had drained of color. She sat staring at the dagger. "I don't...don't understand...."

"Couldn't you be mistaken?" asked Jordan.

"No," said Mr. Jacobs. "I assure you, it's a reproduction."

"I demand a second opinion."

"Certainly. I'll recommend a number of gemologists—"

"No, we'll make our own arrangements," said Jordan.

Mr. Jacobs reacted with a look of injured dignity. He slid the dagger to Jordan. "Take it to whomever you wish," he said, and rose to leave.

"Mr. Jacobs?" called Vauxhall. "We hold the policy on the Eye of Kashmir. Shouldn't we retain this dagger until this matter is cleared up?"

"I see no reason to," snapped Mr. Jacobs. "Let them keep the thing. After all, it's nothing but a fake."

Chapter Eleven

Nothing but a fake.

Clea clutched the wrapped bundle in both hands as she and Jordan rode the elevator to the first floor. They walked out into the fading sunlight of late afternoon.

Nothing but a fake.

How could she have been so wrong?

She tried to reason out the possibilities, but her brain wouldn't function. She was operating on autopilot, her feet moving mechanically, her body numb. She had no evidence now, nothing to back up her story. And Van Weldon was still in pursuit. She could change her name a hundred times, dye her hair a hundred different shades, and still she'd be looking over her shoulder, wondering who might be moving in for the kill.

Victor Van Weldon had won.

It would almost be easier just to walk into his office, meet him face-to-face and tell him, "I give up. Just get it over with quick." She wouldn't last much longer, anyway. Even now she was scarcely aware of the faces on the street, much less able to watch for signs of danger. Only the firm guidance of Jordan's hand kept her moving in any sort of purposeful direction.

He pulled her into a taxi and directed the driver to Brook Street.

Gazing out dully at the passing traffic, she asked, "Where are we going?"

"To get that second opinion. There's a chap I know, has a shop in the area. He's done some appraisals for Uncle Hugh in the past."

"Do you think Mr. Jacobs could be wrong?"

"Wrong. Or lying. At this point, I don't trust anyone."

Does he trust me? she wondered. *The dagger's a fake. Maybe he thinks I am, as well.*

The taxi dropped them off at a shop in the heart of Mayfair. From the exterior it did not look like the sort of establishment any family as lofty as the Tavistocks would patronize. A sign in the window said, Clocks and Jewellery—Bought and Sold. Behind the dusty plate glass was arranged a selection of rings and necklaces that were obviously paste.

"This is the place?" asked Clea.

"Don't be fooled by appearances. If I want a straight answer, this is the man I ask."

They stepped inside, into a dark little cave of a room. On the walls were hung dozens of wooden cuckoo clocks, all of them ticking away. The counter was deserted.

"Hello?" called Jordan. "Herr Schuster?"

A door creaked open and an elderly gnome of a man shuffled out from a back room. At his first glimpse of Jordan, the man gave a cackle of delight.

"It's young Mr. Tavistock! How many years has it been?"

"A few," admitted Jordan as he shook the man's hand. "You're looking very well."

"Me? Bah! I am twenty years on borrowed time. To be alive is enough. And your uncle, he is retired now?"

"As of a few months ago. He's enjoying it immensely." Jordan slid an arm around Clea's shoulders. "I'd like you to meet Miss Clea Rice. A good friend of mine. We've come to ask you for some help."

Herr Schuster shot a sly glance at Clea. "Would this perhaps be for an engagement ring?"

Jordan cleared his throat. "It's rather...your expert opinion we need at the moment."

"On what matter?"

"This," said Clea. She unwrapped the bundle and handed him the dagger.

"The star sapphire in the hilt," said Jordan. "Is it natural or man-made?"

Gingerly Herr Schuster took the dagger and weighed it in his hands, as though trying to divine the answer by its touch. He said, "This will require some time."

"We'll wait," said Jordan.

The old jeweler retreated into the back room and shut the door behind him.

Clea looked doubtfully at Jordan. "Can we trust his opinion?"

"Absolutely."

"You're that sure of him?"

"He used to be the leading authority on gemstones in East Berlin. In the days before the wall came down. He also happened to work as a double agent for MI6. You'd be amazed how much one can learn from chats with the wives of high Communist officials. When things got dangerous, Uncle Hugh helped him cross over."

"So that's why you trust him."

"It's a debt he owes my uncle." Jordan glanced at the door to the back room. "Old Schuster's been keeping a low profile here in London ever since. Touch of paranoia, I suspect."

"Paranoia," said Clea softly. "Yes, I know exactly how he's lived." She turned to the window and stared out through the dusty glass at Brook Street. A bus rumbled past, spewing exhaust. It was early evening now, and the afternoon crowd had thinned out to a few shop girls straggling home for the night and a man waiting at the bus stop.

"If it is a fake," she said, "will you...still believe me, Jordan?"

He didn't answer at first. That brief silence was enough to send despair knifing through her. He said at last, "Too much has happened for me *not* to believe you."

"But you have doubts."

"I have questions."

She laughed softly. Bitterly. "That makes two of us."

"Why, for instance, would Delancey have bought a replica? He certainly had the money to spend. He would have insisted on the genuine item."

"He might have been misled. Believed it was the real Eye of Kashmir."

"No, Guy was a discerning collector. He'd get an expert's advice before he bought it. You saw how easily Mr. Jacobs identified that stone as man-made. Guy would have learned that fact just as easily."

She gave a sigh of frustration. "You're right, of course. He would have had it looked at. Which means whoever appraised it was either crooked or incompetent or..." Suddenly she turned to him. "Or he was right on the money."

"I told you, Guy would never buy a reproduction."

"Of course he wouldn't. He bought the real Eye of Kashmir."

"Then how did he wind up with a fake?"

"Someone switched it for the real one. *After* Guy bought it." She was moving around the room now, her mind racing. "Think about it, Jordan. Before you buy a painting or antique, aren't you very careful to confirm it's genuine?"

"Naturally."

"But after you've bought it—say, a painting—and you've had it hanging on your wall for a while, you don't bother to have it reauthenticated."

Slowly Jordan nodded. "I think I'm beginning to understand. The dagger was replaced sometime after Guy bought it."

"And he didn't realize! He has so many collectibles in that house. He'd never notice that one little dagger wasn't quite the same."

"All right, time for a reality check here. You're saying that our theoretical thief commissioned an exact replica. And then he managed to switch daggers without Guy's knowledge? That would require a hell of a lot of inside knowledge. Remember how much trouble we had, locating the Eye? Without Whitmore's help, we never would've found that hiding place."

"You're right, of course," she admitted with a sigh. "A thief would have to know exactly where it was hidden. Which means it had to be someone very close to Delancey."

"And that would eliminate an outside thug. Van Weldon's or otherwise." He shook his head. "I don't want to say 'the butler did it.' But I think the list of suspects is rather short."

"What about Guy's family?"

"Estranged. None of them even live in the neighborhood."

"One of his lovers, then?"

"He did have a few." He aimed an inquiring glance her way.

"I wasn't one of them," she snapped. "So who *has* Guy romanced in the last month?"

"Only one woman I'm aware of. Veronica Cairncross."

There was a long silence. "You're the one who knows her, Jordan," said Clea. "You two are friends...."

He frowned, troubled by the possibilities. "I've always considered her a bit wild. Impulsive. And not altogether moral. But a thief..."

"She's someone to consider. There's the household staff, as well. Come to think of it, anyone could've slipped into that bedroom. I got in. So did you. If it hadn't been for old Whitmore, we would have slipped out without anyone being the wiser."

Jordan went very still. "Whitmore," he said.

"What about him?"

"I'm thinking."

She watched in bewilderment as he muttered the name again, more softly. With sudden comprehension he looked at her. "Yes, Whitmore's the key."

She laughed. "You're not back to saying the butler did it?"

"No, it's the fact he was *home* that night! Veronica assured me it was Whitmore's night off. That the house would be empty. But when I broke in, he was right there. All this time I assumed she'd made a mistake. But what if it wasn't a mistake? What if she *wanted* the butler home?"

"Why on earth would she?"

"To raise the alarm. And notify the police."

"What would be the point?"

"There'd be an official record of a break-in. If Guy ever discovered the real Eye of Kashmir was gone, he'd assume the theft occurred that night. The night Whitmore raised the alarm."

"A night Veronica had an airtight alibi. Your sister's engagement party."

Jordan nodded. "It'd never occur to him that the switch was made earlier. *Before* that night. By an acquaintance so intimate she knew exactly where the Eye was hidden. An acquaintance who'd been in and out of that bedroom." Jordan slapped his temple in frustration. "All this time I thought *she* was the thick one. *I'm* the idiot."

Clea shook her head. "You're giving Veronica an awful lot of credit. How would she manage to commission such an accurate replica? It would take time. The forger would need to work from the original. I hardly think Guy would let her borrow it for a week. So where would this replica come from?"

"There's always the previous owner," said Jordan.

Clea's mouth went dry. *Van Weldon. The previous owner was Van Weldon.*

She went to stand beside him, close enough to lean her cheek against the fine wool of his jacket. Softly she said, "Veronica. Van Weldon. Could there be a link?"

"I don't know. She's never mentioned Van Weldon's name."

"He has connections everywhere. People who owe him. People who are afraid of him."

"It seems unlikely."

"But how well do you really *know* her, Jordan? How well do we really know anyone?"

He said nothing. He stood very still, not reaching for her, not even looking at her. Aching, she thought, *Oh, Jordan. How well do I really know you? And what little you know of me is the very worst....*

They stood just inches apart, yet she felt cold and alone as they both gazed out at that street where the shadows crept toward dusk. She reached out to him. His shoulder was rigid. Unresponsive to her touch.

"Clea," he said softly. "I want you to go into the back room. Ask Herr Schuster if there's a rear door."

"What?"

"There's a man standing at the bus stop. See him?"

She focused on the street. And on the man standing there. He wore a brown suit and carried a black umbrella, and every so often he glanced at his watch, as though late for some appointment. No wonder. He'd been waiting for his bus a long time now.

Slowly Clea backed away from the window.

Jordan didn't move, but continued to gaze out calmly at the street. "He's let two go past now," he said. "I don't think he's waiting for a bus."

She fought the impulse to run headlong through that rear door. She had no idea if the man could see them through those dusty front windows. She managed to stroll casually to the rear of the shop, then she pushed through the door, into the workshop.

Herr Schuster was at his jeweler's bench. "I am afraid the news is disappointing. The star sapphire—"

"Is there a back way out?" she asked.

"Excuse me?"

"Another exit?"

Jordan stepped in behind Clea. "There's a man following us."

Herr Schuster rose to his feet in alarm. "I have a back door." At a frantic shuffle, he led them through the workshop's clutter and opened the door to what looked like a closet. Dusty coats hung inside. He shoved the old garments aside. "There is a latch at the rear. The door leads to the alley. Around the corner is South Molton. You wish me to call the police?"

"No, don't. We'll be fine," said Jordan.

"The man—he is dangerous?"

"We don't know."

"The dagger—do you want it back?"

"It's not genuine?"

Regretfully Herr Schuster shook his head. "The sapphire is synthetic corundum."

"Then keep it as a souvenir. But don't show it to anyone."

A buzzer suddenly rang in the workshop. Herr Schuster glanced toward the front room. "Someone has come in the door. Hurry, go!"

Jordan grabbed Clea's hand and pulled her into the closet. Instantly the coats were slid back in place and the door shut on them. In the sudden darkness they blindly fumbled along the rear door for the latch and pushed.

They stumbled out into an alley. At once they tore around the corner onto South Molton Street. They didn't stop running until they'd reached the Bond Street Underground.

Aboard the train to Tottenham Court Road, Clea sat in stunned silence as the blackness of the tunnel swept past her window. Only when Jordan had taken her hand in his did she realize how chilled her fingers were, like icicles in the warmth of his grasp.

"He won't give up," she said. "He'll never give up."

"Then we have to stay one step ahead."

Not we, she thought. *I'm the one Van Weldon wants. The one he'll kill.*

She stared down at the hand now holding hers. A hand with all the strength a woman could ever need, could ever want. In a few short days she'd come to trust Jordan in a way she'd never trusted anyone. And she understood him well enough by now to know the gentleman's code of honor by which he operated—an absurd concept under these brutal circumstances. He would never abandon a woman in need.

So she would have to abandon him.

She chose her words carefully. Painfully. "I think it

would be better if…" The words caught in her throat. She forced herself to stare ahead. Anywhere but at Jordan. "I think I would be better off on my own. I can move faster that way."

"You mean without me."

"That's right." Her chin slanted up as she found the courage to keep talking. "I can't afford to spend my time worrying about you. You'll be fine holed up in Chetwynd."

"And where will you go?"

She smiled nonchalantly. "Some place warm. The south of France, maybe. Or Sicily. Anywhere I can be on a beach."

"If you live long enough to climb into a bathing suit."

The train pulled in to the next stop. Abruptly he pulled her to her feet and snapped, "We're getting off."

She followed him off the train and up the station steps to Oxford Street. He was silent, his shoulders squared in anger. So much for self-sacrifice, she thought. All she'd managed to do was turn him against her. And why the hell was he mad at her, anyway? It wasn't as if she'd rejected him. She'd simply offered him the chance to leave.

The chance to live.

"I was only thinking of *you,* you know," she said.

"I'm quite aware of that."

"Then why are you ticked off at me?"

"You don't give me much credit."

"There's nothing more you can do for me. You have to admit, it doesn't make sense for both of us to get our heads blown off. If we split up, they'll forget all about you."

"Will *you* forget all about me?"

She halted on the sidewalk. "Does it matter?"

"Doesn't it?" He turned to face her. They stood looking at each other, an obstruction to all the pedestrians moving along the sidewalk.

"I don't know what you're getting at," she said. "I'm sorry it has to end this way, Jordan. But I have to look out for number one. Which means I can't have you around. I don't *want* you around."

"You don't know what the hell you want."

"All right, maybe I don't. But I do know what's best for *you*."

"So do I," he said, and reached for her. His arms went around her back and his mouth came down on hers in a branding kiss that held no gentleness, brooked no resistance.

Far from protesting, she welcomed the assault, thrilled to the surge of his tongue into her mouth, the hungry roving of his hands up and down her back. She could not hide her desire from him, nor could he from her. They were both helpless and hopeless, lost to the crazy yearnings that always burst forth whenever they touched. It had been this way from the start. It would always be this way. A look, a touch, and suddenly the tension would be sizzling between them.

His lips slid to her cheek, then her ear, and the tickle of his hot breath sent a tremor of delight down her spine. "Have I made myself clear?" he whispered.

She moaned. "About what?"

"About staying together."

The need was still too strong between them. She pulled away and took a step back, fighting the urge to touch him again. *You and your crazy sense of honor,* she thought, staring up at his face. *It will get you killed. And I couldn't stand that.*

"I'm not exactly helpless, you know," she said.

He smiled. "Still, you have to admit I've come in handy on occasion."

"On occasion," she agreed.

"You need me, Clea. To beat Van Weldon."

She shook her head. "I've already tried. Now there's nothing else I can do."

"Yes, there is."

"The dagger's gone. I have no evidence. I can't see any way to get at him."

"There is a way." He moved closer. "Veronica Cairncross."

"What about her?"

"I've been trying to piece it all together. And I think you're right. She could be the key to all this. I've known Ronnie for years. She's a jolly girl, great fun to be around. But she's a gambler. And a big spender. Over the last few years she's run up a fortune in debts. A scam like this could've saved her skin."

"But now we're back to the problem of how she commissioned that reproduction," said Clea. "How'd she get her hands on the original? It belonged to Van Weldon. Did she buy it from him? Borrow it from him?"

"Or steal it from him?"

Clea shuddered at the thought. "No one's stupid enough to cross Van Weldon."

"Somehow, though, that dagger found its way from Van Weldon into Delancey's hands. Veronica could be the link between them. That's what we have to find out." Jordan paused, thinking. "She and Oliver have a town house here in London. They spend their weekdays here. Which means they'd be in town now."

Clea frowned at him. She didn't like this new shift of conversation. "What, exactly, are you thinking?"

He eyed her hair. "I'm thinking," he said, "that it's time for you to try a wig."

ARCHIE MACLEOD HUNG up the phone and looked at Richard Wolf and Hugh Tavistock. "They're in London. My man just spoke to an official from Lloyd's. Jordan and Clea Rice paid a visit there around four o'clock today. Unfortunately the man they met with—an Anthony Vauxhall—wasn't aware of the investigation. He just happened to mention their visit to his superior. By the time we found out, Jordan and Clea Rice had already left."

"So we know they're still alive," said Hugh.

"As of this afternoon, anyway."

They were sitting in Chetwynd's library, the room they'd turned into a crisis headquarters. Hugh had hurried back to Chetwynd that morning, and all day the three of them had sat waiting for word from their police contacts.

This last news was good. Jordan had made it safely to London.

Not that Richard was surprised. In the few months he'd known his future brother-in-law, he'd come to appreciate Jordan's resourcefulness. In a pinch there were few men Richard would rather have at his side.

Clea Rice, too, was a survivor. Together, they might just stay alive.

Richard looked at Hugh. The older man was looking drained and weary. The worry showed plainly in Hugh's round face. "That price on Clea Rice's head will be drawing every contract man in Europe," said Richard.

"Surely, Lord Lovat," said MacLeod, "you can marshal some help from your intelligence contacts. We have to find them."

Hugh shook his head. "My Jordan was reared in the lap of the intelligence business. All these years he's been listening. Learning. He's probably picked up a trick or two. Even with help, it won't be easy to track him down. Which means it won't be easy for Van Weldon to track him down, either."

"You don't know Victor Van Weldon the way I do," said

MacLeod. "At this point, he'll be willing to pay a fortune to get rid of Clea Rice. I'm afraid money is the world's best motivator."

"Not money," said Richard. "Fear. That's what will keep Jordan alive."

"Blast it all," said Hugh. "Why do we know so little about this Victor Van Weldon, anyway? Is he so untouchable?"

"I'm afraid he is," admitted MacLeod. He sank into a chair by the fireplace. "Victor Van Weldon has always operated on the fringes of international law. Never quite crossing the boundaries into illegality. At least, never leaving any evidence of it. He hides behind a regiment of lawyers. Keeps homes in Gstaad, Brussels and probably a few places we haven't found out about. He's like some rare bird, almost never sighted, but very much alive."

"You can't dredge up any evidence against him?"

"We know he's involved in international arms shipments. Dabbles in the drug trade. But every time we think we have hard evidence, it disintegrates in our hands. Or a witness dies. Or documents vanish. For years it's been a source of frustration for me, how he manages to elude me. Only recently did I realize how many friends in high places he has, keeping him apprised of my every move. That's when I changed tactics. I picked out my own team of men. An independent team. We've spent the past six months gathering information on Van Weldon, ferreting out his Achilles' heel. We know he's sick—emphysema and heart failure. He hasn't much longer to live. Before he dies, I want him to face a little earthly justice."

"You sound like a man on crusade," said Richard.

"I've lost...people. Van Weldon's work." MacLeod looked at him. "It's something one doesn't forget. The face of a dying friend."

"How close are you now to building a case?"

"We have the foundations. We know Van Weldon took big losses last year. The European economy—it's affected even him. With his empire on the brink of ruin, he was bound to try something desperate. That's when the *Havelaar* went down. Eight men dead, a fortune lost at sea—all of it fully insured. I couldn't convince the Spanish authorities to foot the bill for a proper investigation. It would've required a salvage crew, ships and equipment. Van Weldon, we thought, had slipped away again. Then we heard about Clea Rice." MacLeod sighed. "Unfortunately, Miss Rice is not the sort of witness to base any prosecution on. Prison record. Family of thieves. Here we finally find a weapon against Van Weldon, and it's one that could backfire in court."

"So you can't use her as the basis of any legal case," said Hugh.

"No. We need something tangible. For instance, the artwork listed on the *Havelaar*'s manifest. We know bloody well it didn't go down with the ship. Van Weldon's stashed it somewhere. He's waiting for an opportunity to sell it off piece by piece. If we just knew where he's hidden it."

"It was supposedly shipped from Naples."

"We searched his Naples warehouse. We also searched— not always legally, mind you—every building we know he owns. We're talking about large items, not things you can just hide in a closet. Tapestries and oil paintings and even a few statues. Wherever he's keeping it, it's a large space."

"There must be a warehouse you don't know about yet."

"Undoubtedly."

"Interpol's not authorized to handle this alone," said Hugh. "You're going to need assistance." He reached for the telephone and began to dial. "It's not the customary way of doing things. But with Jordan's life at stake..."

Richard listened as Hugh made the contacts, called in old favors from Scotland Yard's Special Branch, as well as MI5—domestic intelligence. After he hung up, Hugh looked at Richard.

"Now I suggest we get to work ourselves," said Hugh.

"London?"

"Jordan's there. He may try to reach us. I want to be ready to respond."

"What I don't understand," said MacLeod, "is why he hasn't called you already."

"He's cautious," said Richard. "He knows the one thing Van Weldon expects him to do is contact us for help. Under the circumstances, Jordan's best strategy is to keep doing the *unexpected*."

"Precisely the way Clea Rice has operated all these weeks," observed MacLeod. "By doing the unexpected."

VAN WELDON WAS waiting for the call. He picked up the receiver. "Well?"

"They're here," said Simon Trott. "They were spotted leaving Lloyd's of London, as you predicted."

"Is the matter concluded?"

There was a pause. "Unfortunately, no. They vanished off Brook Street—a jewelry store. The proprietor claims ignorance."

The news made Van Weldon's chest ache. He paused a moment to catch his breath, the whole time silently cursing Clea Rice. In all his years he'd never known such a tenacious opponent. She was like a thorn that couldn't be plucked out, and she seemed to keep burrowing ever deeper.

When he'd managed to catch his breath again, he said, "So she did go to Lloyd's. Did she take the dagger?"

"Yes. She must have been rather peeved to learn it was a fake."

"And the real Eye of Kashmir?"

"Safely back where it belongs. Or so I've been assured."

"The Cairncross woman brought us to the brink of disaster. She cannot go unpunished."

"I quite agree. What do you have in mind?"

"Something unpleasant," said Van Weldon. Veronica Cairncross was an opportunistic bitch. And a fool as well to think she could slip one over on them. Her greed had taken her too far this time, and she was going to regret it.

"Shall I see to Mrs. Cairncross myself?" asked Trott.

"Wait. First confirm the collection is safe. It must go on the market within the month."

"So soon after the *Havelaar?* Is that wise?"

Trott raised a good point. It was risky to release the artwork onto the market. To think of all those assets bundled away, untouchable, just when he needed them most! Last year he had overextended himself, had made a few too many commitments to a few too many cartels. Now he needed cash. Lots of it.

"I cannot wait," said Van Weldon. "It must be sold. In Hong Kong or Tokyo, we could fetch excellent prices, and without much notice. Buyers are discreet in Tokyo. See that the collection is moved."

"When?"

"The *Villafjord* is scheduled to dock in Portsmouth tomorrow. I will be on board."

"You…are coming here?" There was an undertone of dismay in Trott's voice. He *should* be dismayed. What had started as a minor difficulty had ballooned into a crisis, and Van Weldon was disgusted with his heir apparent. If Trott could not handle such simple matters as Veronica

Cairncross and Clea Rice, how could he hope to assume the company's helm?

"I will see to the shipment myself," said Van Weldon. "In the meantime, I expect you to find Clea Rice."

"We have the Tavistocks under surveillance. Sooner or later, Jordan and the woman will surface."

Perhaps not, thought Van Weldon as he hung up. By now Clea Rice would be weary, demoralized. Her instinct would be to run as far and as fast as she could. That would take care of the problem—temporarily, at least.

Van Weldon felt better. He decided there was really no need to worry about Clea Rice. By now she'd be long gone from London.

It's what any sensible woman would do.

Chapter Twelve

At twelve-fifteen Veronica Cairncross left her London flat, climbed into a taxi and was driven to Sloane Street where she had lunch at a trendy little café. Afterward she strolled on foot toward Brompton Road, in the general direction of Harrods. She took her sweet time in one shop to purchase lingerie, and in another shop to try on a half-dozen pairs of shoes.

A disguised Clea observed all of this from a distance and with a growing sense of exasperation. Not only did this exercise seem more and more pointless, but also her long black wig was itchy, her sunglasses kept slipping down the bridge of her nose and her new short-heeled pumps were killing her. Perhaps she should have slipped into that same shoe shop where Veronica had spent so much time and picked up a pair of sneakers for herself. Not that she could have afforded anything in there. Veronica clearly frequented only the priciest establishments. *What is it like to be so idle and so rich?* Clea wondered as she trailed the elegant figure up Brompton Road. *Doesn't the woman ever get tired of constant partying and shopping?*

Oh, sure. The poor thing must be bored to tears.

She followed Veronica into Harrods. Inside she lingered a discreet distance away and watched Veronica sample perfumes, browse among scarves and handbags. Two hours

later, loaded down with purchases, Veronica strolled out
and hailed a taxi.

Clea scurried out after her and after a few frantic
glances, spotted another taxi, this one with tinted windows. She climbed in.

Jordan was waiting in the back seat.

"There she goes," said Clea. "Stay with her."

Their driver, a grinning Sikh whom Jordan had hired
for the day, expertly threaded the taxi into traffic and
maintained a comfortable two-car distance behind Veronica's vehicle.

"Anything interesting happen?" asked Jordan.

"Not a thing. Lord, that woman can shop. She's way out
of my league. Any trouble staying with me?"

"We were right behind you."

"I don't think she noticed a thing. Not me or the taxi."
Sighing, Clea sat back and pulled off the wig. "This is getting us nowhere. So far all we've found out is that she has
time and money on her hands. And a lot of both."

"Be patient. I know Ronnie, and when she gets nervous,
she spends money like water. It's her way of blowing off
stress. Judging by all the packages she was carrying, she's
under a lot of stress right now."

Veronica's taxi had turned onto Kensington. They followed, skirting Kensington Gardens, and headed south-
west.

"Now where's she going?" Clea sighed.

"Odd. She's not headed back to the flat."

Veronica's taxi led them out of the shopping district,
into a neighborhood of business and office buildings. Only
when the taxi stopped and let Veronica off at the curb did
Jordan give a murmur of comprehension.

"Of course," he said. "Biscuits."

"What?"

"It's Oliver's company. Cairncross Biscuits." Jordan nodded at the sign on the building. "She's here to see her husband."

"Hardly a suspicious thing to do."

"Yes, it seems quite innocent, doesn't it?"

"Are you implying otherwise?"

"I'm just thinking about Oliver Cairncross. The firm's been in his family for generations. Appointment to the queen and all that…."

She studied Jordan's finely chiseled face as he mulled it over. *Such eyelashes he has,* she thought. No man had a right to such long eyelashes. Or such a kissable mouth. She could watch him for hours and never tire of the way his face crooked up on one side when he was thinking hard. *Oh, Jordan. How I'm going to miss you when this is over….*

"Cairncross biscuits are internationally known," said Jordan. "They're shipped all over the world."

"So?"

"So I wonder which firm is used to transport all those cookie crates. And what's really inside them."

"Uzis, you mean?" Clea shook her head. "I thought Oliver was supposed to be the innocent party. The cuckolded husband. Now you're saying *he's* the one in league with Van Weldon? Not Veronica?"

"Why not both of them?"

"She comes out again," said their driver.

Sure enough, Veronica had reappeared. She climbed back into her taxi.

"You wish me to follow her?" asked the Sikh.

"Yes. Don't lose her."

They didn't. They stayed on Veronica's tail all the way to Regent's Park. There Veronica alighted from the taxi and began to walk across Chester Terrace, toward the Tea House.

"Back into action." Clea sighed. "I hope it's not another two-hour hike." She pulled on a new wig—this one shoulder length and brown—and climbed out of the cab. "How do I look?"

"Irresistible."

She leaned inside and kissed him on the mouth. "You, too."

"Be careful."

"I always am."

"No, I mean it." He pulled her around by the wrist. His grip was insistent, reluctant to let go. "If there was any other way I could do it instead of you, I would—"

"She knows you too well, Jordan. She'd spot you in a second. Me, she'd scarcely recognize."

"Just don't let your guard down. Promise me."

She gave him a breezy grin that masked all the fears she had rattling inside. "And you promise not to vanish."

"I'll keep you right in view."

Still grinning, Clea turned and crossed Chester Terrace.

Veronica was well ahead of her. She seemed to be merely wandering, strolling toward Queen Mary's Rose Garden, its season of bloom now past. There she lingered, every so often glancing at her watch. Oh, Lord, not waiting for another lover, Clea thought.

Without warning Veronica turned and began walking in Clea's direction.

Clea ducked under an arbor and pretended to inspect the label on the climbing rose. Veronica didn't even glance her way, but headed toward the Tea House.

After a moment Clea followed her.

Veronica had seated herself at a table, and she had a menu propped open in front of her. Clea took a seat two tables behind Veronica and sat facing the other way. At this hour the Tea House was relatively quiet, and she could hear Veronica's whiney voice ordering a pot of Darjeeling and iced cakes. *Now I'll waste another hour,* thought Clea, *waiting for that silly woman to have her tea.*

She glanced toward Cumberland Terrace. Sure enough, there was Jordan sitting on a bench, his face hidden behind a newspaper.

The waiter approached. Clea ordered a pot of Earl Grey and watercress sandwiches. Her tea had just arrived when a man crossed the dining terrace toward Veronica.

Clea caught only a glimpse of him as he moved past her table. He was fair haired, blonder than Jordan, with wide shoulders and a powerful frame—just the sort of hunk Veronica would probably go gaga over. Clea felt a spurt of irritation that yet another hour would be wasted while Veronica made cow eyes at her latest admirer.

"Mr. Trott," Veronica said crossly. "You're late. I've already ordered."

Clea heard the man's voice, speaking behind her, and in the midst of pouring tea, her hand froze.

"I have no time for tea," he said. "I came only to confirm the arrangements."

That was all he said, but his tone of command, the English coarsened by some unidentifiable accent, was enough to make Clea suck in a breath in panic. She didn't dare glance back over her shoulder; she didn't dare let him see her face.

She didn't need to see *his;* his voice was all she needed to recognize him.

She'd heard it before, floating above the sound of lapping Mediterranean waves and the growl of a boat's engine. She remembered how that same voice had cut through the darkness. Just before the bullets began to fly.

All her instincts were screaming at her to lurch from

this table and flee. *But I can't,* she thought. *I can't do anything to draw his attention.*

So she sat unmoving, her hands gripping the tablecloth. So acutely did she sense the man's presence behind her, she was surprised that he didn't seem at all aware of *her.*

Her heartbeat thudding, she sat motionless at the table.

TROTT WATCHED VERONICA light a cigarette and take in an unhurried drag of smoke. She seemed not in the least bit worried, which only proved what a stupid bitch she was, he decided. *She thinks she's untouchable. She thinks her husband's too important to our operations. What she doesn't know is that we've already found a replacement for Oliver Cairncross.*

Casually she exhaled a cloud of smoke. "The cargo's all there. Nothing missing. I told you it would be, didn't I?"

"Mr. Van Weldon is not pleased."

"Why, because I borrowed one of his precious little trinkets? It was only for a few weeks." Calmly she exhaled another cloud of smoke. "We've been stuck with your bloody crates for months now—at no small risk to ourselves. Why shouldn't I borrow what's in them? I got the dagger back, didn't I?"

"This is not the time or place to speak of it," cut in Trott. He passed a newspaper across the table to Veronica. "The information is circled. We'll expect it to be ready and waiting."

"At your beck and call, your highness," said Veronica, her voice dripping with mockery.

Trott pushed his chair back, preparing to leave. "What about compensation?" asked Veronica. "For all our trouble?"

"You'll have it. After all items are accounted for."

"Of course they will be," said Veronica. She blew out another cloud of smoke. "We're not fools, you know."

CLEA HEARD THE man's chair scrape back. He was rising to his feet. Instinctively she huddled closer to the table, afraid to be noticed. She forced herself to take a sip of tea, to pretend no interest whatsoever in the monster standing behind her.

When she heard him walk away, she went almost limp with relief. She glanced back.

Veronica was still sitting at the table, gazing down at a newspaper. After a moment she ripped off half a page, folded it and stuffed it in her purse. Then she, too, rose and left.

It took a while before Clea's nerves steadied enough for her to stand. Veronica was already walking out of the park. Clea started to follow, but her legs were shaking too hard. She took a few steps, faltered and stopped.

By then Jordan had realized something was wrong. She heard his footsteps, and then his arm was around her waist, supporting her, steadying her.

"We can't stay here," she whispered. "Have to hide—"

"What happened?"

"It was him—"

"Who?"

"The man from the *Cosima!*" Wildly she glanced around, her gaze sweeping the park for sight of the blond man.

"Clea, what man?"

She focused at last on Jordan. His gaze seemed to steady her. He held her face in his hand, the pressure of his fingers warming through her numbness.

"Tell me," he said.

She swallowed. "I've heard his voice before. The night

the *Havelaar* went down. I was in the water, swimming alongside the lifeboat. He was the one who—the one who—" She blinked, and tears spilled down her face. Softly she finished, "The one who ordered his men to shoot."

Jordan stared at her. "The man with Veronica? You're absolutely certain?"

"He passed by my table. I recognized his voice. I'm sure it was him."

Jordan gave a quick glance around the park. Then he pulled Clea close, wrapping his arm protectively around her shoulder. "Let's get into the car."

"Wait." She went back to Veronica's table and snatched up the discarded newspaper.

"What's that for?" asked Jordan.

"Veronica left it. I want to see what she tore out."

Their taxi was waiting. As soon as they climbed in the back seat, Jordan ordered, "Move. See that we're not followed."

The Sikh driver grinned at them in the mirror. "A most interesting day," he declared, and sent the cab screeching into traffic.

Jordan draped his jacket over Clea's shoulders and took her hands in his. "All right," he coaxed gently. "Tell me what happened."

Clea took a shaky breath and sank back against the seat. No one was following them. Jordan's hand, warm and steady, seemed to radiate enough courage for them both.

"Did you hear what they were saying?"

"No. They were speaking too softly. And I was afraid to get any closer. After I realized who he was…" She shuddered, thinking of the man's voice. In her nightmares she'd heard that same voice drifting across the black Mediterranean waters. She'd remember the explosion of gunfire. And she'd remember Giovanni, slumping across the lifeboat....

Her head came up. "I do remember something. Veronica called him by name. Mr. Trott."

"You're sure that was it? Trott?"

She nodded. "I'm sure."

Jordan's grip tightened around hers. "Veronica. If I ever get my hands around her elegant little neck..."

"At least now we know. She's the link to Van Weldon. Delancey paid for the Eye. She stole it back. Someone earned a nice profit. And the only loser was Guy Delancey."

"What about the newspaper?"

Clea looked down at the folded pages. "I saw Veronica tear something out."

Jordan glanced at the newspaper's date, then tapped their taxi driver on the shoulder. "Excuse me. You wouldn't happen to have a copy of today's *Times?*"

"But of course. And the *Daily Mail,* as well."

"Just the *Times* will do."

The driver reached over and pulled out a slightly mangled newspaper from the glove compartment. He handed it back to Jordan.

"The top of page thirty-five and six," said Clea. "That's what she's torn out."

"I'm looking for it." Jordan thumbed quickly through the driver's copy. "Here it is. Top of page thirty-five. Article about the Manchester slums. Building renovations. Another about horse breeding in Ireland."

"Try the other side."

Jordan flipped the page. "Let's see. Scandal in some ad agency. Drop-off in the fishing harvest. And..." He paused. "Today's shipping schedule for Portsmouth." He looked at Clea.

"That's it! That has to be it. One of their ships must be arriving in port."

"Or leaving." He sat back, deep in thought. "If Van Weldon has a vessel in Portsmouth, then it's here for either a delivery..."

"Or a pickup," she finished for him.

They looked at each other, both struck by the same startling thought.

"It's taking on cargo," she said. "It must be."

"It could be purely legitimate cargo."

"But there's the chance..." She glanced up as they pulled in front of their hotel. At once she was climbing out the door. "We have to call Portsmouth. Check which vessels are Van Weldon's."

"Clea, wait—"

But she was already hurrying into the building.

By the time he'd settled with their driver and followed her up to the room, Clea was already on the phone. A moment later she hung up and turned to Jordan in triumph.

"There's a *Villafjord* scheduled to dock at five this afternoon. She sails again at midnight. And she's registered to the Van Weldon company."

For a moment he stared at her without speaking. Then he said flatly, "I'm going to call the police." He reached for the phone.

She grabbed his hand. "Don't! Jordan."

"We have to alert the authorities. It could be the best chance they'll have to nail Van Weldon."

"That's why we can't blow it! What if we're wrong? What if his ship's here to take on a cargo of—of undies or something? We'll look like a pair of idiots. So will the police." She shook her head. "We can't tell them until we know *exactly* what's on board."

"But the only way to learn that is…" He froze in the midst of that thought. "Don't you even dare suggest it."

"Just one little tiny peek inside."

"*No.* This is the perfect time to call in Richard. Let him—or someone else—handle it."

"But I don't trust anyone else!"

Again he reached for the phone.

Again she grabbed his hand and held on tightly. "If we let too many people in on this," she said, "I guarantee there'll be a leak. Van Weldon will hear about it, and that'll be it for our big chance. Jordan, we have to wait till the last minute. And we have to be sure of what they'll find."

"You don't really think you can stroll aboard that ship and have a look around, do you?"

"When it comes to making unauthorized entries, I had the world's best teacher."

"Uncle Walter? He got caught, remember?"

"*I* won't get caught."

"Because you're not going anywhere *near* the *Villafjord*." He shook off her hand and began to dial the telephone.

Desperately she snatched away the receiver. "You're not doing this!" she cried.

"Clea." He heaved a sigh of frustration. "Clea, you have to trust me on this."

"No, you have to trust *me*. Trust *my* judgment. *I'm* the one with everything to lose!"

"I know that. But we're both tired. We're going to make mistakes. Now's the time to call the police and put an end to all this. To get back to our lives—our *real* lives. Don't you see?"

She looked into his eyes. *Yes, I see,* she thought. *You've had enough of running. Enough of me. You want your own life back, and I don't blame you.*

Defiantly she raised her chin. "I want to go home, too. I'm sick of hotels and strange beds and dyed hair. I want this all to be over with just as much as you do. That's why I say we do it *my* way."

"Your way's too bloody risky. The police—"

"I told you, I don't trust them!" Agitated, she paced over to the window, paced back. "I've survived this long only because I didn't trust anyone. *I'm* the only one I can count on."

"You can count on me," he said quietly.

She shook her head and laughed. "In the real world, darling, it's every man for himself. Remember that. You can't trust anyone." She turned and looked at him. "Not even me."

"But I do."

"Then you're crazy."

"Why? Because you're an ex-con? Because you've made a few mistakes in your life?" He moved toward her and took her by the shoulders. "Are you *afraid* to have me believe in you?"

She gave a nonchalant toss of her head. "I'd hate to disappoint anyone."

He cupped her face in his hands and lowered his mouth to hers. "I have complete faith," he whispered. "And so should you."

His kiss was sweet enough to break her heart. And that frightened her, because she knew now there could be no clean parting between them, no easy goodbyes. The break would be painful and haunting and bitter.

And inevitable.

He pulled back. "I'm going to have to trust you now, Clea. To do as I ask. To stay in this room and let me take care of this."

"But I—"

He silenced her by pressing a finger to her lips. "No arguments. I'm going to assert a little male authority here. Something I damn well should have done ages ago. You're going to wait for me. Here, in this room. Understood?"

She looked at his unyielding expression. Then she gave a sigh. "Understood," she said meekly.

He smiled and kissed her.

She smiled, too, as he walked out of the room. But when she went to the window and watched him leave the building, her smile faded. *What makes you think I'm so damn trustworthy?* she thought.

Turning, she saw Jordan's jacket, which she'd left draped over a chair. Impulsively she thrust her hand in the pocket and pulled out the gold watch. She flipped open the dented cover and looked at the name engraved inside: Bernard Tavistock.

And she thought, This will end it. Here and now. It's going to end anyway, and I might as well do it sooner than later. If I take this watch, something he treasures, I'll cut the ties. Cleanly. Decisively. After all, that's what I am. A thief. An ex-con. He'll be relieved to see me go.

She thrust the watch into her own pocket. Maybe she'd mail it back to him someday. When she was good and ready. When she could think of him without feeling that painful twist of her heart.

Glancing out the window, she saw that Jordan was nowhere in sight. *Goodbye,* she thought. *Goodbye, my darling gentleman.*

A moment later she, too, left the room.

Chapter Thirteen

Richard Wolf was on the telephone to Brussels when the doorbell rang. He paid it no attention—the butler would see to any visitors. Only when he heard Davis's polite knock on the study door did Richard break off his conversation.

The butler, looking oddly uncertain, stood in the doorway. It was something Richard hadn't gotten the hang of, dealing with all these servants. His Yankee sense of privacy was always being violated by all the maids and butlers and underbutlers whom the Tavistocks insisted upon keeping underfoot.

"Pardon the interruption, Mr. Wolf," said Davis. "But there's a foreign gentleman at the door. He insists upon speaking to you at once."

"Foreign?"

"A, er, Sikh, I believe." Davis made a whirling gesture over his head. "Judging by the turban."

"Did he say what his business was?"

"He said he would speak only to you."

Richard cut the call short and followed Davis to the front door.

There was indeed a Sikh waiting on the front step, a short, pleasant-looking fellow with a trim beard and a gold tooth. "Mr. Wolf?" he inquired.

"I'm Richard Wolf."

"You called for a taxi."

"I'm afraid I didn't."

Without a word the Sikh handed an envelope to Richard.

Richard glanced in the envelope. Inside was a single gold cuff link. It was inscribed with the initials J.C.T.

Jordan's.

Calmly Richard nodded and said, "Oh, right. Of course. I'd forgotten all about that appointment. Let me get my briefcase."

While the Sikh waited on the doorstep, Richard ducked back into the study, slid a 9 mm automatic into his shoulder holster and reemerged carrying an empty briefcase.

The Sikh directed him to a taxi at the curb.

Neither of them said a thing as the car moved through traffic. The Sikh drove exactly the way one expected of a cab driver—calmly. Recklessly.

"Are we going some place in particular?" asked Richard.

"Harrods. You will stay there half an hour. Visit all the floors. Perhaps make a purchase. Then you'll return to my taxi. You will recognize it by the number—twenty-three. I will wait for you at the curb."

"What am I to expect?"

The Sikh grinned in the rearview mirror. "I do not know. I am only the driver." He paused. "We are being followed."

"I know," said Richard.

At Harrods Richard got out and entered the store. Inside he did as instructed, wandering about the various departments. He bought a silk scarf for Beryl and a tie for his father back in Connecticut. He was aware of two men lingering nearby, a short man and a blond man. They were good—it was a full five minutes before he noticed them, and only because he'd glimpsed them in a mirror as he tried on top hats. He lost them briefly in the gourmet foods section, but picked them up again in housewares. If Jordan hoped to make contact, it was going to be difficult. Richard knew he could shake these guys if he wanted to. But then he'd probably shake Jordan, as well.

A half hour later he walked out of Harrods. He spotted taxi number twenty-three parked across the street, the Sikh driver still sitting patiently behind the wheel.

He crossed the street and climbed in the back seat of the taxi. "No luck," he said. "I was watched the whole time. Is there a backup plan?"

"This *is* the plan," said a familiar voice.

Richard glanced up in surprise at the rearview mirror, at the face of the bearded, turbaned driver. Jordan's brown eye winked back at him.

"Gotcha," said Jordan, and pulled the taxi into traffic.

"What the hell's going on?"

"Little game of wits. How am I doing so far?"

"Splendidly. You outsmarted me." Richard glanced back and spotted the same car following them.

"I see them," said Jordan.

"Where's Clea Rice?"

"A safe place. But things are coming to a head. We need help."

"Jordan, Interpol's already stepped in. They want Van Weldon's head. They'll arrange for the woman's safety."

"How do I know we can trust them?"

"They'd been watching over her for weeks. Until you two shook them off."

"Veronica's working for Van Weldon. Oliver may be, as well."

Richard, stunned, fell momentarily silent.

"You see, it reaches all levels," said Jordan. "It's like

an octopus. Tentacles everywhere. The only people I can really count on are you, Beryl and Uncle Hugh. And you may regret hearing from me at all."

"We've been waiting for you to contact us. Hugh's calling in old favors. You'll be in good hands, I'll see to it myself. MacLeod's just waiting for the chance to move on Van Weldon."

"MacLeod?"

"Interpol. That was his man on the train platform. The one who saved your lives."

Jordan chewed on that piece of information for a moment. "If we come in, how will it be arranged?"

"Through your uncle. Scotland Yard will oversee. Whenever you're ready."

Jordan was silent as he dodged around a tight knot of traffic. "I'm ready," he said at last.

"And the woman?"

"Clea'll take some convincing. But she's tired. I think she's ready to come in, too."

"How shall we do it, then?"

"Sloane Square, the Underground. Make it an hour from now—eight-thirty."

"I'll let Hugh know."

They were coming up on the Tavistocks' London residence, one in a row of elegant Georgian town houses. The car was still following them.

Jordan pulled over to the curb. "One more thing, Richard."

"Yes?"

"There's a ship docking this afternoon in Portsmouth. The *Villafjord*."

"Van Weldon's?"

"Yes. My guess is, she'll be taking on cargo tonight. I

suggest the police perform a little unannounced inspection before she leaves port."

"What's the cargo?"

"It'll be a surprise."

Richard stepped out and made a conspicuous point of paying for the ride. Then he walked up the steps and entered the house. As Jordan drove off, Richard saw that the car that had followed them remained parked outside the Tavistock residence. It was just as he'd expected. The men were assigned to watch him; they had no interest in any Sikh driver.

All the tension suddenly left his body. Only then did he realize how edgy he'd been.

And how close to the precipice they'd been dancing.

BACK AT THE hotel, Jordan parked the taxi a block away, and sat for a moment in the driver's seat, watching to see if any cars had followed him. When he saw nothing suspicious, he stripped off his beard and turban, got out and headed for the building.

Trust me, he thought as he climbed the stairs. *You have to learn to trust me.* He knew it would be a long, slow process, one that might take a lifetime. Perhaps it was too late. Perhaps all the damage done in childhood had robbed Clea forever of her faith in other people. Could they live with that?

Could she?

Only then did he realize that, lately, all his thoughts of the future seemed to include *her.*

Sometime in the past week, the shift had occurred. Where once he would have thought *I,* now he thought *we.* That's what came of sharing so much, so intensely. It was both the reward and the consequence, this link between them.

Trust me, he thought, and opened the door.

The room was empty.

He stood staring at the bed, suddenly, painfully aware of the silence. He went into the bathroom; it was empty, as well. He paced back to the bedroom and saw that her purse was gone. And he saw his jacket, lying draped across a chair.

He picked up the jacket and noticed at once that it was lighter than usual. That something was missing. Reaching into the pocket, he discovered that his father's gold watch was missing.

In its place was a note.

"It was fun while it lasted. Clea."

With a groan of frustration, he crumpled the paper in his fist. Blast the woman! She'd picked his pockets! And then she'd headed for...where?

The answer was only too frightening.

It was eight o'clock. She'd had a solid three hours' head start.

He ran back down the stairs to the taxi. First he'd swing past Sloane Square, to pick up some Scotland Yard assistance. And then it'd be on to Portsmouth, where a certain little burglar was, at this moment, probably sneaking up the gangplank of a ship.

If she wasn't already dead.

THE FENCE WAS higher than she'd expected. Clea crouched in the thickening gloom outside the Cairncross Biscuits complex and stared up in dismay at the barbed wire lacing the top of the chain link. This was not the usual penny ante security one expected for a biscuit warehouse. What were they afraid of? An attack by the Cookie Monster? The fence ringed the entire complex, interrupted only by the main gate, which was padlocked for the night. Floodlights shone down on the perimeter, leaving only intermittent patches of shadow. Judging by the fortune invested in security, there was more than just biscuits being stored in that warehouse.

Right on the money, she thought. *Something else is going on in there besides the manufacture of teatime treats.*

It had required only a small leap of logic to lead her to the Cairncross warehouse on the outskirts of London. If Van Weldon's ship was taking on illicit cargo tonight, then here was the obvious holding place for that cargo. Legitimate trucks were probably in and out of here all the time, pulling up to that handy warehouse platform. If a truck showed up tonight to pick up a load of crates, no one in the neighborhood would bat an eyelash.

Very clever, Van Weldon, she thought. *But this time I'm one step ahead of you.*

She'd be ahead of the authorities, as well. By the time Jordan and his precious police converged on that Portsmouth dock, there'd be no telling how many people would know about the forthcoming raid. Or how much warning Van Weldon would have. Now was the time to view the evidence—before Van Weldon had a chance to change plans.

The sound of someone whistling sent Clea scrambling for the cover of bushes. From her hiding place she watched a security guard stroll past, inside the fence. He had a gun strapped to his hip. He moved at a leisurely pace, pausing to flick away a cigarette and crush the butt with his shoe. Then, lighting up another, he continued his circuit.

Clea timed the gap between his appearances. Seven minutes. She waited, let him go around again. This time it was six minutes. Six minutes, max, to get through the fence and into the building. The fence was no problem; a few snips of the wire cutter she'd brought and she'd be in the complex. It was the warehouse that worried her. Those locks might take a while to bypass, and if the guard circled around too early, she'd be trapped.

She had to take the chance.

She snipped a few links in the fence, then hid as the guard came around. The instant he vanished around the corner she cut the last link, scrambled under with her knapsack and dashed across the expanse of pavement to the warehouse side door.

One glance at the lock told her she was in for some trouble. It was a brand-new pin tumbler, and six minutes might not be enough to bypass it. She set her watch alarm for five minutes. Holding a penlight in her teeth, she set to work.

First she inserted an L-shaped tension wrench and gently applied pressure to slide apart the plug and cylinder plates. Next she inserted a lifter pick, with which she gingerly lifted the first lock pin. It slid up with a soft click.

One down, six pins to go.

The next five pins were a piece of cake. It was the seventh one—the last—that kept tripping her up. She felt the minutes tick by, felt the sweat beading on her upper lip as she struggled to lift that seventh pin. Just one more click and she'd be in the door. Interrupt the effort now, and she'd be back to square one.

Her watch alarm gave a beep.

She kept working, gambling on the chance she'd conquer that last pin in the seconds that remained. She was so close, so close.

Too late, she heard the sound of whistling again. The guard was approaching her corner of the building!

She'd never make it back under the fence in time. Neither was there any cover along the building. She had only one route of escape.

Straight up.

Sheer panic sent her clambering like a monkey up a flimsy-looking drainpipe, seeking the cover of the shadows above.

As the guard rounded the corner, she pressed herself to the wall, afraid to move a muscle, afraid even to breathe. A few feet below, the guard stopped. Pulse hammering, Clea watched as he lighted a fresh cigarette and inhaled deeply. Then, with a satisfied sigh, he continued his circuit. He rounded the next corner without a backward glance.

Clea had to make a quick choice: should she try that bloody lock again or keep climbing? Glancing up, she traced the course of the drainpipe to the three-story-high roofline. There might be another way in from there. Though the drainpipe looked flimsy, so far it had supported her weight.

She began to climb.

Seconds later she scrambled up over the edge and dropped onto the rooftop.

A shadowy expanse of asphalt tile lay before her. She started across it, moving past the whirring fans of vents. At last she came to a rooftop door—locked, of course. Another pin tumbler. She set to work with her tension wrench and lifter pick.

In two minutes flat she had the door open.

At her feet a narrow stairway dropped away into the darkness. She descended the stairs, pushed through another door and entered the vast cavern of the warehouse. Here the area was lighted, and she could see rows of crates. All of them were stamped Cairncross Biscuits, London.

She grabbed a crowbar from a tool bin and pried open one of the crates, releasing the fragrant waft of cookies. Inside she found tins with the distinctive red-and-yellow Cairncross logo. The crate did, indeed, contain biscuits.

Frustrated, she glanced around at the other crates. She'd

never be able to search them all! Only then did she spot the closed double doors in the far wall.

With mounting excitement she approached the doors. They were locked. There were no windows, so it was unlikely there was an office beyond.

She picked the lock.

A rush of cooled air spilled out the open door. Air-conditioned, she thought. Climate control? She found the light switch and flicked it on.

The room was filled with crates, each stamped with the Cairncross Biscuits logo. These crates, however, were a variety of sizes. Several were huge enough to house a standing man.

With the crowbar she pried off one of the lids and discovered a fluffy mound of wood shavings. Plunging both arms into the packing, she encountered something solid buried within. She dug into the shavings and the top of the object emerged, its marble surface smooth and gleaming under the lights.

It was the head of a statue, a noble youth with a crown of olive leaves.

Clea, her hands shaking with excitement, pulled a camera from her knapsack and began to snap photos. She took three shots of the statue, then reclosed the lid. She pried open a second crate.

Somewhere in the building, metal clanged.

She froze, listening, and heard the growl of a truck, the protesting squeal of a bay door being shoved open along its tracks. At once she killed the room lights. Opening the door a crack, she peered out into the warehouse.

The loading gate was wide open. A truck had backed up to the platform, and the driver was swinging open the rear doors.

Veronica and the blond man were walking in Clea's direction.

Clea jerked back and shut the door. Frantically she waved her penlight around the room. No other exit. No place to hide except...

Voices were speaking right outside the door.

She grabbed her knapsack, scrambled into the open crate and pulled the lid over her head.

Through the cracks in the wood she saw the room's lights come on.

"It's all here, as you can see," said Veronica. "Would you care to check the crates yourself, Mr. Trott? Or do you trust me now?"

"I have no time for that. They must be moved immediately."

"I hope Mr. Van Weldon appreciates the trouble we've gone to, keeping these safe. He did promise there'd be compensation."

"You've already taken yours."

"What do you mean?"

"Your profit from selling the Eye. That should suffice."

"That was *my* idea! *My* profit. Just because I borrowed the bloody thing for a few weeks..."

There was a momentary pause. Then Clea heard Veronica suck in a sharp breath. "Put the gun away, Mr. Trott."

"Move away from the crates."

"You can't—you wouldn't—" Suddenly Veronica laughed, a shrill, hysterical sound. "You *need* us!"

"Not any longer," said Trott.

Clea flinched at the sound of a gun firing. Three bullets in rapid succession. She pressed her hand to her mouth, clamped it there to stifle the cry that rose up in her throat. She felt as if all the air had been sucked out of the crate and she was suffocating in her fear, choking on silent tears.

Then she heard the sounds of terrified sobbing. Veronica's. She was still alive.

"Just a warning, Mrs. Cairncross," said Trott. "Next time, I'll hit my target."

Trott crossed to the doorway and called out, "In here! Get these crates in the truck!"

More footsteps approached—two men and a squeaky loading cart.

"The large one first," said Trott.

Clea heard the cart move closer, then the men grunted in unison. She braced herself as the crate tilted. She found herself wedged between the side of the crate and something cold and metallic: the bronze torso of a man.

"Christ, this one's heavy. What's in here, anyway?"

"That's not your concern. Just get it moved."

Every little bump seemed to squash Clea into a tighter and tighter space. Only when the crate at last thumped to a rest in the truck was she able to take in a deep breath. And take stock of her predicament.

She was trapped. With the men constantly shuttling back and forth, loading in the rest of the crates, she couldn't exactly stroll out unseen.

The scrape of a second crate being slid on top of hers settled the issue. For the moment she was boxed in.

By the glow of her watch she saw it was 8:10.

At 8:25, the truck pulled away from the warehouse. By now, Clea's calves were cramping, the wood shavings had worked their way into her clothes and she was battling an attack of claustrophobia. Reaching up, she strained to push off the lid, but the crate on top was too heavy.

She pressed her face to a small knothole and took in a few slow, deep breaths. The taste of fresh air took the edge off her panic. *Better,* she thought. *Yes, that's better.*

Something hard was biting into her thigh. She managed

to worm her hand into her hip pocket and found what it was: Jordan's watch. The one she'd stolen.

By now he knew she'd taken it. By now he'd be hating her and glad she was out of his life. That's what she'd wanted him to think. What he should think. He was a gentleman and she was a thief. Nothing could close that gap between them.

Yet, as she huddled in that coffin of a space and clutched Jordan's pocket watch in her fist, her longing for him brought tears to her eyes.

I did it for you, she thought. *To make it easier for you. And me, as well. Because I know, as well as you do, that I'm not the woman for you.*

She pressed the watch to her lips and kissed it, the way she longed to kiss *him,* and never would again. She wanted to curse her larcenous past, her transgressions, her childhood. Even Uncle Walter. All the things that would forever keep Jordan out of her reach. But she was too weary and too frightened.

So she cried instead.

By the time the truck wheezed to a stop, Clea was numb in both spirit and body. Her legs felt dead and useless.

The other crates were unloaded first. Then her crate was tipped onto a cart and began a roller coaster ride, down a truck ramp, up another ramp. She knew there were men about—she heard their voices. An elevator ride brought her to the final destination. The crate hit the floor with a thump.

After a while she heard nothing. Only the faint rumbling of an engine.

Cautiously she pushed up on the lid. The weight of the other crate had redriven the nails into the wood. Luckily she still had the crowbar. It took some tight maneuvering, but she managed to work the tip under the lid and yanked on the bar.

The lid popped open.

She raised her head and inhaled a whiff of diesel-scented air. She was in a storage bay. Beside her were stacked the other crates from the warehouse annex. No one was around.

It took her a few moments to crawl out. By the time she dropped onto the floor, her calves were beginning to prickle with renewed circulation. She hobbled over to the steel door and opened it a crack.

Outside was a narrow corridor. Beyond the corner, two men were laughing, joking in that foul language sailors employ when they're away from the polite company of women. Something about the whores in Naples.

The floor lurched beneath Clea's feet and she swayed sideways. The engine sounds were grinding louder now.

Only then did she focus on the emergency fire kit mounted on the corridor wall. It was stamped with the name *Villafjord*.

I'm on his ship, she thought. *I'm trapped on Van Weldon's ship.*

The floor swayed again, a rolling motion that made her reach out to the walls for support. She heard the engine's accelerating whine, sensed the gentle rocking of the hull through the swells, and she understood.

The *Villafjord* was heading out to sea.

Chapter Fourteen

Hugh Tavistock's limousine was waiting at the side of the road just outside Guildford. The instant Jordan and his two Scotland Yard escorts pulled up in a Mercedes, the limousine door swung open. Jordan stepped out of the Mercedes and slid into the limousine's rear seat.

He found himself confronting his uncle Hugh's critical gaze. "It seems," said Hugh, "that I retired from intelligence simply to devote my life to rescuing *you*."

"And a fond hello to you, too," answered Jordan. "Where's Richard?"

"Present and accounted for," answered a voice from the driver's seat. Dressed in a chauffeur's uniform, Richard turned and grinned at him. "I picked up this trick from a certain relative-to-be. Where's Clea Rice?"

"I don't know," said Jordan. "But I have a very good idea. Did you confirm the shipping schedule for Portsmouth?"

"There is a vessel named *Villafjord* due to sail at midnight tonight. That gives us plenty of time to stop the departure."

"Why all this interest in the *Villafjord?*" asked Hugh. "What's she carrying?"

"Wild guess? A fortune in art." Jordan added, under his breath, "And a certain little cat burglar."

Richard pulled onto the highway for Portsmouth. "She'll jeopardize the whole operation. You should have stopped her."

"Ha! As if I could!" said Jordan. "As you may have surmised, she doesn't take to instruction well."

"Yes, I've heard about Miss Rice," said Hugh. "Uncooperative, is she?"

"She doesn't trust anyone. Not Richard, not the authorities."

"Surely she trusts *you* by now?"

Jordan gazed ahead at the dark road. Softly he said, "I thought she did…."

But she didn't. When it came down to the wire, she chose to work alone. Without me.

He didn't understand her. She was like some forest creature, always poised for flight, never trusting of a human hand. She wouldn't *let* herself believe in him.

That lifting of his pocket watch—oh, he understood the meaning of that gesture. It was part defiance and part desperation. She was trying to push him away, to test him. She was crazy enough to put him to this test. And vulnerable enough to be hurt if he failed her.

I should have known. I should have seen this coming.

Now he was angry at himself, at her, at all the circumstances that kept wrenching them apart. Her past. Her mistrust of him.

His mistrust of *her.*

Perhaps Clea had it right from the start. Perhaps there was nothing he could do, nothing she could do, that would get them beyond all this.

With renewed anxiety he glanced outside at a passing road sign. They were still thirty miles from Portsmouth.

MACLEOD AND THE police were already waiting at the dock.

"We're too late," said MacLeod as Hugh and Jordan stepped out of the limousine.

"What do you mean, too late?" demanded Jordan.

"This, I take it, is young Tavistock?" asked MacLeod.

"My nephew Jordan," said Hugh. "What's happening here?"

"We arrived a few minutes ago. The *Villafjord* was scheduled to sail at midnight from this dock."

"Where is she, then?"

"That's the problem. It seems she sailed twenty minutes ago."

"But it's only nine-thirty."

MacLeod shook his head. "Obviously they changed plans."

Jordan stared out over the dark harbor. A chill wind blew in from the water, whipping his shirt and stinging his face with the tang of salt. *She's out there. I feel it. And she's alone.*

He turned to MacLeod. "You have to intercept them."

"At sea? You're talking a major operation! We have no firm evidence yet. Nothing solid to authorize that sort of thing."

"You'll find your evidence on the *Villafjord.*"

"I can't take that chance. If I move on Van Weldon without cause, his lawyers will shut down my investigation for good. We have to wait until she docks in Naples. Convince the Italian police to board her."

"By then it may be too late! MacLeod, this could be your best chance. Your only chance. If you want Van Weldon, move *now.*"

MacLeod looked at Hugh. "What do you think, Lord Lovat?"

"We'd need help from the Royal Navy. A chopper or

two. Oh, we could do it, all right. But if the evidence isn't aboard, if it turns out we're chasing nothing but a cargo of biscuits, there's going to be enough red faces all around to fill a bloody circus ring."

"I'm telling you, the evidence *is* on board," said Jordan. "So is Clea."

"Is that what you're really chasing?" asked Hugh. "The woman?"

"What if it is?"

"We don't launch an operation this big just because some—some stray female has gotten herself into trouble," said MacLeod. "We move prematurely and we'll lose our chance at Van Weldon."

"He's right," said Hugh. "There are too many factors to weigh here. The woman can't be our first concern."

"Don't give me any bloody lecture about who's dispensable and who isn't!" retorted Jordan. "She's not one of your agents. She never took any oath to protect queen and country. She's a civilian, and you can't leave her out there. *I* won't leave her out there!"

Hugh stared at his nephew in surprise. "She means that much to you?"

Jordan met his uncle's gaze. The answer had never been clearer than at this very moment, with the wind whipping their faces and the night growing ever deeper, ever colder.

"Yes," said Jordan firmly. "She means that much to me."

His uncle glanced up at the sky. "Looks like some nasty weather coming up—it will complicate things."

"But…they'll be miles at sea by the time we reach them," said MacLeod. "Beyond English waters. There's no legal way to demand a search."

"No *legal* way," said Jordan.

"What, you think they'll just invite us aboard to comb the ship?"

"They're not going to know there *is* a search." Jordan turned to his uncle. "I'll need a navy helicopter. And a crew of volunteers for the boarding party."

Troubled, Hugh regarded his nephew for a moment. "You'll have no authority to back you up on this. You understand that?"

"Yes."

"If anything goes wrong—"

"The navy will deny my existence. I know that, too."

Hugh shook his head, agonizing over the decision. "Jordan, you're my only nephew…."

"And with a bloodline like ours, we can't possibly fail. Can we?" Smiling, Jordan gave his uncle's shoulder a squeeze of confidence.

Hugh sighed. "This woman must be quite extraordinary."

"I'll introduce you," said Jordan, and his gaze shifted back to the water. "As soon as I get her off that bloody ship."

THE MEN'S VOICES moved on and faded down the corridor.

Clea remained frozen by the door, debating whether to risk leaving the storage area. Before they docked again, she'd have to find a new hiding place. Eventually someone would check the cargo, and when that happened, the last place Clea wanted to be was trapped in a crate.

The coast looked clear.

She slipped out of the storeroom and headed in the opposite direction the men had taken. The below-decks area was a confusing maze of corridors and hatches. Which way next?

The question was settled by the sound of footsteps. In panic, she ducked through the nearest door.

To her dismay she discovered she was in the crew's quarters—and the footsteps were moving closer. She scrambled across to the row of lockers, opened a door and squeezed inside.

It was even a tighter fit than the crate had been. She was crammed against a bundle of foul-smelling shirts and an even fouler pair of tennis shoes. Through the ventilation slits she saw two men step into the room. One of them crossed toward the lockers. Clea almost let out a squeak of relief when he swung open the door right beside hers.

"Hear there's rough weather comin' up," the man said, pulling on a slicker.

"Hell, she's blowin' twenty-five knots already."

The men, now garbed in foul-weather gear, left the quarters.

Clea emerged from the locker. She couldn't keep ducking in and out of rooms; she'd have to find a more permanent hiding place. Some spot she'd be left undisturbed...

The lifeboats. She'd seen it used as a hiding place in the movies. Unless there was a ship's emergency, she'd be safe waiting it out there until they docked.

She scavenged among the lockers and pulled out a sailor's pea coat and a black cap. Then, her head covered, her petite frame almost swallowed up in the coat, she crept out of the crew's quarters and started up a stairway to the deck.

It was blowing outside, the night swirling with wind and spray. Through the darkness she could make out several men moving about on deck. Two were securing a cargo hatch, a third was peering through binoculars over the port rail. None of them glanced in her direction.

She spotted two lifeboats secured near the starboard gunwale. Both were covered with tarps. Not only would she be concealed in there, she'd be dry. Once the *Villafjord* reached Naples, she could sneak ashore.

She pulled the pea coat tighter around her shoulders. Calmly, deliberately, she began to stroll toward the lifeboats.

SIMON TROTT STOOD on the bridge and eyed the increasingly foul weather from behind the viewing windows. Though the captain had assured him the passage would present no difficulties for the Villafjord, Trott still couldn't shake off his growing sense of uneasiness.

Obviously, Victor Van Weldon didn't share Trott's sense of foreboding. The old man sat calmly beside him on the bridge, oxygen hissing softly through his nasal tube. Van Weldon would not be anxious about something so trivial as a storm at sea. At his age, with his failing health, what was there left for him to fear?

Trott asked the captain, "Will it get much rougher?"

"Not by much, I expect," said the captain. "She'll handle it fine. But if you're that concerned, we can turn back to Portsmouth."

"No," spoke up Van Weldon. "We cannot return." Suddenly he began to cough. Everyone on the bridge looked away in distaste as the old man spat into a handkerchief.

Trott, too, averted his gaze and focused on the main deck below, where three men were working hunched against the wind. That's when Trott noticed the fourth figure moving along the starboard gunwale. It passed, briefly, under the glow of a decklight, then slipped into the shadows.

At the first lifeboat the figure paused, glanced around and began to untie the covering tarp.

"Who is that?" Trott asked sharply. "That man by the lifeboat?"

The captain frowned. "I don't recognize that one."

At once Trott turned for the exit.

"Mr. Trott?" called the captain.

"I'll take care of this."

By the time Trott reached the deck, he had his automatic drawn and ready. The figure had vanished. Draped free over the lifeboat was an unfastened corner of tarp. Trott prowled closer. With a jerk he yanked off the tarp and pointed his gun at the shadow cowering inside.

"Out!" snapped Trott. "Come on, *out.*"

Slowly the figure unfolded itself and raised its head. By the glow of a decklight Trott saw the terror in that startlingly familiar face.

"If it isn't the elusive Miss Clea Rice," said Trott.

And he smiled.

THE CABIN WAS large, plushly furnished and equipped with all the luxuries one would expect in a well-appointed living room. Only the swaying of the crystal chandelier overhead betrayed the fact it was a shipboard residence.

The chair Clea was tied to was upholstered in green velvet and the armrests were carved mahogany. *Surely they won't kill me here,* she thought. *They wouldn't want me to bleed all over this pricey antique.*

Trott emptied the contents of her pockets and her knapsack onto a table and eyed the collection of lock picks. "I see you came well prepared," he commented dryly. "How did you get on board?"

"Trade secret."

"Are you alone?"

"You think I'd tell you?"

With two swift steps he crossed to her and slapped her across the face, so hard her head snapped back. For a moment she was too stunned by the force of the blow to speak.

"Surely, Miss Rice," wheezed Victor Van Weldon, "you don't wish to anger Mr. Trott more than you already have. He can be most unpleasant when annoyed."

"So I've noticed," groaned Clea. She squinted, focusing her blurred gaze on Van Weldon. He was frailer than she'd expected. And old, so old. Oxygen tubing snaked from his nostrils to a green tank hooked behind his wheelchair. His hands were bruised, the skin thin as paper. This was a man barely clinging to life. What could he possibly lose by killing her?

"I'll ask you again," said Trott. "Are you alone?"

"I brought a team of navy SEALs with me."

Trott hit her again. A thousand shards of light seemed to explode in her head.

"Where is Jordan Tavistock?" asked Trott.

"I don't know."

"Is he with you?"

"No."

Trott picked up Jordan's gold pocket watch and flipped open the lid. He read aloud the inscription. "Bernard Tavistock." He looked at her. "You have no idea where he is?"

"I told you I don't."

He held up the watch. "Then what are you doing with this?"

"I stole it."

Though she steeled herself for the coming blow, the impact of his fist still took her breath away. Blood trickled down her chin. In dazed wonder she watched the red droplets soak into the lush carpet at her feet. *How ironic,* she thought. *I finally tell the truth and he doesn't believe me.*

"He is still working with you, isn't he?" said Trott.

"He wants nothing more to do with me. I left him."

Trott turned to Van Weldon. "I think Tavistock is still a threat. Keep the contract on him alive."

Clea's head shot up. "No. No, he's got nothing to do with this!"

"He's been with you this past week."

"His misfortune."

"Why were you together?"

She gave a shrug. "Lust?"

"You think I'd believe that?"

"Why not?" Rebelliously she cocked up her head. "I've been known to tweak the hormones of more than a few men."

"This gets us nowhere!" said Van Weldon. "Throw her overboard."

"I want to know what she's learned. What Tavistock's learned. Otherwise we'll be operating blind. If Interpol—" He suddenly turned.

The intercom was buzzing.

Trott crossed the room and pressed the speaker button. "Yes, Captain?"

"We've a situation up here, Mr. Trott. There's a Royal Navy ship hard on our stern. They've requested permission to come aboard."

"Why?"

"They say they're checking all outbound vessels from Portsmouth for some IRA terrorist. They think he may have passed himself off as crew."

"Request denied," said Van Weldon calmly.

"They have helicopter backup," said the captain. "And another ship on the way."

"We are beyond the twelve-mile limit," said Van Weldon. "They have no right to board us."

"Sir, might I advise cooperation?" said the captain. "It sounds like a routine matter. You know how it is—the Brits are always hunting down IRA. They'll probably just want to eyeball our crew. If we refuse, it will only rouse their suspicions."

Trott and Van Weldon exchanged glances. At last Van Weldon nodded.

"Assemble all men on deck," said Trott into the intercom. "Let the Brits have a good look at them. But it stops there."

"Yes, sir."

Trott turned to Van Weldon. "We'd both better be on deck to meet them. As for Miss Rice..." He looked at Clea.

"She will have to wait," said Van Weldon, and wheeled his chair across the room to a private elevator. "See that she's well secured. I will meet you on the bridge." He maneuvered into the elevator and slid the gate shut. With a hydraulic whine, the lift carried him away.

Trott turned his attention to Clea's bonds. He yanked the ropes around her wrists so tightly she gave a cry of pain. Then quickly, efficiently he taped her mouth.

"That should keep you," he said with a grunt of satisfaction, and he left the room.

The instant the door shut behind him, Clea began straining at her bonds. It took only a few painful twists of her wrists to tell her that it was hopeless. She wasn't going to get loose.

Shedding tears of frustration, she slumped back against the chair. Up on deck, the Royal Navy would soon be landing. They would never know, would never guess, that just below their feet was a victim in need of rescue.

So close and yet so far.

She gritted her teeth and began to strain again at the ropes.

"You're certain you want to go in with us?"

Jordan peered through the chopper windows at the deck

of the *Villafjord* below. It would be a bumpy landing into enemy territory, but with all this wind and darkness as cover, there was a reasonable chance no one down there would recognize him.

"I'm going in," Jordan said.

"You'll have twenty minutes at the most," said the naval officer seated across from him. "And then we're out of there. With or without you."

"I understand."

"We're on shaky legal ground already. If Van Weldon lodges a complaint to the high command, we'll be explaining ourselves till doomsday."

"Twenty minutes. Just give me that much." Jordan tugged the black watch cap lower on his brow. The borrowed Royal Navy uniform was a bit snug around his shoulders, and the automatic felt uncomfortably foreign holstered against his chest, but both were absolutely necessary if he was to participate in this masquerade. Unfortunately the other seven men in the boarding party—all naval officers—were plainly doubtful about having some amateur along for the ride. They kept watching him with expressions bordering on disdain.

Jordan ignored them and focused on the broad deck of the *Villafjord,* now directly beneath the skids. A little tricky maneuvering by the pilot brought them to a touchdown. At once the men began to pile out, Jordan among them.

The pilot, mindful of the hazards of a rolling deck, took off again, leaving the crew temporarily stranded aboard the *Villafjord.*

A man with blond hair was crossing to greet them.

Jordan slipped behind the other men in his party and averted his face. It would be bloody inconvenient to be recognized right off the bat.

The ranking officer of the naval team stepped forward and met the blond man. "Lieutenant Commander Tobias, Royal Navy."

"Simon Trott. VP operations, the Van Weldon company. How can we help you, Commander?"

"We'd like to inspect your crew."

"Certainly. They've already been assembled." Trott pointed to the knot of men huddled near the bridge stairway.

"Is everyone on deck?"

"All except the captain and Mr. Van Weldon. They're up on the bridge."

"There's no one below decks?"

"No, sir."

Commander Tobias nodded. "Then let's get started."

Trott turned to lead the way. As the rest of the boarding party followed Trott, Jordan hung behind, waiting for a chance to slip away.

No one noticed him duck down the midship stairway.

With all the crew up top, he'd have the below-decks area to himself. There wasn't much time to search. Slipping quickly down the first corridor, he poked his head into every doorway, calling Clea's name. He passed crew's quarters and officers' quarters, the mess hall, the galley.

No sign of Clea.

Heading farther astern, he came across what appeared to be a storage bay. Inside the room were a dozen crates of various sizes. The lid was ajar on one of them. He lifted it off and glanced inside.

Swathed in fluffy packing was the bronze head of a statue. And a black glove—a woman's, size five.

Jordan glanced sharply around the room. "Clea?" he called out.

Ten minutes had already passed.

With a surging sense of panic he continued down the corridor, throwing open doors, scanning each compartment. So little time left, and he still had the engine room, the cargo bays and Lord knew what else might lie astern.

Overhead he heard the sound of rumbling, growing louder now. The helicopter was about to land again.

A mahogany door with a sign Private was just ahead. Captain's quarters? Jordan tried the knob and found it was locked. He pounded on it a few times and called out, "Clea?"

There was no answer.

She heard the pounding on the door, then Jordan's voice calling her name.

She tried to answer, tried to shout, but the tape over her mouth muffled all but the faintest whimper. Frantic to reach him, she thrashed like a madwoman against her bonds. The ropes held. Her hands and feet had gone numb, useless.

Don't leave me! she wanted to shriek. *Don't leave me!*

But she knew he had already turned from the door.

In despair, she jerked her body sideways. The chair tipped, carrying her down with it. Her head slammed against an end table. The pain was like a bolt of lightning through her skull; it left her stunned on the floor. Blackness swam before her eyes. She fought the slide toward unconsciousness, fought it savagely with every ounce of will she possessed. And still she could not clear the blackness from her vision.

Faintly she heard a thumping. Again and again, like a drumbeat in the darkness.

She struggled to see. The blackness was lifting. She could make out the outlines of furniture now. And she realized that the thumping was coming from the door.

In a shower of splinters the wood suddenly split open,

breached by the bright red blade of a fire ax. Another blow tore a gaping hole in the door. An arm thrust in, to fumble at the lock.

Jordan shoved into the room.

He took one look at Clea and murmured, "My God…"

At once he was kneeling at her side. Her hands were so numb she scarcely felt it when he cut the cords binding her wrists.

But she did feel his kiss. He pulled the tape from her mouth, lifted her from the floor and pressed his lips to hers. As she lay sobbing in his arms he kissed her hair, her face, murmuring her name again and again, as though he could not say it enough, could never say it enough.

A soft beeping made his head suddenly lift from hers. He silenced the pager hung on his belt. "That's our one-minute warning," he said. "We have to get out of here. Can you walk?"

"I—I don't think so. My legs…"

"Then I'll carry you." He swept her up into his arms. Stepping across the wood-littered carpet, he bore her out of the room and into the corridor.

"How do we get off the ship?" she asked.

"The same way I got on. Navy chopper." He rounded a corner.

And halted.

"I am afraid, Mr. Tavistock," said Simon Trott, standing in their path, "that you are going to miss your flight."

Chapter Fifteen

Clea felt Jordan's arms tighten around her. In the momentary silence she could almost hear the thudding of his heart against his chest.

Trott raised the barrel of his automatic. "Put her down."

"She can't walk," said Jordan. "She hit her head."

"Very well, then. You'll have to carry her."

"Where?"

Trott waved the gun toward the far end of the corridor. "The cargo bay."

That gun left Jordan no choice. With Clea in his arms he headed up the corridor and stepped through a doorway, into a cargo bay crammed full with packing crates.

"The landing party knows I'm on board," said Jordan. "They won't leave without me."

"Won't they?" Trott glanced upward toward the rumble of the chopper rotors. "They're about to do just that."

They heard the roar of the helicopter as it suddenly lifted away.

"Too late," said Trott with a regretful shake of his head. "You've now entered the gray world of deniability, Mr. Tavistock. We'll claim you never came aboard. And the Royal Navy will have a sticky time admitting otherwise." Again he waved the gun, indicating one of the crates. "It's large enough for you both. A cozy end, I'd say."

He's going to shut us inside, thought Clea. And then what?

A ditching at sea, of course. She and Jordan would drown together, their bodies locked forever in an undersea casket. Suddenly she found it hard to breathe. Sheer terror had drained her of the ability to think, to act.

When Jordan spoke, his voice was astonishingly calm.

"They'll be waiting for you in Naples," said Jordan. "Interpol and the Italian police. You don't really think it's as simple as tossing one crate overboard?"

"We've bought our way into Naples for years."

"Then your luck is about to change. Do you like dark, enclosed places? Because that's where *you're* going to find yourself. For the rest of your life."

"I've had enough," Trott snapped. "Put her down. Pry the lid off the crate." He picked up a crowbar and slid it across the floor to Jordan. "Do it. And no sudden moves."

Jordan set Clea down on her feet. At once she slid to her knees, her legs still numb and useless. Dropping down beside her, Jordan looked her in the eye. Something in his gaze caught her attention. He was trying to tell her something. He bent close to her and the flap of his jacket sagged open. That's when she caught a glimpse of his shoulder holster.

He had a gun!

Trott's view was blocked by Jordan's back. Quickly she slipped her hand beneath Jordan's jacket, grabbed the pistol from the holster and hugged it against her chest.

"Leave her on the floor!" ordered Trott. "Just get the bloody crate open!"

Jordan leaned close, his mouth grazing her ear. "Use me as a shield," he whispered. "Aim for his chest."

She stared at him in horror. "No—"

He gripped her shoulder with painful insistence. *"Do it."*

Their gazes locked. It was something she'd remember for as long as she lived, that message she saw in his eyes. *You have to live, Clea. For both of us.*

He gave her shoulder another squeeze, this one gentler. And he smiled.

"Come on, get the lid off!" barked Trott.

Clea hooked her finger around the pistol trigger. She had never shot anyone before. If she missed, if she was even slightly off target, Trott would have time to squeeze off his entire clip into Jordan's body. She had to be accurate. She had to be lethal.

For his sake.

His lips brushed her forehead and she savored their warmth, knowing full well that the next time she touched them they might carry the chill of death.

"It seems you need a jump start," said Trott. He raised his pistol and fired.

Clea felt Jordan shudder in pain, heard him groan as he clutched his thigh. In horror Clea saw bright red droplets spatter the floor. The sight of Jordan's blood seemed to cloud her vision with rage. All her hesitation was swept away by a roaring wave of fury.

With both hands she aimed the pistol at Trott and fired.

The bullet's impact punched Trott squarely in the chest. He stumbled backward, his face frozen in surprise. He weaved on his feet like a drunken man. The gun slipped from his grasp and clanged to the floor. He dropped to his knees beside it, made a clumsy attempt to pick it up again, but his hands wouldn't function. As he sank to the floor, his fingers were still clawing uselessly for the gun. Then they fell still.

"Get out of here," gasped Jordan.

"I won't leave you."

"I can't leave, period. My leg—"

"Hush!" she cried. On unsteady legs she stumbled over to Trott's body and snatched up his gun. "There's no getting off this ship, anyway! They've heard the shots. They'll be down here any minute, the whole lot of them. We might as well stick together." She tottered back to his side.

He sat huddled in a pool of his own blood. Tenderly she took his face in her hands and pressed a kiss to his mouth.

His lips were already chilled.

Sobbing, despairing, she cradled his head in her lap. *It's over,* she thought as she heard footsteps pounding toward them along the corridor. *All we can do now is fight till the bitter end. And hope death comes quickly.* She bent down to him and whispered, "I love you."

The footsteps were almost at the cargo door.

With a strange sense of calmness she raised the gun and took aim at the doorway....

And held her fire. A man in a Royal Navy uniform stood blinking at her in surprise. Behind him stood three other men, also in uniform. One of them was Richard Wolf.

Richard shoved through into the room and saw Jordan and the growing pool of blood. Turning, he yelled, "Call back the chopper again! Have the Medevac team standing by!"

"Yes, sir!" One of the naval officers headed for the intercom.

Clea was still clutching the pistol. Slowly she let the barrel drop, but she did not release the grip. She was almost afraid to let go of the one solid thing she could count on. Afraid that if she did let go, she would drop away into some dimensionless space.

"Here. I'll take it."

Dazed, she looked up at Richard. He regarded her with an almost kindly smile and held out his hand. Wordlessly she gave him the pistol. He nodded and said softly, "That's a good girl."

Within fifteen minutes a team of medics had appeared, helicoptered in from the nearby Royal Navy ship. By then, Clea's legs had regained their circulation and she was able to stand, albeit unsteadily. Her head was aching worse than ever, and a medic tried to pull her aside to examine the bruises on her temple, but she shrugged him away.

All her attention was focused on Jordan. She watched as IV lines were threaded into Jordan's veins, as he was lifted and strapped onto a stretcher. In numb silence she squeezed onto the elevator that carried his stretcher up to the deck.

Only when one of the officers held her back as they lifted Jordan into the chopper did she understand they were taking him from her. Suddenly she panicked, terrified that if she lost sight of him now, she would never see him again.

She shoved forward, elbowing aside the naval officer, and would have run all the way to the chopper were it not for a grip that firmly closed around her arm.

Richard Wolf's.

"Let me go!" she sobbed, trying to fight him off.

"He's being transported to a hospital. They'll take care of him."

"I want to be with him! He needs me!"

Richard took her firmly by the shoulders. "You'll see him soon, I promise! But now *we* need you, Clea. You have to tell us things. About Van Weldon. About this ship."

The roar of the rotor engine drowned out any other words. With despairing eyes, Clea saw the chopper lift away into the wind-buffeted darkness. *Please take care of him,* she prayed. *That's all I ask. Please keep him safe.*

She watched the taillights wink into the night. A moment later the rumble had faded, leaving only the sounds of the wind and the sea.

"Miss Rice?" Richard prodded gently.

Through tears Clea looked at him. "I'll tell you everything, Mr. Wolf," she said. And an anguished laugh suddenly escaped her throat. "Even the truth."

IT WAS TWO days before she saw Jordan again.

She was told that Jordan had lost a great deal of blood, but that the surgery had gone well, without complications. She could learn no more.

Richard Wolf installed her in an MI6 safe house outside London. It was a sweet little stone cottage with a white fence and a garden. She considered it a prison. The three men guarding the entrances did nothing to dispel that impression.

Richard had told her the men were a necessity. The contract on her life might still be active, he'd explained. It was dangerous to move her. Until Van Weldon's topple from power became general knowledge, Clea would have to be kept out of sight.

And away from Jordan.

She understood the real purpose of the separation. It did not surprise her that his aristocratic family would, in the end, prevail. Clea was not the sort of woman one allowed into one's family. Not if one had a reputation to uphold. No matter how much Jordan cared about her—and he *did* care, she knew that now—her past would come between them.

The Tavistocks had only Jordan's well-being in mind. For that she could not fault them.

But she did resent them for the way they had taken control of her freedom. For two days she tolerated her pleasant little prison. She paced in the garden, stared at the TV, leafed without interest through magazines.

By the second day in captivity, she'd bloody well had enough.

She picked up her knapsack, marched outside and announced to the guard posted in the front yard, "I want out."

"Afraid that's quite impossible," he said.

"What're you going to do about it, Buster, shoot me in the back?"

"My orders are to ensure your safety. You can't leave."

"Watch me." She slung the knapsack over her shoulder and was pushing through the gate when a black limousine rolled into the driveway. It came to a stop right in front of her. In amazement she watched as the chauffeur emerged, circled around and opened the rear door.

An elderly man stepped out. He was portly and balding, but he wore his finely tailored suit with comfortable elegance. For a moment he regarded Clea in silence.

"So you are the woman in question," he said at last.

Coolly she looked him up and down. "And the man in question?"

He held out his hand in greeting. "I'm Hugh Tavistock. Jordan's uncle."

Clea momentarily lost her voice. Wordlessly she accepted his handshake and found the man's grip firm, his gaze steady. *Like Jordan's.*

"We have much to talk about, Miss Rice," said Hugh. "Will you step into the car?"

"Actually, I was just leaving."

"You don't wish to see him?"

"You mean...Jordan?"

Hugh nodded. "It's a long drive to the hospital. I thought it would give us a chance to get acquainted."

She studied him, searching for some hint of what was to come. His expression was unreadable, his face a cipher.

She climbed into the limousine.

They sat side by side, not speaking for a while. Outside the window, the countryside glided past. The brilliant hues of fall were tingeing the trees. *What do we possibly have to say to each other?* she wondered. *I'm a stranger to his world, as he is to mine.*

"It seems my nephew has formed an attachment to you," said Hugh.

"Your nephew is a good man," she said. She stared out the window and added softly, "A very fine man."

"I've always thought so."

"He deserves…" She paused and swallowed back tears. "He deserves the very best there is."

"True."

"So…" She raised her chin and looked at him. "I'll not be difficult. You must understand, Lord Lovat, I have no demands. No expectations. I only want…" She looked away. "I only want him to be happy. I'll do whatever it takes. Even if it means vanishing."

"You love him." It was not a question but a statement.

This time she couldn't keep the tears at bay. They began to fall slowly, silently.

Sighing, he sat back in the seat. "Well, it's certainly not without precedent."

"What do you mean?"

"A number of women have fallen for my nephew."

"I can see why."

"But none of them were quite like you. You do realize, don't you, that you are almost single-handedly responsible for bringing down Victor Van Weldon? For smashing an arms shipment empire?"

She shrugged, as if none of it mattered. And at the moment, it didn't. It all seemed irrelevant. She scarcely listened as Hugh outlined the ripple of developments since the *Villafjord* was boarded. The arrests of Oliver and

Veronica Cairncross. The new investigation into the *Max Havelaar*'s sinking. The cache of surface-to-air missiles found in the Cairncross Biscuits warehouse. Unfortunately, Victor Van Weldon would probably not live long enough to go to trial. But he had, in some measure, met justice. The final rendering would have to come from his Maker.

When Hugh had finished speaking, he looked at Clea and said, "You have performed a service for us all, Miss Rice. You're to be congratulated."

She said nothing.

To her surprise he chuckled. "I've met many heroes in my time. But none so uninterested in praise."

She shook her head. "I'm tired, Lord Lovat. I just want to go home."

"To America?"

Again she shrugged. "I suppose that *is* my home. I...I don't know anymore...."

"What about Jordan? I thought you loved him."

"You yourself said it's not without precedent. Women have always been falling in love with your nephew."

"But Jordan's never fallen in love with them. Until now."

There was a silence. She frowned at him.

"For the past two days," said Hugh, "my normally good-natured nephew has been insufferable. Belligerent. He has badgered the doctors and nurses, twice pulled out his intravenous lines and commandeered another patient's wheelchair. We explained to him it wasn't the right time to bring you for a visit. That contract on your life, you know—it made every transfer risky. But now the contract's off—"

"It is?"

"And it's finally time to fetch you. And see if you can't restore his good humor."

"You think I'm the one who can do that?"

"Richard Wolf thought so."

"And what does Jordan say?"

"Bloody little. But then, he's always been close-mouthed." Hugh regarded her with his mild blue eyes. "He's waiting to speak to you first."

Clea gave a bitter laugh. "How distressing it must be for you! A woman like me. And your nephew. You'd have to hide me in the family closet."

"If I did," he said dryly, "you'd find half my ancestors lurking in there with you."

She shook her head. "I don't understand."

"We Tavistocks have a grand tradition of choosing mates who are most...unsuitable. Over the centuries we've wed Gypsies, courtesans and even a stray Yank or two." He smiled. For the first time she recognized the warmth in his eyes. "You would scarcely raise an eyebrow."

"You'd...allow someone like me in your family?"

"It's not my decision, Miss Rice. The choice is Jordan's. Whatever will make him happy."

How can we predict what will make him happy? she thought. *For a month, or a year, he might find contentment in my arms. But then it will dawn on him who I was. Who I am...*

She clutched her knapsack in her lap and suddenly longed for escape, longed to be on the road to somewhere else, anywhere else. That was how she'd survived these past few weeks—the quick escape, the shadowy exit. That, too, was how she'd always resolved her romantic relationships. But now there was no avoiding the encounter that lay ahead.

She'd simply have to be straight about this. Lay her cards on the table and be brutally honest. She owed it to Jordan; it was the kindest thing she could do.

By the time they reached the hospital, she had talked

herself into a benumbed sense of inevitability. She stood stiff and silent as they rode up the service elevator. When they got off on the seventh floor and walked toward Jordan's hospital room, she was composed and prepared for what she knew would be a goodbye. Calmly she stepped into the room.

And lost all sense of resolve.

Jordan was standing by the window, a pair of crutches propped under his arms. He was fully dressed in gray trousers and a white shirt, no tie—casual for a Tavistock. At the sound of the door's opening, he turned clumsily around to face her. The crutches were new to him, and he wobbled a bit, struggling to find his balance. But his gaze was steady on her face.

Her escorts left the room.

She stood just inside the door, longing to go to Jordan, yet afraid to approach. "I see you came through it" was all she said.

He searched her face, seeking, but not finding, what he wanted. "I've been trying to see you."

"Your uncle told me. They were afraid to move either one of us." She smiled. "But now Van Weldon's gone. And we can go back to our lives."

"And will you?"

"What else would I do?"

"Stay with me."

He stood very still, watching her. Waiting for a response.

She was the first to look away. "Stay? You mean…in England?"

"I mean with *me*. Wherever that may happen to be."

She laughed. "That sounds like a rather vague proposition."

"I'm not being vague at all. You're just refusing to recognize the obvious."

"The obvious?"

"That we've been through bloody hell together. That we care about each other. At least, I care about *you*. And I'm not about to let you run."

She shook her head and laughed—not a real laugh. No, it felt as though her heart had gotten caught in her throat. "How can you possibly care about me? You're not even sure who I am."

"I know who you are."

"I've lied to you. Again and again."

"I know."

"Big lies. Whoppers!"

"You also told me the truth."

"Only when I had to! I'm an ex-con, Jordan! I come from a family of cons. I'll probably have kids who'll be cons."

"So...it will be a parenting challenge."

"And what about *this?*" She reached into her knapsack and took out the pocket watch. She dangled it in front of his face. "I *stole* this. I took something I knew you cared about. I did it to prove a point, Jordan. To show you what an idiot you are to trust me!"

"No, Clea," he said quietly. "That's not why you stole it."

"No? Then why did I take it?"

"Because you're afraid of me."

"I'm afraid? *I'm* afraid?"

"You're afraid I'll love you. Afraid you'll love *me*. Afraid it'll all fall apart when I decide you're hopelessly flawed."

"Okay," she retorted. "Maybe you've got it figured out. But it does make a certain amount of sense, doesn't it? To get the disillusionment over with right at the start? You can put a nice romantic spin on all of this, but sooner or later you'll realize what I am."

"I know what you are. And I know just how lucky I am to have found you."

"Lucky?" She shook her head and laughed bitterly. "Lucky?" Holding up the pocket watch, she let it swing in front of his face. "I'm a thief, remember? I steal things. I stole this!"

He grabbed her wrist, trapping it in his grip. "The only thing you stole," he said softly, "was my heart."

Wordlessly she stared at him. Though she wanted to pull away, to turn from his face, she found that her gaze was every bit as trapped as her hand.

"No, Clea," he said. "This time you don't run away. You don't retreat. Maybe it's the way you've always done things. When life gets rough, you want to run away. But don't you see? This time I'm offering you something different. I'm giving you a home to run *to*."

She stopped struggling to free herself and went very still. Only then did he release her wrist. Slowly. They stood looking at each other, not touching, not speaking. His gaze was all that held her now.

That and her heart.

So many times I've tried to run away from you, she thought. *And it was really myself I was running from. Not you. Never you.*

Tenderly he stroked her face and caught the first tear as it slid down her cheek. "I'm not going to force you to stay, Clea. I couldn't, even if I wanted to. But I've already made a decision. Now it's time you made one, too."

Through the veil of tears blurring her vision, she saw his look of uncertainty. Of hope.

"I…want to believe," she whispered.

"You will. Maybe not now, or next year, or even ten

years from now. But one of these days, Clea, you will believe." He edged his crutches forward and pressed his lips to hers. "And that, Miss Rice," he whispered, "is when your running-away days will finally be over."

She looked at him in wonder through her tears. *Oh, Jordan, I think they already are.*

She threw her arms around his neck and pulled him close for another kiss. A sealing kiss. When she pulled away, she found he was smiling.

It was the smile of the thief who had stolen *her* heart. And would forever keep it.

* * * * *

A ringing phone in the middle of the night...

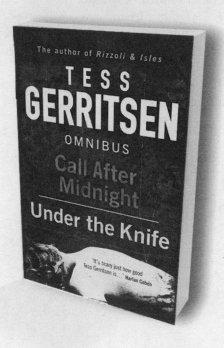

Trying to stay one heartbeat ahead of a dangerous killer might prove fatal...

Guilty until proven innocent

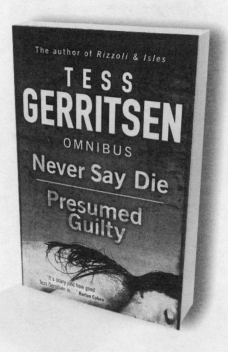

When you're investigating secrets that people would kill to protect, knowing who to trust can be far from clear cut...

A deadly truth...

'It's scary just how good Tess Gerritsen is...'
—Harlan Coben

www.mirabooks.co.uk

'FANS OF *GONE GIRL* WILL EMBRACE THIS' —LISA GARDNER

Mia Dennett can't resist a one-night stand with the enigmatic stranger she meets in a bar.

But going home with him will turn out to be the worst mistake of her life.

An addictively suspenseful and tautly written thriller, *The Good Girl* reveals how, even in the perfect family, nothing is as it seems.

Loved this book?
Let us know!

Find us on **Twitter @Mira_BooksUK**
where you can share your thoughts, stay up
to date on all the news about our upcoming
releases and even be in with the chance of
winning copies of our wonderful books!

Bringing you the best voices in fiction

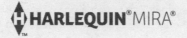